D1553936

# ROMANCING THE ARTIST

# ROMANCING
*the*
# ARTIST

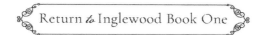

Return *to* Inglewood Book One

# SALLY BRITTON

Romancing the Artist © 2023 by Sally Britton. All Rights Reserved.

No part of this book may be reproduced in any form or by any electronic or mechanical means including information storage and retrieval systems, without permission in writing from the author. The only exception is by a reviewer, who may quote short excerpts in a review.

Published by Pink Citrus Books
Edited by Jenny Proctor
Cover design by Blue Water Books

This book is a work of fiction. Names, characters, places, and incidents are either products of the author's imagination or are used fictitiously. Any resemblance to actual persons living or dead, events, or locales is entirely coincidental.

Sally Britton
www.authorsallybritton.com

First Printing: May 2023

*To Marilee.*
*She Saved the Day.*

# CHAPTER 1
## JUNE 1823, DUNWICH

Picturesque. Most who visited the countryside surrounding Dunwich, a village beside the sea, called it picturesque. But beneath the shade of a cherry tree orchard, Caroline Clapham scowled at the canvas before her, upon which she had painted a depiction of sheep wandering beneath the orchard's trees. Her landscape didn't at all capture that lovely, dream-like quality that so many felt when they walked in that very same orchard.

"I cannot understand why my paintings lack the emotion I wish to invoke in them." She examined the depiction of the fluffy white shapes nestled in the long brushstrokes of grass. "This is supposed to look peaceful. Instead, it is insipid. I can feel it, even if you won't tell me that you see it." She glared accusingly at her companion.

A pair of baleful brown eyes stared back at her, then blinked slowly. The aged audience to her rant, a brown dog with a curling coat and white fur upon her snout and around her eyes, hadn't much to say on the matter. The dog whined, sensing the distress of her mistress.

Caroline's shoulders fell, and she dropped her paintbrush upon the easel. "Sweet Muse. It isn't your fault, of course. You're not a classically trained artist." Caroline knelt next to her dog, a beloved companion in all her pursuits for the last eight years.

Muse's tail thumped against the ground happily as she leaned into Caroline's gentle touch. There they sat, together in the shade of a cherry tree, upon a faded quilt liberally sprinkled with paint from hundreds of Caroline's artistic projects.

At all of nineteen years of age, Caroline hadn't yet found the secret to creating true masterpieces. Somehow, it still eluded her, that special something her mentor promised Caroline would one day find within herself. Yes, she possessed a talent and had turned it into a skill through a great deal of practice.

But the sheep on her canvas were only sheep. The trees, only trees.

"Maybe it's the light," she murmured to herself, tilting her head to the side as she studied the canvas. Muse whined again. The dog wanted more attention before Caroline focused on her task and wasn't shy about letting her mistress know.

"Spoiled," Caroline said softly, fondness in her voice. The dog had come into Caroline's life the same summer as her papa. Everything had changed for her, her mother, and her grandmother, in those precious weeks that a lord's son had stumbled onto their property looking for directions and a meal.

Caroline released a deep sigh, her eyes sweeping across the meadow between the orchard and the cottage where her family lived. That cottage had changed, too. After Mama and Papa married, they built on to the thatched building. There were more rooms with new purposes, including a bedroom for Caroline's little sister and another for her twin brothers.

Leaning back on her elbows, Caroline narrowed her eyes at the cottage. She had sketched and painted that building a dozen times or more, and still she hadn't possessed the skill to transmute the love contained within those walls to canvas or paper.

What was wrong with her?

Muse's head turned, and her tail thumped happily against the blanket. Caroline followed the dog's gaze to find her papa coming through the trees, rolling his sleeves down his forearms, his coat tucked under one arm. He spotted her at nearly the same moment and his expression brightened.

Caroline raised her hand in greeting, and he adjusted his direction to come to her side. She turned her attention back to her canvas. She kept both hands in her lap, though. There was nothing more she could think to do with this particular attempt at artistry.

"How goes the creative endeavor today, Cara?" Papa stood beside the blanket, peering down at her canvas while Muse's tail thumped all the faster at his nearness. The dog adored Neil Duncan more than any other member of the family. He turned his attention to the animal long enough to give her a reassuring pat on the head.

Releasing a frustrated sigh, Caroline gestured to the blanket, inviting her stepfather to join her. "I am not certain you want the answer to that question. It will sound a great deal like complaining."

Papa took a seat on the other side of Muse, keeping his boots well away from the fabric. "I don't mind hearing complaints, now and again. What ails my artist, hm? Too much sunshine? Or is the sky not the right shade of blue today? Perhaps you need better brushes, made of silver and the hair of an exotic goat of some sort?"

She smiled despite herself, his familiar teasing somehow reassuring. She stuck her nose in the air. "You obviously do not understand the delicate temperament of an artist, Papa. I require a diet of raspberries and cream to perform the greatest work with my paints."

"Ah, I see. You must excuse me. How did I not guess?" Papa studied her painting, his expression thoughtful. Without looking at her, he said, "Are you nervous about the summer?"

She considered his words, studying the profile of the man who had taken on the role and responsibility of fatherhood with more enthusiasm than most would, especially given she'd been a rather precocious child of ten when they'd met. "Not really. Not about spending the time away from home. But...what if Lady Inglewood cannot help me?" She looked down at her hands, seeing only one smudge of paint on her index finger. She rubbed her thumb over the dried dollop of white. "What if I can do no better, or learn no more, than I know now?"

Her papa's large hand appeared, covering her own. She looked up to see him regarding her with gentle eyes and a smile that had soothed away her childhood worries on many occasions. "You have a gift, Caroline. Lady Inglewood was the first to see it, and your mother and I are proud of all the work you have done to turn that gift into a talent. You have grown so much already. Be patient with yourself."

Though they were not the answer she wanted, his words soothed her enough that she managed a weak smile. "Thank you, Papa."

"I am not certain you should thank me for anything." He grimaced. "I would much rather you stay home with us. We will miss you, Cara."

"Summer will not last forever, and you will have plenty to do with the other three children underfoot during the cherry harvest."

Papa wrinkled his nose. "Yes. My three little helpers. Perhaps I should come with you to Inglewood and take up art myself."

Caroline laughed softly. Lady Inglewood was an old friend of Lord Neil. It was through their connection that the countess had first seen Caroline's childish attempts at drawing and offered to mentor the budding artist. "Too late for that. I'm beginning to think you will only miss me for all the work I do around here."

"Not at all. You barely lift a finger." He winked at her. They all helped when it was time to harvest the cherries, but it was true that Caroline did little else that could be called work. Her mother owned the farm, and her stepfather was the third son of a marquess. After their marriage, and a generous gift from her step-grandmother, life on their land was less about survival and more about enjoyment.

Caroline had been given more time to study and play, to practice her painting, and to grow from a child who ran barefoot through the fields to a woman with aspirations of one day seeing her artwork in a London gallery. Grand dreams, indeed, for someone who still milked the family cow every day.

A stick cracked, and Caroline tilted her head back until she could see the upside-down scene taking place behind her.

A girl of six with blonde curls streaming down her back stood as still as a statue, her green eyes wide.

"Caught you, Amelia," Caroline said, not restraining the laughter in her voice.

Papa turned to look over his shoulder. "Here now, how long have you been creeping up on us?"

"Not even a minute." The little girl's eyebrows came down and her entire frame drooped with defeat. "I didn't see the twig." She came the rest of the way to the blanket, collapsing somewhat dramatically on her knees when she arrived at its edge.

"I don't know *why* you are determined to sneak up on people." Caroline flicked one of her sister's curls over her shoulder. "If you wished to give me a fright, you'd only have to put a toad in my bed."

The child shivered. "But then I would actually have to catch one. And *touch* it."

"That is true." Papa sighed sympathetically. "The poor toad wouldn't enjoy it either."

Caroline closed her sketchbook, then shifted about to tidy her brushes and paints while her Papa and Amelia discussed the feelings of toads. There was no use in struggling through her work anymore today. Whatever creative spirit had overtaken her had fled the moment she painted the fluffy white sheep.

"What are you doing out here?" she asked her sister. "I thought you were visiting Grandmama today."

"I already visited her. I was gone all morning. Didn't you notice?" Amelia's eyes narrowed at her older sister.

Caroline raised her eyebrows as she checked lids on her paints one more time before placing them in her box.

Papa sounded thoughtful as he said, "Is that why it was so quiet around here?"

Amelia huffed and rolled onto her back. "I am not the noisy one. Those *boys* are the reason the house is so loud."

"I suppose that is the way of things with twins. Perhaps it is time we go rescue your mother from them?" Papa stood and picked up the blanket, giving it a shake before folding it up, and tucked it under the same arm where he carried his coat.

Caroline put all her artist's trappings into a large basket with handles that made it easy for her to slip the whole of it over her shoulder. The three of them, with Muse following dutifully behind, left the shade of the orchard for the cottage.

"Must you really leave tomorrow, Cara?" Amelia asked, her wide hazel eyes as sad as a pup's. "And must you really be away, all summer?"

A thrill of excitement shot from Caroline's heart all the way to her fingers and toes. Tomorrow. She had packed and repacked half a dozen times for the journey to the most marvelous place on earth.

*Inglewood.*

Even the name made her shiver with anticipation.

Papa answered before she could. "Yes, she must go. And yes, she will be away all summer. But we will have the best time we can while your sister is bored to tears without us."

Amelia's little nose wrinkled. "Won't you write letters, Cara?" Her lips turned down and her shoulders drooped.

Caroline exchanged a glance with her papa, smiling at her sister's sweet disappointment. To her surprise, she caught a look of concern in her papa's eyes before he looked away.

"I will," Caroline promised, pouring her cheer into her words. "As often as I can. And you can practice your letters by writing me back."

As though a woman of eighty instead of a girl of six, Amelia heaved an enormous sigh. "I suppose that will have to do."

Hiding her grin with a turn of her head, Caroline took in the scene of her home again. The barn, the chicken coop, her cat sunning himself beside the paddock fence. Cider, though nearing ten years of age, was still a champion mouser.

They entered the house through the kitchen, then walked through to the family's front room where they spent most of the time. The queen of their house, Teresa Duncan, sat in her favorite chair with a book in her lap. She looked up as they came through, then stood and held her hand out to her husband.

"Here you are at last." She lifted her cheek for her husband to press a kiss against it. Mama's hair was dark, like Caroline's, with the occasional silver strand amid the deep brown waves. "All of you smell like sunshine and spring meadows. What has everyone been doing while the boys and I took our nap?"

"Let me put my things away, Mama, and then I will join everyone." Caroline walked on her toes around the two boys playing with wooden animals on the floor, depositing her things by the staircase to take up with her later. Amelia, exhibiting her youth, walked through the carved menagerie to hang her apron on the stair rail.

"Amie!" Alfred, the more vocal of the two brothers, protested loudly. "You'll crush our lion."

Victor, younger by a quarter hour, swiped up the lion before it could meet an ill fate.

Caroline didn't pause to watch the rest of the scene, though she heard the children's indignant tones and her mother's soothing voice as she took her things up the stairs to her room. She entered her bedroom, which had once upon a time been her mother's room, and opened the wardrobe that acted as storage for all her art supplies. She tucked her paints and brushes away with tenderness equal to a mother caring for a babe. Then she removed her paint-covered smock and went to work cleaning her hands and nails in the basin of water on her nightstand.

Sometimes, she wished she had a lady's maid. Her mother had told her all about how a servant of that sort would see to the ladies of the house. Helping them with their hair, their clothes, drawing them baths. It sounded like an incredible luxury, though why someone would want help to do something as simple as bathing she couldn't imagine. The life Caroline had lived since the death of her father—her mother's first husband—hadn't included many servants.

Even years after her mother remarried and their farm grew prosperous, they hadn't "taken on airs," as her friend Jill Martin liked to say.

Jill had a lot to say on all matters concerning Caroline. What she had said about Caroline leaving for the summer had stung. "You're only going to confuse yourself, spending time with nobility when you're nothing more than a farmer's daughter."

Caroline checked her hair in the mirror above her modest dressing table. Though born a gentleman's daughter, she couldn't remember what life had been like before her father's death and her move to the farm. Though technically incorrect about her station in life, perhaps Jill was right about something else. Perhaps Caroline's dreams were too far removed from her upbringing.

She tucked a loose, curling strand of dark brown hair behind her ear and patted the rest to ensure it would stay put. When all appeared in place, she left her bedroom with a light step.

When she walked into the room, her father sat on the floor with the children, marching the animals back into their wooden box. The boys giggled as their father purposefully made the wrong noises for each of the animals. He roared for the ducks, squeaked for the lion, and crowed for the horse.

Amelia sat on one of the chairs, watching, and pretending to be above it all. Though she giggled as Caroline made eye contact with her.

Mama had resumed her place in the chair, the book tucked in her lap. Caroline found a place on the sofa and released an inelegant sigh as she leaned back into the cushion. There was nothing left for her to do, to prepare for her journey in the morning, other than wait. But the minutes felt like hours when one anticipated something especially exciting. She closed her eyes and willed the sun to set faster.

"What is Caroline doing?" Alfie whispered. "She looks bored."

Caroline popped one eye open to look at her little brother, then to her papa, who stared at her with feigned surprise. He tipped his head to the side, regarding her with unconcealed curiosity. "Teresa? Does it seem to you as though our eldest is bored?"

"Is that what she is?" Mama's eyes twinkled, and Caroline opened both eyes to look from one parent to the other as they spoke as if she was not present. "I cannot imagine what would cause such a thing."

Amelia jabbed a needle through the sampler she had picked up. "It's because she's leaving tomorrow."

Papa crossed his arms and leaned his back against his wife's chair. "Is that true? Caroline, are you leaving us tomorrow?" He shook his head, his eyes wide. "You would never!"

She glared at him while the twins snickered. Her papa was excellent at acting out scenes for the family's amusement. She didn't mind joining in the fun at all. She placed the back of her hand on her forehead. "Oh, Papa. I am afraid I must. I cannot stay here on the farm another day."

He covered his heart with both hands. "But why, child? Have your mother and I not given you a roof over your head? A warm bed? And..." He trailed off, looking at the twins with wide eyes, asking for them to supply the words.

"Puppies," Victor said with a decisive nod.

"And her cat," Alfred added.

"Yes. We've given you puppies and a cat. What more could we do to induce you to stay?" Papa asked, both hands now clasped before him.

Mama watched with a mild smile, her posture correct and her eyes gleaming. Mama was everything a lady ought to be: lovely, kind, and compassionate. Everything Caroline hoped to be, someday in the future. After she became a *real* artist.

With pursed lips and a finger tapping her chin, Caroline finally delivered her next line. "Perhaps if you could secure an elephant, I would be tempted to stay."

"An elephant?" Papa repeated, then looked at both boys. "Do either of you have an elephant?" They both shook their heads, solemnly. "And you, Amelia? Do you have an elephant?"

"Of course not." The little girl frowned at him. "And if I did, I wouldn't give it to Cara. I'd use it myself, to ride around the country. And I would paint it blue, so everyone would want to come and see it. I might even let other people ride it."

"Would you?" Mama asked, amusement coloring her words.

Blonde ringlets bobbed as Amelia nodded. "I would charge a penny for each ride."

Papa broke character and laughed, the sound rich and rolling and one of Caroline's favorite things about him. "You would be a rich business woman in no time." Then he nodded to the twins. "What do you think? Since we haven't any elephants, should we let Caroline go on her visit?"

"Will she come back?" Alfred asked, while Victor stilled to hear the answer.

"Yes, at the end of summer," Caroline said, her heart beating an excited rhythm once again. "And I will bring you presents."

Alfred nodded, as though that decided everything. "She can go."

It took a moment for Caroline to suppress her laugh. "Thank you, Alfie. That is most kind of you."

Victor's solemn gaze rested on her a moment longer before he asked, "Will you miss us?"

Caroline looked from one familiar face to the next, drinking in the sight and feel of her family surrounding her. Loving her. Supporting her, even if it meant letting her go her own way for a little while. Her mother's eyes softened, and Papa's smile seemed wistful. They probably understood her need for this journey better than she suspected.

"Yes, darling. I will miss all of you. Very, very much." Though her heart squeezed painfully with that truth, it also whispered to her of the excitement she would face when stepping into the world at last, all on her own. To Inglewood for the summer.

# CHAPTER 2

E verly Refuge had been in the family for four generations, but
it hadn't been christened until Edward's father took on the
estate. When Edward shuffled into the parlor, his eyes
naturally went to the Latin inscription etched into the stone
mantel: *Refugium a tribulationibus mundi.*

"Refuge from the troubles of the world," he translated aloud,
then snorted. They were each the authors of their own troubles. He
had ample evidence of that in his own four-and-twenty years of life.
He dropped into a chair near the hearth, exhausted despite a full
night's rest. His previous evening's activity had taxed him, mentally
if not physically; he hadn't quite recovered from the taxing requirements foisted upon him as a dinner guest.

He hadn't had much choice in regard to attending the dinner,
thanks to a long-standing notion that the family he'd visited and his
own had fostered for well on a decade.

Five minutes or so after Edward sat, glaring at the family motto,
his father came into the room—his spectacles perched on the edge
of his nose and humming to himself. Mr. Samuel Everly took the
chair across from Edward's, also near the fire.

"Good morning, my boy. I didn't see you at breakfast."

"I haven't much of an appetite this morning, sir." Edward half-smiled, though his father wasn't even looking his direction. Edward shared dark hair and blue eyes with his father, as did his elder sisters, but there was little else about them that was similar. He was just as tall as the older man, but Edward was far less practical and prone to distraction.

"Don't neglect your nutrition, son." His father patted his rounded middle to drive home his point. Leaning forward in his seat, he fixed his gaze upon Edward. "How was your dinner at the Kimballs' home yestereve?" His voice carried a note of curiosity tinged with concern. "Did Miss Kimball seem well?"

Edward's gaze dropped, and he sank deeper into his chair, feeling the weight of the situation pressing upon him. "She appeared to be in the best of health," he replied, his voice tinged with a touch of resignation. Mariah Kimball had made every effort to maintain a distance, to avoid any hint of affection or interest towards him, be it as a friend or otherwise.

Edward knew all too well the reasons behind her actions. Mariah, despite her own desires, had yet to find a way to convince her parents that she and Edward were not suited for each other. It was an imperative task for her, as she harbored deep feelings for someone else, someone whom her parents would never approve of.

It was a shame she felt the need to go to such lengths when they'd always been friendly toward one another in the past. But neither of them saw an alternative means without Edward giving insult to the family, and angering his own parents in the process.

"Such a bright young lady," his father remarked before opening his book. "Your mother had her to tea three days ago. She told your mother that she had no wish to ever leave Alderton. Not like other young women who are always speaking of Paris as though it is the center of the world." He scoffed. "Miss Kimball is a practical woman."

"I know." Edward fought against the impulse to grit his teeth. His parents made it obvious to everyone in the neighborhood how fond they were of Mariah, and how much they hoped for Edward to grow fond of her, too. His father thought Mariah a safe match, due to her pragmatism. Mother praised Mariah's dedication to domestic skills an angelic virtue. They were as determined as Mr. and Mrs. Kimball were to make a match of Edward to Mariah.

In fact, it seemed everyone believed Edward and Mariah were a perfect pair. Apparently, they need only exist near one another in order to qualify for assured marital bliss. Edward had nothing against his neighbors. They were everything decent and correct, as far as society went. And he knew the good qualities of Mariah's character, because they had grown up as friends.

What no one other than Edward seemed to know was that she had fallen in love with someone her parents were unlikely to accept as a future son-in-law while they yet viewed Edward as a viable choice.

It didn't matter if her parents would never approve of her choice. Not to Mariah. But sworn to secrecy on the matter by Mariah before the matchmaking had begun in earnest, Edward couldn't disabuse their parents of their hopes without giving his friend away.

"They had a fine wheat harvest last winter," his father muttered, turning pages in his book until he came to the right one. "Rich land. Well-tended. Unentailed, too."

Ah, yes. The ever-important consideration of land. Another virtue in his father's eyes. If Edward made an offer for Miss Kimball, her parents were bound to tie up some of their land in the dowry or bridal agreement.

"Not like our estate," Edward noted, keeping his eyes on the family motto carved into the hearth. The weight of his words made the momentary silence between parent and child heavy. He felt his father's gaze boring a hole into his skull.

They had argued about the entailment and what it meant for the family's future before.

It felt as though they were about to revisit that argument.

"It will still pass to you. The whole of it. Unencumbered by debts. Because I have done my duty by the family." It was a point of pride for Mr. Everly that he had never found himself in debt to another man, and that he'd cleared all the debt his father left when he'd passed. But Samuel Everly hadn't taken risks, either. Never invested in something that might improve their lands or their family coffers. *"Speculating in the stock exchange, investing in risky ventures, is no better than playing cards in a gambling hell,"* he had said time and again.

Edward's father spoke often against the things he viewed as vices. Travel, for one. *"A waste of time and money. And look at your sister Hope. Her obsession with travel nearly killed her, marooned as she was on that island. Lucky she got off of it in one piece. But then what did she do? Married an ambassador, and we haven't seen her since."* Then there were his views on art. *"Imagine spending hundreds of pounds on a portrait of yourself. Vanity. Better to spend those funds on an education or land improvements."*

His father had no use for everything Edward liked or dreamed of.

*"Nothing matters so much in this world as family honor and upholding your family's name. Respect for that, for your mother, for me, is what will make you an honorable and successful man, Edward."*

The memories of those lectures blended with his father's current words. "I've raised you better than my father raised me or my brother—God rest both their souls. You know your duty, as you should."

Edward ground his teeth together briefly, then muttered, "Why must marriage be part of that duty?"

This was the other reason he kept silent on the truth of his and Mariah's mutual disinterest in a marriage between them. Because his parents had lately made every conversation with him about marriage. Their every hope and expectation hinged on Edward settling down, when he had no wish to settle.

Restlessness stirred within him. His imagination was captivated by the allure of unknown places that he read about in books and monthly journal publications. In his heart, a yearning, aching need grew day by day to walk out of the door and be swept along strange roads and pathways. And he didn't dare tell his father. Not when the ghost of his late uncle, Matthew Everly, haunted every mention of the world outside of England.

His father closed his book with a snap, bringing Edward back to the present. "Why are you so averse to the idea of matrimony? Have your mother and I not proven what a well-made match can mean? Respect, devotion, familial affection! Don't you want those things, Edward?"

He met his father's gaze, reading impatience and incredulity there, but not curiosity. Not even a father's desire to understand the son's point. "Not presently, sir."

Edward couldn't marry. Not when it would add tethers to his soul. The thought of being tied down, whether to a wife, the weighty responsibilities of the estate, or the expectations of his parents, stifled him.

There were dreams within Edward's heart that whispered of distant lands, of adventures yet to be embarked upon, of knowledge waiting to be acquired. He longed to chase the horizon, to witness the breathtaking beauty of foreign landscapes, and to engage in intellectual pursuits that would broaden his understanding of the world.

But Edward's father thought the six weeks Edward spent exploring the Tuscany region enough for any "man of sense." His father hadn't ever wished for an adventure. And he seemed to resent those who wanted one for themselves.

The argument hadn't ended with Edward's quiet comment.

"And what happens when I die, hm?" His father scowled and one hand balled into a fist where it rested on the arm of his chair. "What will your opinion be then? How will you expect to live here, without a wife, without settling down?"

Perhaps he ought to tread carefully, even if his father had held the subject of his mortality over Edward's head on other occasions. "I will care for my mother and sisters as you have, sir. I needn't be married to do that."

"The house needs a mistress, Edward. You need a companion. And there must be an heir."

"We are not a noble house, Father. An heir isn't necessary."

A muscle over his father's left eye spasmed. "If *you* die without a son, you know who inherits the whole of it! Your cousin Claude Everly. The gambler. The unprincipled offspring of my wastrel brother, the very brother who likely drank himself into his grave not even *two* years past." They didn't know what Matthew Everly had died from. He hadn't spoken to Edward's father, or any of the family, in over two decades. Though he had sent his wife and son to visit the family estate when Edward's mother extended the invitation. She had tried to mend whatever had broken between the brothers, to no avail. "Do you want Claude sitting in this house? Casting your mother or your unwed sisters out?"

His father spoke as though he expected both himself and Edward to succumb to the plague that very summer. Edward dropped his gaze to the carpet. "No, Father. That is not what I want."

"Then stop wasting everyone's time," the older man snapped, opening his book harshly enough that the spine protested with an audible creak of thread and glue. "And don't neglect your duty or Miss Kimball's interest."

Edward didn't say another word. He stayed slumped in his seat a few minutes more, so as not to appear frightened off by his father's temper, then rose at last with a quiet farewell and left the room.

He needed fresh air and time away from home. A ride would be just the thing. Perhaps he would visit his sister, Grace, at the vicarage. She had the patience of a saint, though how she had put up with their parents' interfering in every aspect of her life, he hadn't any idea. His sister had managed to stave off marriage until the man she cared for finally realized that he and Grace were a perfect match.

The events leading up to that realization had become something of a local legend. Most in the family laughed about it now. But Edward's father always grew quiet and somber when the story arose. Whether because he hadn't forgiven himself to pushing his daughters to that extreme or because he still harbored disappointment in their actions, no one knew. No one dared ask.

Edward had been away at school at the time. He had the feeling that Grace, his brother-in-law Jacob Barnes, and his father left a lot of details out of the story when they told it, too. But that was neither here nor there at present.

If anyone could give him advice on how to avoid his father's plans for him, it was Grace.

He arrived at the vicar's cottage where it was nestled close to a hill, across the lane from the church. The air here, even close to his family's home as it was, tasted more strongly of the sea. The vicarage was but a short distance from the shore. Only a small rise of the land kept the gray waves from view.

He sat a moment on his horse, looking toward that rise. Gulls flew above, gliding on invisible waves of their own and calling to one another in gentle squeaks and caws. Perhaps their lives weren't peaceful, but it certainly appeared as though they hadn't any cares so long as they were soaring above land.

The cottage door opened, and Edward turned to see his sister standing there, one hand on the doorway and the other on her hip. Though a decade older than her brother, Grace's cheerful demeanor always made him feel they were much closer in age. "Do you intend to sit on your horse all day, or will you come inside and keep me company?"

Edward chuckled as he dismounted, leading his horse closer to secure it to the pole and ring meant for that very purpose. "Haven't you children for that sort of thing?"

Grace raised her dark eyebrows at him, her blue eyes sparkling merrily. "A four-year-old and a two year old are *very* good company, but even I occasionally like to discuss things other than bunnies and the sounds cows make."

"What a shame. It is precisely with cattle in mind that I came to see you." He followed his sister into her home, a modest dwelling filled with all the trappings of a young family. They passed Jacob's office, the door open to reveal the vicar wasn't presently at work or at home, then along the narrow corridor into the sitting room.

A maid-of-all work appeared with a curtsy and took Grace's request for a tea tray, then disappeared again while Edward and his sister took their places. He sat in a chair near the window, and she perched on the end of her sofa with her hands folded demurely in her lap.

"Where are my nieces at present?" he asked, eyeing a small doll wrapped in muslin and tucked into the corner of his sister's couch.

"Napping," she informed him with a tired smile. "Where I should like to be, in all honesty, except I cannot seem to settle long enough to so much as daydream. The moment I close my eyes, I think of a dozen things that need to be done. And when better to do them than when the children are asleep?"

"Am I keeping you from something?" Edward started to rise. "I can return another time."

She shook her head and waved him down. "No, please stay. You see, as soon as I rise to get something done, I am weary all over again. It is rather vexing that my mind cannot choose between sleep or activity. Sitting and conversing with you is the best answer. I may rest and still engage in good conversation."

"You are a study in contradiction today, Grace." Edward relaxed again into his seat and stretched his legs out before him, crossing one booted ankle over the other. "I will admit I came for entirely selfish reasons, though I am glad my presence will do you some good."

"Selfish?" She cocked her head to one side. "I'm not certain you can admit to being selfish. Not to a vicar's wife. I am positively duty bound to tell you to go forth and think of others, rather than your-self." Her lips turned upward, the admonishment more teasing than serious. "Or solicit a donation to the poor, perhaps. Or maybe there is a proverb we ought to recite."

"Please leave the preaching to your husband," Edward begged, unable to hide a smile of his own. His sister was the perfect vicar's wife, in all honesty. She had a quiet way about her, whether she was encouraging good behavior in another or doing a kind deed of her own. Grace never made a fuss about things, either. She was calm and gentle, mindful of others' feelings and circumstances.

"Well?" She held a hand out, soliciting his explanation. "Out with it. What selfish thing is in your thoughts?"

Edward shifted again in his chair. "It's about Father."

The maid reentered the room with a tea tray and set it on the table nearest Grace, then left again. Grace rose to prepare a cup for him. "What has our father done to inspire selfishness? Given that he is a creature of comfort, I cannot imagine he denied you something." She spoke without judgment, merely a matter-of-fact knowledge of the parent.

He accepted the cup and saucer from her and noted she'd tucked a biscuit onto the tiny plate. Shortbread. His favorite. "It is more that he is forcing a thing on me that I do not want."

"Really?" Grace settled with her cup and a biscuit. She nibbled on the shortbread more daintily than a bird took up a crumb. "What might that be? A business responsibility of some sort?"

"The business of marriage."

The words floated between them a moment, Grace staring at him with her eyes wide and her cup frozen midway to her mouth. "He is forcing you to marry?" She lowered her cup to her saucer with a clatter. "Oh, no. Not the Kimball girl, surely? Mama was here speaking of her only yesterday."

Edward put his cup down on the small table at his elbow and dropped his forehead into his hand, rubbing at his temples. "She is doing her best to couple our names together all over the neighborhood. If Mama could speak my marriage into existence, she would." Then he looked between his fingers at his sister. "Wait one moment. What do you have against Mariah Kimball?"

His sister's lips pressed together, her eyes widening drastically.

"Come now, Grace," he cajoled, genuinely amused by her response. "Even you can admit that not everyone is perfect."

"I know that," she spluttered, then took a hurried sip of her tea, her gaze sliding away from his. "And I think Miss Kimball is a lovely person. Talented in all the ways a young lady ought to be talented. Fashionable, too, without being ostentatious. Everything I know of her character is acceptable. I merely think—that is to say, Edward, that I…" Her voice trailed away as she lowered her eyes guiltily to the ground. Her cheeks lost all color. "I think I am going to be ill."

Edward's heart twisted for his sister's discomfort. All because he had teased her. "You needn't fear telling me your thoughts, Grace. I wouldn't betray your trust, and—"

"No." She rose abruptly and put her cup and saucer down with a clatter. "I mean *physically* ill." She rushed out of the room before he could say another word, leaving him to stare after her. Belatedly, he rose from his chair and put his cup down.

Ought he to follow in case she needed help? Or call the maid? He took a step to the door before indecision froze him in place. What if his sister's sudden illness was of a delicate, female nature?

Four sisters had taught him more than he wished to know about the sometimes volatile nature of a woman's emotions. He greatly loved and respected his sisters. So much so, that he knew when it was best to stay out of their way.

He sat back down and crossed his arms. He would wait. Grace hadn't asked for any help. Merely fled. Obviously, she did not think him capable of assisting in whatever ailed her.

The clock on the mantel showed ten minutes passed before Grace returned, still a little pale.

"Edward. I am terribly sorry."

He had risen again and eyed her with concern. "Are you unwell, Grace? Should I send for Jacob? Or a doctor?"

She shook her head and picked up a biscuit from the tray—a ginger biscuit this time—and retook her seat. Hesitantly, Edward did the same. Her smile wasn't nearly as cheery as before. "You needn't wear that gloomy mask of worry. My stomach had an indelicate moment. That is all."

"I cannot help but worry. I have never seen you charge out of a room like that."

She lifted one shoulder in a shrug. "It has passed. I am quite composed now." She took a bite of her ginger biscuit and visibly relaxed after she swallowed.

But what if she couldn't keep that down either? If she rushed out again, he would track down Jacob and bring him back to look after his ill wife. Vicar or no, Grace shouldn't be ill on her own.

"What were we speaking of before?" Her eyebrows drew together as she thought, and Edward finally had to remind her.

"Miss Mariah Kimball."

"Oh. Yes." Grace sighed and leaned a little against the arm of the couch. "As I was saying, there is nothing wrong with Miss Kimball. She will make someone a perfectly adequate wife someday. But I cannot imagine that you would be happy together. I watched you grow up, Edward. You are so much like our sister Hope, eyes so often on the horizon and what might be over its edge." Her tone became wistful when she spoke of her twin. "I may not know who to match you with, but I know for certain it would not be Miss Kimball."

"Father thinks I need someone practical to anchor me to home and hearth," he muttered, trying to keep resentment from his voice.

"A ridiculous notion. We ought to have learned our lesson on that matter by observing Hope and Alejandro's union. Hope's spirit hasn't at all been tamed, or anchored if you prefer." She waved the last of her biscuit at him. "If anything, Alejandro is more like the sails of her ship than an anchor. He provides direction and guidance to her free-spirited nature. He empowers her, allowing her to harness her wildness and navigate life's currents with purpose and excitement. And that is the same sort of person you need, Edward." She took a decisive final bite of the biscuit, punctuating her speech with a satisfied smile as she chewed.

"And I should be the one to decide when I find that person."

"Precisely. Such a process should not be rushed or decided by the whims of others," Grace declared.

He almost laughed in his relief. "Will you tell our parents your opinion? Perhaps it would help them reevaluate their own."

"I doubt it." Grace took a sharp bite of her biscuit, and her eyes glazed over as she chewed. "Our father is stubborn. Our mother is single-focused. I cannot think either of them would hear my differing opinion without pointing out that it is, in fact, merely an *opinion*. Have you told them, outright, that you believe the two of you are poorly suited?"

"I have." He let his gaze settle on a painting on the wall opposite him, one sent by Hope as a gift from Spain. The painting depicted an old Spanish windmill, with a man on a horse gazing at it from a distant hill, dressed like a knight. He wanted to go there. He wanted to see Spanish meadows and Grecian temples, climb French mountains, and explore German castles. While he was still young enough to enjoy such things.

Grace's voice interrupted his musings. "Our parents will not change their minds until they see a clear reason for it."

Edward's mind caught that thought and turned it over. "They need proof that it is a bad idea."

"Precisely. If your appeals for reason have fallen on deaf ears, they need to see with their own eyes that it is not a good match. Or..." The single word trailed away, and Grace hurried to take another bite of her biscuit rather than finish her thought aloud.

Edward raised his eyebrows. "Or?"

Color returned to Grace's cheeks. "Nothing. It was an unhelpful idea."

"You may as well say it aloud." Edward tried to hide his smile as he watched his sister, a vicar's wife, squirm in her seat as though caught speaking during a sermon.

"If someone else caught your interest," she said at last, wincing somewhat, "our parents would stop encouraging you toward Mariah."

"Someone else?" Edward groaned and dropped his face into his hands. "Grace. I have no wish to marry at all, at present. And even if I did, you know all the eligible women of the neighborhood as well as I do. Better, even."

"Yes." She sighed and took another bite of her treat. "I cannot imagine you with any of them, really."

22

All he could do was hope for his parents to come to their senses. Or for Mariah Kimball to tell her parents that her affections were already engaged elsewhere. Seeing how miserable he was in Miss Kimball's presence might help. Maybe the answer was to spend more time with the woman rather than less, but only in his parents' view. Showing them at every opportunity how ill-suited Mariah Kimball would be as his wife. How unprepared *he* was to marry anyone, in fact.

His mind whirled with ideas, but his confidence remained low as he disregarded one half-formed plan after another. Nothing suited his circumstances. He muttered to himself, "If Hope were here, she would suggest something outrageous."

Grace studied her brother intently, her gaze sharp and discerning, as she delicately brushed away the remnants of gingerbread from her fingertips. There was a flicker of concern in her eyes. "Edward," she cautioned, her voice tinged with a mix of amusement and worry. "I implore you, do not let your impulsive nature lead you to do something rash."

Edward's features instantly transformed into a mask of feigned innocence, his brows raising in a mock display of surprise. "Me? Rash?" he laced his words with a mischievous undertone. "Never."

"You have a look about you that reminds me far too much of Hope."

Edward was not one to let an opportunity slip through his fingers. If there was a way to extricate himself from his current predicament, he was determined to seize it.

She frowned at him and opened her mouth, perhaps to question him or admonish him, but Edward never found out which. Above them, a babyish voice called out for "Mama," and Grace looked to the ceiling with a sigh.

"Naptime is over."

# CHAPTER 3

The carriage that brought Caroline to Inglewood Castle would take her father home again. He'd hired it for the occasion rather than send her along with a mail coach or drive their little gig the distance from Dunwich to Woodbridge. The journey of twenty-nine miles on narrow country roads had never felt so long to Caroline, even if it brought them to the edge of Inglewood's Estate mid-afternoon.

They passed beneath the branches of the silver birch trees that lined the main path, and Caroline moved to the edge of her seat, holding her breath. Her papa had grown quiet over the last half hour, but she'd hardly noticed. Now that they were so near, a temptation to leap from the carriage and run the rest of the way up the lane nearly moved her to act. Surely, she could move faster than the horses at this point!

"Steady on, Cara," Papa said, as though sensing her words. He laid his hand over hers, where she gripped the edge of her seat with tight fingers. "We are nearly there, and you will have all summer with the countess. You needn't rush things."

Of course he was right. But her smile remained tight, and her worries continued to race like a horse on a track through her mind, round and round, over and over. What if she had grown worse since the last time Lady Inglewood had viewed her work? What if there was no way to improve? What if Jill Martin was right when she said Caroline's head was turned the wrong way round? What if she shouldn't be any kind of artist at all? What if the only thing waiting for her was marriage to a farmer?

On and on the worry went.

Her father undid her grip on the seat with gentleness, then tucked her hand into both of his, drawing her attention to him. His clear blue eyes were soft with his care for her, and his words were likewise compassionate. "If you find yourself missing home, you need only write, and I will come for you. Though I doubt you will wish to leave even an hour earlier than what we've planned, Caroline. You have worked hard for this, my dear. Lady Inglewood took you under her wing all those years ago because she could see better than anyone how much you love your art. Trust her judgement and have faith in yourself, *ma fille*."

*His girl.* A heavy sigh, one filled with relief, escaped her. He had started calling her that after he'd married her mother, in part to tease her as well as to show his love.

Because she had so hated learning French when they first met. But her Papa hadn't let her give up those lessons, either. Her parents believed in her, and they had sacrificed much for her to pursue her passion.

"Thank you, Papa. I will do my best to make you proud."

He gave her gloved hand a gentle squeeze. "You already have, Cara. We are always proud of you."

Tears welled up in her eyes and her throat tightened before any coherent sound escaped her, then the carriage stopped, making them both rock forward. Her papa released her hand and opened the door himself, rather than wait for their hired driver or an Inglewood servant.

Neil Duncan wasn't a man used to others waiting upon him. An observation that often made Caroline wonder what his life as a marquess's son had been like, when such had been his due.

She took Papa's hand, accepting his help to step down from the box where they'd spent the last several hours bouncing about on dusty roads. Then she looked up at Inglewood castle, and her heartbeat sped along with excitement.

Though she had visited before, the castle never failed to make her catch her breath. It rather looked like three completely separate buildings had been pushed together to make one grand edifice. There was the wing to the left of their entry that was made with white stone and blue-roofed turrets. The wing on the right of dark red brick that was older and had something of a Tudor style. And between the two differing structures was one of gray, with white columns, that if it stood alone would only be called a grand *house,* without any castle-like features at all.

The earl's predecessors had vastly differing tastes when it had come to adding onto their ancestral home.

"Perhaps we should add some turrets to our cottage," her papa remarked, studying the castle himself.

Caroline darted a quick look at him, and he winked at her. Teasing, of course. "Do *not* make fun in front of Lord Inglewood, Papa, please."

He raised his eyebrows at her and grinned. The expression wasn't reassuring at all. He and the earl had a history she couldn't begin to understand, as her papa was quite tight-lipped about his past.

Servants appeared, as if by magic, even before the main doors to the castle opened. They bustled about, unloading Caroline's two small trunks and a crate of her art supplies. She carried her portfolio of paintings herself, the canvases inside rolled carefully into the leather cylinder before she left home. She fixed the long strap over her shoulder, holding tightly to it with one hand, while looping the other through her papa's arm.

The front door opened as Caroline's eyes fell upon it, and out stepped the most sophisticated and elegant couple she knew. The Earl of Inglewood and his countess. When Caroline and her father drew near, she sunk into an appropriately deep curtsy while her father bowed more like a lord than a gentleman farmer.

The earl spoke first, his words more clipped than her papa's, though his accent every bit as refined. "Lord Neil, Miss Clapham, welcome to our home."

"Thank you, your lordship." Her papa's smile was friendly. "We are grateful that you extended an invitation to our Caroline. Knowing your lady wife, my daughter's summer will be quite memorable."

"We hope so," Lady Inglewood said, stepping forward with arms outstretched to embrace Caroline, ending the formalities necessary for those of rank when greeting one another. As she enfolded Caroline in the welcome hug, she murmured, "I am glad you are here, Caroline. We will have a wonderful time. You can ask Silas." She nodded her head to her husband. "He has heard me talk of little else these last weeks."

"True enough," the earl said, one corner of his mouth ticking upward. "We are grateful you are here at last, Caroline." Then he met her father's gaze. "Lord Neil."

Her papa arched an eyebrow at the earl. "We have been over that, Inglewood. Mr. Duncan is my preference now."

"I know." The earl's smile shifted into a good-natured smirk. "But it's always difficult to reconcile the indolent lordling with the hard-working farmer. I can never quite believe my eyes."

"Perhaps you should invest in spectacles. I have heard aging can rob even the nobility of their sight."

"Given you are—what?—eight or nine years my senior, I must return your advice."

"Five years, Inglewood. Only five," Neil Duncan responded cheerfully, rocking back on his heels.

Though mortified by her step-father's irreverence for the earl, Caroline did her best to ignore it. The two men always greeted each other as though they were enemies, though their antagonism never went farther than a few barbed words.

"The two of you are going to make Caroline fret," Lady Inglewood said by way of chastisement. "Behave yourselves, or I will cancel dessert for both of you, the same as I would my little boy for misbehavior."

They went inside, the earl walking with Lord Neil, and Caroline's arm looped through her mentor's. She listened with delight as the countess informed her of all the changes to the castle since the last time they had visited, and spoke with enthusiasm of a new supply of paint ingredients she had ordered from Paris.

Though she had visited Inglewood before, Caroline had never stayed a night within its walls. They had always taken a room at a nearby inn, stayed only for a day or two, then returned home. As a family. But this time, everything was different. The countess herself led Caroline to a room in the family wing, while a footman took her papa away to the guest wing since he would stay only a single night.

"I thought of putting you up on the other side of the castle," Lady Inglewood said as they turned down a long corridor with walls the color of a summer sky and a long rug with looping silver and blue patterns to soften the sound of their footfalls. "But having you near will be so much nicer for both of us. Besides, you are practically family. And we will be acting as your guardians while you are with us."

"I am grateful for any place in your home, my lady." Caroline's heart thrilled at the richness surrounding her, not so much for its expense as for its beauty. Gilded frames held beautiful works of art, portraits of people from the past, and tables here and there held statuettes and busts of subjects she itched to examine in detail.

Lady Inglewood's gentle, dark eyes accepted Caroline's enthusiasm without a blink, though they crinkled at the corners with her smile. "I have assigned one of our maids to look after you while you are with us."

"A maid?" Caroline sounded far more provincial than she liked, but hurried to recover in a more even tone. "Thank you. That is most kind of you."

The countess smiled anyway, the look understanding rather than amused. "Her name is Emily."

CAROLINE HADN'T any idea what she'd missed by doing her own hair. Not until that evening, before dinner, when she sat before a mirror twice as large as the one she had at home. Emily, a woman near Caroline's own age, had curled and twisted Caroline's hair into a style befitting a princess. She'd brought flowers, too, to weave in here and there to elevate the style.

Caroline wore no other ornaments. She had very few. A small amber cross, a simple silver chain, and that was all. She hadn't ever needed much else. She wore her favorite gown, too. One her family had commissioned especially for her to wear at the earl's home. It was cream-colored with enough ruffles near the hem to satisfy even the most fashionable of country ladies.

"Though I cannot say I like the direction we are going with sleeves," her mother had said of the fashion plates they examined together, "I am grateful there is more fabric to gowns now. When I was your age, thin white dresses that barely covered our bosoms, let alone our arms, were all the rage."

A soft knock drew Emily to the door, which she opened a bare crack at first. Then she stepped back and curtsied as Caroline's Papa stepped inside with one hand behind his back. He'd dressed in one of his finest suits for the evening, looking less and less the part of a farmer with his regal bearing. Emily fluttered away like a butterfly, lighting on little messes to tidy while Neil spoke.

"Cara, you look beautiful."

She turned in a circle for him. "Do you think I'll do?" Though she managed to keep the question light, a knot had formed in her midsection. Eating at a table with an earl and countess, no matter how familiar they were to her, wasn't something she was accustomed to. Her mother had always been there before, on their previous visits to the castle, and Caroline had followed her mother's lead in every move she made.

"Indeed, you will. And it seems I have arrived just in time for the finishing touch."

Caroline smoothed out the front of her gown. "Finishing touch?" Had she missed something in her preparation?

Her papa drew his arm out from behind his back and held out a rectangular case, made of wood, with a small silver clasp at one side. "A gift for you, my dear."

Caroline crossed the room, looking at the case with confusion. "Papa, you needn't give me anything. I have everything I could need."

"Stop protesting and take the present." He turned the box and held the underside in both hands, nodding to the clasp. She gave him one more suspicious glance before flipping the little latch up and raising the lid of the box with both hands. Then she practically turned into a statue as she stared down into the box.

Jewels rested on a plush, velvet lining.. The most beautiful, sparkling jewels she had ever seen. Sapphire earbobs with a matching pendent and chain, and a pair of pearl earrings with the smallest of light blue stones dangling beneath them.

"Where did these come from?" she whispered. Certainly they must be made of paste. They could not be real. Her family wasn't poor, but they certainly didn't keep jewels lying about. She had only seen such beauty once before, when her mother and her papa wed, and a trunk had come from his mother. Her eyes came up to meet his, and she saw the mischief in the way his eyes crinkled at the corner. "Are these your mother's?"

"They were. Once." He closed the box and held it out to her. "Now they are yours. I kept a few small pieces to pass on to my daughters. I chose these for you the first time I saw them."

Her gratitude made her eyes grow wet and a thick lump of emotion form in her throat. He'd never once made her feel like she wasn't truly his. Though they hadn't been bound by blood, Lord Neil had been her father in every way that mattered. "Papa. It's too much. I don't need them."

"No one needs jewels, Cara." He motioned to the maid, who

31

came with a quick step. "Wear them as you wish. But I think the pearls would look lovely on you this evening. And every time you put them on, I hope you will remember that your mother and I are thinking of you." The maid took the box, and the moment it left her papa's hands, Caroline threw herself into his arms and started to cry.

"What's this? Tears?" Papa tutted and returned her embrace. "I didn't think you the sort to cry over pearls? Or perhaps they are too ugly—"

"Papa, hush." She laughed at his lame attempts at teasing. "They are perfect, and you know it because you are perfect, too." She stepped away from him. "Thank you, Papa. I will put the pearls on right away."

Once the earrings were in place, with Emily's help, Caroline accepted her father's escort to the dinner table. He walked through the halls of the earl's home with the same confidence he strode through their orchards at home. His surety bolstered her own, and Caroline tilted her chin up and recalled the lessons her grandmother and mother had given her on decorum.

"So much of being a lady is in how one comports herself," her grandmother had told her. "A lady walks with confidence and grace, always aware of her surroundings."

Papa had been born a lord. Caroline had been born a gentleman's daughter. Though she had spent summers running barefoot through the orchards, and winters curled up in the hay loft with her kitten while she read aloud or sketched, she had every right to be a guest in a fine home.

And perhaps, if she told herself that often enough, she would begin to believe it.

# CHAPTER 4

"Have you seen Edward?"

The moment he heard his mother ask that question, Edward paused in his steps. He'd been about to open the door from the Blue Room, the west-facing sitting room, and step into the adjacent music room. His mother's voice had come from across the narrow corridor where his father's study was located.

"Not for hours." His father's tone was low, and he seemed distracted. "Have you need of him?"

"Mrs. Kimball and her daughter are coming to visit at 2 o'clock."

Edward's eyes darted to the mantel in the room behind him, noting it was but a quarter hour until the scheduled visit. He grimaced.

"I was hoping he might sit with me while they are here."

He slowly backed away from the door, alarm rising as he made his way to the open window. He needed to get out of that room, and out of the house, before his mother found him. As of yet, he'd not come up with a viable plan—to show his parents how unsuitable a match he and Miss Kimball were for one another—and if his mother asked him to stay, he had no reasonable excuse to deny her request. Mrs. Everly was too good a mother to easily reject her wishes. Edward sacrificed much to see his mother happy.

And she knew it.

"Perhaps he is in the music room. You know he likes to practice the pianoforte on occasion."

Edward's eyes darted to the door he had nearly passed through.

"Yes, of course. I will look there." His mother's voice drew closer.

If she stepped into the music room, it would be quite natural for her to try the sitting room next. Perhaps he could leave through the smaller door that led to the dining room—

"Would you like to join us, too, my dear?" His mother asked of her husband.

The door to the sitting room cracked open.

His mother meant to access the music room through the very room in which Edward stood! He held his breath, staring at the six inches of open doorway, glimpsing his mother's fingers on the handle as she waited for her husband's reply to her invitation.

In a moment of sheer madness, Edward leaped to the open window, then launched himself out of it, vaulting his legs out first with little care as to how he landed. His feet hit the ground, hard, and his knees nearly buckled underneath him. He looked up and winced.

The window had to be at least nine feet off the ground, and he'd hurled himself out of it like a rat leaving a sinking ship. Really, he ought to be ashamed of himself.

"Edward?" his mother's voice called again.

He pressed himself to the wall and winced. Did hiding from his mother make him a coward, or merely a poorly behaved son?

He didn't linger to debate the matter with himself. Instead, he kept close to the house as he went around it to the back, the better to avoid the arriving Kimballs. He'd need to leave his family's house by a way other than the road, or else risk an awkward encounter. The stables weren't out of reach, but he hadn't thought to take a hat with him. Nor was he dressed for riding.

A walk, then. Even if walking about bareheaded might be rather daft. He'd manage. Taking a route that would lead him off his family's property altogether seemed the safest course.

"I'll walk to the beach," he muttered aloud. One could walk on the beach without a hat, especially in fine summer weather.

He tilted his chin up and set the goal firmly in his mind. Two miles would take him off his family's inland property, down a road that was little more than a lane for carts, and to the Earl of Inglewood's property. As the earl and his wife were friends of the Everly family, they certainly wouldn't mind if he accessed the shoreline via their estate. All told, he would have a fine jaunt on a fine day, and he wouldn't return for an hour or more. Long enough for the Kimballs to have come and gone.

Proving to his parents that Mariah Kimball wasn't the right match for him wouldn't be a simple matter. He'd already tried reasoning with his father, and he'd dropped hints to his mother. But they wanted him to marry.

And for some reason, they had decided Miss Kimball was the very woman Edward needed. And Mariah wasn't about to tell anyone she had no intention of marrying Edward, because the man who held her heart would be deemed unsuitable by her family.

What was she hoping to achieve by buying more time? Would it truly make a difference in the grand scheme of things? He found himself uncertain of the outcome, questioning the effectiveness of their arrangement. Yet, he was willing to comply with her wishes, to honor her plea for secrecy regarding her unrequited love. For now, he would play his part, keeping her confidence without fully understanding the reasons behind her actions.

He kicked a large rock into the brush. His frustrations mounted, and his feet took him down the path faster than normal. He knew the way and navigated it without paying heed to his surroundings. What did it matter if the sky above was cloudless and blue? Or if the birds sang especially bright notes from tree to tree?

If only he had spent more time abroad before coming home. If he'd had an adventure or two more, perhaps he'd feel ready to settle.

And then he'd choose a bride of his own rather than have his parents thrust the nearest neighbor into his way at every opportunity.

"Perhaps I could go to London," he said, glaring at the ground as it changed from the hard-packed earth to softer, grass-strewn dirt. He stepped beneath the shade of birch trees, their leaves full and green for the summer. The cool shadows cast by the tree's limbs, combined with the heavier feel of the salty sea air, made Edward realize sweat had broken out across his brow. That awareness made him grimace, and he looked upward for the first time since leaving his home.

After two o'clock in the afternoon, on a cloudless day in June, meant he'd been walking through the heat. Without a hat. But in a coat more suited to a cool parlor than the summer sun. He grumbled and tugged at buttons and sleeves until he had the coat off and tucked beneath his arm.

A breeze carrying the scent of the sea brushed by him, instantly cooling his skin.

Edward closed his eyes and leaned into the soft caress, then kept walking.

As a child, he'd thought it terribly unfair that his family lived so near the sea without having a beach of their own. He loved the water, the sand, the pebbles, all of it. He had sneaked away from lessons as a child to make the two and a half mile walk from his home to the nearest beach, on the Inglewood property.

He'd driven his governess and his parents to fits of worry when he disappeared, and he'd received lectures and punishments when he returned hours later with sand in his shoes and salt on his skin.

The freedom of childhood had given way to the responsibilities of an adult, and he couldn't remember the last time he'd walked barefoot on the sand.

At the same moment the melancholy thought sailed through his mind, he stepped into a small clearing within the Birchwood. A familiar old boat, small enough that someone dragged it far inland, waited with empty seats and faded paint on its side, declaring the boat and its place in the world *The Silver Birch Society*.

A group of children, three decades ago, had pulled the broken boat to its current place. Painted it. Spent hours and hours sitting on its benches and dreaming up games and futures that they now lived. Edward's sisters, Grace and Hope, had been two of those children. The other three were men Edward, and the community, respected and looked up to. He'd been too young to follow them to this place, though he'd ventured there often enough in his youth and on his own.

On this day, the boat wasn't the only thing in the clearing.

A young woman sat against a tree, a blanket spread beneath her, and a sketchbook in her hands. She'd propped the book against her knees, and she'd drawn her legs up close to herself. She peered over the edge of that sketchbook, looking at him with two dark eyebrows raised.

Perhaps twenty feet separated them.

"You are rather loud, sir."

Edward stared at her. "I beg your pardon?"

"And so you ought. I suppose I will forgive you for disturbing my peace, and you may go on about your business." She waved toward the trees from which he'd emerged, then turned her attention back to her sketch, dismissing him with her manner as much as her words.

Who was this strange sprite, sitting all alone, and with enough confidence to dismiss him from a place he had as much right to be as she did? He'd never seen her before. Nor had he heard that Lord Inglewood expected guests.

Edward took a step toward her, and her gaze came up.

"Yes?" She tilted her head to the side. "Was there something you needed?"

What a strange person. "Not from you, Miss...?" He waited expectantly for her to provide a name.

"Then I'm not certain why you linger. I am quite busy." She tapped the top of her sketchbook with her pencil. "I did not settle out here in hopes of a conversation with a stranger." This time, Edward caught something else in her expression. Not the indifference he thought he'd seen, but a slight twist to her lips and the barest narrowing of her eyes that suggested at a sense of humor.

He'd amused her, merely by happening upon her in the birchwood.

"We could introduce ourselves. Then it would not be a conversation between strangers." Though he found his proposal rather clever, the young woman shook her head with an unimpressed toss of her dark curls.

"I am afraid that simply isn't done, sir. If we are not properly introduced, it wouldn't count, and we must remain strangers even while knowing one another's names. It is a hopeless matter." She pointed to the boat. "Much like the idea of that boat ever making it out to sea again."

"This boat? It's been here twenty years or more." He looked it over, vaguely remembering his older sisters bringing him to the boat to play when they were tasked with his care. He'd liked the beach more than an old boat. "I'd like to think an introduction won't take us that long to obtain. Perhaps, if you tell me who you are visiting, I can appeal to them to right matters between us."

She sniffed daintily and bent over her sketchbook. "Now you go too far, sir. You assume I am a visitor. How do you not know that I haven't recently purchased the whole of the grove? Indeed, I might intend to live here the rest of my days."

Edward's smile twitched into a grin. "You have a gift for making ridiculous statements, miss."

"If only my gift in artistry was as well practiced." She sighed, somewhat dramatically. Then she adjusted her grip on the sketchbook and held it toward him. "Here. See what you think of this."

Cautiously, Edward approached. He accepted her sketchbook and turned it about to peer down at her subject matter. It was, unsurprisingly, a sketch of the boat at rest among the trees. An incongruous scene, made somehow sad on her paper. The boat appeared lonely. "It looks like enough." He turned to study the boat, then the paper. "I'd say this shows at least a little talent."

"Thank you," she responded, tone somewhat dry.

She made as if to come to her feet, and Edward held his hand out to her, as he would assist any woman coming from sitting on the ground to standing. She accepted his hand, her own as bare as his, and when his fingers wrapped around hers—Edward's stomach tightened. A strange buzzing began between his ears as he looked down into dark brown eyes that glittered up at him with good humor.

This close, he realized that she wasn't a tiny sprite. She had delicate enough features—wide eyes, a nose that turned up the barest bit at the tip, and pink lips that tilted a little to one side when she smiled. But she was tall. Nearly as tall as he was. And when he'd pulled her to her feet, he'd felt strength in the arm and hand that came from more than plying a needle or playing a pianoforte.

Who was this woman? Her accent wasn't familiar. Educated, but not clipped. She had the bearing of a lady, now that she stood, but when she'd sat on the ground she'd not seemed to care at all about posture or display. And her skin wasn't the pale alabaster so many women of his age and acquaintance strove to protect. Instead, she looked as though she'd spent a fair amount of time in the sun.

"Again, thank you." She took her hand back and used it to brush back a curl from her forehead, tucking it behind a braid that looped from one ear to the other atop her head. "Look." She pointed to her sketch, at the hull of the boat. "As you said, the image is accurate. But I feel it is missing something."

"Really?" He forced himself to look away from the sun-kissed cheeks of the mystery woman and back to her drawing. "What could you add that isn't already there? Color, perhaps."

"Color comes later." She tapped the paper again. "First a sketch, then an outline on canvas, and then the color. I have to know all the lines and details first." She studied her work and shook her head. "Do you know what time it is?"

The question caught him off guard, and it took his mind a

moment to form an answer. "Half past two, or a little more, I think."

"Oh, bother." She turned and looked about the ground, then turned over a corner of the blanket she'd sat on, revealing a wide-brimmed straw hat. Not a lady's hat. It was too simply made and lacked any kind of embellishment. But she still put the thing on her head and kept it in place by tying a dark blue ribbon under her chin. "I must be going. I have an appointment at three o'clock." She gathered up the blanket, rolling it up tightly before tucking it under one arm. She held her free hand out, and he put the sketchbook into her grasp.

"It was...interesting. To meet you, I mean." He'd almost said it had been nice, but really she had made him feel so wrong-footed he wasn't certain he could use the word with any honesty. "Will you be here long?"

"What, in the woods?" She laughed. "Of course not. But if you mean to ask if I will be in the neighborhood, then yes. I am here all summer."

"Oh." He tried on a smile, and then laughed with her. "Good. Then perhaps we will be lucky enough to have a proper introduction in the near future. And then I'll know your name."

She gave him a considering look, and her eyes still danced with humor. "Perhaps. I am told I will meet all sorts of people while I am here. I suppose you could be one of them." She turned in the direction of Inglewood Castle.

He couldn't let her leave without another word. It didn't feel right. Edward called out to her, after she'd stepped into the trees. "I hope I get to see your finished scene—with the color added."

She peeped from behind the tree she'd barely passed. "Have you a great interest in art?"

Her strange boldness inspired some of his own. "When it is created by pretty ladies, I suppose I do." The moment the flirtatious comment left his lips, Edward felt his ears turn warm. Why had he said such a thing to a woman he'd known less than ten minutes? A woman who hadn't even given him her name, in point of fact.

She neither laughed nor took offense. Instead, she bestowed a slow, curious smile upon him. One that made the warmth leave his ears and fill his chest instead. "Is that so? How interesting. Farewell for now, Sir Stranger." She left without another word, and Edward stared after her for several long moments. Wondering if he had imagined her, so quickly had she gone.

Until he realized how stupidly he had behaved. "I could have offered to carry her things," he muttered aloud to the clearing. Would it be odd if he hurried after her? Yes. Yes, he felt certain it would.

He took a different path to the shore. One that wove around the edge of the Inglewood estate rather than through it. Because coming upon the lovely woman a second time in the same afternoon, without a proper introduction, would likely turn him on his head.

No matter how pretty the woman, he ought not flirt with her. Even if curiosity about her tugged at his thoughts.

The waves crawled upward to the shore, slowing and leaving remnants of white foam before hurrying backward again, back to the sea. The gulls overhead dipped toward the water, then let the wind take them up again. For a time, Edward stood still, breathing in the salt-heavy air and closing his eyes.

He had no plan. Despite his ramble through the woods. And instead of trying to untangle the mess of his mind, he was thinking about the sprite in the woods.

It was Mariah Kimball he had to worry about. His friend had asked for his help in keeping a secret. A secret that had taken root in his life, despite the fact that it belonged to another. How best could he assist Miss Kimball whilst still keeping his parent's expectations in check?

He opened his eyes again, staring out across the blue-gray water to the horizon, where a ship sailed far in the distance. Steadily forward, on course in a way Edward's life ought to be.

He needed to devise a plan to convince his parents that marriage wasn't on his agenda. And soon. He turned on his heel to return home, but Inglewood stood before him, the woods just behind it.

The mysterious woman's smile, tilted and teasing, remained painted upon his mind, surfacing the moment he let his guard down. And he couldn't help returning the imagined smile, even as he shook his head at himself. "Stop being a fool, Edward," he muttered aloud, and above him a gull burst into its laughter-like call.

CAROLINE'S HEART didn't slow its rapid pace until she walked through one of the side doors of the castle, out of the sun and away from any possibility of that man coming upon her again. She'd acted ridiculously. All the lessons her grandmother and mother had given her, trying to teach her how to look and behave ladylike, had emptied from her head the moment that man had stepped out of the trees.

He'd made an awful noise, stepping on leaves and snapping twigs beneath his feet. She'd known someone was about to interrupt her quiet sketching, and she'd prepared herself to greet either a noisy child or a loose donkey.

When a man had appeared, without hat or coat on his person, Caroline hadn't quite believed her eyes.

Hadn't anyone ever taught him how to move quietly in the woods?

And then he'd come closer, his attention on the boat before he looked her way, and Caroline had found herself staring at a tall, broad, handsome gentleman with chestnut brown hair and eyes the color of the sea on a bright summer's day. His bearing, his clothing, marked him as a gentleman. But the figure he cut—it quite addled her thoughts.

Until he looked at her directly, and Caroline realized what he saw.

She walked up one of the smaller staircases, trying not to

breathe like an overburdened ox and still keep hold of both blanket and sketchbook. Climbing two flights of stairs after crossing what felt like a mile of property just to enter the house, Caroline wondered how the countess ever accomplished anything. The lady likely spent most of her time traveling from one destination to another.

She paused for breath at the top of the stairs, realizing she still had half the length of the castle to cross before she came to her room.

The man in the woods had seen her sitting on the ground, in a plain brown dress she'd brought from home, without gloves, parasol, or even a bonnet atop her head. She'd looked like a country mouse, no doubt about it. Not like a guest of the earl and his wife.

Caroline glowered at the bust of a man with more curls in his hair than she'd ever managed on her own. Even with tongs.

"I cannot keep acting like a farm girl," she told the stone figure, then gave his stern scowl a deep nod. "You are quite right. It is most unbecoming." An artist learning her trade ought to try for a measure of sophistication in her appearance. Even when working out of doors.

Lady Inglewood came around the corner at that moment, and Caroline hastily straightened her posture before dipping a polite curtsy. "My lady."

"Caroline." Lady Inglewood put a hand over her heart. "Goodness, where did you come from? Here, let me help you."

"That isn't necessary, my lady." Caroline hugged both book and blanket tight to her chest. "I was outside, sketching. But I think I must be late for our meeting in your workroom."

"Time runs differently in a large home, does it not?" Lady Inglewood gestured for Caroline to walk with her. "We will go in together. And I'll have someone fetch the blanket for you."

Caroline's cheeks burned. She'd created work for the staff, carrying things about with her. And nearly arrived late to the first lesson of the summer. Lady Inglewood had spent the morning with her housekeeper, and then given time to her children, and kept another appointment with her husband. She had told Caroline the details of her schedule the evening before, ensuring that Caroline knew she could spend her morning hours on her first full day at the castle however she wished.

And still, even with all that time, Caroline had arrived late, disheveled, and out of breath.

They went down a long corridor, Lady Inglewood's gentle voice filling the vast space. "I am terribly sorry I wasn't available this morning, but it will not happen again. I have made certain that we will spend much more time together the rest of the week. There is so much I wish to know about your work. And I have a surprise for you, too."

"A surprise?" Caroline repeated, walking down a different, wider flight of stairs to the ground level. "You needn't go to any trouble, my lady. I have no wish to disturb your schedule."

Lady Inglewood responded with a cheerful laugh. "My dear, this summer, you *are* my schedule. We will spend as much time on art as we can stand, and then we will walk the beach for inspiration and create even more. We will visit my friends, so I may tell them how accomplished you are, and they will visit us here to better marvel at your skill."

Tingles of anticipation crept up Caroline's neck, down her arms, and made her fingertips twitch. She clutched the sketchbook tighter. Was she ready for this amount of focus on her work?

"But that is not the surprise, of course." Lady Inglewood pushed open the last door between them and Caroline's favorite room in the castle. Lady Inglewood had called it the Solarium. It was her workroom for her art, a room filled with light. Glass panes made up half the ceiling, allowing sunlight to flood the room. Easels stood in half a dozen places, along with comfortable but paint-speckled couches and high-backed chairs. Potted plants stood on columns, trailing ivy down to the floor. The windows stood open, letting in a breeze that came directly off the nearby sea.

The moment Caroline passed through the door into the room that smelled of the sea, of linseed oil, and earth, her soul expanded and all the pressing concerns in her mind lightened. In that room, anything was possible and most of her worries slipped away.

Caroline caught the countess's secretive smile from the corner of her eye. "Do you not wonder about your surprise?"

She released a happy sigh and turned her full attention to her hostess and mentor. "Yes, my lady. I do very much."

"I have invited Sir Thomas Lawrence to stay for a week at the end of August."

For a long moment, Caroline could do nothing but stare. The name sank into her mind slowly, the significance of it not immediately present. Her tongue loosened when her thoughts finally caught up. "The president of the Royal Academy?" she whispered. "I will meet him?"

Sir Thomas Lawrence, a portrait painter, was the most talented and sought after artist in England. His advancement to president of the Royal Academy, patronized by members of the royal family, had occurred three years before.

The countess appeared positively giddy and rather unlike her usual graceful self as she rocked forward onto the tip of her toes. "Indeed. And we will show him your work. With what you have brought with you, and what we will work on this summer, we should have an excellent sampling of your capabilities."

Caroline dropped the blanket on the floor and took a step back, then another, and slowly lowered herself into one of the chairs. She wasn't ready. Her work wasn't nearly good enough. Why would anyone connected with the Royal Academy give her even a moment's attention? The humiliation of a man like Sir Thomas seeing her childish attempts at painting would surely make it impossible for her to ever hold a brush or appear in public again.

"Oh dear." Lady Inglewood approached slowly, one hand outstretched in a calming gesture. "I have shocked you. Frightened you? Caroline, you are quite pale."

Caroline's first attempt to respond was merely a squeak, but then she managed to whisper, "No, my lady. I am all right. It is only that it is a most unexpected piece of news." She started to babble, a thing she couldn't stop herself from. "Sir Thomas Lawrence is rather famous, isn't he? Everyone knows who he is. Of course you would be friends with an artist such as himself. And he must enjoy looking at your work, my lady. It will be such an honor to meet him."

"Perhaps you will feel better about it when you have grown used to the idea." The countess sounded hesitant rather than hopeful. "Your art is beautiful, Caroline. We will work to improve where you struggle, and Sir Thomas may help you find your purpose in art when he visits."

That was the crux of the matter. Caroline wanted to find a home for her talent. Would it only ever be an amusement for her? Could she teach others? Would anyone ever commission her to create artwork for their homes?

She swallowed back all those fears as well as she could, but a sizable lump remained at the back of her throat. Forcing a smile, and hugging her sketchbook to her chest, she said, "I am certain you are right, my lady." But she couldn't speak of the impending visit and judgement a moment longer. "What are our plans for today?"

# CHAPTER 5

S pending every waking hour in the solarium seemed the most intelligent use of Caroline's time. Especially if she meant to prove herself a capable artist. But after three days of sketching ideas and learning new methods of mixing her own colors, she didn't mind in the least when Lady Inglewood suggested they visit one of her dear friends.

Lady Inglewood drove them herself in a pony cart that somehow did not diminish her elegance in the slightest. Between the two women, Lady Inglewood's four-year-old daughter kept them giggling with her observations of the world.

"The sky isn't as dirty today, Mama. Yes'erday, it was all gray. Like soot."

"Isn't it wonderful when it is bright and blue? Though I do love the rain," the mother answered her child, as interested in the conversation as she would be with a person her own age. In many ways, Lady Inglewood reminded Caroline of her own mother. The countess had two children. Isaac, whose place as his father's heir gave him the title Baron Marham, and little Lady Irene.

The vicarage wasn't far, and Irene spoke of her good friend the vicar's daughter with enthusiasm. "Eliz'beth has acorn cups in the garden. May we play in the garden today?"

"If Mrs. Barnes doesn't mind, neither shall I," her mother answered.

Caroline had met Mrs. Barnes once, years before, on a previous visit with her family to Inglewood.

"You will like my friend, Miss Clapham. Will you play in the garden with us, too?"

"I think today your mother wishes me to keep her and her friend company," Caroline said.

"Oh. Aunt Grace," the child gave a somber nod of approval. "She is *lovely*. She will be your friend."

Lady Inglewood's light laugh made her daughter grin up at her. "I think you are right, my darling."

The vicarage was a picture-perfect house of two stories, with ivy climbing up its bricks and a touch of moss upon the roof tiles. So near the sea, almost within sight of the shore were it not for a small, grassy rise, the house doubtless never dried out. The cottage itself was quite welcoming with the flowers along the path and the gentle swirls of smoke curling from the chimney, and the vibrant green of the door and shutters.

"Lady Inglewood," a deep voice called. "Allow me to assist you." The vicar had come from around the corner of the house, hat in one hand and a little girl holding the other, skipping along beside him.

"Auntie Essie," the child shouted, waving her hand with enthusiasm. "Did you bring Irene?"

Lady Irene jumped from her place between the two grown-ups. "Here I am! Good day, Marianne." She waited, though with some impatience given the sway of her shoulders, for the vicar to help first her mother down and then take her up in his hands and put her on her two feet again.

"Miss," he said to Caroline, holding out his hand. "Might I assist you as well?"

"Thank you, Mr. Barnes." She took his hand and stepped down, noting that the only thing that even hinted at his place as vicar might be the somber color of his coat and waistcoat.

He seemed to remember her all at once, and his expression

immediately brightened. "Ah, Miss Clapham. Lord Neil's daughter. Come to stay for the summer at last? Welcome. We are delighted to have you."

The front door opened on the last word, and the vicar's wife came outside. She curtsied, as was proper, but then immediately enveloped Lady Inglewood in an embrace as though they were sisters. "Esther, I am so glad you came today. And Miss Clapham, you have certainly grown since we last met."

With unhurried cheer, the vicar's wife led them all into the home she shared with her husband and two daughters. Caroline caught shades of blue and green throughout the home, and water-color paintings of flowers on the walls, before she settled in a comfortable chair near a large window. The vicar had taken charge of the two little girls, taking them all the way out the back of the house to the garden.

Soft yellow papered the sitting room, and the ladies settled on rose-petal pink furniture. Mrs. Barnes deftly produced rose-sprigged teacups for her guests in a trice.

"And how have you two been getting on?" she asked as she settled on the sofa beside Lady Inglewood. "Your hands are not paint-splattered. I cannot tell if that is a good thing or a bad." The twinkle in her eyes hinted that this was a usual way in which she teased her friend.

Caroline kept quiet, enjoying her tea and smiling as she listened to the friends trade news of their households. She let her gaze roam from one corner of the room to another, appreciating the soft feminine touches of the room as much as she did the combination of colors in paintings and the ribbons from which they hung.

Small oval portraits took up a large portion of one wall, and they all appeared quite recent rather than depictions of ancient ancestors from centuries past. Caroline rose and went closer, to study the watercolors with appreciation. It only took her a moment to recognize the methods of her mentor, and she could not help a squeak of surprise.

"Caroline?" Lady Inglewood asked. "Do you like the portraits?"

"I thought you did not work in water colors, my lady." She looked over her shoulder at her mentor.

"Not usually, though they used to be my favorite medium." Lady Inglewood didn't rise from her seat. "I do find them more forgiving when I create smaller portraits."

Mrs. Barnes appeared relaxed as she asked, "How long did it take to complete the set of my family and Jacob's? He has so many siblings, and with four of my own all trying to sit for you—it was the better part of a month, was it not?"

"Two Christmases past, yes." Lady Inglewood huffed. "And the men were difficult about it, of course. They all wanted to be off doing other things, and stealing away one at a time they treated like an act of kidnapping."

Amused with that idea, Caroline leaned closer to study the gentlemen. She found the vicar's portrait and realized the men nearest him were likely brothers. Then she moved along the wall, pausing a moment when she came upon two images of Mrs. Barnes, though the smiles on each was quite different. An identical sister? Extraordinary.

Then she came to another gentleman and paused. She leaned closer. He was quite familiar. The tight-lipped, half-smile and slight curl of his dark hair, and the cut of his jaw, made her feel as though she had studied his likeness before—no. It couldn't be.

The handsome man from the clearing, who'd walked about bare-headed and in his shirtsleeves, as though he owned the whole of the outdoors. His deep blue eyes stared back at her from the small portrait, and she realized that half-smile he wore was akin to a teasing smirk.

The cheek of the man! Appearing here, in a vicar's cottage.

Mrs. Barnes had risen to fetch more tea, but drifted first to Caroline. "Which of my family has caught your interest? My twin, perhaps?"

Caroline stepped back, a blush warming her cheeks though she could not say why. "Oh, no. I mean, yes, I did find that odd for a moment. An identical sister? Does she live nearby? Does it ever cause trouble for the neighbors?"

"It did when we were younger, but now my sister Hope lives abroad with her husband." Mrs. Barnes studied the portraits as well, then pointed to two younger women. Girls, really. "These are my sisters, Charity and Patience. And our poor brother, in the middle of us all." She tapped the oval frame with the man Caroline felt she knew.

"Your brother—?" That explained his presence on the vicarage walls.

"Yes, Edward Everly. You know, he came to visit me recently. And in such a state! It seems our parents want him to court Mariah Kimball." She raised her eyebrows high. "And Edward would most certainly rather not." Mrs. Barnes went back to her seat and took out her fan. She closed her eyes and took a deep breath. "Do forgive me. I have not been myself of late. As the weather grows warmer, I cannot seem to help feeling fatigued in the afternoons."

Leaning back as well, proper posture seemingly not a necessity between friends, Lady Inglewood closed her own eyes. "Yet another good reason for us to have escaped the solarium today. As helpful as the light is, even with the windows open, it grows unbearably warm inside in the afternoons."

Caroline had to bite back a smile, even though neither woman had their eyes open at that moment. "My mother says summers are for napping beneath the trees, not working indoors."

The vicar's wife nodded without shifting in her position. "Your mother is a wise woman. That sounds like a delightful way to spend the afternoon. That or at a picnic with lots of lemonade."

"Thank goodness your family's picnic is tomorrow." Lady Inglewood opened her eyes and smiled brightly at Caroline. "We always attend. You will enjoy it, Caroline. And there is no better time to introduce you to the neighborhood."

Caroline nodded her agreement as she murmured her assent, but her stomach gave an odd sort of flutter. The Everly family hosted a picnic. Edward Everly would be present.

She would see him again and gain a proper introduction.

Good heavens.

A maid appeared at the door with a curtsy. "Excuse me, Missus. There are visitors at the door asking for you. Mrs. Kimball and Miss Kimball."

"How unexpected," Lady Inglewood murmured, her posture immediately what one would expect from a countess. "It is as though we summoned them with our conversation."

Mrs. Barnes brushed at her gown, then folded her hands in her lap. "Show them in, Anna." The maid curtsied and disappeared, returning a moment later with a formidable looking blonde woman in her fifties or so and a woman nearer Caroline's age with similar coloring but a friendly smile.

Everyone rose and Mrs. Barnes made the necessary introductions for Caroline's benefit, then invited the Kimball women to join them for conversation and refreshment. For her part, Caroline kept a curious eye on Miss Mariah Kimball. This was the woman that the handsome Edward Everly was meant to court and wed? She supposed there wasn't any way to know, merely by looking at two people, if they would suit one another. Yet she wondered what his objection to the woman could be, when she seemed as charming as anyone Caroline had met before. Certainly she was upon the same rung of society as the gentleman who had crashed into Caroline's clearing.

Miss Kimball caught her watching at one point and smiled, then put her teacup down on its saucer and interrupted the steady flow of conversation by saying, "Mrs. Barnes, has Miss Clapham had the pleasure of seeing the seaside from the hill? I think it one of the dearest views. Might I show her? If you have no objection, Miss Clapham."

"I think that is a lovely idea," Mrs. Barnes said, looking first to Caroline and then the countess. "If the two of you have really been shut up inside the conservatory all this time, a little fresh air would be good for Miss Clapham."

"I agree," the countess said with a firm nod. "And that will give the two of you a chance to become acquainted. Miss Kimball can tell you everything about the doings of the younger generation in our neighborhood."

Caroline rose without protest. As much time as she spent out of doors as a child, she still enjoyed the open air more than she did enclosed spaces. No matter how lovely they were. "I would enjoy that. Thank you, Miss Kimball, for the suggestion."

The two of them left the vicarage, tying bonnets beneath their chins and carrying parasols above them. Miss Kimball did not waste time in trivialities. She immediately went about performing an exchange of information, asking Caroline about her family and in return sharing similar stories of her own as they climbed the little rise toward the seashore.

"It is always wonderful to have new people visiting us, especially at summertime. There is much to do, and a new perspective brought by a new friend makes everything that much better." She paused at the top of the hill and took in a deep breath, her eyes staring out at the sea. "Here now. Isn't it beautiful? I know you said you are from a seaside village, too. Do you ever grow tired of such a view? I do not think I will. No matter how old I grow."

"I agree with you, with my whole heart." Caroline pulled in a deep breath, filling her lungs with the air and the scent of the sea. "I find it a shame so many people live inland and never catch a glimpse of the waves and the sunlight on the water. I have tried many times to capture it with my paintings, but it is so difficult to convey all that I feel using only one sense."

"Shall we continue?" Caroline pointed to the beach below their little rise. "We can pay our respects to Neptune before we return to the cottage."

Down they went, clasping hands to steady one another as they ambled down a steeper portion of the land. Caroline twirled the parasol she carried over her shoulder and lifted her face to the sun. She never freckled. Instead, her skin tended toward bronzing. Something she hadn't minded as a child, and she couldn't quite understand the fashion for pale arms and faces. The beach, devoid of the bustle of human activity, belonged solely to the graceful flight of gulls overhead and the two women.

"Are you attending the picnic tomorrow?" Caroline asked her newfound friend. "The one the Everly family hosts?"

"Yes, of course. We would never miss it." Miss Kimball's smile wasn't as bright as before. "When I was younger, still Miss Mariah with several older sisters still unmarried, I never counted summer as started until the Everly picnic. It used to be such fun. We would play games all day long. Tag beneath the trees. Foxes and hounds. That sort of thing. Always running and laughing, and not minding getting dirt on our gloves or our hems."

"That sounds like a perfect picnic," Caroline agreed, facing the other woman. "Do you not enjoy them anymore, now that you are grown?"

Miss Kimball's weak smile and shrug answered the question well enough. "They are still wonderful. I enjoy being with my friends. Though of late, my parents make it difficult to enjoy such an outing. They have expectations of me, now. And I wonder if my sisters went through the same thing I go through now." She held her parasol in both hands, gripping it and turning her gaze to the horizon. "You seem a kind person, Miss Clapham. Might I confide something in you?"

Taken aback, Caroline blurted the first thought she had. "Of course, but you needn't feel the need to. We are strangers yet, but you have my word I will not repeat anything you say to me in confidence."

The other woman laughed, the sound soft against the background of waves and wind. "I count myself a good judge of character, but I see I have alarmed you."

"Surprised rather than alarmed," Caroline said. She studied the other woman's profile, noting the weariness in Miss Kimball's eyes and the tightness at her jaw. Something weighed on the charming woman. "Please. If it would help you to speak what is on your mind, I will listen."

The sea breeze gently tousled their hair, as if nature itself sought to lend an empathetic ear to Miss Kimball's words.

"You are kind." Miss Kimball released a sigh. "Very well. The truth of why it is difficult for me to enjoy the things I used to, the picnic as an example, is that my parents are completely fixated on me marrying the man they have chosen for me. A man they have thought, since my childhood, would be the best and only candidate for my hand. They have teased me since I was a little girl, but I always thought it was just that. Teasing. 'Did you have fun playing with Edward today? Wouldn't it be wonderful if the two of you married? Imagine, having a friend like him all your life!' As though marrying a man is the only way to have a friendship." The beautiful woman snorted.

Caroline winced. Her parents had never made such remarks. If anything, they had cautioned her against mistaking friendship for something more complex, an emotion necessary between a man and woman to form a lasting union. "That must make things uncomfortable. For both of you."

"Yes." Miss Kimball's gaze fell to the sand beneath them. "Among other things. My parents' desire for Mr. Everly to make a match with me has complicated my own hopes for my future. They will not hear me, no matter how often I say we will not suit. And I have hope that someone else..." She swallowed and Caroline's alarm rose when she saw tears in Miss Kimball's eyes. She laughed, the sound trembly and damp. "I apologize, Miss Clapham. We have barely met, and I am making a confession to you I ought not. Forgive me."

As they walked along the sandy shoreline, their steps left fleeting imprints upon the soft terrain, momentarily marking their passage. Miss Kimball's voice, hushed yet filled with earnestness, carried on the gentle breeze, unveiling her vulnerabilities.

It hurt to see someone in pain. Caroline had always had a difficult time, whether it was man or beast, physical or mental anguish made her heart ache for others. Miss Kimball's difficulty, whatever it was, mattered.

"There is nothing to apologize for." Caroline wrapped an arm around Miss Kimball's shoulders in a friendly embrace, the same as she would for any of her friends in a difficult moment. "You are troubled, and I am willing to listen. Sometimes, talking things out can help a situation. And I give you my word, again, I will say nothing of what you tell me to anyone else."

Miss Kimball sniffled and withdrew a handkerchief from the reticule at her wrist. "You are very kind. Perhaps you are right." She lifted her chin. "You see, there is a man I have come to care for, indeed, I have given him my heart. He loves me. But he does not feel *worthy* of me. Silly, ridiculous man. He is the best person I have ever known. He is kind, gentle, and intelligent. He makes me laugh, and he always knows what to say when I am sad. But because our stations are different, he will never dare ask to court me, let alone marry me." She sniffled again. "I am ashamed to say that so long as my parents have Edward Everly in their sights, they wouldn't entertain even the thought of me, their youngest daughter, marrying *beneath* my station. Though I do not see it that way at all."

Caroline kept her arm around the other woman, sensing the contact helped. "That is a difficult position for you and for the man you love." What could she say? There was no way to repair this hurt. Only time could make a difference. "Have you told your parents you do not want to marry Mr. Everly?"

"Yes." Miss Kimball shivered. "They were quite angry. Then they assured me I didn't know what I wanted. And they haven't given up. And..." She met Caroline's eyes. "If I push the matter too much, they will send me away. I know they will. Especially if they ever find out about my secret suitor. I have a great aunt in Scotland. She is horrid. I would be sent to her." She shivered as though speaking of dungeons and torture. "If they didn't see Mr. Everly as an option anymore, and if I had time to convince my suitor to speak to my father, I know I could reason with them."

An alarming thought came to Caroline. Truly, it was a thought formed in a moment of desperate empathy. And she bit her tongue rather than say it aloud. Except...What if...? Another soft sob from

Miss Kimball undid Caroline's reservations. "Would Mr. Everly be willing to turn his attentions elsewhere, if you asked?"

Miss Kimball laughed, without humor. "To whom? Everyone in our neighborhood, all of our friends, know that his parents and mine are determined to have this match. And I would not want one of my friends to have to pretend at a romance she knew would never come to fruition. Edward—Mr. Everly—has no intention of marrying. He has told me that quite plainly. He knows my secret too, you see. And we both thought it best that he does not say anything against the match, so his parents will not grow angry, mine will not be offended, and no one will be punished." She brushed hair away from her face. "I know he grows impatient, though. And I am sorry I am the cause of his discomfort."

"It sounds as though he offered to help you, so you mustn't make yourself feel guilty on that account. Friends are usually willing to sacrifice for one another." Caroline turned over her idea again. "What if you found a woman willing to help? Someone who knew from the start that she played a part in a ruse. Someone the neighborhood does not know well. A woman who will be gone again at the end of the summer." Caroline drew in a deep breath as Miss Kimball's eyes widened with comprehension. "I would be willing to help you."

"But why?" Miss Kimball shook her head. "Your reputation—"

"It would be fine. A courtship isn't an engagement. And I am a stranger here. Who would care?" She raised her shoulders in a shrug, then spoke with sincerity. "I believe it is only right that you should be free to love whomever your heart desires. Would the summer be enough time to convince your suitor to ask for your hand?"

Miss Kimball's eyes welled with tears again, though this time she was smiling. "Your willingness to help me is truly selfless. I cannot express what this even means to me. There must be something I can do for you in return."

At this, Caroline shook her head. "There is no need for any sort of repayment, Miss Kimball. I am doing this because I believe in the importance of following your heart." Her parents had given her everything she could want for her to follow her own. If she could pass on such a gift, in such a simple way, why wouldn't she? "If this brings you happiness, that is enough."

Miss Kimball nodded, her eyes drying and a glow of hope replacing the damp. "I will speak to Edward about this, Miss Clapham. I will explain the situation, and we will find a way to repay you for your kindness. It is only right."

Caroline didn't bother arguing the point a second time. "Please. Call me Caroline. I think we must be friends now."

"Indeed. Then I am Mariah." Her new friend looked out over the sea. "I will make certain Edward understands the depth of your kindness. He will agree to this plan. I haven't any doubt on that account."

Thinking of the man who charged through the trees to find her, a stranger in the wood, and then studied her sketches with genuine interest, Caroline had to agree. He would go along with the plan. And Caroline now had more to worry about this summer than she'd thought possible on the day she left her family's land.

A summer of improving her art had grown more complex than she thought possible. A meeting with the President of the Royal Academy and a pretended romance to allow a real one to blossom sounded more suitable to a comic play than her life. If everything ended happily, though, she would not complain.

The women turned back on their path, returning to the vicarage. Somehow, they found their way to laughing again as they spoke of childhood adventures on beaches, soaking their dresses when they fell into the waves, and how much they wished it still proper for them to wander about barefoot on the sand. When they took their leave of one another, Caroline could not regret her offer. Mariah Kimball's eyes gleamed with hope and determination.

Caroline's heart lifted. Helping Mariah was the right thing to do. As long as she remembered that, everything would be fine.

# CHAPTER 6

E dward Everly stood beneath the shade of a large apple tree, watching his family's servants march to his mother's commands as they set up each and every food item or cushion to her liking.

For Edward's part, since the moment he'd left Inglewood land several days before, he'd only had one hope for this picnic.

He wanted to see his woodland sprite again.

Perhaps thinking of her as *his* sprite was presumptive. But that was who she was in his thoughts and memory, since that was the only place she lived at present. At least until he had a proper name for her.

Her loveliness attracted him, of course. What man wouldn't find someone with her features and teasing smile alluring? But more than that, as soon as she spoke he knew she possessed a sharp wit and intelligence that would make for engaging conversation, and that intrigued him. Even still, he couldn't quite articulate, even to himself, exactly why he hadn't been able to stop thinking about her.

He'd nearly asked his sisters if they knew of any guests at Inglewood or nearby. But she hadn't dressed quite like a lady. More like an upper-servant, or a governess, or some such thing that hinted at gentle breeding but lacking in funds.

He forced himself to bite his tongue rather than make inquiries. At least until after the picnic. If she wasn't among their guests, he would look for her.

After uncovering her identity, there would be no need to dwell on her any longer. She was merely a mystery to be deciphered, albeit an attractive one.

Edward shook his head to rid himself of his ridiculous thoughts. And just in time, too. His mother had left the servants to themselves for a moment and strode toward him with a rather determined gait.

Usually, he didn't have much to do with picnic preparations, even though his family had put together such events every season of the year. Sometimes every-other month of the year, for as long as Edward could remember. His assignments, since boyhood, had consisted of a list of things *not* to do.

He wasn't to muddy his shoes, or boots, or coat. He wasn't to let the dogs loose on accident or on purpose. He wasn't to sample any of the food prior to their guests' arrival. And today, despite his age and maturity, he'd been given yet another thing not to do. She had told him the evening before he wasn't to "sneak away" from the picnic.

His mother made an inspection of his person the way a general inspected their troops. Thoroughly and with a sharp eye.

"Edward, mind what I told you before. I want you here from this moment until the last guest steps into their gig and waves farewell. You will one day be master of this house, the lands, and it will fall to you to be a good host to your neighbors. Do you promise me you will stay at the picnic until it ends?"

She faced him with the same eyes he saw in the mirror every day, wearing an expression she had used with great effect to instill in him respect for her desires. What choice did he have but to say, "Yes, Mother. I am yours to command today."

She gave a satisfied, succinct nod. Then gave her attention to a servant bearing a large tray of fruits, directing him to a table set up beneath a stretch of fabric meant to mimic a medieval tent. The large blue and cream colored fabric billowed like sails when the breeze caught itself inside, but softened again the next moment to add a fairy-tale quality to the center of the oldest part of the orchard.

His mother had outdone herself, and Edward hated knowing the reason for her excess care. Large cushions with gold tassels were scattered about under the nearest trees, along with old rugs the maids had spent the better part of the previous day beating into dustless submission. Chairs made to fold up cleverly were set about the area, too, and three local musicians took up a place in the shade behind the tent where they couldn't be seen, but certainly were heard.

Two violins and a flute, played by footmen on loan for the occasion, filled the air with cheerful—if not always perfectly musical—notes as they warmed up until the moment the guests arrived.

"Here you are, Edward." He started and looked down into the laughing blue eyes of his youngest sister. Patience was all of seventeen years old, and she loved pranks far too much for a young lady of her standing. She had taken after their eldest sister, Hope, in terms of her humor. "I thought you'd have run for it the moment the sun came up this morning."

He snorted and folded his arms across his chest, surveying the scene of bustling servants and his mother following everyone about like a mother hen, clucking admonitions at everyone in her vicinity. "I am certain, had I tried, Mother would have run me to the ground in less than an hour's time."

"I am only glad it is you and not me," Patience noted with a wry smile. "Thank goodness Father thinks seventeen too young for marriage."

"Twenty is the ideal number," another soft voice said as Charity stepped around to Edward's other side. In six months, she would have the birthday that made her that very age. "Though apparently, boys can wait half a decade longer."

Edward smirked. "Never you fear. I don't intend to give in to our parents' matchmaking before the year is out. They will have me to focus all their ambitions upon for some time yet."

Charity's lips twitched. She was the most unique among the siblings. Even Grace, a vicar's wife, was not so somber and serious-minded as Charity. She looked the definition of the word *"staid."* Steady, sober, and sedate. "Do not make me any promises, brother dearest. Not when our mother and father have joined forces against you."

"And wish to enlist the entire neighborhood's help," Patience added. "This has all been done to inspire romance, you know."

"I know." Edward looked at the flapping blue tent, then let his eyes drift to the hammock his mother had insisted on displaying with a spray of roses at each of its ends. "I am well aware we are setting the stage for Romeo and Juliet to have one of their famed meetings."

Charity and Patience simultaneously cringed. Patience looked up at him, her expression pained. "You know they both die rather stupidly at the end of that story, do you not?"

Edward caught sight of bonnets bobbing from behind a stone wall that separated the house's gardens from the orchards. "I am familiar with the tale of how they escaped one another, yes." He drew in a deep breath, then extended his arms outward, one for each sister.

They accepted his escort, and Edward led them to the rug in front of the tent his mother had declared where they must stand to welcome the guests. Their father appeared, leading the first of their guests with a broad smile beneath his somewhat ridiculous wide-brimmed hat. Edward's sisters behaved themselves perfectly, greeting all their neighbors by name or title, making brief but welcoming conversation with everyone who came through their informal receiving line.

The moment Miss Kimball arrived, his mother would expect him to perform as though the young woman was their most honored guest. Such a performance would, in the eyes of most if not all of their neighbors, signal his interest in Miss Kimball. An interest neither of them felt toward each other.

How was he to depart from his mother's plans without offering the Kimballs insult, or calling attention to the fact that Mariah's heart belonged elsewhere?

Lord Inglewood arrived, with his wife on his arm and his young son holding his hand. No one would officially outrank the earl that day, as the Marquess of Alderton and his family were in France for the season.

Edward put his full attention into welcoming the nobility. Even if the earl and his wife were friends with Edward's sisters and brother-in-law, he stood in some awe of the prestige and power such a man wore as easily as Edward wore a waistcoat.

It was only when Lady Inglewood stepped in front of Charity and gestured slightly behind her that Edward realized someone new had joined the earl's family.

A familiar someone. He'd hoped he'd exaggerated her looks in his memory.

But he hadn't. His sprite remained as lovely as the first time he saw her.

"Allow me to present my friend and protege, Miss Caroline Clapham. She is staying with us this summer. Her family is from Dunwich. Miss Clapham, here are some of the young people I so hoped for you to meet. Mr. Edward Everly, and his sisters, Miss Charity Everly and Miss Patience Everly. They are, of course, Mrs. Barnes's siblings."

Her dark eyes met his, alight with amusement even though her lips remained politely pressed together as she curtsied.

The artist from the clearing—a guest of Lady Inglewood?

Edward's luck had shifted. Not only did he now know the identity of the mysterious, pretty woman, but her status also gave him the best possible reason to slip free of his mother's plans. Absolutely no one would fault him for taking up the honor of ensuring the countess's guest enjoyed her first foray into their society. In fact, most would expect the duty to fall to him and his sisters. At least at this event.

The grin he wore, informal and entirely honest, made Miss Clapham's eyes widen. "It is a pleasure to meet you, Miss Clapham.

We are fortunate to have you visiting, and I dare say you have come at the best season. Summer near the sea is always enchanting."

"Yes, I know. My own home is near the sea," she informed him, her voice low and soft. Not the same as it had been when they were alone, yet still quite pleasant to his ears.

"Then you know precisely what I mean." He couldn't take his eyes from hers as she studied him, perhaps wondering if he would reveal their prior meeting. Did she also compare that moment to this one?

He thought he'd imagined how charming she was in appearance, with the shadowed wood providing atmospheric enhancements. Yet the bright sunshine revealed he hadn't invented the curve of her cheek or the sweep of her raised eyebrows. And he couldn't help staring at her.

An elbow to his ribs, followed by Patience's voice, pulled him out of the silent communication with the near-stranger. "You must excuse my brother, Miss Clapham." Patience darted him a surprised glance. "He doesn't make a habit of gawking at people, usually."

Miss Clapham's smile finally slipped free. "Thank you, Miss Patience. I cannot blame anyone for showing exuberance today. The weather is perfect for a picnic."

Charity stepped forward to eclipse Edward as she expressed her own welcome to the newcomer. "Miss Clapham, I couldn't agree more. And our friends delight in celebrating the warmer months, especially on days such as this. I hope you will enjoy yourself."

"Thank you for your kind welcome, Miss Everly. Mr. Everly. Miss Patience." She curtsied to them, and the earl's daughter appeared as if from the air, snatching up Miss Clapham's hand.

"You must come, all my friends are here, and you will meet everyone," the four-year-old Lady Irene insisted. "Won't you, Caroline?"

Edward's ears would have stood on end, had he been a fox. Caroline. What a lovely name.

"Leave her be, Irene," her older brother, Isaac, said with a shake of his head. "She probably wants to be with the grownups."

"I haven't any objection to meeting all of your friends," the woman said to the children before turning her smile back to Charity. "If you will excuse me, please," Miss Clapham said, her voice soft and light with merriment. "It seems there are more introductions awaiting me."

Edward watched her move away to sit beneath a tree where little girls in pastel gowns and bonnets had already claimed a half dozen cushions. It wouldn't be difficult to steal her away from them. Not once he'd finished his duty to his mother by greeting the rest of the guests.

Charity took a step back to her position beside her brother. "Edward," she whispered, her lips barely moving. "What was that all about?"

"Hm?" He looked down at her solemnly concerned expression. "What?"

"You looked like you planned to pounce on poor Miss Clapham," Patience informed him, and Edward saw she studied him from the corners of her eyes. "You showed more teeth than a fox sighting a rabbit."

Charity tilted forward on her toes enough to peer around her brother to her youngest sister. "How would you know what that looks like?"

"Hush, both of you." Edward smiled and greeted the baronet, Sir Isaac, his wife, and the two children they brought. The youngest was still an infant, at home with his nurse. But Luther and Faith Fox made their way to sit under the tree where Miss Clapham now held court for the youngest guests of the picnic. Sir Isaac was brother to Lady Inglewood, and the little Isaac who'd gone away with Miss Clapham was named after his uncle.

"Oh, Lord Neil's daughter," Lady Fox said when she spied where her children had gone. "I haven't seen Caroline in ages."

"You have met her before?" Patience asked before Edward could express his surprise. She seemed as startled as he was. Lord *Neil's* daughter? Neil Duncan? The Marquess's wayward son?

He'd been a favorite topic of neighborhood gossip for years. His journey from scoundrel to outcast to a prosperous farmer had become part of local folklore in the decade since he'd left his father's home.

Lady Fox raised her gold-red eyebrows at them. "I am surprised you have not spoken to her before now. But then, I suppose their visits here were always rather short and contained." She waved a hand somewhat dismissively. "Having awkward family relationships will do that, I fear. But it is good they have sent her here at last. Isn't it, darling?" She smiled up at her husband, who nodded his agreement as they stepped away.

"Grace didn't mention that anyone else knew her," Patience murmured as she cast a curious glance in Miss Clapham's direction.

Edward started. "Grace mentioned Miss Clapham before? To you?"

"To all of us, silly." Patience shook her head at him, appearing rather disappointed. "Do you never listen at dinner? When Grace and her husband ate with us a fortnight ago, she told us that Lord Neil Duncan's stepdaughter was coming to pay a visit to the countess."

Charity gave him a reproving glare, too. "You really ought to listen to news about our neighbors, Edward. It will keep you from making ridiculous mistakes."

He shook his head. "A disgraced lord's stepdaughter doesn't qualify as a neighbor," he muttered, distracted by the large yellow bonnet coming his way—one resting atop a head of blonde ringlets.

"Lady Inglewood *is* a neighbor, and therefore my advice stands," Charity said with a firm nod of her head. Then she said louder, and more cheerfully, "Mr. and Mrs. Kimball, we are delighted you could come. And Miss Kimball, welcome."

Edward kept his countenance friendly as Mariah curtsied to him and his sister. "Mr. Everly," she greeted him, nothing suggestive in tone or expression. "Good afternoon."

How had a childhood friendship created such an awkward situation for him? And why had he agreed to keep her secret? "Miss Kimball. So good to have you here."

His mother emerged from the tent, both arms extended in welcome to the Kimballs. "Oh, I am so glad all of you are here. This is wonderful. You know, children, I think most of our guests have arrived. You are excused to go and enjoy yourselves. I will be certain to welcome anyone else."

The timing his mother executed was something of a marvel. Dismissing her children from their places at that exact moment guaranteed that one of them would take Miss Kimball in hand, at least offering conversation. He looked first to Patience, who sent him a pitying smile before calling to a friend, leaving him behind. Then Edward turned his pleading gaze to Charity. But their mother took her arm before Charity could come to his assistance.

Mr. and Mrs. Kimball had likewise slipped away. Leaving Edward and Miss Mariah Kimball facing one another, standing in the middle of the gathering, within easy view of all the guests. Much like actors on a stage.

She had the decency to wince, and mouth the words, "Sorry, Edward," to him.

The musicians started playing a lively tune, appropriately chipper, and Edward wished the flautist would swallow his instrument. Or that someone would cause a scene. Because the weight of all his neighbors' stares rested squarely on him as he offered Miss Kimball his arm.

"Allow me to fetch you something cool to drink, Miss Kimball." He did not grit his teeth, nor stumble over the words.

Instead, he searched for any possible escape. For both of them.

She could not reveal that her heart belonged to another. Not yet, she had insisted when last he asked it of her. And he would not expose her secret.

"Edward." Mariah's voice remained soft as she walked with him to the refreshments. "I have come upon a scheme to relieve us both of my parents' expectations. Rather, someone else presented a plan to me that I think has merit."

"I am all ears," he murmured, stepping beneath the tent that protected food and drink from the sun.

"You have met Miss Clapham?"

He paused, mid-motion, with a ladle in hand to serve punch into a cup. "Yes. Moments before you arrived." She couldn't know about his less-than-formal first conversation with the countess's guest, could she?

Mariah glanced at the opening of the tent, her eyes flickering from those outside the shelter back to him. "We have become fast friends. In fact, I confided our plight to her."

Plight? He supposed it was that. "You must have been quite taken with her to share your secret." He handed her the cup of punch, a heady mix of fruit juices and mint. He had no reason to object to Mariah entrusting her secret to others. Though it was somewhat odd.

Then again, Caroline Clapham made a strong first impression on others. He'd been thinking of her ever since their meeting in the woods, hadn't he?

"She is a kind woman." Mariah looked down at her cup and turned it about in her hands rather than drink it. Years of friendship gave Edward enough experience for him to recognize that his friend had more to say, but hesitated.

"Mariah," he said, voice low. "Stop stalling and tell me what it is you wish to tell me."

She raised her eyes to his with a helpless shrug. "I am not certain you will like what I have to say. You see, Miss Clapham is clever as well as kind. And she came up with a plan to help us." When he said nothing, merely crossed his arms and waited for the explanation, Mariah began speaking with quiet urgency. "Miss Clapham suggests that you pretend to court her while she is here for the summer. This would be a way for us to avoid any further speculation about an engagement between us without causing any undue harm or blame on either of our parts. My parents' plans will be quite undone, and your parents will stop pressing you to make an offer for me if you are at the beginning of a courtship with another."

He stared at her, the hope shining in her eyes urging him to agree to the mad plan without even thinking on it. "A pretend courtship." Edward turned the idea over in his mind, and his conversation with Grace returned to him. Though his rule-following sister hadn't stated it outright, if people thought that *his* affections had been engaged elsewhere, both he and Mariah would benefit.

His parents would be surprised if he turned his attention to Miss Clapham. But could they protest, when they had claimed all they wanted was for him to find someone to wed? And since there was no spoken understanding, no true courtship, no betrothal between Miss Kimball and himself, the Kimball family couldn't claim he'd ill-used their daughter.

In fact, they might halt their own campaign to marry her off if their chosen bridegroom was no longer available. That could give Miss Kimball the time and opportunity she needed to persuade them to her way of thinking about the man who *had* captured her heart.

He had to ask at least one question as he led Mariah out into the sunlight again. "What does Miss Clapham gain from helping us?"

"She denied any form of repayment or favor," Mariah said, turning and pretending to study the orchard. "If there is any chance of us breaking free of our parents' expectations, I am willing to try anything. Aren't you, Edward?"

"Yes. I am." He ought to take time to consider the matter. Weigh and measure possible outcomes to engaging in such a ruse with a woman he'd laid eyes on only twice. And yet...hadn't he been captivated by Caroline Clapham? Even though he had no desire to tie himself to a wife, he had no objection to enjoying the company of a charming and intelligent woman. "It could work," he murmured.

"And she leaves at the end of summer," Mariah reminded him again. "There is already an end date to your play-acting. Do you think you could manage it?"

Could he? Edward wasn't known for his ability to act. He was rubbish at cards, and everyone who played with him made certain he knew it. His face, they said, gave everything away. But this was different. Because he needn't feign love. Only interest. And he certainly found Miss Clapham interesting enough already. "I believe I could."

Mariah grinned happily up at him, then quickly schooled her features into a more demure expression. "Then we had better inform her of your agreement before any of us can change our minds."

Edward's gaze went to where the children had gathered beneath the tree, surrounding Caroline Clapham, who appeared quite content in their company.

Miss Kimball's gaze followed his. "There is no better time than now, I think."

They were fortunate, indeed. Caroline Clapham had arrived at the right moment. A woman Edward could pretend held his full romantic attention. Someone safe, who didn't have parents about to approve a match. Someone who would be gone before autumn.

"Then by all means, let's speak with her," he said, offering his arm to his friend.

"I think you will like her." Mariah accepted his arm.

Edward didn't spend another moment thinking on their plan. Sometimes, following one's instinct was best. No matter what his family said.

# CHAPTER 7

Even demanding children were not as intimidating as an orchard full of strangers, and Caroline took her perch on a chair surrounded by boys and girls with ease. She wasn't shy. Not precisely. But she could not remember mixing among a crowd made up of so many people whose lives were far above her own, in social standing if nothing else.

There were no farmers present. No orchard laborers. No merchants, either, that she could tell. Only those who possessed lands or titles made up the guest list. She hadn't realized it would be that way until Lady Inglewood told her many of the guests' names while they rode over in the earl's carriage.

How silly she had been, to think an earl and countess would attend a picnic with anyone of the working class.

Not that she thought less of them for it, of course. They could no more help their position in the world than a farmer's daughter could. Yet even wearing her best day dress, Caroline had felt somewhat out of place when she stepped from the carriage to behold Everly Refuge.

A fine, tall, gray stone house had faced her, with ivy crawling up one side. Deep green shutters surrounded the large windows, and a long green lawn dotted with wooly white sheep had immediately reminded Caroline of home.

Walking along the winding path to the orchard, bordered on one side by a low stone wall, had given her time to compose herself. And then the trees came into view, planted in rows and already showing signs of the fruit they would bear. Caroline took in a deep breath, the same as she would in the cherry orchards of her home.

They turned the corner, and as peace settled upon her heart once more, she met the direct, blue-eyed gaze of Edward Everly. The peaceful feeling didn't flee, precisely. It stayed, but slowly curled around her heart like a lazy kitten, and everything grew warmer.

Especially when the gentleman smiled at her without the least measure of decorum and stared as though he found her the most fascinating woman in the world. For one horrid moment, she'd both feared and hoped he'd recognize her and mention their first meeting. But he didn't say a word about it. And his sisters stepped in before Caroline grew brave enough to mention it herself.

Had Mariah Kimball managed to speak with him already? It didn't seem possible, given they had made their plan the day before the picnic. Perhaps the gentleman had grinned at her not because he recognized her, but because he thought her plan ridiculous. She had no way to ask the meaning behind the look, though.

When Irene and Isaac took her hand to lead her away, Caroline had breathed a sigh of relief. Letting a child direct her seemed easier than trying to find her own way in the crowd of strangers. And the now-properly-introduced Edward Everly.

That vibrant grin he'd given her had made her blush without quite knowing why.

"Tell them about your dog," Lady Irene begged, and soon Caroline spun tales of puppies, kittens, the family milk cow, and her father's horse. The children listened with delight, talking of their own adventures with domesticated animals. The conversation wasn't sophisticated, but it was familiar and simple. Caroline's younger siblings had prepared her for this exact circumstance. All children loved animals.

"I rode an elephant once," a little boy with dark eyes and red hair declared. "But I can't 'member it. We were in France."

"France?" Caroline repeated, shocked that a child of his age had ever lived so far from English shores. "Goodness. What was an elephant doing in France?"

"I don't know." The boy shrugged, one corner of his mouth tipping down as he frowned. "But my papa tells me stories about it all the time."

The gaggle of children nearly took her mind off Edward Everly and the plan she had made with Mariah. A bright yellow bonnet, however, soon drew Caroline's eye. Mariah Kimball wore the bonnet, her perfectly oval face framed by golden curls and the cheerful hat. She walked arm-in-arm with Edward as though it came quite naturally to her. She drifted at his side, her gown the color of daffodils, and everything perfectly in place.

It was no wonder their families expected them to make a match. They seemed quite comfortable with one another.

Caroline looked down again at her simple cream-colored dress with its limited flounces and single pink ribbon sash around her waist. Her arms were sun-bronzed, and her hands, spotted with the paint she couldn't remove with soap and water, were covered by lace gloves the countess had gifted her a few days before.

Perhaps her idea hadn't been as sound as she supposed.

Mariah and Edward Everly came nearer, Caroline realized Edward and the lady on his arm were taking a route toward friends to come to her. She stood when they arrived, her hands tucked against her side, and a genial expression upon her face. One of the children had proposed a game of tag, and they left her there moments ago after she declined their invitation to join them.

"Miss Clapham," Edward said, his dark blue eyes alight with mischief. "I understand you've met one of my oldest friends. Miss Kimball speaks quite highly of you, too."

Miss Kimball's cheeks had turned rosy. "Indeed. We became fast friends. I hope we will spend a great many hours together." Her voice was pitched to carry, as though she wanted others to overhear their conversation. Caroline followed suit.

"Thank you. I am at her ladyship's mercy while I am here, though she has assured me she wishes to fill our schedule with diverting events." Even if Caroline would much rather stay on Inglewood's grounds, filling her days with ink and paint.

Miss Kimball took the lead in the conversation, her eyes alight with good cheer as she went on to describe the sorts of ways the neighborhood celebrated the warmer weather. She spoke of outings in the country, bonfires, parties that filled gardens, evenings of storytelling and cards, and Caroline's stomach twisted itself in knots as she heard of each and every thing that could separate her from her purpose.

And Mariah kept giving significant glances, as though hoping he would say something.

Caroline let her gaze flicker to the silent Edward Everly, noting he smiled steadily at her even while he made no effort to add to Miss Kimball's exuberance. He appeared amused, and she caught a smirk on his lips that nearly stole her attention with its suggestive tilt.

"What are your favorite things to do, Miss Clapham?" the enthusiastic woman asked at last, her gold eyelashes batting with her curiosity. She sent a frustrated, side-eyed glance in Edward Everly's direction.

Here at last, the silent man answered before Caroline could speak. "She looks like an artist to me," he stated with confidence. "Something about the way she carries herself, you see. Perhaps it is in the way she places her hands."

Caroline's eyebrows shot up while Miss Kimball blinked at the man in confusion.

"I hold myself no differently than other ladies brought up well," Caroline corrected. "And my hands have been folded this whole conversation."

"And hardly a clever supposition, Edward," Mariah added, narrowing her eyes at him. "As a guest to the countess, it would be natural to suppose such a thing." She seemed quite annoyed with him. Mariah didn't intend to play along with whatever game her friend had concocted. She lowered her voice, "This is a horrid way to begin, you know. Miss Clapham will think you troublesome and change her mind about everything."

At last, evidence that Mr. Everly and Mariah had spoken of Caroline's idea! She relaxed at once, then smiled. "I can withstand a little teasing, Miss Kimball. It would take more than that to dissuade me from our agreement."

Mariah's relief tinted her response. "That is too kind of you." She raised her voice again. "You must be an artist of some talent, to be a guest to the countess."

They were having two conversations at once, it would seem. Caroline was perfectly equal to that task. "Lady Inglewood has been my mentor and teacher for a number of years. I still have much to learn, though."

"Oh, you needn't be modest, Miss Clapham." Mr. Everly folded his arms across his chest and tipped his head forward, as though making an examination of her. "If Lady Inglewood has made you her guest on merit of your artistic capabilities alone, you will have a superior talent compared to most."

"But not all." Caroline had no intention of comparing herself to anyone in present company. Even if she had passable skills with paint, she couldn't play pianoforte very well. Nor did her alto-voice lend itself well to most popular music of the day. And she highly doubted Miss Kimball spent her summers climbing cherry trees. Best move the conversation along. "It is a lovely day for a picnic, isn't it?"

"Absolutely." Mariah gave Edward another pointed look. "A perfect day for a picnic. And perhaps a walk in the orchard. Wouldn't you agree, Mr. Everly?"

He readily nodded. "Indeed. Perhaps you would like a tour of the orchard, Miss Clapham?"

"And an opportunity for a more private conversation," Mariah added quietly, then startled when Miss Patience Everly appeared at her brother's elbow. "Edward, Mama would like to ask Miss

Kimball's opinion on something regarding their ladies' sewing circle."

Even Caroline knew what that meant. Mrs. Everly wanted Edward to escort Miss Kimball to her side, bringing son and potential daughter-in-law into her sphere. The lack of subtlety, accompanied by a slight wince from both the gentleman and lady, affirmed Caroline's guess.

Miss Kimball hadn't exaggerated the maneuvering of her parents or his, it seemed. She was the hoped-for bride, but Edward Everly wasn't the man of her choice. The knowing look she shared with him turned to one of commiseration.

The two of them needed help, and neither was eager to disappoint parents or cause gossip. Caroline resisted shaking her head in despair of them both.

The gentleman's next words were a willful misunderstanding of the summons. "Wonderful. Miss Kimball, while you speak with my mother, I will give our new acquaintance a tour of the orchard. As you have seen it so many times on your visits, you will not mind saving yourself the walk." In one fluid motion, he moved from Miss Kimball's side to Caroline's, and offered her his arm.

Caroline hesitated somewhat awkwardly, her hand frozen at her side and her gaze upon Miss Kimball's expression. Miss Kimball's eyebrows raised a touch, but she didn't appear the least perturbed. Instead, her smile quirked up higher on one side than the other and she gave her erstwhile escort a single nod of acceptance.

It was Miss Patience, the youngest of them, who covered her brother's graceless retreat. "Precisely what I hoped, Edward. Miss Clapham's welcome tour cannot be neglected. Come, Miss Kimball. Mama and I are both interested in what you think of the new embroidery patterns she received from France."

If Caroline hadn't been watching carefully, she would have missed the sharp look of censure the girl aimed at her brother as she turned away, leading Miss Kimball by the hand. Miss Patience hadn't caught the silent agreement that passed between the other two.

Edward waggled the elbow he held out to Caroline, a grin in place of the smile that had barely reached his eyes before. "Come along, my mysterious artist. I have an orchard to show you."

Caroline at last accepted his proffered escort, slipping her hand through the crook of his elbow and resting it lightly on his forearm. Children of all ages darted among the roots and branches of the apple trees, and other couples were strolling beneath the shade, too.

Despite the unlikeliness of eavesdroppers, Caroline lowered her voice as she walked with him beneath the trees, away from the picnic area. "There is nothing subtle about you, is there? First you crash through the woods to disturb my afternoon, now you dismiss a young lady when you were clearly meant to remain by her side. Tell me. Are you always so reckless?"

He put his free hand to his heart and affected a hurt expression, his eyebrows drawn sharply together. "Your aim is true, Miss Clapham. I am wounded. Though perhaps you cannot blame me overmuch. I did not know I disturbed anyone in the woods that day, besides the handful of squirrels in the trees. As for Miss Kimball—" He shrugged and frowned at the path ahead of them, winding through the trees. "She told me of the plan you concocted."

"That is a relief," she told him, "as it saves me from explaining the whole of it to you."

He stopped walking with such abruptness that she took another step without him, her arm catching his in a way that made her stumble. He tightened his hold on her, steadying her with ease.

"Do you truly mean to help us?" he demanded, his brow creased and lips turned downward.

Two young girls a few feet away from them paused in their clapping game to look their way. Caroline cast them a reassuring smile, then gave Edward enough of a yank that he had to start walking again. She whispered, "As I said, you have no talent for subtlety."

He grumbled, "Skirting around an issue never helps anyone. And we are desperate, Miss Clapham." He finally lowered his voice to match hers, drawing her along to a place where the orchard gave way to older, different sorts of trees. Caroline stopped him beneath the shade of an oak.

"You hardly appear desperate." Caroline pulled her arm from his and barely resisted the inclination to put both hands on her hips, as she would to take her younger siblings to task for poor behavior. "The two of you promenaded through that picnic as though you were already a comfortable old married couple. If you keep up such behavior, you will end your stroll at a church altar with your brother-in-law pronouncing you 'man and wife.'"

"What would you have us do?" he asked, both hands coming up to ward off her prediction of future events. "I haven't any intention of marrying anyone. But Mariah's parents have expectations, as do my own, and neither of us want to hurt our families or force their hands." He shuddered and took a step away before turning, his back to her. "I apologize for drawing you into our personal affairs."

He no longer seemed like the man in the woods. Quick to smile and tease. Charming her with his deep blue eyes. Instead, his whole being radiated tension and impatience. "You needn't apologize. If Miss Kimball told you of my plan, I hope she told you it was my decision to help. If you still want my help, Mr. Everly."

His shoulders dropped and he chuckled, the sound without much mirth. "For all that I lack delicacy in conversation, Miss Clapham, you have a talent for frankness."

"That doesn't sound like much of a compliment," she responded, then had to cover her smile. He was correct, of course. Though she knew when to mind her words well enough around others. Something about this man, perhaps due to the unexpected way he had entered her life without any regard for the niceties of society, had made her forget to curb her tongue. She spoke to him the way she did to her family.

When he turned around again, eyebrows raised, she spoke with sincerity. "I apologize, Mr. Everly. We are strangers. I will refrain from speaking so freely in future."

"Zeus, Miss Clapham, I hope not."

She blinked. Had she ever heard someone invoke the Greek god of thunder that way? Her stepfather had a colorful vocabulary that he regularly apologized for, but his references to the things above and below earth were always quite biblical.

He misinterpreted her confusion, given his sheepish smile and the way he averted his eyes. "What I meant was, I find it refreshing to hear someone speak as candidly as you do. It was one of the things I immediately liked when we met."

Her cheeks warmed. Was he flirting? She couldn't tell. She knew when Jill's brother attempted to flirt with her, and she never blushed at his clumsy compliments. Perhaps the excitement of the day and discomfort of the situation had finally taken effect. Caroline ignored the blush. Hopefully, he wouldn't pay it attention either.

"Thank you. I think." She looked through the trees, seeing only slivers of the picnic they had left behind amid the trunks and branches. "I must ask you what I asked Miss Kimball. Why not tell your parents that you have no matrimonial intentions toward her? For one who admires candor, it ought to be a simple matter of one conversation."

"One would think that." He shoved his hand through his hair, making the artistic wave near his forehead into a shabby likeness of a birds' nest instead. "But our families have been connected for generations, in friendship and as neighbors. If her family thought I had insulted her, it would damage the relationship between the two households." He met her gaze. "My parents wouldn't be able to do much to me, of course. One of the benefits of being a man in his majority." His smile was bitter. "But there are ways they could exercise their displeasure. It is Mariah I am worried for. She believes her parents would send her away if she defied them outright."

"Ridiculous," Caroline muttered, crossing her arms in front of her. "You have both let expectations, gossip, and a lack of honesty to bring you to this most unfortunate point."

He rubbed the back of his neck, an incredulous smirk on his lips. "It is a rather convoluted mess." He stepped closer, and Caroline realized how lovely it was to stand up straight while speaking with a gentleman and have his eyes slightly above the level of her own. Tall as she was, most gentlemen of her acquaintance met her gaze eye-to-eye. "Perhaps the two of us are trapped because we care about our families and one another."

"You are speaking in riddles," she told him. Then she tilted her chin up and allowed herself one hand upon her hip. "I want to know one thing only. Do you intend to go through with my plan or not? If not, we have nothing more to say and we ought to return to the picnic, Mr. Everly."

"I intend to go through with your plan."

Caroline's gasp escaped despite herself. Then she pressed her lips together and nodded once. "Good."

His eyebrows drew together. "Because of your earlier candor, and the intelligence I can sense you possess, you will not mind if I ask a few questions."

Caroline couldn't doubt the sincerity in his voice. He sounded desperate, and his whole body bent toward her with a beseeching posture. "I will not mind, Mr. Everly. I would be alarmed if you didn't have questions." She folded her arms across her chest. "Go on."

"How do you benefit from helping us?"

"In no way at all," she answered easily. "I like Mariah. When she confided her troubles in me, a complete stranger, I wanted to help. My own parents have provided me with everything I need to achieve my dreams, my happiness. It seems a shame that she believes her family cares nothing about her ability to do the same."

"Mariah is as good as she seems. It makes sense you would want to help her, even after a short acquaintance." He relaxed and the tension drained from his expression. His grin had disappeared, but so had the worried furrows in his brow. The poor man. In keeping his word to a friend, he had tied himself to a situation over which he had no control. Because he was a concerned friend.

"Our conversation is remarkably honest, considering what strangers we are to one another." Caroline said, more gently than before, "I think you must be a good man, too, Mr. Everly. I am happy to help you, too."

"You cannot be a real person," he stated simply, staring at her with open confusion. "You must be that sprite I found in the woods. Or else, I suppose, an artist of great integrity in both her craft and in her words."

Warmth spread upward from her chest and into her blood. That they barely knew one another made his words weigh more, at least in that circumstance. He had identified her as what she wanted to be more than anything in the world. An artist. And he used that identification to deduce what mattered to her.

"I am not an artist. Not really."

He chuckled and turned slightly away. "So you are a woodland, fey creature?"

"It isn't good manners to call someone a fairy."

"A sprite."

"Still a type of fairy," she countered as an invisible hand closed around her heart and squeezed. Despite her protests, he had given her a gift with the title she so longed to claim. And she *did* have sympathy for him and for Mariah.

"Do you have any other questions?" Caroline asked.

"Your reputation might suffer if we do this. Doesn't that worry you?"

"I have no history with the people in your community. With Mariah's family or yours. I am leaving at the end of summer, too. That gives me a great deal of freedom that neither of you may feel. As the guest of the earl and the countess, I imagine that grants me a buffer of sorts, too. So no. I am not concerned about my reputation, so long as you promise you are an honorable man."

"I am." His smile faded away. "We may still be asking too much of you."

"No one asked. I offered." A mixture of anxiety and excitement twisted about inside of her. This was happening. He was about to agree to her idea. Her ridiculous scheme that suddenly loomed larger than she thought it would in her mind.

Edward cleared his throat, and the way he tapped his fingers against his leg made her think he had as many complex emotions about the path ahead as she did.

"Miss Clapham," he began, his voice a little unsteady. "I know we have only just met, but I feel that we understand one another. I trust you. So does Mariah." He paused for a moment. "It doesn't sit well with me that you do so much for us. I will insist that you have something from me. A favor of your naming, whenever you wish, in return for your kindness."

"If it makes your mind easier, I will agree to that." Caroline looked through the trees, where children now called to one another in a new game. "I know it sounds unconventional," she said, "this plan of mine."

"I think it will work." He surprised her with a smile. "My parents will be satisfied that I am making progress towards a marriage, and it will buy time for Mariah to convince her parents of her own plans for happiness. It is only one summer." He looked at her earnestly, and Caroline reassured him once more.

"A pretend courtship cannot be too difficult."

"Perhaps not. I promise, I will do all I can to make your summer enjoyable and interesting. Don't artists require unusual things to motivate their creation? Perhaps this is the sort of adventure that will lead to inspiration."

She hadn't thought of it that way. And her inspiration had run quite thin of late. Perhaps this strange idea would stimulate her creativity in a way nothing else had.

"It wouldn't be fair to either of us to enter into something like this lightly." She smiled at him, giving him one more chance to think things through. "If you need more time to think on it—"

"I don't," he admitted, ducking his head. "This is the right thing to do." He didn't appear much comforted as he offered her his arm. "When shall we begin?"

The feeling in her stomach reminded her of something strange. After she finished using a paintbrush, she would swirl it about in a mixture of turpentine, agitating the brush with quick, sharp movements. Then she removed it, and pressed the bristles between her cloth, squeezing the damp out.

Her stomach had been quite thoroughly agitated by Edward Everly's conversation, and his acceptance of her idea had finished the job, leaving her wrung dry and uncertain as to whether she had done the right thing in proposing their strange arrangement.

"There is no time like the present," she quipped, ignoring the increase of heat in her cheeks. "Are you a capable flirt, Mr. Everly?"

He chuckled. "Call me Edward. We are allies in battle, Miss Clapham. And you will have to judge my abilities yourself."

"You must call me Caroline." She lifted her chin as they left the shadows of the orchard, her heart racing. Her brazen, impractical, outlandish idea had been accepted by Mariah and Edward. And now, though she had no experience with romance whatsoever, her first courtship was about to begin.

What would her family think of her decision? Her mother wouldn't approve. But her papa might well find the whole idea amusing. They had praised her for thinking outside of conventional dictates before, but had she taken a step too far this time? Edward returned her to the picnic, speaking to her of the apple trees, and she said nothing about how much they reminded her of her orchard at home or the family she had left behind in pursuit of her dream.

# CHAPTER 8

L ady Inglewood and Caroline examined a scattered selection of sketches and paintings spread across the largest table in the library while they waited for the morning's guests. Though they had guests arriving soon, the countess had sent for Caroline earlier than their agreed-upon time.

Nearly a week had passed since the picnic, which had been wholly unremarkable after Caroline's conversation with Mr. Everly. They would put their plan in motion for the first time this day, when he arrived with his sisters and Miss Kimball for a painting exercise dreamed up by the countess. Caroline had tried to prepare herself for what she suspected would be an attempt at flirtation amid watercolors and paintbrushes.

She hadn't prepared herself for whatever had sent Lady Inglewood into a state of distraction. A furrow creased her brow, revealing her deep concern. Her lips, usually adorned with a gentle smile, were now pressed together in a contemplative line.

"What is it?" Caroline asked, *not* twisting her fingers with anxiety. She kept them clamped on the edge of the table, her eyes searching her work for whatever had made Lady Inglewood's brow pucker. "Is something wrong?" She couldn't imagine what glaring deficiency she had that would necessitate a look at all the work she had brought with her. Rolled canvases were held open and down by small paperweights, sketchbooks were open to display profiles of her father and farmers who had sat patiently while she captured their likenesses.

One of her favorite sketches was of a man she had known for many years, though he had died the year before. A grizzled farmer, his face lined with wrinkles, and a soft smile on his lips. It certainly wasn't an elegant work, but she loved it and didn't understand why the countess picked it up only to frown at it.

"Nothing is wrong, my dear." Lady Inglewood put the sketchbook down and raised both hands to her temples. "Your work is excellent. But I had a sudden realization not an hour ago about all I have seen. There are no paintings here of the male form, other than the formal portrait of Lord Neil. No full-length depictions. And no depictions of classical themes, events, characters, or stories."

Caroline looked down at the table, her eyes taking in what she had spent days and weeks creating. Examining her work, Caroline saw a portrait of her grandmother, her mother, her stepfather, an image of her twin brothers playing with a puppy, her little sister walking on a beach, landscapes of orchards and sheep, and studies of cathedral ruins and cottages.

But Lady Inglewood was correct. Caroline had nothing like what Lady Inglewood described. "I don't understand. Why is this troubling you?"

The countess lowered herself into a chair pulled up to the table. She tapped the arm of the chair, meeting Caroline's gaze with a serious one of her own. "Sir Thomas has a marked preference for paintings that are dramatic and evocative of history, myth, and legend. He has stated in the past that he believes no one can count themselves a true artist until they have delved into subjects that touch on the minds of men throughout history."

And as the President of the Royal Academy, Sir Thomas's preferences mattered to everyone in the art world of Great Britain.

"This is almost Madonna-like," Lady Inglewood said as she lifted a watercolor of Caroline's mother holding one of the twins, her tone absent as though she spoke more to herself than to Caroline. "A gentle theme of divine motherhood might satisfy him."

The doubt in Lady Inglewood's tone was enough to make a prick of fear touch Caroline's heart. "But you doubt it."

"It isn't truly a lack," Lady Inglewood said after several silent moments of thought. "Young, unmarried ladies aren't expected to study the male form in any detail. Some might think it scandalous." Her expression turned neutral as she turned another page in one of the sketchbooks.

"Would Sir Thomas think it scandalous, if I had a male model doing something other than sitting?" Caroline watched her mentor carefully, and the countess's frown reappeared.

"No. He would find such societal limitations on an artistic mind restricting. I have heard him say as much about women who show a gift for painting or sculpting." The countess shook her head. "I am not certain that we could have something new for him by the end of summer and still improve upon other areas that are essential to your progress." She put down the sketchbook gently. "Even if he wouldn't be scandalized, your stepfather and mother likely wouldn't approve if we hired someone to model for a more...adventurous pose."

Caroline's cheeks grew warm. "It wouldn't have to be a nude—"

Lady Inglewood laughed. "Of course not. Dear me. Lord Neil would certainly *not* approve of that." The countess pointedly looked up at a painting in her library, above a small bust of Athena. "If only we could combine the two things. A classical depiction of a man's form."

Caroline looked at the picture, too. It was a painting of the Greek hero, Herakles, wearing a tunic that covered one shoulder and left the other bare. He reached for golden apples upon a tree, one of the impossible tasks set for him by the gods.

"You do not think it possible?"

"We could never find a model who I could approve of, given that you are an unattached young lady." Lady Inglewood sighed, her shoulders falling. Her tone grew softer as she mused aloud, "Silas wouldn't agree to such a thing. Not a second time. And my brother...well. He has already granted me all favors owed."

The thought of asking either of those men, an earl and baronet closer in age to her parents than to her, made Caroline shudder. If they were her only options, she would rather not attempt a classical piece or anything to do with the male form.

"What of a younger man?" Caroline asked, her mind racing down numerous paths. "Perhaps someone without the status or age of the other two might be braver about posing for such a thing."

Lady Inglewood shook her head. "I fear it would be the opposite. Men are temperamental models as it is." She looked at the mantel clock. "Our guests will arrive at any moment. We can discuss your options another time. For now, we ought to adjourn to the garden."

Caroline didn't quite manage to disguise her impatient sigh. Then she blushed as the countess laughed, the sound light and without censure.

"Dear Caroline. I know you see today's activity as a distraction. But one of the best ways to improve our knowledge of a subject is to teach that subject to another." Lady Inglewood led them out of the library. She wore a clean cotton apron over an unadorned, simplistic gown. Clean paintbrushes poked up out of narrow pockets against her thighs. "Which is why I invited young ladies to paint with us today."

The two of them took up their bonnets, in a sitting room with doors that led out to the gardens. Their reflections stared back at them from a large, gilded mirror that hung beside the doors as they tied the ribbons of the hats beneath their chins.

Linked arm-in-arm, they went out into the late-morning sun. Despite the bonnet, Caroline had to blink several times before her vision adjusted to the bright glow of sunlight from above and its reflection on the white stone of the path they followed. Five ladies and a single gentleman waited for them on a lower part of the terraced gardens. A large wall of shrubbery between them and the sea protected the fountain and its occupants from any wind that might come off the water.

Vases of flowers were placed on the fountain's low-wall. Each lady had an easel with paper clipped or pinned in place, along with pedestal-like tables holding paints and jars of water.

Mrs. Kimball and Miss Kimball were both present, as were Miss Everly and Miss Patience Everly, and Lady Fox, wife to Sir Isaac. Lady Fox and her husband had visited Caroline's home on many occasions, as Lady Fox was a good friend to Papa.

And on a bench near the fountain, with a book in hand, was the only gentleman. Edward Everly. He rose as they approached, bowing to Lady Inglewood and Caroline both.

"Edward," Lady Inglewood greeted him with a smile. "You will not join us in painting today?" Her tone made it clear she teased him, the same as an affectionate aunt might.

Edward feigned a deep sigh of disappointment. "Alas, your ladyship, you know I have no talent for brushwork. It is best I remain as unobtrusive as possible."

"If you didn't wish to paint, I cannot understand why you came," Miss Everly said, giving her brother an impatient glance. "Unless you mean to be a distraction."

He chuckled and sent Caroline a glance so quick no one else could have noticed, but she saw the mischief there. Three of them at that moment knew precisely why Edward had not only agreed to accompany his sisters on their visit, but why he would be insistent on remaining throughout the course of their activity.

Still anxious and impatient after the conversation about Sir Thomas's preferences, Caroline couldn't muster more than a brief smile for him. He would have to carry the weight of the ruse today. She had other things to concentrate on. Even if his charming smile tempted her to take a second glance at him.

The expense of all the supplies made the party a unique one, and the sort of thing only someone of a generous mind or large fortune would think to invent. Lady Inglewood presented Caroline with a polite reintroduction. "You have all met my dear friend

Miss Clapham by now. She has graciously agreed to take part in your instruction today. Miss Clapham is an apt student, and a talented artist. We will benefit from her artistic insight, I am certain."

Whether the ladies had the usual level of expertise one could expect from females of gently bred households, Caroline couldn't say. She hadn't worked with anyone outside of Lady Inglewood, her mother, grandmother, and an instructor her mother had hired two years previous. Having few to measure against her own abilities, Caroline couldn't be certain what the ladies themselves would consider well done or in need of improvement.

Edward Everly settled on his bench, one leg crossed over the other, his book in hand. He didn't appear the least interested in the painting party.

For a time, Caroline strictly observed and worked upon her own paper. Settled as she was between Miss Kimball and Miss Everly, she had an excellent view of their work. Lady Fox and Miss Patience were on either side of Lady Inglewood. It became apparent at once that Miss Everly over-saturated her color with water, making her reds into pinks and all other colors into pastels. Was it on purpose? She also had a difficult time adding detail to her roses. Miss Kimball had started her work with the blooms, too, and her chosen hues were perfect. Yet she had the tendency to linger overlong on a brush stroke.

First Caroline went to Miss Everly's aid. "Your technique is lovely," she said first, and the woman's cheeks turned the same shade of pink as her roses. "May I make one small suggestion?" She held her hand out for the other's brush, then showed how to remove excess water from the bristles after taking in some color.

"Oh, thank you." Miss Everly said, beginning a new rose. "I much prefer quilling, but my mother assures me it is no longer in fashion."

Lady Fox sniffed and spoke with confidence from her side of the fountain. "And what do we care for fashion when it comes to our artistic pursuits, Miss Everly? Quilling has long been a favorite of mine, along with inking wood in the deepest blacks. Shall I invite your mother to come and play at quilling with us some afternoon?"

Miss Everly's cheeks turned pinker still. "I would enjoy that, my lady. I believe my mother would, too."

Lady Fox nodded firmly, as though that settled things, and Caroline stepped behind her easel to hide her smile. Then she peeped over at Mariah's work. The other woman had continued her slow, steady progress, and her mistake took effect. Her colorful wash of red dried, uneven and with small, dark streaks.

Caroline laid her brush down. She walked around Miss Kimball to stand on her side furthest from Miss Everly. She watched for a moment in silence, contemplating how best to explain the problem to the other lady.

Mariah, not looking up from her work, spoke before Caroline made up her mind on what to say. "The paint dries too quickly for me," she murmured softly, glancing briefly to where her mother worked on the other side of the fountain. "But when I add more water, it dilutes the color, as you saw with Miss Everly."

"Watching you, I don't think your problem is in the amount of water you use. The colors are perfect. Quite vibrant." Caroline offered a sympathetic smile to the other woman, noting the dimple that appeared when Mariah sucked in her cheeks. The woman was an absolute beauty. No wonder Mr. Edward Everly's parents wanted her for a daughter-in-law.

"Is my brush the wrong size?" she asked, looking at her work critically.

"No, indeed. Your strokes are even, precise. You are using the same brush I would use." Caroline pointed along the heavy, dark line of one rose petal. "Your handling of the brush is near perfect. I can only find fault with the speed at which you work. While I understand the desire to move slowly, to perfect each detail, it is not a supportable way to work with watercolors. The paint dries before you finish with it, creating edges that will only grow darker if you attempt to correct it. You will overwork the area and compound the problem. You must move faster, Miss Kimball."

The other woman chewed on her bottom lip, looking from Caroline to the paper. "But what of the lost detail? Or a blunder? Hasty work can lead to mistakes," she added, softer still.

Perhaps she wasn't truly speaking of the painting. Caroline glanced over her shoulder and noted Edward Everly had lowered his book to watch them, his eyebrows raised.

"In some cases, that is true. You must strike a balance between hurried work and efficiency." Caroline nodded to the thick paper before Miss Kimball. "Create another petal. A different rose. But think only of making one, fluid motion with your wrist first one direction, and then the other, drawing the paint along with the brush rather than trying to place it exactly where you wish it to be."

Mariah took the brush and drew in a slow, deep breath. "Very well." She checked the color in its well, adding more pigment to the water until satisfied with the hue, and then held the brush close to the paper.

A movement at the corner of her eye heralded Edward's rise from the bench. He approached them without sound and stood just behind them both. Caroline sensed his watchful gaze on the back of her neck the same as she would feel the sunlight warming her.

"One fluid motion, Miss Kimball," Caroline repeated softly, ignoring the man.

Miss Kimball, with her delicate wrists and long, tapered fingers, gracefully gave shape to a rose petal the color of her shapely lips. Her lips parted with surprise as she drew the brush back the opposite way, and then she released her breath in a small, cheerful puff. "That looks much better."

"Watercolor can be concerned with the details, of course," Caroline admitted, smiling to herself. "But more often it is about the proper feel of the thing you wish to paint. Roses are less bothersome about having perfect edges than we are. If you work with the colors before they dry on the page, you have time to correct mistakes, too. Once they dry, things are less amendable."

"One would think the passage of time makes it easier to mend mistakes," Miss Kimball murmured, her gaze on the painting. Her sunny smile returned, though Caroline realized it did not quite reach the woman's eyes. She looked over her shoulder and her eyes widened. "Mr. Everly. When did you creep up behind us?"

Edward chuckled. "When I sensed an important lesson being taught."

"I thought you hadn't any enjoyment in painting," Caroline countered, her eyebrows raised at him. "Of what use is instruction on the subject to you?"

"I said I haven't any talent for it," he corrected with a crooked grin. "I am an admirer of art, though. I can appreciate the work that goes into the creation as much as I do the final product. Thus I find your instruction to Miss Kimball enthralling."

"Enthralling," she repeated, letting skepticism drip from each syllable. His grin appeared, and Caroline chanced a look at his sister nearest them to find her watching with interest. The show had started.

"Interesting," he amended, the grin still in place.

"Edward," Miss Everly said, eyes on her canvas again. "Stop being a distraction."

The gentleman folded his arms and shared a glance with Mariah and Caroline. "Am I distracting the two of you?"

Mariah heaved a sigh. "You so like being at the center of attention, don't you? Here." She put her brush in the crook of his arm. "You try."

He took the brush and shook his head. "I haven't any wish to harm your painting, Miss Kimball."

"Then come have a go on mine," Caroline offered, gesturing to her painting. "I have no need for this particular piece, so you needn't protest that you will cause any damage to it."

From the other side of the fountain, his sister Patience said in a sing-song voice, "Edward is in trouble."

He waved his paintbrush at his sister and then squared up against the easel Caroline had abandoned to him, as though he meant to box it rather than put brush to paper. "This will not be too terrible. I can simply copy what you have already done." He dipped the brush in the paint and Caroline said nothing. She only watched.

Like most gentlemen of education, he knew enough to get the general shape of the flower correct. And he didn't ask for help. Merely went through the motions. But after a few moments of quiet, he asked, "How did you come to be such a talented and patient painter?"

Though she hadn't expected the questions, the explanation came without Caroline giving it much thought, each word as warm and true as the summer sun. "I have always thought of painting as an act of love. That it is a talent to nurture as much as it is a thing to correct."

Edward chuckled and dipped his brush into the paint again. "I can understand nurturing talent, but I find I don't comprehend the rest. Perhaps it is because I do not have the same artistic passion as you do, Miss Clapham. To be in love with your work must change how you perceive it."

"Oh." Caroline's cheeks grew warm and she discreetly checked that her bonnet's brim still shaded her from the sun. "I don't mean I am in love with my work. That sounds entirely too romantic. It is more of a nurturing love. Like that of a mother toward a child. My art is something to tend to and take care of, a thing that exists because of my efforts."

His brow furrowed, but whether the reaction was due to her words or his concentration on the roses, Caroline couldn't tell.

Mariah spoke before Edward did. "That is a lovely way to put it. When I play a new piece on my harp, I feel that way about learning the music. I am devoted to my harp. I care for it. I treat it almost as I would an extension of myself. Every time I touch the strings, bringing the notes on the page to life, I am determined to have everything turn out well. Even the most difficult pieces, even the music I never quite master as I should wish, I love and devote myself to the music."

Caroline's artist heart recognized in Mariah's a kinship. They were different, of course. They came from wholly unrelated backgrounds and families. But they understood one another perfectly as Mariah's gentle eyes met Caroline's.

"I hope I may hear you play someday," Caroline said, voice soft.

"Whenever you wish it, Miss Clapham." Mariah nodded her agreement.

Edward took a step back from his painting. "There. What do you think?"

The colors ran into one another, from dark pink to light, and a stem of green that wavered. It wasn't the worst thing Caroline had ever beheld. But it still took her a moment to say, "There now, Mr. Everly. You are not so terrible as you said."

Miss Everly put down her brush and came to see her brother's work, her expression one of puzzlement. "Edward, that looks terrible." Sisters were not prone to mincing words, it would seem. "I am terribly sorry, Miss Clapham, but I think he is beyond even your assistance. Though I do thank you for helping me. Look, how beautiful my roses are now!"

Caroline came to look over and approve of the other woman's work, as did Miss Kimball. "This is excellent, Miss Everly. Well done."

"We were speaking of our devotion to our chosen arts," Mariah said, giving a brief summary of the subject to Miss Everly before she asked, "Do you have a thing you love to do above all else, Miss Everly?"

"Of course. Dancing." Miss Everly tossed her head merrily. "But I cannot see how one could relate dancing with handsome gentlemen to motherhood, of all things." She brushed at her nose with one finger, transferring paint from the brush in her hand to her temple in the process.

"According to our society," Edward put in, picking up a cloth to dab away the paint on his sister's face while she made faces at him, "you cannot have one without the other."

"Cynical Edward," his sister said with a sigh, brushing aside his help and taking the cloth from him to tend to the matter herself.

"What is it *you* love above all else, Edward? What talent or entertainment?"

Given the way Mariah raised her eyebrows in expectancy, Caroline realized she didn't know what her friend would say. Curious, Caroline repeated the question. "Indeed, Mr. Everly. To what idea do you devote your heart?"

He met her gaze without reserve, his blue eyes darkening just enough for her to believe him ready to give a serious response. Something lurked in the depths of his thoughts and in his heart. She felt his answer rising, but then he seemed to recall himself. He blinked and turned away from the ladies. "At the moment, I must devote my mind to my book. *A Treatise on Seaside Agriculture.* Riveting subject."

"Is that the book Papa put on your breakfast plate?" Miss Everly asked without looking away from her painting.

He picked it up. "Indeed." Then sat back down on his bench. "A required text to be a landowner, it would seem."

Caroline blinked at him, then looked to Mariah, whose lips were pursed as though Edward's reaction had disturbed her. She met Caroline's gaze and offered a small shrug. She hadn't any idea what had changed his mood, either.

A pretended courtship between Edward and Caroline would have to be convincing. Thus far, their steps were quite small. But at least they had made a start of it.

Caroline studied Edward's attempt at a rose. She couldn't fix it, exactly, but with a few added flowers and more greenery, she could make it blend well into her bouquet. If nothing else, it gave her a bit of a challenge while the others worked on their pieces. Something to keep her hands busy while her mind worked through other problems.

Everyone who saw Edward and Caroline together had to believe the two felt an attraction toward each other. And that would mean spending yet more time away from her art, which she had to focus on more than ever. Especially if she was going to impress the president of the Royal Academy. Already she began with a disadvantage, having nothing in a classical style—

Caroline's brush stilled, a wet green blot of paint growing beneath its bristles that she hardly noticed.

Edward had insisted that he owed her a favor. A marvelously *large* favor. And she had thought of something that she needed. A favor which no other man would have reason to perform for her.

With a sudden gasp, Caroline pulled her brush from the thick paper and used a dry handkerchief to blot up her mistake. A mistake she didn't actually mind making, since it had come about in the moment her rather brilliant idea had come alive. Her plan to help Edward Everly, Mariah Kimball and her mysterious suitor, and to help herself appear to best advantage when Sir Thomas Lawrence arrived at Inglewood.

All she needed was an opportunity to speak to Edward about it. Alone. She looked to where he sat, frowning at his book as he turned a page. Her hope rose and a flush of excitement warmed her inside and out. He would help her. He simply *had* to.

# CHAPTER 9

Summer had always been Edward's favorite season, full as it was of fine weather and sun. He found freedom in escaping the confines of his family's house to enjoy the company of others. Winter kept too many at home with its chill winds and frost-covered fields, and spring made the roads more nuisance than convenience.

But now, with the sun out later and the weather enlivening the neighborhood, evening parties were far more common. The invitation to such a party at Inglewood had come, only a week after his family's picnic. And Edward had struggled to hide his enthusiasm at his inclusion, considering it was "a party for young people to come to know the esteemed guest of the Earl and Countess of Inglewood, Miss Caroline Clapham."

His sisters had spent the two days since the invitation's arrival debating on a gown choice for Charity. Patience was not yet out in society, especially for formal engagements away from home. She still uttered the complaint that evening, "I would be a better guest than Edward, who is frightfully dull and keeps telling us he doesn't want to spend time in company with unwed ladies."

Their mother had given Patience a stern lecture, but Edward received one as well. Mrs. Everly had told Edward, before he went upstairs to dress, "Make certain you pay attention to Miss Kimball this evening. Do not neglect her in favor of the guest of honor. And do mind your manners, Edward."

Edward smirked into the mirror as his valet fixed his cravat in place with a sapphire stickpin. His mother knew him well. Though manners would not be the issue. Putting Caroline Clapham's plan —a good plan he wished he had come up with himself—into action, in public, was what worried him.

He'd nearly run mad, thinking his way through the evening and all possible paths to take. Planning conversations and a public flirtation in advance were not to his liking.

Lord and Lady Inglewood had issued their invitation to dine and play games to all the young members of their community who were out in society, including chaperones where necessary.

"Your coat, Mr. Edward." His valet held out the black evening coat. The staff would call him by this name until Edward inherited. He didn't much mind. He'd prefer to be Mr. Edward for many years yet. At least when at home. He slipped into the coat. The only color other than his stickpin came from the dark blue waistcoat beneath the black frock-coat. The blue always brought out his eyes, he knew. And the eyes he shared with his sisters were one of their most attractive features. Everyone said so.

"Thank you. That will be all for this evening." He brushed at his sleeves one last time before he left the mirror and his room, his valet tidying up behind him. He strode down the corridors of his home with a confident step, and nearly gave in to the urge to whistle as he descended the staircase.

It was well he refrained.

"Oh, how handsome you are, son." His mother waited in the front hall, where she had fussed over all her children for years. Charity waited, too, with an exasperated grimace.

"He had better look resplendent, given how long he took to ready himself." Charity wore a gown of pale blue, with her hair framing her face in tight ringlets. "What has come over you,

Edward? You are usually the one at the door, begging the rest of us to make haste."

Had he taken longer than usual to dress? Perhaps asking to try on three different waistcoats, and then picking different shoes, hadn't been precisely necessary.

He shifted uncomfortably on the last step. He didn't usually object to whatever his valet laid out. Tonight had been different. Though he couldn't precisely say why. Only that he felt it important to look his best.

"I would rather have a man who cares about his appearance in public than one who does not," their mother said as she stepped back, taking in the sight of them. "How grown up you are, both of you. Mind your manners at the earl's table and be gracious to your hosts."

"Yes, Mama," Edward said, coming forward to kiss his mother on the cheek.

"We are not infants, Mama," Charity said with a teasing smile. "I will tell you all about it when we return."

"I have no intention of being awake that late. One of the benefits to staying behind on an evening such as this is getting a full night's rest." Their mother laughed and followed them outside when the footman held the door open. "Look after your sister, Edward. Have a wonderful time!" She waved as the coach pulled away, and Edward exchanged one look with his sister before they both started laughing.

"For all that our parents may vex us, I feel we are quite fortunate to have them." Charity smoothed her skirt over her knees. "They worry because they care, that is all."

"Agreed. Most of the time." Edward put his hat in his lap, giving it as little chance as possible to crease his hair. His valet regularly expressed dismay in Edward's ability to destroy whatever the man managed to create of the short, curling mess, but Edward had inherited the stubborn waves his sister Hope had to contend with. Were his hair any longer, even his valet would have no say in how it behaved.

"Why did you take so long to dress?" Charity asked, more curious than annoyed this time. "You never care what you look like at these things. Surely, you aren't trying to impress anyone?"

"Not at all." He avoided meeting his sister's eyes. Why had he rejected the valet's first choice of evening costume? And the second? "I merely lost track of the time."

His sister didn't sound convinced. "Mm. I haven't known you to be anything less than punctual before."

With his sister examining his motives, Edward allowed himself to do the same. But only for a moment before he realized he needed to put a stop to that direction of thought before he ran directly into a pair of pretty eyes and dark curls. Caroline had done him a great service. One he hoped to repay. That made him grateful to her. Intrigued by her, too, perhaps. But *not* anything more.

Even if she was attractive, that didn't mean he had to be attracted *to* her.

Wives were anchors. No matter what Grace had said about sails and wind and whatever else she thought about good matches. Edward had things yet to do. If only he could convince his father that they were as worthwhile as sitting at home and minding the estate.

But that would mean telling his father Edward wanted to leave. And the senior Mr. Everly had made his thoughts on his son's future abundantly clear. Family duty came above all else, and travel for the sake of travel was the mark of a frivolous mind.

Charity continued to stare at him, her nose wrinkled. "Should I worry for you, Edward?"

"No," he said quickly, forcing himself to laugh. "Perhaps I ought to worry over you and why you were in such a hurry that I did not have to pace the corridor for half an hour waiting for you. Is there a gentleman in attendance this evening I ought to give attention to?"

Charity protested at once, as he knew she would, and the two of them let the conversation devolve into laughing with one another about the way their peers continually fell in and out of love, or fancied themselves to do so. Charity took the idea of matrimony no more seriously than Edward did, and when they weren't beneath their parents' gaze it was something of a relief to find the ridiculous in future marital plans.

When they arrived at Inglewood Castle to the sight of blazing torches, Charity and Edward were in the best of humor with each other and their neighbors. The servants moved with precision to pass guests from coaches into the house, and up again into a large common room littered with chairs and people, all of them laughing and talking amiably with one another. Someone murmured in his ear who he was expected to take into dinner, and then he and his sister were left to their own devices.

Charity broke away from Edward the moment she saw friends amid the two dozen young people crowding the room, but Edward hardly noticed. As soon as they entered, one person had drawn his entire attention. The guest of honor, Miss Caroline Clapham, stood before the empty hearth, her hands folded before her, and her face nearly as pale as the gloves she wore.

People clustered together on either side of her. Men and women he had grown up with and knew quite well. But they were all talking to one another, as though unaware she stood still and mute among them.

He had thought it curious, how quickly she gave her attention to children at the picnic. He hadn't seen her speaking to anyone else after he had parted from her, either. She had hovered at the countess's elbow or followed little Lady Irene from one side of the orchard to the other. When they had spoken, first in the woods and then during the picnic, she hadn't been shy.

Why then did she appear as though she wished herself anywhere but there, as a guest in an important household?

Edward made his way to her, forgoing subtlety. He smiled at himself. Perhaps Miss Clapham was right about him. He did tend to charge into whichever direction he meant to go. A few friends looked up as he arrived in their circle, some offered greeting.

"Everly, good to see you. Did your sister come?"

"Everly, old chap. Didn't think you liked these sorts of parties."

"Merrell. Oddsen." He nodded to both, but pointedly broke eye contact to fix it on the woman who stared at him as though he'd found her hiding place. She shifted to one side as he turned his shoulder to slide in between her and the person standing nearest.

Then he bent his head and spoke softly, "Your impression of a Greek statue is a marvel, Miss Clapham. You must be a champion when you take part in charades."

The shock on her face transformed into amusement. "Couldn't you tell? The whole room is playing. The tableau is called *Being Late to Dinner*."

He scoffed. "I am *not* late."

The room quieted as the earl and countess entered the room, making their way to the middle. "Welcome, young friends, to our home," the earl said in his deep, booming voice, and Caroline gave Edward a meaningful raise of her eyebrows the instant before the earl drew attention to her.

"We thank you for coming this evening to meet our guest, a dear friend to Lady Inglewood, Miss Caroline Clapham." The guests responded with a smattering of applause, and those who hadn't seemed to notice Caroline before turned toward her with polite smiles in place.

Caroline turned into a statue again, with a strained smile. The earl kept speaking, and attention drifted away from her. Enough so that Edward felt comfortable bending toward her to whisper, "Courage, sprite. A dinner party is nothing to fear."

She blinked up at him once, and Edward grinned at her. "I am not a sprite—"

The earl had finished speaking, applause followed again, and Sir Isaac Fox appeared with a wide smile.

"Here we are, Miss Clapham. I have the honor of taking you into dinner this evening." He nodded to Edward. "How does everyone at Everly Refuge, Edward?"

"We are all well, sir," Edward answered with a slight bow of his head. "I thank you for asking."

"Wonderful to see you here this evening." Sir Isaac offered his arm to Caroline, who took it with a grateful smile. As though she already knew him quite well.

The baronet was married, equal in age to the hosts, but he and his wife were both present. Likely to assist in chaperoning the crowd of misses and gentlemen who weren't yet tied up in matrimonial strings. Edward had always liked Sir Isaac and looked up to him as he did the earl and the vicar who had married one of his sisters. Those three men, now pillars of their community, had treated him as they would a little brother when they spent time at Everly Refuge.

Sir Isaac would set Caroline at ease. Indeed, while Edward watched them lead the procession into dinner, Sir Isaac whispered something that made Miss Clapham laugh. A feat Edward had attempted but hadn't yet achieved that evening.

He pushed away the disappointment and went in search of the lady he had to escort through to dinner. With any luck, he'd be near enough Caroline to keep an eye on her. Perhaps help her navigate the evening.

It was the least he could do, after all her kindness. It would help begin gossip in their favor, too, if those in attendance noticed his attentiveness.

When his assigned lady took his arm, Edward caught a glimpse of Mariah Kimball. He hadn't even thought to look for her. Which wasn't the best behavior for a friend. Tonight, she wore a deep green gown lovely enough to draw the gaze of everyone in the room, though he doubted that was her intention. It likely had been her mother's.

Thankfully, Edward and Mariah were put at opposite ends of the table. The long, elegant, wide table, which held four-and-twenty unwed youths, eight married chaperones, and the host and hostess at either end.

Miss Clapham sat across the table and one to Edward's left, properly at the center of all the guests where she might see and be seen. Far away, too, from the earl and his countess.

SALLY BRITTON

As always, the countess's table boasted the finest dishes Edward had ever seen or tasted. He wasted no time in attending to the ladies on either side of him, serving them whatever they wished, before filling his plate too. The conversation rose and fell in natural eddies and flows, much like the waves lapping on the not-too-distant shore. Among friends, Edward relaxed more than he had in days.

Nearly finished with his meal, Edward listened attentively to Miss Parr at his left, when his ear caught part of the conversation happening across the table.

"You mean to say what, precisely, Miss Clapham?" The tone of the gentleman who spoke caught him as much as the use of the guest of honor's name. Because there was something unpleasant about it. Almost mocking. "In your village of Dunwich, is the society so dwindled that you rely on farmers' daughters to make up a dinner party?"

Caroline's sun-kissed cheeks reddened as Edward turned in her direction, and her gaze dropped to the plate in front of her. She answered too softly for him to hear, but the slight shake of her head and shape of her mouth as she spoke allowed him to make out the words "not what I meant."

Mr. Penrose put his fork down, his expression incredulous. "What then did you mean? That you take dinner with farmers and their families? At their own tables?"

A few others had hushed, their attention as caught by the strange line of questioning as Edward's. At either end of the long table, everything went on as normal. The earl and countess had no idea their guest had stumbled in her conversation.

"I have done so before," she admitted, easier to hear now that others near her fell silent. "I see nothing wrong with enjoying a meal when it is offered by a kind, well-respected family, whatever their position in society may be."

At her other side, Mr. Howard—a man three years Edward's junior with a jovial nature—chortled as though she'd told a singularly amusing jest. "Come now, Miss Clapham. You are trying to put one over on us. No one of your good breeding can have so

106

much as entered a farmer's hovel. One has only to see your fine manners and pretty grace to know such a thing impossible."

Miss Clapham appeared neither amused nor comfortable. Her whole face had turned the color of cherries. She no longer stared at her plate. Indeed, her chin had come up as though she prepared to do battle.

"What is so terrible about knowing a farmer, be he tenant or a gentleman? Agriculture is the foundation of our nation, Mr. Howard. Where do you think this food came from?" She gestured with her bare hand to the basket of rolls in front of her plate. "Wheat grown in fields, harvested by farmers and their daughters. Beans plucked from runners, tended by men and women who work long days. Fish from those who put boats and nets in water. If it is shameful work for them to do all the things which feed you, perhaps you should also be ashamed to eat the outcome of their labors."

Admiration for the young woman's bold declaration swelled in Edward's chest. She reminded him of Hope, speaking up like that, and yet he had never seen his sister defend a humble farmer before. Miss Clapham's singular response ought to put anyone who had agreed with Penrose or Howard to the blush.

Except it did not. Miss Parr tittered, covering her mouth delicately as her amusement escaped her. "Oh, Miss Clapham, you hold exceedingly progressive ideas in your head."

"I think it sounds rather noble," Mariah spoke next, a few seats away from Edward, her voice barely raised. He saw from where he sat the distressed expression of his childhood friend.

"Or soft-hearted," Mr. Penrose muttered.

Edward's fist tightened where it rested on his knee.

Mr. Howard added, "And this is why women are best kept out of politics, my dear Miss Clapham. While your kind heart makes you well-suited to charitable works, you cannot understand the complications of society well enough to see why the association of the gentry with the working class is a danger to the correct order of things."

"Human kindness ought not be a purely feminine trait."

Edward didn't realize he had spoken until several pairs of eyes turned toward him. Even then, he barely noticed their attention, as his was riveted on the young woman who had turned pale and quiet during Mr. Howard's lecture. "I would rather have someone of Miss Clapham's compassionate and thoughtful turn of mind representing my interests in government than someone ashamed to know the farmer whose labor provided the feast before us. A feast, I might add, that we enjoy in honor of Miss Clapham's presence." He lifted his glass as he said the last, "To your health, Miss Clapham."

Others swiftly raised glasses, repeating his words, until the whole table became aware of the impromptu salute Edward had offered and did the same.

This time, a smile accompanied the pinkness of her cheeks, and her dark eyes settled on Edward with a gleam of gratitude. She tipped her head forward in the smallest of nods, and Edward responded in kind.

AFTER DINNER, Caroline drifted into the cardroom with the other ladies. The rest of the meal had passed without further incident. Mr. Penrose had even seemed somewhat apologetic after Edward Everly raised a glass to her health, as though he had recalled the good manners with which he began the evening. Mr. Howard did not speak to her again, though. She didn't mourn that loss, given the pompous nature he revealed at the table.

How had Edward known precisely what to do to quiet the conversation that had left her feeling exposed? She hadn't looked for a rescue from him or anyone else, but gratitude and relief had overcome her the moment she'd realized she wasn't alone. Though she had to remind herself that Edward hadn't been the only one to speak on her behalf. Mariah had ventured a defense first.

They were both kind. And evidence of their good nature reassured her in her offer to help them.

Caroline studied Mariah, watching the blonde woman sit at a table and pick up a deck of cards. She chatted amiably while shuffling the deck in her ungloved hands, then dealt the cards to the three women who had joined her. She appeared perfectly at ease with herself and her company.

Who was it, if not Edward, who had captured Miss Kimball's affection? Neither of them had so much as hinted at the man's identity, except to say the Kimball parents would find him unsuitable. Though it wasn't her business, Caroline couldn't help her curiosity.

Not especially fond of cards, Caroline drifted to the edges of the room. She studied a wall with portraits hanging from ceiling nearly to the floor. Old portraits, whose subjects wore thick ruffles about their necks and plumy feathers in their caps. Their features were quite uniformly oval, the expressions somewhat flat, lips thin and mostly unsmiling. The composition appeared somewhat stiff and formal, adhering to traditional rules of symmetry and balance. The colors and tonal variations, though skillfully rendered, seemed muted and restrained compared to what Caroline had been taught.

Thank goodness art had come away from making everyone appear as though their heads were mere eggs with faces painted upon them.

When the men rejoined the ladies, Caroline had drifted from the portraits to the corner farthest from the hearth. Perhaps she would return to that position. It would be the most comfortable, given that Lady Inglewood and Lady Fox were seated comfortably near the low fire. With no wish to intrude on their conversation presently, Caroline turned her attention to the small bookcase in that corner, reading the spines with their tiny gold-embossed titles.

Caroline sensed Edward's approach when he was within a few feet of her. The sensation was as it had been the day at the fountain, with warmth slipping through her until her fingertips tingled with awareness. She pressed her lips together and did not turn. Perhaps it was someone else—?

"Do you often spend your time at parties hiding in the corners?"

Her first instinct proved correct. Edward had found her.

Caroline lifted one shoulder in a careless shrug, removing a book titled *Of The Kings and Queens of Britannia*, then placing it elsewhere in the row. "Only when I am the guest of honor, I suppose." She took another book out, *The History of Wicked Plots*. She shelved that one in a new spot, too. "I do not mean to sound ungrateful, you must understand, but I did not ask for this party. I cannot think why it necessary to acquaint myself with people I will likely never see again after this summer."

"I am given to believe that three things matter in this world. Land, money, and connections. Given that the first two can be had as a result of the third, you might reconsider the value of many acquaintances." Edward leaned one shoulder against the side of the bookcase. "Are you well, Caroline?"

She met his gaze briefly. The concern in his dark blue eyes made the witty remark she thought to make die upon her lips. She looked down at the books again. "I am well, Mr. Everly. I appreciate your defense at dinner. You came speedily to my rescue when the conversation grew discomfiting."

She felt his gaze on the top of her head before she glanced up to confirm his careful scrutiny. "I wish I could do more for you, Caroline. I must apologize for the behavior of the other men. You must have a poor opinion of our neighborhood, given their manners. I hope my own are better, even if I do occasionally come crashing through the woods at you and ruin your paintings."

His heavy sigh coaxed a smile from her. Though she could not explain the ease she felt around him, Caroline could certainly repay him for it by sharing a part of herself.

"I find your behavior preferable to what my dinner companions displayed this evening. Though I suppose they had the right to be shocked." She moved another book. "I do regularly take meals at a farmer's table. And the farmer's daughters come to my home in their turn."

"Do they?" He didn't sound shocked. Merely curious. He kept his shoulder against the bookcase and his gaze on her. "Are they better company than what you enjoyed this evening? I must imagine so."

"My closest friend is a farmer's daughter," she said. "Her name is Jill Martin. Her family leases the farm across the lane from my home. My mother owns our land, through an inheritance. And though I am a gentleman's daughter, I have few memories of a time before I spent every summer picking cherries from our orchard to sell at market." She braced herself, unmoving, staring at the books she had reordered and waiting for his judgement. For him to scoff or excuse himself.

He moved slowly, standing fully upright, then took a step to her side. They stood nearly shoulder-to-shoulder, both facing the leather and cloth spines of books. "Your family has a cherry orchard? Why on earth did you let me lecture you about fruit orchards when you were at the picnic?" He shook his head and took it upon himself to move yet another book from one place to another —a final book from the top shelf to the middle one she had spent time ordering just-so.

"I did not mind hearing what you said of them," she admitted. "Mr. Everly?"

"Edward," he reminded her. "We are quite alone here. Unless you prefer we return to formality?"

"No." She swallowed. "Though I am too nervous this evening. Formality suits me better."

"I see. Very well, Miss Clapham. Here is our construct." He pointed to the first book in the row and read the spines aloud, from right to left, inserting an occasional word.

"*A History of Wicked Plots - Of the Kings and Queens of Britannia* - and their *Whole Comical Works* -caused all in their kingdoms to make *Curious Remarks and Observations* until- *A Great and Terrible Curse* swept across the land, and then - *Within the Prophecies Fulfilled* - a fate that not even - *Experiments and Observations on Electricity* - could offer relief or - *A Vindication of*

*Man."* He grinned and nudged her arm softly with his elbow. "Not bad, is it?"

She turned her head enough to stare at him from the corner of her eye. "You have played this game before?"

"And suffered the consequences of putting my father's library out of order, yes." He grinned back at her, clearly unrepentant. "What else is an ill-mannered boy to do when he is home from school for the summer and all it does is rain?"

She couldn't help returning his smile. "We must hope the earl is more forgiving."

"Since this is but one shelf, I imagine he will not see any harm done." Edward Everly winked at her, and such a thing might have shocked Caroline were she not so used to the way her papa winked every time he wished to tease her. What surprised her instead was the way he lowered his voice and said, "It doesn't matter whether you pick cherries or have picnics with farmer's daughters, Caroline Clapham. You are a guest of Lord Inglewood and his lady. That ought to be enough for everyone here to know themselves in the best of company."

A glance over her shoulder ensured no one was about to come upon them. They were, despite being in a room full of people, quite alone. It wouldn't last long. And who knew when she would see Edward again? She had to ask her favor of him.

Caroline took a deep breath, gathering her courage. "Mr. Everly, I have been thinking about what you offered before," she said, trying and likely failing to cover her nerves with confidence. "When you offered me a favor."

Edward's expression changed rapidly from surprise to careful examination. "I hoped you would. You have thought of something? I find myself anxious to find out what you have in mind."

She met his gaze steadily and kept her tone serious. "It isn't anything horrid. I promise. And you can decline if you are uncomfortable. What I want most is something that will help me achieve my goals this summer."

He turned and leaned his shoulder against the bookcase again, though he seemed less certain of himself despite the leisurely pose. "I suppose that is fair. I'm not certain what I could do to be of assistance to you."

"I know exactly what I need," she assured him. Even as she felt a twist of discomfort in her stomach. That wrung-out feeling that made her miss her home, her mother, her papa, and their constant reassurance. "I have an idea for a painting, Mr. Everly. A painting that I believe is important to my future as an artist. But I need a model. A gentleman model."

His eyebrows drew together sharply. "You wish me to sit for a portrait? Of course. That is simple enough."

Caroline shook her head and twisted her gloved fingers together. "Not a portrait. And you certainly will not be sitting. This is different. I need someone who is willing to pose as Atlas, with the weight of the world on their shoulders. I have been told no gentleman would willingly do such a thing. Men don't want to model in a way that looks silly, you see."

Edward stood to his full height, gaping at her. His mouth opened and closed again. He made a strange sound, like a protest, but his lips remained clamped shut. Finally, a strangled, single word escaped from him. "Atlas?"

"The Titan holding up the earth." She added in a rush, "I will still help with the pretend courtship, even if you cannot help me. I wouldn't ask anything of you if it is upsetting, or—"

"Yes."

She couldn't quite believe it. Had he agreed, so quickly? "You will do it? You may take time to think on it, if you'd like."

Edward looked at her for a long moment, his expression inscrutable. Caroline looked away from him, watching the room again. Edward's sister stood with other young ladies, but she watched them with a curious tilt of her head.

Their time alone in the corner was nearly over. Caroline felt it keenly.

Finally, he let out a deep sigh. "I must confess, Miss Clapham, I'm not entirely certain what I'm getting myself into," he said, his voice tinged with amusement. "But if it means helping you achieve your artistic vision, I will pose for you. I trust it will be a fair trade for what you are willing to do for me and for Mariah."

Caroline wanted to sag with relief into the nearest chair. Instead, she gave a sharp, succinct nod. "Thank you."

He grinned at her, a mischievous glint in his eye. "Promise me you won't make me look too foolish, will you? I don't know if my reputation could stand it."

"You will look as Atlas ought to look, Mr. Everly." Caroline had no intention of letting him set the terms on her work. Though she had a new problem to solve. How would she explain Edward's willingness to model for her to Lady Inglewood? And convince the countess that there was nothing inappropriate about Caroline using Edward for her work.

He offered her a slight bow, then tilted his head toward the other guests. "I had better make certain my sister is behaving herself. Perhaps we could play Whist later?"

"I would like that. Thank you."

And then he was gone, leaving her in the corner, facing a room full of people who had come to Inglewood Castle to meet her. Caroline squared her shoulders, lifted her chin, and rejoined the party.

# CHAPTER 10

E dward sifted through the mail at breakfast with more than his usual interest. He had some slim hope, some idea, that there might be invitations in the morning post. Invitations to parties, dinners, picnics, or something of the like where he had a chance of encountering Caroline.

Their plan was underway. And their secretive conversation in the corner hadn't gone unnoticed.

Charity had attempted to question him about his *tete-a-tete* during their carriage ride home. Edward evaded her questions by informing Charity of Mr. Howard and Mr. Penrose's rudeness at the dinner table. "I wanted to be certain she wasn't upset," he told his sister, who accepted that as reason enough before she shared her thoughts on the inexcusable behavior of the other two gentlemen, who—according to Charity—were undeserving of that title.

A letter in an unfamiliar hand waited for his father, another was addressed to his mother, and a third—in his elder sister's hand— had Charity and Patience's names swirled upon its face, and the seal of the Córdoba family keeping the paper closed against prying eyes. Hope Córdoba always wrote her mother and sisters, but she often put a word or two for Edward in her letters. He supposed married sisters had little to say to bachelor brothers when they lived several countries apart from one another.

There was nothing addressed to him, or to the family as a whole. Which meant he couldn't justify breaking seals in the hope of finding himself invited to the same evening's entertainment as Caroline.

Edward experienced a complex blend of emotions, a mingling of nervousness and excitement intertwining within him. There was a sense of relief that he would be free from his parents' matchmaking, accompanied by a tinge of uncertainty that coursed through his being. It was as if he stood at the precipice of a great adventure, brimming with anticipation yet aware of the unknown that lay ahead.

What was Caroline thinking, now that they had a firm agreement? How did she see their plan unfurling? Curiosity drove him to impatience, and they had barely started their ruse. There was so much he didn't yet know about Caroline. Was there a possibility of regret creeping into her mind, or did she revel in the thrill of embracing a self-imposed challenge?

Edward had barely slept, but instead of worrying, he found himself anticipating their next meeting. Even if he couldn't plan how he would act. There were too many variables to even attempt such a thing. Best to go with his instinct, to follow his first inclination, to convince others around them that he and Caroline were venturing into the early stages of a romantic relationship.

Because if Edward ever pursued a lady in truth, he couldn't imagine treading carefully. Not if his heart was at stake. Love would be an adventure of its own. He knew that instinctively. The same way he knew his heart wouldn't be content until he'd seen more of the world and its wonders.

As to the matter at hand, it was a lark. A game. Of course, Edward doubted he would face any difficulties when it came to public flirtation or expressing his admiration of her to others. As Edward contemplated Caroline's beauty, he couldn't help but feel a certain attraction to her. He found her dark hair, dark eyes, and sun-kissed complexion quite lovely, and he appreciated the way she carried herself with confidence and poise. Yet her smile hinted at good humor, or at mischief she held in reserve.

Sprite, indeed.

Already, he found her fascinating. The way Caroline Clapham spoke to him, without reserve or false modesty, had surprised him. Even if she compared him to a wild boar, charging through trees and drawing rooms both.

He needed a reason to see her again.

Slouching in his chair, one elbow on the table, Edward poked at the fried ham on his plate.

Perhaps he ought to go for a walk toward the Inglewood estate. He might encounter Caroline as he had before, completely by chance. No one could accuse him of impropriety if he came across her while enjoying a ramble toward the shoreline.

Was it too early to call at Inglewood? He looked up at the long-case clock hanging at the center of the dining room wall. It confirmed the hour was yet inappropriate for making neighborly visits.

Mr. Everly came into the room, spectacles atop his head and newspaper already tucked under his arm. He made the usual sighs and grumbling noises of a man in his sixties settling in at a dining table. Once seated, he bestowed a nod and low greeting to his only son. "Edward. Good to see you up early."

"Father. Are you well today?" They had not spoken of Edward's marital prospects in several days. The silence on the subject ought to have left Edward with a sense of relief. Instead, every time he and his father occupied the same room, he had the unsettling impression that his father spent that silence in scheming.

Which struck him as odd, since he hadn't ever thought his father the scheming type. His mother had a knack for orchestrating plans without informing the family of her intentions, but not his father. If Edward was as unsubtle as a boar in the woods, he likened his father to a bull elephant in a jungle. Unconcerned as to how his path might impact the smaller creatures beneath his feet, or what inner turmoil his plans created for his children.

"Has the post arrived?"

Edward took the small stack of folded paper and handed it to his sire. "There isn't much. Something for Mother, and Hope sent a letter for my younger sisters. There is a letter addressed specifically to you."

His father, with the missive in his hand already, lowered his spectacles from his forehead to the bridge of his nose. He frowned down at the paper, then sighed as he turned it over and broke the seal.

Edward turned his attention to his breakfast and slathered a thin piece of toast with the apple preserves the whole family had been raised to eat at nearly every meal.

Charity entered the room at the same moment that Mr. Everly said a sharp, vulgar word that his daughter had never heard him utter. Consequently, she froze in place a mere two steps from the table, just as Edward had risen to greet her. Both children stared at their father, whose face had turned a shade of puce that made Edward fear for a long and uncomfortable moment that his father had choked on something.

"The audacity of it," Mr. Everly muttered, slamming the letter to the table. Only then did he see Charity, her deep blue eyes round in shock. "Oh. Charity. I didn't see you come in." He stood and gestured to her usual chair. "Forgive me, my dear. I ought not to have—but the shock, you see. And the very audacity!"

Edward and Charity exchanged a confused glance, then Edward gestured with a tip of his chin. "Does the letter have bad news, Father?"

"Yes." Mr. Everly pointed Charity to her seat again. "You had better sit, my dear. As the eldest children at home, you must know at once. Then I will go to your mother—if this brings on the headache or megrims, I will blame him, you know."

"Whom will you blame, Papa?" Charity asked as a footman helped her into her chair. "The person that wrote you the letter?"

"The very same." Mr. Everly retook his seat, and Edward did the same, but slowly. What was his father muttering about?

"Are my sisters well?" Edward asked. "Hope? Grace? Their families?" What else could put his father in a temper such as the one he had seen, but the tragic news of family illness or pain?

"This isn't about them, thank God for that." Mr. Everly closed his eyes and went to rub at them, forgetting his spectacles were in the way until he had knocked them askew. He muttered less offensive words of impatience as he resettled the spectacles on his nose. "You must both bear up. Though it is you, Edward, I must depend upon. This letter is from your cousin Claude."

That explained the reaction Edward thought only death or family tragedy might bring from his father. Claude Everly, though unlikable, was still family.

"What does he want?" Charity asked, sitting back in her chair even though her eyes blazed with indignation.

"A roof over his head," their father muttered. "Our roof. He will arrive at the Refuge in two days' time."

"Oh, Papa." Charity groaned and bent forward, imploringly, toward their father. "Can you not prevent him? Last time he came, my friends thought they were in love with him. And he *encouraged* them. When he left after making half a dozen near-promises, every girl in the neighborhood despised me."

"There will be greater danger of that this time," Edward muttered, and when his sister gave him a curious glance he added, "Your friends are all old enough to marry now."

Charity looked as though she wished to repeat the word her father had used minutes ago. "He wouldn't dare, surely. There would be fathers or brothers after him if he trifled with any of them."

"Claude has a secret talent for dancing on the edge of a cliff without ever falling to natural consequences." Edward had seen it many times, when the two of them had been at the same schools or London parties in their youths. Association with Claude had made Edward unpopular for a time, until he found friends who took him at his own merits and didn't think sharing a surname akin to sharing vices.

"Be that as it may," their father said, folding the letter up again. "He is coming. He is my nephew. Your cousin. And I trust you will make sure everything is in order for his visit." Then Edward's father turned his eye on him, the weight of his gaze heavy with purpose. "As you know, he is next in line to inherit should anything happen to you, Edward. I hope you will take this as a reminder to consider your future, and to make the necessary plans to secure the legacy of our family."

Charity gaped at their father as he left the room, letter in hand, without having touched so much as a crumb of breakfast.

Edward couldn't blame his father for a lack of appetite. He'd lost all interest in his plate and cup the moment his cousin's name had polluted the air they breathed.

"At this moment, I am most relieved I am not the heir." Charity shivered, then gave Edward a gentle, crooked smile. "You needn't wear that morose expression, Edward. Claude has visited before, and we all lived to tell the tale. He is horrid, but he cannot mean to stay long. He thinks the country is boring."

If Claude took after his late father, it was no wonder Samuel and Matthew Everly hadn't spoken in the decades prior to Matthew's death.

"Father will use every one of Claude's vices to prod me into matrimony." Edward grasped the table knife at his place setting and motioned with it as though poking some unseen enemy with small, subtle jabs.

A giggle escaped his sister, and Edward lowered the knife with a sigh. "You are a man, Edward. And men in this world have far more advantages than my sex. No one can stop you from pursuing your own happiness. If you have no wish to marry, you will not be forced to the altar. Father's fears for continuing the family line might be justifiable, but they needn't consume you."

Edward blinked at her, then folded his arms and leaned back in his chair. "You sound rather mutinous when you put things that way." And innocent. Though he'd reached his majority, his father held the purse strings. Beyond that, Edward would not act in a way that would drive a divide between him and his family. Despite his disagreements with his father, he had no wish to harm their relationship.

She shrugged one shoulder upward, then picked up the apple preserves. "No matter what you choose to do about your future, Edward, know that I support you. Father's opinion isn't the only one that matters. As his heir, you may have a duty to consider the well-being of everyone in our family. That includes *you*, too. And the future Mrs. Edward Everly, whomever she may be. As much as Mama wishes for Miss Kimball to take the position, the decision is yours alone. You know best who will suit you."

Though he generally acknowledged Charity to have good sense, Edward hadn't heard her opinions on the matter stated quite so clearly before. Or so cheerfully. "I appreciate your support," he said at last, while she took a large bite of her apple-slathered toast.

She chewed with a thoughtful expression, staring at him until after she swallowed her bite. "You and I both know how it is when Papa is being stubborn. He *will* use Claude's visit to convince you that he is right about settling down. I have watched you successfully avoid our parents' wishes on that account for months now. There hasn't been any need to worry about your ability to stand up for yourself. But when Claude is involved, he acts as a thorn in your side, and your judgement isn't always the best. Keep your wits about you, Edward."

She had a fair point. The constant irritant of Claude's presence and Mr. Everly's stubborn insistence could cause enough distraction to impair Edward's judgement in all manner of ways. Including making a fool of himself, agreeing to things he shouldn't, or forgetting his own good breeding and boxing his cousin during a formal dinner. Not that the last item had ever happened. But Edward had come quite close to leaping over a table to knock a smug grin off of Claude's face.

"I'll do my best to maintain my composure. And if things get too heated, I will remind myself that giving Claude a facer is likely not the best course of action." He gave her a wry smile, though it didn't do much to lighten his mood.

"It is odd," Charity said, chewing thoughtfully at her toast again, "for Claude to invite himself for a visit. I cannot think he has ever done that before. He only ever attended us with the rest of his family. Do you suppose he said why he wished to come in the letter to Papa? There was a great deal of ink on those pages, considering how little we were told about the matter."

Edward rubbed at his temples as tension built behind his eyes. "Claude is a pompous, arrogant lout. No doubt he filled every inch of paper with descriptions of his own self-importance." He stood from the table. "I'm sorry to leave you alone at the table, but I cannot sit still at this moment."

He needed air. And room to think.

"Patience will be along soon enough. Take care, Edward." She waved her toast at him in farewell, and he returned the gesture with an absent-minded nod.

First his parents and their obsession with Mariah Kimball, now Claude coming to visit. He had counted on spending his summer in leisure, enjoying the comforts of home, the pleasure of time spent among friends, and all of it without complication.

"I'd have avoided more trouble had I gone on a jungle expedition," he muttered to himself as he left his family home behind him, making for the stables, thinking only of the pleasure of riding away from all of it well into the afternoon.

# CHAPTER 11

Edward hadn't stumbled upon the sprite in the grove of birch trees. Nor had he seen her anywhere along the path to the beach, though he rode his horse slowly enough that there was ample opportunity to come across another person. When he glanced up to the terraced gardens of Inglewood Castle, they were empty save for a single gardener.

He couldn't return home. Not yet. Not while the idea of his cousin Claude's smirks made Edward want to quit the entire county. He needed to calm himself still. Distract his mind from the unpleasant knowledge of the impending invasion. And his father's expectation that Edward thwart his cousin's hopes of inheriting the Refuge.

But what else could he do? After giving his horse a half hour more of exercise, Edward returned home. Yet no sooner did he enter the stable yard than he realized the small gig his sisters drove about the country roads stood waiting. He dismounted and dismissed the groom who came forward to take his horse. "I think he and I are going out again," Edward said, giving the gelding a pat on his neck. "If my sisters will accept my escort."

"You are only invited if you promise not to be dull company," Patience said from behind him, and Edward turned back toward the house to see his sisters had come out, still adjusting gloves and reticules.

"We are bound for a shopping expedition," Charity informed him, a little smile upon her lips. "Mama has requested more smelling salts from the apothecary, and we have a mind to look in on every shop in the village to purchase whatever strikes our fancy."

"I hadn't thought either of you possessed the nature of a spendthrift." Edward tipped his hat up higher on his forehead.

Charity raised her eyebrows at him while Patience snorted and stepped into the gig, with the helping hand of a groom.

"Why is it that men accuse women of such things when they take even the smallest delight in a purchase?" Charity asked. "And today is a special circumstance. There are frustrations to work from our minds. Neither of us are pleased about our impending visit from Cousin Claude."

"He is as oily as an eel," Patience said from her seat, giving her head a toss.

"The purchase of a book or fan, or perhaps ordering an entirely new bonnet, will go far in soothing our spirits." Charity stepped into the gig next. "You ought to try it, Edward. Shopping can be a lovely distraction from unwanted thoughts or undesirable circumstances." She winked at him.

Though their reasoning lacked all sense or logic, Edward shrugged and mounted his horse. "What sort of brother would I be if I did not offer you my escort during this trying time?"

Patience and Charity exchanged wide smiles, then Charity gave the horses the command to drive on.

The village of Alderton wasn't all that large, but it boasted enough shops to entertain a handful of nobles and two dozen families of the gentry. As it was but three miles from their home, it made for easy comings and goings for the Everly family, too. Their nearest town of greater import and size was Ipswich at twenty miles distance.

Edward and his mount trotted along in front of his sisters,

listening to the murmur of their voices as they conversed, though he was unable to join in the conversation himself.

His horse didn't mind that they were off again. The mount stepped lightly, his ears perked forward. Whether it the fine weather, or simply something new to occupy his mind, Edward found himself relaxing to near-enjoyment.

What a fool he'd been to suppose he needed to encounter Miss Caroline Clapham to rescue himself from agitation. All the time out of doors had cured him.

Somewhat.

Well. Mostly.

Claude was still coming. And the last time his cousin had spent more than five minutes in the same room with Edward, he'd said a dozen things that still crept into Edward's thoughts at night and made him grind his teeth. Or punch his pillows, imagining his cousin's smug face in place of the downy cushions.

*"You know, Edward, I've always admired your ability to persevere despite your limitations."*

Infuriating. That's what Claude was.

*"I suppose I find your company dull merely because we have such different interests. Such opposite views when we look at the world."*

Claude's views only encompassed card tables, finish lines, and naive young ladies. Sometimes, glasses filled to the brim with liquid that burned like fire. And still, Claude sauntered through life as though all of it was made for his pleasure, and any pain he caused was merely a matter of course.

Edward's body stiffened, and his gelding's ears flicked back, picking up on Edward's mood and mind. Edward soothed his horse with a few words and realized they had entered Alderton without him realizing it. He looked over his shoulder and saw his sisters had stopped in the road, a youth in apron assisting them with their horses.

His cheeks warm, Edward turned his mount around and joined them. The boy, in the employ of the shop that sold bonnets downstairs and served tea in the rooms above, took charge of Edward's gelding, too. Edward gave the lad a coin, promised more when they returned, then offered his arms to his sisters.

"What is our first destination, ladies?"

For nearly an hour, Edward let them order him about. They hadn't jested when they'd mentioned going into every single shop in the village. And nearly everywhere, they made a purchase. Buttons, ribbons, a small toy horse for their nieces at the vicarage, a tin of sweets, an order placed for smelling salts, another for new music, two used books, a dozen sweet rolls wrapped in brown paper, a bottle of rose oil, and on the list went. Every shop benefitted from his sisters' attempts to cleanse their mind of Claude's impending visit.

They had started the walk down the opposite side of the street, moving back to their gig, and Edward carried several small parcels in his arms behind them. He wondered how his sisters had managed to spend so little of their own money and so much of his, when he heard Charity exclaim in front of him.

"Isn't that Miss Clapham? Whatever is she doing in Alderton, all alone?"

Edward's gaze swept the street and shops, and he saw Miss Clapham exiting the apothecary he and his sisters had visited first upon their arrival. She carried a single parcel of her own and wore a gentle smile as she spoke to someone inside the shop. Then she closed the door, and Edward's heart performed an odd sort of leap the moment she turned and caught his stare with hers.

"At the apothecary, no less. I hope she is well," Charity murmured. Then she looked over her shoulder at Edward. "Do you mind if we speak to her, Edward?"

He rapidly shook his head. "Not in the slightest. It is the neighborly thing to do."

Patience gave him an odd look. "You said a moment ago you were tired of playing the part of our pack horse."

Edward glowered at her and said, "A jest. Besides, I can put these things in the gig." He looked across the street again but caught Charity and Patience exchanging a glance. "She is waving. Quick, wave back." His hands and arms were full, yet he was tempted to drop everything to return the salutation.

Patience saved her parcels from a sorry fate by waving, then locked her arm about Charity's. "Come, the road is clear. Mind your step, Edward."

He followed his sisters, and the parcels in his arms made it awkward when he bowed in greeting to Caroline. She appeared in good health, with pink in her cheeks and the usual brightness in her eyes. Her dark hair peeked out from beneath her bonnet, which had a spray of peach-silk flowers around its brim. She wore a dress in a color to match, and the shade made her sun-bronzed skin appear to excellent advantage. She quite glowed with health.

"Good afternoon, Miss Everly, Miss Patience, and Mr. Everly." Her lips tilted up, hinting at a smile. "How lovely to see all of you."

His sisters exchanged pleasantries, giving and receiving news of the health of everyone in both Inglewood Castle and the Refuge. Caroline gave his sisters most of her attention, hardly glancing at Edward. Though left out of the conversation, he didn't mind. He hadn't anything pressing to say. He and Caroline were yet at the beginning of their play; their proximity to one another was enough for the moment.

Standing there, listening, watching the play of emotion on Caroline's face as she spoke with his sisters, made him quite forget about Claude.

"Have you been to the tea shop yet? The one above the milliner's? Mr. and Mrs. Raleigh own both businesses, of course, but their eldest daughter, Mrs. Belton, sees to the tea," Charity explained.

"And they have the most delicious little cakes," Patience added. "Oh, do take tea with us. This very moment, if you can spare the time."

Finally, Caroline's eyes caught Edward's, and this time, her gaze lingered. "If your brother doesn't mind, that would be wonderful."

"I don't mind," he said, nearly before she'd finished speaking. "So long as I might put my baggage away beforehand." He smiled over the parcels at her, and she returned his smile with a broad one of her own.

"You mean you prefer to take your tea *without* half a dozen boxes in your lap? How very conventional of you."

He chuckled. "Indeed, they would hinder my ability to get my fair share of the tea cakes. Beware, Miss Clapham. My sisters are notorious for taking a second cake before anyone else has had their first."

"Retract that accusation at once," Charity demanded.

"Not true at all, Edward," Patience said at the same time.

"It seems you know the plight of having younger siblings as well as I do, Mr. Everly." Caroline's dark eyes laughed while his sisters gasped in feigned horror.

Edward took the parcels away to the gig but didn't miss when Charity said, "I will forgive you for taking his side, Miss Clapham, but only because you put him in a better mood. You do not know him as we do, but he is most unpleasant when he is out of temper."

If he had thought of lingering over his brief errand, his sister's words made him move with greater haste. He didn't need to give Charity or Patience any time to fill Caroline's head with misrepresentations of Edward's character. Tease though they might, he liked Caroline. And he wanted her to like him.

Yes, he was willing to admit he liked her. Despite their few meetings, he liked her a great deal. Enough to consider her a friend. Though their acquaintance was quite new, of course. And she had undertaken a rather daunting task, and that situation had forced a bond of trust upon them. Hadn't it?

And yes, he found her pretty. But he'd admitted that much about any number of women. *Pretty* was a simple descriptor for a woman of pleasant countenance.

Though, why he stood outside the tea shop sorting through his thoughts, he didn't know. Especially when he had told himself he couldn't allow his sisters time alone with Caroline. Edward removed his hat as he stepped inside and went directly to the staircase to take him above, where the ladies had already settled at a small table, sitting upon delicate chairs with spindly legs.

Edward took the last remaining chair, the one across from Caroline and between his two sisters. They were already speaking on the subject of bonnets, and he hadn't any way to enter the conversation without sounding remarkably stupid or overly eager.

So he waited for the topic to change.

By the time the tea arrived, his sisters had moved into discussing the number of ruffled hems a woman might wear on the bottom of her skirt before it became ridiculous. Yet another matter he knew nothing about. Somehow, though, Caroline made the subject interesting.

"My papa claims you can accurately estimate a lady's dowry based on the number of flounces at her hem," she said with a twinkle in her eye. "Two flounces, a respectable amount. Three, modest but nothing that would encourage a fortune hunter. When you come to six of those ruffled lines, you have found an heiress." Edward lowered his head to hide his grin but his sisters giggled appreciatively.

Caroline poured for everyone, and Edward had a moment to thank her before Charity pressed to know more about Caroline's lace gloves from the picnic.

He'd wondered once how ladies spent so much time talking of their clothing. He'd never spent more than a minute to tell a man where he bought his boots or ask another for the name of his tailor. But the women at his table had touched on every item of their wardrobes that they could feasibly speak upon, at least in public. And for each article, Caroline had a quip that was either self-deprecating or comically obvious.

"Have you seen those dreadful bonnets that look as though they were inspired by the plague doctor masks?" she asked, holding her hands in a cup around her cheeks. "Or are they meant to be like blinders on cart horses?"

Edward knew what she spoke of. "I've seen bonnets that kept

gentlemen from catching so much as a glimpse of a woman's face unless they were directly in front of one another."

To this Caroline replied, "Ah, perhaps that is the reason for them, then. They annoy unwanted suitors."

Laughter from Charity and Patience made others in the tearoom turn to look at them with censorious glances. At least from the married women in the room. Edward noted one unmarried gentleman among them who was smiling in Charity's direction. Perhaps he needed to purchase such a bonnet for his sister.

"The worst of it is dancing slippers," Charity said, shaking her head. "They always look so lovely when we first put them on. Soft satin, pretty embroidered toes, and ribbons that shimmer tied on our ankles. And then we actually *dance* in them, and they are ruined."

Patience sighed. "At least you get to attend balls and assemblies to dance."

"When will you be out?" Caroline asked, taking a sip of her tea.

"I am only seventeen." Patience's smile turned to a glum frown. "Charity wasn't permitted to attend public assemblies until she was nineteen."

"But private balls at eighteen," Charity reminded her sister with a soft smile. "And you are not missing much. You know all the gentlemen who attend such things from church and market days."

Caroline met Edward's gaze and raised her eyebrows. "Are there many private balls here?"

"More than enough, if you ask me," he answered.

"Edward complains every time there is a dance," Patience informed their new friend.

"I find many gentleman share those sentiments." Caroline cast him a knowing glance and Edward crossed his arms. "What activities do you enjoy when it comes to socializing with your friends and neighbors, Mr. Everly?"

"Picnics," he said with raised eyebrows. "Perhaps a walk in the woods."

The slow curl of her smile robbed him of whatever clever thing he'd meant to say next. Instead, he cleared his throat and turned to ask Charity if she wanted another morsel of cake. His sister already stared at him more intently than she ever had a teacake. Edward blinked at her, confused, and she abruptly shifted her gaze to their younger sister.

"Patience, dear, I have suddenly remembered. Mama needed one more thing from the shop downstairs. Will you come with me? Your tastes are more attuned to hers than my own."

Patience's eyebrows raised. Within their family, they all knew how often their mother and her youngest child argued over fashion. She glanced toward Edward and stood up. "Yes, of course. Do stay and finish your cake, Miss Clapham. Edward will keep you company until we return."

"We will not be long," Patience affirmed with an overly bright smile. "Do not bore her to pieces, Edward."

The two of them left, weaving between tables occupied by others, then down the steps.

Caroline watched them go, then turned back to Edward with her eyebrows drawn together. "That seemed rather abrupt. I certainly hope I didn't offend—"

"No, of course not. You did nothing wrong." Edward put his hands on his knees beneath the small table, steadying himself as he searched for a way to excuse his sisters. But was this not what they wanted? He had to laugh, though he winced when he realized how he had to force the sound. "I think they suspect I have an interest in you. They have left us alone to create an opportunity for private conversation. Unobserved flirtation, perhaps."

Her cheeks flushed. "It is as easy as that for a couple to be left to themselves? I thought the trick near impossible."

Some of the tension in the air eased. "I have excessively affectionate sisters. And they still believe in romance and love."

"You are doing well, I think," she said. When he stared at her blankly, Caroline clarified. "You were quite attentive in our conversation, though I cannot imagine a gentleman enjoying the topics of bonnets and gowns. It is no wonder your sisters think you have a genuine interest in me."

It took Edward a moment to shift his thoughts. Had he been pretending? At any point in the conversation? No. He hadn't. He'd genuinely enjoyed every moment of it. And he'd forgotten—or nearly forgotten—their ruse. Unnerved by his realization, Edward spoke in as flat a tone as possible. "Thank you. You did well, too."

Caroline looked down at the cake he had served her a moment before and smiled. "They did give us an excellent opportunity to discuss another private matter." She kept her tone low, where it would not carry to others in the room.

It took Edward a moment to recall what other private matter she meant, and when he remembered, he winced. "Have you spoken to Lady Inglewood about painting me, then?"

"Indeed. She approves of the idea and wants you to visit as soon as possible, so we might compare schedules and make arrangements to be properly chaperoned." Caroline's nose wrinkled slightly, and he had the absurd desire to wrinkle his own back. But he resisted. "I imagine we will need to consult on other parts of our social calendar, too. I do have one more concern," she said.

His heart had deviated from its steady rhythm, though Edward hadn't any idea why. Even if he hadn't meant to begin their plan, it was already going well. "What is it?" he ventured at last.

"I haven't a great deal of time for socializing, though Lady Inglewood is determined that I attend every picnic and fete from here to Ipswich," Caroline said, using a small fork to halve her little cake. "At the end of August, Sir Thomas Lawrence is coming to Inglewood Castle as the countess's guest. Do you know who he is?"

"The name sounds vaguely familiar," Edward admitted with a small shrug. "Ought I to know him?"

"He is the president of the Royal Academy and one of the most talented artists of our time. The royal family has employed him since the start of the century. He's painted every important person you can think of for nearly three decades."

"I see. And you will meet him when he comes?"

"Not only that. He will view my work, and his opinion of it will determine my future in art." Her expression turned anxious; her eyes less bright than before and her jaw tight. "That is another reason the painting is important. I haven't many samples of gentlemen, and nothing fantastic, such as representation of biblical or mythical figures. I need to show that I am capable of more than domestic scenes of sheep and orchards."

The painting he had agreed to pose for meant more to her than he had guessed. And it was daunting to know it, too. As much as he wanted to avoid the needling of his parents and stop their misguided matchmaking for Mariah's sake, as a man, he could simply tell them "no" and suffer few consequences.

Upholding his end of their agreement meant considerably more to Caroline and Mariah. It meant everything to them both. Mariah's heart depended on him. Caroline's dreams were at stake, too, and Edward knew well enough how sharp-edged an unfulfilled dream rested in a person's heart.

"I understand. I promise I will take you from your work as little as possible, and I will put myself completely at your disposal, Miss Clapham."

"Thank you." Caroline relaxed, at least enough that the crease left her brow. "Have you given any thought to how best we will go about our feigned courtship?"

"Some." Edward shifted in his chair and glanced toward the open staircase, ensuring himself his sisters hadn't yet returned. He glanced across the room and nodded to one of his mother's friends, sitting at a table with her husband. She'd been staring at him throughout the course of their tea. "Being seen together like this is enough to create gossip, and my sisters already suspect something."

Caroline's smile, though slight, still reached her eyes. "Our conversation the other evening certainly helped matters. How long did we stand in that corner?"

"Not even a quarter of an hour," he insisted, folding his arms across his chest. "But that, and my eagerness to speak to you today, made an impression." And she didn't need to know how little he

SALLY BRITTON

had feigned that eagerness. The moment he had spied her upon the street, he'd wanted to speak with her. He hadn't even minded his sisters taking the reins in the conversation. Realizing that now made his chest feel tight. Surely, he'd only been eager to begin their ruse. But then, why had he forgotten about the whole thing until the moment his sisters left the table?

She smoothed a small wrinkle from the tablecloth, not looking at him. "I am glad we happened upon each other, then."

Was that the only reason she was glad, or had she enjoyed his company?

Why did he care?

Edward studied the woman in front of him. Admitting she fascinated him felt dangerous, and yet he wouldn't deny it. At least not to himself. "When I come to visit you at Inglewood to determine our schedule, I will be certain my parents are aware that I am intrigued by spending more time in your company."

Caroline's amusement grew. "What will they think of that? I am a little nobody to them."

At this he shrugged and barely resisted giving a tug to his cravat. "I'm not concerned on that end, so long as it distracts them from Mariah. You will leave at the end of summer, and whether they are relieved or disappointed, it hardly matters." At least, he kept telling himself that. If his parents were going to meddle in his life, they well deserved the consequences of such a thing.

The woman's expression briefly turned to surprise, but then she lowered her gaze to her plate and took up her fork. "You seem quite calm about all of this," Caroline murmured, still cutting her cake into smaller and smaller pieces. "I suppose you will yet face a great deal of opposition from them."

"Yes. Perhaps." Edward forgot himself and ran his hand through his hair and then placed it on the table again to tap his fingers. "Mariah will face the worst of it if she cannot manage her parents' reaction to my courting another woman. At least they cannot perceive it as a deliberate move on her part. If they did, I'm certain they would send her away. I know she lives in terror of a certain Scottish great-aunt."

"So I have heard," Caroline murmured. "Do you think Mariah is right? Do you think they will be shocked enough, muddled enough, that she will be able to introduce an alternative suitor and gain their approval?"

"I cannot say. Mariah believes it. I suppose I must, too." He abruptly leaned forward, meeting her eyes and hoping she read the sincerity in his own. "Thank you, truly, for offering to help us. I am grateful to you, and I will fulfill my end of our bargain to the best of my ability. You have my word that I will do anything within my power to help you. You have only to ask it of me."

Her eyebrows rose and one corner of her mouth tilted upward. "Goodness. It sounds as though I could ask you to slay a dragon. A pity there aren't any about."

He chuckled and leaned back. "And what have you against poor dragons?"

"Nothing at all. I am rather fond of the creatures in storybooks," she said, her teasing smile fully apparent. "I will hold you to your word, sir. Though I have the feeling you do not yet understand how much I have asked of you already."

"Indeed. I haven't sat for a complicated portrait before. This will be an interesting experience, even if it takes all summer for you to create your masterpiece." He smiled, and then the weight settled in the pit of his stomach again. All summer. And he would have at least part of that summer with his dreadful cousin. He found freedom from parental matchmaking only to leash himself to Claude.

"You see, it is an expression like that which makes me think I haven't helped you at all."

He looked up at Caroline and allowed a sigh to escape him. He glanced to the staircase, but his sisters had not yet reappeared. That gave him a little time to explain himself. "It is nothing to do with your service to me, Caroline. I am quite relieved on that account. It is another matter entirely. I learned this morning that one of my relatives, a cousin, is coming to stay with us for an undetermined length of time." He tapped his fingers against his knees. "And he's an unpleasant houseguest. In truth, he is an altogether unpleasant person."

"Oh dear." Caroline gave him a sympathetic frown. "I haven't any cousins, pleasant or unpleasant," she said. "Is he difficult to get along with?"

"For me, yes. Others don't often see my cousin for what he is. He has a gift for charming people." Edward rubbed his hand over his face, then studied Caroline's expression. She didn't seem eager, as one would look when anticipating gossip. Nor did she seem indifferent or bored. Instead, she leaned slightly toward him, her expression open and even a touch concerned. "He has a reputation, in some circles, for gambling. He wins often enough at cards and horses that this isn't usually noted as a vice. And then...he flirts, outrageously, with genteel women. With those of lower status, he doesn't limit himself to flirtation." He winced and looked down. "I apologize. I shouldn't speak of such things to you."

Her hand appeared upon the table, palm down, but reaching toward him. He looked first at her hand and then raised his gaze to hers. She gave him a small, discreet smile. "My papa, he had a terrible reputation once. A lot of it undeserved. Because of all the things he knew of the world, he never shielded me from the truth of what is out there. He taught me how to tell a good man from a bad one. I understand what you mean, Edward. You needn't apologize."

His cheeks warmed, but he nodded. His parents hadn't explained such things to his sisters until the last time Claude had visited. They had warned his sisters to keep watch on their cousin when near their friends, and moved their maids to sleep in cots in the same rooms as the girls if they could not sleep in their parents' homes nearby.

Caroline tapped her hand on the table once, then withdrew it, her expression thoughtful. "I am terribly sorry for the discomfort he causes during his visits."

The softness and the sincerity in her voice made him look up, and when he met her gaze this time, he felt something strange. A sensation he couldn't explain, though it reminded him of the way his stomach dropped when he stood on the edge of a precipice or leaned too far over a railing to find the ground far beneath him.

"If it was only that, I might well endure it," Edward admitted, surprising himself. But she had listened with so much sympathy and understanding. Why not tell her the rest? "He is the cousin who will inherit if I don't have an heir of my own. Someday." He swallowed and reached for his cup. The tea was cold, but he didn't care. He needed something to ease the dryness in his mouth.

If anything, Caroline's expression indicated an even greater understanding. "He represents all the things your parents fear and are using to encourage you to marry."

He lowered his cup. "Precisely."

"That is rather awful."

"Immensely awful." He stretched his arm out on the table, then tapped his fingers in the same spot she had tapped a moment ago. "Cousin Claude is awful. The worst sort of man. And when he is around, my judgment can sometimes suffer."

"How?" she asked, her gaze on his fingers. "Surely, he doesn't influence you to act as he does. I cannot imagine you behaving as anything other than a gentleman."

"Even when I crash through trees like a boar?" he asked, raising his eyebrows at her. She blushed, but smiled, too.

"You are a very gentleman-like boar."

He laughed, though it was quiet and short. "No. I haven't any desire to act as my cousin does. He makes it difficult to keep my temper in check. We have come to blows in the past, or he pokes and prods me until I say or do something, in public usually, that leads to gossip or scandal."

"And he looks like the victim of your temper rather than the villain that he is," she surmised.

"Precisely."

Caroline's hand returned to the table. Smaller than his. Delicate, and without its glove since she had removed it to take tea. Without hesitation, she laid her slim fingers atop the back of his hand, the touch featherlight and soft. "You must do better this time, Edward. Prove to your family, and yourself, that your cousin cannot goad you into anything. Not poor behavior, and not into taking a wife as a means only to disinherit him."

Edward wanted to turn his hand over and grasp her fingers in his own. He wanted to know how those delicate fingers would feel, laced with his. And the wanting of those things shocked him so much that he withdrew his hand, though not so fast as to startle her, and tucked it safely beneath the table where he clenched it into a tight fist. Her touch had done something. Stirred movement within, and his thoughts had turned in a dangerous direction.

"You are right, of course." Why did he sound suddenly hoarse? Had the tea done nothing to help his throat? "I will take your advice to heart. I will do better this time."

Her eyes brightened, and she gave a firm nod of agreement. "You will. I have complete faith in your abilities."

That made one of them, at least. Would she still have that faith in him if she knew how he worked to avoid revealing his dream to his father? Caroline had worked hard, had obviously sacrificed time and energy, to devote herself to her art. And he hadn't even the bravery, the cleverness, to tell his father he wanted to leave England and see the rest of the wide world. His father would spit fire, most likely. And forbid it.

His sisters finally returned, exclaiming over the time and an appointment with a friend. Edward had no choice but to lead all three of them away from the table, through the shop, and onto the street again. It was there they took their leave of Miss Clapham, who went in search of the driver who had brought her from Inglewood Castle to Alderton.

As Edward handed his sisters into their gig, he finally asked, "Why did you two abandon us at the table? It doesn't look as though you made any more purchases, despite being away for an age."

Charity and Patience exchanged a knowing glance, then

Patience answered, "It didn't look as though you minded us being gone. In fact, you and Miss Clapham appeared rather cozy."

He crossed his arms and stood there, in the street, looking up at his sisters. "What can you mean? We were merely having a conversation. And running out of things to say, at that." It wasn't precisely true. He had found himself unable to speak because his thoughts had run away with him, making him think excessively about holding Caroline's hand. If he admitted as much to his sisters, it would help their ruse and harm nothing. Charity and Patience were already shaping a romance for him in their minds, given the evidence before him of their glances and smiles.

"Is she too clever for you?" Patience teased in a false whisper. "Is that why she is difficult to talk to?"

He heaved a sigh. He may as well add a few more lines to the story they were telling themselves. "Rather she is too lovely and charming." At least he could speak with sincerity. That would be his only chance at getting away with things. To tell half-truths rather than attempt to bluff his way through the farcical relationship.

Charity's lips parted. "Edward. Do you hear yourself?"

Patience put her chin in her hand and widened her eyes to a comical size. "I knew we hadn't imagined the twinkle in your eye when Miss Clapham joined us for tea. Doth your heart skip a beat at the sound of her voice?" As she teased, her eyes sparkled with amusement.

Edward started and dropped his arms in his alarm. He could answer that question, quite honestly, with a *yes*. But he wouldn't. He refused to go that far. "That's—it's ridiculous. To say—"

Charity chimed in, "You needn't deny it, Edward. It is obvious to us that there is an attraction between you."

"Yes, you positively *glowed* the moment you saw her on the street," Patience added with unconcealed glee. "She's witty, too. Though we really must come to know her better before you decide on a match."

He opened his mouth to deny it again, to argue—and then recalled himself to his senses yet again. He *needed* his sisters to think such a thing. Because if they believed it, his parents would believe it, too. Denial didn't serve his purpose, though his stomach flipped and turned, and he dearly wanted to tell them both to mind their own business.

Charity continued where her sister left off. "A match? Edward can hardly hope for such a thing. He is abysmal at flirtation. I doubt he would have said two words to Miss Clapham if we hadn't left them alone together."

"Are you saying I'm shy?" Edward spluttered.

His sisters shrugged, in unison. Had it not occurred to them he couldn't speak so much as a sentence while they had discussed fashion without ceasing?

"I am not shy." No one had ever accused him of such a thing before. Until he grew from youth to adult, many would have said the opposite thing to be true. He'd been accused of brazen and bold behavior by his professors all through his education.

"Not shy in general terms. Perhaps it is an affliction brought on by finally meeting a woman you like. Such a circumstance is not unheard of," Charity said, taking up the reins. "Will you at least admit that you had an easier time of things when we left?"

"Indeed. Miss Clapham appeared quite refreshed after your conversation," Patience added. "Did you see the twinkle in her eye when she bid us farewell? I think she rather likes you, too, Edward."

Edward's face flushed at his sisters' teasing. "You two are insufferable," he muttered, but he allowed them to see a smile tug at his lips.

He hadn't meant to perform for his sisters, at least at first. Had Caroline? Or had his sisters seen something real when they observed her enjoyment?

That thought had to stop before it fully sunk into his consciousness. Edward dutifully shoved it aside. The sprite didn't like him as anything other than an acquaintance, perhaps a friend. His attraction to her was one-sided and easily overcome, thanks to his determination to remain a bachelor.

"Perhaps we are insufferable," Charity said, a grin on her face.

"But we're also quite observant. You like her." She slapped leather to horse, commanding the animal forward, and she shouted over her shoulder to Edward, "Whether you admit it or not!"

He heard his sisters' laughter. Shook his head. Then accepted the lead for his mount after he handed the boy another coin. He'd follow his sisters home, of course, but not too closely. A man teetering on the edge of...something...didn't need his sisters' teasing to distract him from his purpose. Falling in love, marrying someone, would not grant him freedom. It would take what little he had left.

With Caroline Clapham, there wasn't any truth to a courtship between them. Merely the illusion of one. Even though when he looked into her eyes, he'd had an odd feeling. That feeling of being on the edge of a cliff, anticipating a fall, ought to be unpleasant. Yet Edward's instinct wasn't to pull back. The sensation was too heady. Almost pleasant.

And for once in his life, whatever brink it was Edward stood upon, he wasn't about to let anyone push him over the edge. Not until he knew what consequences waited below.

# CHAPTER 12

As Claude Everly stepped out of the carriage, Edward wished, not for the first time, that Claude's physical characteristics matched the vices of which his cousin was guilty. But instead, those who thought beauty a virtue in and of itself would find no fault with the man.

The family stood in a line, waiting to welcome their cousin and nephew, while he brushed dust from the road from his shoulders and gave commands to his manservant and the Everly footmen.

Claude was a sight to be seen. He had copper-colored hair that shone in the sunlight, longer than fashionable, and curling, framing his hollow cheekbones. His eyes were a deep shade of blue, with a hint of something sharp in their depths. He stood tall and confident, with a lean frame. Edward immediately felt awkward and overly large, and his hands curled into fists behind his back.

Claude looked as fit and athletic as the racing horses he rode into the ground, before he used them until they were spent by his rough ways and constant urging. Edward had heard his mother declare the recklessness an Everly trait, one that Hope had nearly allowed to lead her to ruin. But Hope had never had the cruel tilt to her smile that Claude employed the moment he caught Edward's gaze.

"Ah, my uncle, aunt, and cousins. Greetings." Even his voice had a quality that made Edward's eyes narrow with suspicion as his hackles rose.

The solitary comfort Edward had in that moment was knowing he had reason to leave the household the moment Claude retired to his room. In his coat pocket, a card bearing the Earl of Inglewood's crest rested over his heart. The countess had written, inviting him to come to the castle that afternoon.

Perhaps it was the way Claude moved, with a fluid grace that spoke of a man who either knew his way around a brawl or a ballroom, that made Edward stiffen from head to toe. Or maybe it was the way he held himself, with arrogance others would mistake for confidence. Either way, there was no denying the fact that Claude Everly was a man who commanded attention. Unfortunately, his presence, combined with what many called his rakish charm made the man generally well-liked. Only those close to him recognized him for what he truly was.

Caroline hadn't laughed when Edward expressed his dread over his cousin's visit. At least there was that. She'd listened. Believed him. Encouraged him to do better in the face of his cousin's arrogance and immoral behavior.

The rectangle of paper in his pocket bore the weight of his focus. He would leave soon. He would go to Inglewood. He would speak to Caroline. Their plans would take shape. He would be free of his parents' expectations for courting Mariah.

Edward's Father greeted his nephew first, his expression neither cold nor welcoming. "Claude, welcome to the Refuge. I trust you had a safe journey?"

"Indeed, Uncle. And it is a relief to be at its end and welcomed into the warm embrace of my kin." Claude turned to Edward's mother. "And Aunt Everly, as charming as ever."

Edward's mother managed a smile. "I hope you will find your stay here comfortable, nephew."

Edward was next in line. He kept his posture stiff and didn't bother with a false smile. "Claude," he said, barely tilting his head to acknowledge the other man's focus on him.

"I see you are as pleasant as ever," Claude remarked, a coolness in his eyes and tone. "I understand this is an important summer for you, Cousin Edward. You are on the hunt for a new mistress to the Refuge. What a...thrilling prospect." His smile turned almost simpering. "The ladies in the vicinity must be overcome with excitement."

Though he wanted to tell his cousin, using terms unfit for a gentleman, exactly where he could betake himself, Edward ground his teeth together and said nothing.

Charity, next in their receiving line, spoke before Claude could jab at Edward with another word. "Cousin Claude, it is such a surprise to have you here. I did not think you enjoyed our part of the country, especially in the summer."

He gave his attention to her, his lips curving into a smile that didn't mean anything good. "I have expressed such sentiments in the past, so your supposition is not ill-founded. Cooler climes are more to my liking. But there is always the sea-air to look forward to when venturing to the edge of civilization. I understand it is good for one's health."

The edge of civilization? The man couldn't help but insult others at every turn.

Patience wrinkled her nose, and Claude bestowed a look of amusement upon her before he tugged one more time at the cuff of his sleeve. "The sun is rather unpleasant at this time of day, is it not?"

The family moved from outdoors to indoors, with Father offering the usual polite comments about his guest's stay. When Claude went up the stairs to his room, and everyone else remained on the ground floor, the family released a collective breath. The patriarch of the family said nothing. He grunted, a sound of discontent, then strode down the corridor toward his study.

Their mother gave their offspring a long-suffering glance. "Now, children. I know we haven't got on with Claude in the past. But please be polite and mannerly. How can we hope for a man like him to be better if he has not the proper example for such behavior among his own family?" She glanced in the direction their father had fled. "I better speak to your father about our dinner plans this evening." Then she hurried away, as elegantly as one could while still being in a hurry.

"How did Claude know Papa wants you to marry?" Patience asked.

"I wondered the same," Charity said, her tone thoughtful. "I didn't think our local gossip would carry all the way to someone like him, in London."

"Nor did I." Edward shrugged, attempting to rid himself of the irritation he felt. "Claude has a habit of knowing things he shouldn't and making remarks to purposefully irritate others."

"What do you suppose he means to accomplish, all the way out here, without his friends?" Patience asked, eyes bright with curiosity. "Do you think he is running from the law?"

"Unlikely," Charity answered, smoothing away the wrinkles in her forehead with an amused expression. "Father wouldn't harbor a criminal. Family or not."

"A gambling debt, then, that he cannot pay?" Patience tapped her chin and peered up the staircase. "Or a jilted lover, perhaps, with a brother who demands satisfaction in the form of a duel?"

"Duels are illegal," Edward muttered, shaking his head. "I haven't any desire to speculate on whatever dishonest conduct might've made him flee London. It's more likely he felt the sudden desire to torment people who were innocently minding their own business."

"That would be rather dull reasoning for him to swoop down upon us," Patience said with some dissatisfaction. "I prefer believing he is in hiding."

Charity shook her head and walked to the stairs. "As interesting as it is to speculate on Claude's presence, I have better ways to pass my time until we have to take dinner with the odious man."

Edward needed a distraction, too. Something to keep his mind occupied. His invitation to visit Inglewood couldn't have arrived at a better time. "I think I must be off as well, Patience. I am for Inglewood today. Have you something to keep yourself busy?"

"There are always things for ladies to do," Patience said with a theatrical tilt of her chin. "Why, there is the stillroom to manage, embroidery, the painting of fans, rearranging my combs, arranging flowers, reading sermons, writing letters to all my dearest friends—"

Edward laughed and nudged her with his shoulder. "Quite a list, sister. Though I cannot say I envy your possession of it."

"I cannot say I enjoy everything on my list, either. I have little choice in the matter, though." She sniffed, then followed after Charity, who had paused at the top of the staircase to wait for her younger sister.

With his sisters gone, Edward followed in the tracks of his parents to the study. He meant to remind them of his invitation before leaving, perhaps emphasizing that Miss Clapham's interest in art piqued his curiosity. He would call her charming, too. Give them reason to fret. He approached the study without making much sound, thanks to his father's insistence that a long rug be installed in the corridor.

"Servants and people walking about on the floors, always tapping, tapping, tapping, drives me to distraction," his father had proclaimed the winter before. Now he never heard anyone coming or going—a thing Edward and his sisters had used to their advantage a time or two.

As Edward silently approached the study, he heard his parents talking but didn't listen to their actual words, until he raised his hand to knock.

His fist stilled an inch before making contact.

"I hope you know what you are about, husband," his mother said, her tone somewhat irritable. "When one person has the ability to make our entire household uneasy, he doesn't deserve an invitation to visit."

"I had my reasons," Mr. Everly responded, voice low and

grouse-like. "And Claude knows what's expected of him. He will behave himself, so long as I fulfill my end of the bargain."

No. Edward had to have misunderstood. His parents hadn't invited Claude, had they? He only caught the smallest part of their conversation. And it wasn't gentlemanly to eavesdrop on his own parents.

A long silence followed before Edward heard his mother ask, "What is it you aren't telling me, Samuel?"

Edward lowered his fist to his side, puzzling over his parents' conversation. It sounded as though—but it couldn't be, surely—his parents had *invited* Claude to stay with them? His father had even made some type of arrangement with Claude to ensure his cooperation on some secret matter. Perhaps if he were to go in and ask...?

His father spoke in a tone that closed the subject. "Nothing you need worry about. Old, unsettled business. Claude is exactly like his father. He thinks only of his own pleasure and entertainment. What he wants is more important to him than the family name. After this visit, I doubt we will see him again."

The carpet muffled Edward's backward step, taken in surprise and uncertainty.

Claude *had* been invited. By Edward's father. The letter that had come—it had been in response to something his father sent, something his father had asked of Claude. Then his cousin had made demands in turn, which his father had agreed to, and such was their arrangement that it involved Claude's late father.

He ought to walk through the door and reveal that he had heard what was said. Then demand an explanation. Edward drew in a deep breath, prepared to do just that.

Except...except Caroline had said something that came back to him in that moment. *"You must do better this time, Edward. Prove to your family, and yourself, that your cousin cannot goad you into anything. Not poor behavior, and not into taking a wife as a means only to disinherit him."*

Though tempted to barge into the study and get answers, Edward checked his impulse. Poor behavior, indeed. Listening at doors. Letting his temper guide him. No. He could do better. He *would* do better.

There were not many reasons his parents would have Claude to stay. Caroline had noted that Claude's presence would bring up everything his parents feared would happen if Edward didn't marry and provide himself with an heir.

He backed away from the door another step.

Had his father purposefully brought Claude Everly to their doorstep with the purpose of making those fears more tangible to Edward? Was his cousin simply a pawn in Mr. Everly's game to make Edward see reason and wed sooner rather than later? And wed the person approved of by Edward's parents, most likely.

The obviousness of the plot made Edward grind his teeth together.

His parents thought him unintelligent enough to not see through their scheme. And perhaps he never would have, had he not overheard just enough to make it obvious.

Cursing himself as every kind of fool, Edward withdrew from the corridor in silence. He had to think. And he had to plan how best to endure his cousin's visit as well as his parents' duplicity.

There was no reason for him to linger at home.

The countess's invitation in his pocket drew him away, and he departed with relief. Putting his father, mother, marriage, and Claude out of his mind.

Sadly, Everly Refuge hadn't been a haven for him in a long time.

# CHAPTER 13

The library at Inglewood was modest compared to libraries found in similar households, but it still awed Caroline every time she stepped inside. Today, the curtains at the tall windows were drawn open, letting in bright afternoon sunlight. Lady Inglewood led Edward and Caroline to the room's center, where a table waited with books already upon it.

"Here we are." The countess gestured to the chairs around the table. "Please, sit, both of you. I told Caroline yesterday, Mr. Everly, there are not many artistic representations of Atlas of which I am aware, and I have seen even fewer of them in person. I gathered what I could here."

She moved a large book of maps toward them and turned to the first illustrated page, which featured a black and white woodcutting of a man bent forward, toward the viewer, with a globe upon his back.

"Most of what I have seen is like this," the countess went on. "Not detailed work, but more the impression of the Titan." She moved a larger book to them, one tied with a ribbon. "These are sketches from a holiday my husband and I took three years ago. We were in Rome for two months, and I visited a house with several beautiful sculptures."

Caroline opened the book when Lady Inglewood gave her a nod, then gently turned several pages of charcoaled and penciled sketches until she came to the one the countess wanted them to see. Atlas, bent down to one knee, both hands above his head to support a globe, with the sphere pressed into the place between his shoulders. The sculptor had left the statue nude, except for a robe or cloak wrapped around Atlas's left forearm that draped behind him, over his left side.

"This sculpture is known as the Farnese Atlas, which was discovered in the ruins of Rome. It depicts the mythological figure in stunning detail."

Caroline studied the sketch with fascination, pursing her lips and taking in the man's posture. The Titan was on one knee, with both arms holding up the globe. His muscles bulged and strained under the weight, and his face was contorted with effort and pain.

Lady Inglewood turned the page to show a more detailed sketch of the sculpture's face.

Edward cleared his throat, and when Caroline looked up, she saw him staring at the countess, his cheeks pink.

"We aren't trying to replicate the sculpture, surely?" He avoided Caroline's gaze completely. He released a weak laugh. "I doubt I could manage a beard like that one."

Caroline didn't blame him in the least for his worries, which she knew had little to do with facial hair. And she quickly assured him, "No. No, of course not. This is merely an example of what might be done. You needn't change any aspect of your physical appearance."

"And we will certainly provide more covering than a cape." The countess seemed momentarily amused, then covered her sketchbook with another book, already open. When Caroline looked down, she was somewhat relieved to see no illustrations.

"Here is the myth of Atlas. The earl helped me find it for you." She pointed to the book. "I suggest the two of you read it through together, and then discuss what pose you think best suited to his tale. Knowing what others have done is useful, but the work must be your own, Caroline. And do remember that we can depict the Titan in a variety of ways, including styles of clothing." She looked between them, and Caroline wondered if the countess had somehow enjoyed making her uncomfortable. Perhaps it had been a test, of sorts. As neither Caroline nor Edward had fled the room or had a fit of vapors, they had to have passed.

"Thank you for your advice, your ladyship." Caroline smiled up at her mentor. "I have a few ideas already, and I will certainly take Mr. Everly's comfort into consideration."

"Good. I will be reading over there." The countess pointed to a couch at one side of the large room. "Chaperoning, of course, but also available if you need anything else."

Edward nodded his understanding, but as soon as Lady Inglewood was settled, he leaned toward Caroline and whispered, "I would prefer to keep as much clothing on as possible, Miss Clapham."

Heat flooded her cheeks again. "I prefer the same. Trust me on that account." She pulled the book of Greek mythology closer. "Let us see what we can glean from Atlas's story."

"Is it too much to hope for a full description of his most formal suit of clothing?" Edward asked, and Caroline smirked at him as she ran her finger along the page. Then she read aloud.

"'As a powerful and proud Titan, Atlas was not content to be ruled by the gods. Instead, he sought to overthrow them and claim the heavens for himself. With the help of his brothers, he waged a great war against the gods, hoping to emerge victorious.'"

"I like him so far," Edward interrupted, and Caroline cut him a sharp look with raised eyebrows. "My apologies. Do continue."

"'But the gods were not to be defeated so easily. They unleashed their full wrath upon Atlas and his kin, and in the end, the Titans were defeated and banished to the underworld. For his part in the rebellion, Atlas was punished in a most unusual manner.

"'The god Zeus, in his wisdom, decreed that Atlas would be forced to hold up the heavens on his shoulders for all eternity. The weight of the heavens was immense, and it caused Atlas great pain and suffering. He longed to be free of his burden, but there was no escape from his punishment.'"

Edward released a heavy sigh. "Poor fellow. He has my sympathy."

Caroline kept going. "'For centuries, Atlas held up the heavens, straining under the weight of the celestial sphere. His muscles grew tired and sore, and his back and shoulders became hunched and deformed. But he held on, steadfast and unyielding, for he knew that his punishment was just.'"

"I would rather not be the subject of a painting in which I must appear hunched and deformed," he said aloud, and Caroline looked up at him to see him smiling at her. "But if that is what you need, of course, I will keep my word."

That he said as much made her feel somewhat better, though Caroline had no intention of recreating an old, broken Atlas. "I think I would like to depict Atlas at the beginning of his punishment, rather than the end. Still with a measure of defiance, I think. His punishment new, and his feelings of rebellion still simmering. Perhaps disappointed, but not yet defeated in spirit."

The gentleman at her side raised his eyebrows at her and bent toward the book, his shoulder brushing hers. "You didn't read the last of it. It says, 'To this day, Atlas remains a symbol of the power and pride of the Titans, and a warning of the dangers of rebellion against the gods. His fate serves as a reminder that even the mightiest of beings are subject to the will of the gods, and that defiance can lead only to ruin and suffering.'" He snorted and brought the book closer to himself. "Whoever wrote this wasn't the most cheerful fellow, was he?" He turned to the title page, and Caroline read it over his shoulders.

*Divine Retribution: The Mythological Stories of Gods and Titans by Sir Mortimer Grimsby.*

"The author's name certainly paints a picture, does it not?" Edward grinned at her, and Caroline resisted the impulse to grin back.

She needed Edward to take this seriously.

"Sir Mortimer did us a favor," she noted, reaching over Edward to close the cover, her arm brushing along his in the process. She sat again and cleared her throat. "As I said, I already have a few ideas. I thought we could try them today and find out which pose might be the easiest for you to hold."

"I won't have to stand that way for the whole time, will I?" he asked with a wince. "That fellow in the sketch hardly looked happy with his position."

"Not the entire time," she promised. "And not all at once. I will do some preliminary sketches, of course. Studying you from all sides. Then I will decide the best position overall, and we will spend longer with you in that pose and angle. From there I will be able to draw out most things on the canvas from memory or using my reference sketches. I will need you available to be certain I get other details correct, from time to time."

"All right then. Let us begin." Edward stood, with such an easy willingness that Caroline wondered why Lady Inglewood had thought it so impossible to find a gentleman willing to model. Edward didn't act at all reticent, other than expressing concern about holding one position overly long. And the costume.

Perhaps, as the project went, things would change.

"All right. We needn't worry about proper costuming yet." Caroline stood and went to where several empty picture frames leaned against the wall. All of them were circular, found in attics and corners by the Inglewood servants. They differed in size, from small diameter to large.

"I thought these would do well enough to find the right pose and size for the globe." She picked up a middling-sized frame, the wood heavier than she liked but still lighter than trying to put an actual globe on Edward's back.

She turned around to face him, and found Edward slipping off his coat, revealing the crisp white shirt and waistcoat beneath. Though she had already seen him in shirtsleeves the first time they met, there was something different about watching the act of a man sliding a coat from his shoulders—something that made her grasp the frame tighter and her throat constrict.

She swallowed away the strange feeling as Edward put the coat over the back of a chair, then came to her with arms outstretched to take the frame.

He hesitated, giving her an odd look. "I hope you do not mind. Gentlemen's coats are not made in a way that makes it easy to reach overhead and behind. Not without angering my valet and tailor both when the seams split."

"Of course. Not at all. Here." She thrust the frame toward him, grateful that she hadn't blushed. Men in shirtsleeves had never bothered her before. Ever. She grew up on a farm, with both her father and laborers working in their fields and orchards in their shirtsleeves.

However, Edward was neither employed by her family nor related to her. And they weren't in the fields.

After assuring herself that Lady Inglewood remained quietly reading her book, Caroline shook her head at her own silliness. "Upon your back or shoulders, I think, would be best. Try something that feels natural. Imagining you must carry that frame on a long walk."

Edward gave the frame a spin against the floor, then hefted it up and over his head. She couldn't help but notice how his broad shoulders filled out the fabric of his shirt, and how easily he lifted his arms to hold the large round frame on his back.

"It's not too heavy, is it?" Caroline asked, concerned.

Edward shook his head. "No, I can manage it. But could we create something lighter for me to hold for the longer sessions? I don't want to tire too quickly."

Caroline nodded in agreement. "Yes, that's a good idea. I will think of something before our next session. Perhaps a *papier-mâché* frame?"

Edward rolled the frame upon his back from one shoulder to the other with ease, settled it in the center of his back, but then shook his head. "This is too small. It would be easier to hold it in place if it was larger. My arms wouldn't have to stretch up as much. Have you another frame?"

They went up in size, and Edward's arms and shoulders appeared less taxed. From there, Caroline picked up her sketchbook and sat in a chair, hastily forming a human shape holding a circle. Edward stood upright, frame above his head, bent only slightly forward.

Caroline shook her head. "I think kneeling will be better, both for the painting and for your sake as you pose."

Without a word, he went down to one knee, balancing the frame in the hollow between his shoulders, his head tilted up to look at her.

"Better?" he asked, eyebrows drawn together. His deep blue eyes didn't waver from hers, and she read sincerity and determination in their depths. He wasn't laughing at her, nor was he annoyed. The wonderful man genuinely wanted help, to do his best on her behalf.

Her heart skipped. With delight, she told herself. Because she finally had an exciting project to work upon. "Yes. Now, I need only find the right angle."

"Keep in mind what it is you wish to convey to your viewer," Lady Inglewood said, voice raised to carry across the room. Caroline nearly jumped, having forgotten the countess was there.

Edward must have noticed, because when Caroline met his stare again, his expression had changed. His eyes danced, and he smiled crookedly. She narrowed her eyes at him, and he winked in response but said nothing.

Let him think her silly for getting wrapped up in things. *He* certainly wasn't the reason for her distraction. No. Her work had taken hold of her. And she would prove it.

Caroline approached, sketchbook in hand, and circled Edward where he knelt on the carpet. First clockwise, then counter-clockwise, asking him to make small adjustments as she went. Tilt his head this way, now that. Could he move the leg he knelt on a little more forward. What about shifting his hands a little more? How did that feel? Switch knees. No, switch back.

To his credit, the man obeyed every instruction she gave him, and spoke only when answering a direct question. Until, finally, Caroline thought she had it right.

She angled herself in a way that allowed her to sketch him in profile, his face toward her. Details were not yet important. The pose was what mattered. Then she moved a little more to his front and sketched some more. That was it. Nearly perfect.

Again, she moved to sit directly in front of him. "Now, lift your head to look at me. Imagine, if you please, that you are Atlas facing Zeus as he declares this your punishment for eternity."

Edward lifted his head—the angle couldn't be comfortable given the frame on his back—and raised both eyebrows at her. The puzzlement in his look was so incongruent with what she had asked for that Caroline giggled, then covered her mouth.

Serious artists didn't giggle.

Caroline cleared her throat and tried to school her features into something more serious. "I doubt Atlas appeared confused. Remember, he knew what was coming when his mutiny failed."

The gentleman shifted the weight of the frame, then put it down on the ground with care. He stayed kneeling, though. "What is the emotion you want to convey?"

Thinking of the book's description, of her goals, Caroline lowered her sketchbook to her lap and considered the question carefully. "Defiance," she said, voice soft as she spoke through her thoughts. "Pain. Anger. Rebellion. Everything Atlas wanted had been taken from him. Even his daughters, if I remember the myths correctly. He was a Titan, older than the Greek gods, and struck down when they took control of the heavens and the earth."

Edward studied her, then ran his now-free hands through his hair. "Anger, then. But maybe a measure of sorrow, too." He stood and stretched, then gestured to her sketchbook with a flourish. "May I? Perhaps writing out the idea would help."

"Of course." She turned to an empty page, then handed him paper and a pencil from the table, curious as to what he would come up with.

Edward sat down beside her and jotted down a list along the edge of the paper.

*Pain*
*Anger*
*Devastation*
*Longing*
*Sorrow*
*Defiance*
*Rebellion*

"And you said your depiction will be at the start of his punishment. Before his spirit is broken." Edward wrote this at the top of the page, then tapped the paper with the pencil, creating tiny dots in the process. Caroline stared at his list, then looked up at him, at his furrowed brow.

Was she less of an artist, letting him help with this part?

But then, it was important for the work that she get Atlas's expression perfect.

"When I was on the Continent," he said, still looking at the paper, "I toured several Catholic churches and holy sites. They are full of the most exquisite artwork. You would love them." He smiled briefly, then continued his story. "I went to the *Piazza della Signoria*, where Michelangelo's sculpture of David stands, three hundred years since its creation." He looked down at the words on the paper, and he started writing again. Caroline kept her eyes on his face as he spoke.

"His expression is one of intense concentration. Yet there was something sorrowful about his. A furrowed brow. And he glares, fixedly, at a mark no one else can see. Is he preparing to face Goliath and his awful future at war? Or the king who will betray and try to kill him?" Edward smiled, though the expression wasn't exactly pleasant. "His lips are pressed together, as though he dare not speak. His whole body is tense, and he leans heavily on one leg. He is unwavering. Certain of himself."

Caroline spoke softly, "As you wish to be?" She saw it as she watched him—a longing that did not match his words. What was it that Edward wanted and refused to say aloud? What was the thing that he, like David, dared not speak?

Edward looked up, momentary surprise showing before he winced. Then he shrugged and attempted a smile. "Perhaps. But we cannot all be chosen vessels for greatness." He sighed and looked at all he had written. "Atlas would not feel that sense of calm, I think. Though the rest of it might be there."

He wrote for a moment more, then handed the sketchbook to Caroline. His handwriting wasn't exactly tidy, yet she had no trouble making out his words. A description that had her puzzled.

*Atlas's face is etched with lines of pain and suffering, his brow furrowed in anger and frustration. His eyes burn with intensity, daring anyone to challenge his rebellious spirit. His punishment is unjust, singled out by Zeus for no reason other than his own power and strength. But he refuses to be broken by his burden, to give in to the weight of the heavens on his shoulders. Instead, he holds his head high, defying his fate and challenging the gods themselves with his unwavering spirit.*

"You ought to write professionally," she murmured, smiling at the paper and then looking up at him.

Edward shook his head slowly, his gaze unfocused. "I know so little of true hardship. But I can imagine what it would be like to have a burden too heavy to bear. I have seen it in others often enough."

The depth of his emotions and thoughts on the matter surprised her and put her own thoughts deeper into a river of doubt. What did she know of such heavy burdens? Would painting a scene such as that be dishonest?

Uncertainty filled her mind. Until Edward's hand picked up hers from the table where it rested. Caroline's gaze came up, meeting his with surprise. Both their hands were bare. His skin was warm against hers, his fingers strong, his grasp firm.

"Don't look so worried," he whispered, eyes soft and smile sincere. "You can do this, sprite."

She exhaled a shaky breath as she nodded, and then he released her hand with one last squeeze. Edward rose, lifted his empty picture frame again, and knelt. He looked down for a long moment, gathering his thoughts. She put her sketchbook in her lap and picked up the thin stick of charcoal she preferred for quick, rough outlines.

Edward lifted his head, brow furrowed, and features set in an expression of restrained anger and agony.

Her heart stopped. It must have. The whole world stopped. And there was only a transformed Edward, an Atlas glaring at her with such ferocity that she forgot for a moment that it was not she who deserved his fury.

Her heart began beating again, her stomach dropped, and heat filled her, flooding her chest and limbs, climbing into her cheeks, and making her fingertips tingle. Caroline started sketching, as quickly as she could, in broad, dark strokes that captured the furrowed brow, the darkness in the eyes, the sharp lines of an angry jaw.

There was nothing on her page except Atlas and his anger.

At last she nodded, satisfaction curling around her heart like a contented kitten. "This will be a start," she murmured.

Atlas melted away as Edward's smile returned, though he appeared tired this time.

An hour had passed. Lady Inglewood called a halt to their work. Servants brought in refreshments. Edward was himself again.

Caroline walked him to the door after he enjoyed tea and cake. As Edward put on his hat, he smiled at her. "Thank you for this, sprite. I needed to escape my family. Claude is come, you see. And forgetting about him in the time I was here was immensely helpful."

He hadn't mentioned his troublesome cousin's arrival even once. Caroline's stomach twisted with guilt. "I am sorry, Edward. We should have spent some time in conversation, not the whole of it on my work. I ought to have asked—"

He shook his head, the weariness in his eyes quite plain to see. "As I said, it was a boon to forget for a time." He adjusted his gloves, not looking directly at her. "The time in your company today—well. I would not have changed a moment of it."

She blushed and tucked her hands behind her back, twisting her fingers together where he wouldn't see. "Good. I'm glad." She lifted her head with more confidence. "Will I see you tomorrow?"

"For more sketching? That is a delightful idea," he said, a genuine smile melting away the melancholy before it fully took hold of him. "More opportunity to escape my cousin and spread rumors of our growing attachment."

"Exactly." Caroline brought her hands forward, folding them demurely. "Thank you for coming today, Edward. I look forward to seeing you again."

"Tomorrow," he agreed, bowing. "Good afternoon, sprite."

She didn't object to the fairy-name this time, and he swept out the door to his waiting horse. She leaned against the doorway and watched as he mounted. Edward looked back one last time, and his eyebrows lifted when he saw her yet watching. Then he grinned, rather playfully, and tipped his hat to her before riding away.

Caroline closed the door. They had dismissed the footman after the servant delivered Edward's hat and gloves, so there was no one to see the way she leaned against it, or her little frown when she realized her heart skipped far too happily within her chest.

This time, she knew she couldn't blame it on her painting.

# CHAPTER 14

Having Claude as a houseguest made every moment at home miserable. The hour Edward spent with Caroline each day was the only hour he felt like himself. The rest of the time, he was at his father's beck and call, and subsequently attached to Claude, too. Listening to his cousin's subtle put-downs and innuendo.

Edward came home from another session spent in Caroline's presence, entering the stable yard while his thoughts remained lingering behind him at Inglewood. Today, he had spent a lot of time merely sitting while she studied his face. He worked through a variety of expressions, with her dutifully sketching each one, and speaking all the while to him of her family.

She adored her siblings, despite the difference in their ages. She talked of her sister forever trying to startle her and hoped aloud that the little girl didn't miss her too terribly. She spoke of her twin brothers as having different characters at such a young age and mused at the trouble they would likely cause when they grew older.

Staying still for her study, Edward didn't speak much in return. But he took in every word she said with interest and watched the play of emotion upon her face with growing admiration.

Sprite, indeed. She glowed when she spoke of her family, lit from within by her love. Her smiles, her concentrative frowns, made him wish to lean in closer the better to study the lines of her jaw, the curve of her cheek, the depth to her brown eyes.

Leaving at the end of an hour in her presence already caused a strange, disappointed feeling in his chest. Something pulled, stretched, between him and the artist at Inglewood. Tugging him backward, at least in thought, when he left for home.

Claude was already waiting, his horse saddled and ready, the rider still adjusting his gloves. He had a crop tucked beneath his arm, and his usual expression of boredom on his face. He looked up when Edward rode in, raising one eyebrow.

Riding together had become a daily activity for Edward, his father, and Claude. Every day when Edward returned from Inglewood. This would mark the fourth time they rode out together, with Edward feigning indifference to his cousin's company.

Edward's father had announced the desire to take them hunting for birds on the morrow, perhaps in an effort to dispel the tension and change the routine. Putting a loaded rifle in Edward's hands while he was anywhere near Claude was something of a risk.

"Ah, Edward, good to see you. Pray tell, where have you been gallivanting all morning?" The man's smirk appeared, slow and deliberate. "Or are you attempting to better your horsemanship through practice? You know, I've always admired your ability to persevere despite your limitations."

Maybe they ought to go hunting today instead of tomorrow.

Edward sighed. No. Though Claude was as pleasant as a weasel, Edward wouldn't shoot the man. Even if it put everyone out of their misery.

"I had an appointment, of a personal nature," Edward responded shortly, tone even as he dismounted. He gave his horse a pat and instructed the groom to bring him a different animal for his ride with his father.

They were still waiting when Claude spoke again. "This is the third time I have come out to the stables to find you barely returned from your errand, cousin." Claude's hat tilted across his forehead at an angle the man likely meant to look rakish. Edward hoped a tree removed it before long.

"It is a *daily* appointment," Edward said, doing his best impression of the statue of David, with his face a study in stone. "I cannot imagine it causes you any inconvenience."

"None." Claude dusted off his shoulder with a free hand while the other clutched his riding crop. "I imagine your time spent away from the estate is filled with all sorts of wholesome activities. Making charity visits, perhaps. Teaching the poor to read. Visiting widows and orphans. That sort of thing."

Edward snorted before he remembered he wasn't going to let his cousin rile him. "Any of those things would be better than how you tend to spend your idle hours."

The other man chuckled and gave his riding crop a spin. "I am rarely idle, Edward. In London, I am a busy man. Every hour is spoken for by either delightful recreation or leisure enjoyment."

"The country must not agree with you, then." Edward crossed his arms and turned his full attention to the house. If his father didn't arrive soon, Edward would go inside and drag him out. He wasn't about to go riding alone with Claude. "Perhaps you should return there."

"It would be so much better here if there was a young lady or two who appreciated my charms." Claude sighed wearily. "I applied to your sisters to re-introduce me to the local females, but they never seem to want to visit their friends."

Charity and Patience were not about to sacrifice a friendship at the altar of their cousin's arrogance. They would likely pretend they had no friends for the duration of Claude's visit, rather than expose any unmarried maiden to the man's dubious flirtations.

"Had you attended services with us on Sunday, you may have gained introductions," Edward pointed out with outward calm and inward relief.

"Step foot in a church, and at ten o'clock in the morning?" Claude shuddered. "But we are not speaking of church. We are speaking of leisure hours and ladies. Tell me, Edward. Do you have a woman hidden somewhere? Perhaps tucked away behind some bit of heather or a sand dune?"

A muscle over Edward's eye twitched. "If I did, why would I confide such a thing to you?"

"Perhaps that is where you run off to every day for an hour?" Claude spoke as though he gave thought to his own musings, with no expectation of a response. "That would make an abundant amount of sense, given your father's preoccupation with your bachelorhood. Or perhaps the daily appointment has more to do with an avoidance of your family's plans for you and their lady of choice. Is there already someone who occupies your thoughts?"

Edward ground his teeth together and said nothing, though memories of time spent with Caroline danced through his head.

"Your dear papa and mama would be quite cross if you entertained affections for someone they hadn't deemed suitable," Claude went on, still as though he expected no reply.

A new thought occurred to Edward. What if Claude wasn't merely invited to annoy Edward into marriage? What if his father had asked Claude to investigate Edward's doings? With Edward's refusal to openly court Mariah, his parents might have suspected Edward had promised himself to another.

He wanted people to think he and Caroline were in the first stages of a courtship. Which meant he needed to speak about her, openly. Even though the thought of saying her name in front of his cousin made Edward's skin crawl.

"I must say, you seem awfully secretive compared to the last time we were in company together." Claude sniffed and tilted his head enough to peer at Edward from the corner of his eye. "It's strange for someone as committed to high principles as you to act clandestine about, well, anything."

"There is nothing secretive about how I spend my time. Though I doubt it would be of any interest to you, which is why I kept my explanation short." Edward couldn't seem too willing to share the information. Claude would likely find a sudden change in attitude suspect. "As you seem incapable of setting the topic aside, I will put your overly curious mind at rest. I am sitting for a painting, assisting a friend of mine by acting as a model for her."

"Her?" Claude sounded far too gleeful. "The friend is a lady?"

"Indeed. And an artist of some talent."

"And you are her model?" Claude appeared taken aback.

"As I said. Have you grown hard of hearing, cousin?" Edward raised his eyebrow, mimicking Claude's mocking tone and finding at once it did not suit him. "For a study on a Greek myth." Edward tried to sound unconcerned as he revealed more and more to his cousin.

"Who do you portray in this mythological scene?"

Edward shrugged as he answered, "Atlas."

"Atlas." Claude's face twisted, for once making him appear less than handsome. "You? How many gentlemen turned your friend down before you were asked?"

Edward was saved an answer, or reacting to the implied insult, when his father emerged from the house at last, hat in hand rather than on his head. He came toward them, puffing as though he'd already undergone exercise that day.

"My apologies, lads. The delay could not be helped." He climbed his mounting block and Edward mounted his horse as Claude did the same with irritating ease. They had not long exited the stable yard before Claude took up the conversation again.

"Uncle, you did not tell me that Edward had artistic leanings."

"What is that?" Mr. Everly turned in his saddle to look first at Claude and then at Edward. "Artistic? Edward's never had the talent for drawing, of course, but he took particular notice of the statuary during his time in Rome. Did you not, Edward? Every letter he sent home seemed full of description of ruins and disfigured gods and goddesses. Lot of rot, if you ask me. But then, I never saw need to leave England." The older gentleman ended his monologue on a grumble, giving Edward another glance of disapproval. "Travel is nothing but an aimless pursuit, a frivolous indulgence that accomplishes nothing of importance and empties a man's bank account."

Claude's expression hardened. "I suppose it is a good thing my father had the navy to fund his need for exploration then."

"Indeed. My late brother saw the world while still doing his duty to his country." The senior Everly gentleman didn't take notice of the way Claude's lip curled, though Edward saw it and wondered at it. He knew his late-uncle had made his living as a naval officer. He'd even taken enough prize money in the war to fund his son's education and set him up as a gentleman of leisure, to some extent. Claude never spoke much about it. But given his fine clothing and lifestyle, Edward supposed there had to have been some funds left to his cousin upon his father's death.

"My cousin has an interest in art as well as travel, then?" Claude said, no trace of bitterness in his tone despite his distaste for the last thing his uncle had said.

"I'm not artistic in the least," Edward muttered.

Claude tutted at him. "But you have an *interest* in it," he noted, not to be dissuaded from the subject.

Edward's insides curled with mingled disgust and triumph. Claude had given him exactly the opening he wished for to address his comings and goings to his father. "Cousin Claude has discovered where I go for an hour in the afternoons, and he seems rather perplexed by it. I thought you would have told him, Father, about my posing for Miss Clapham."

Edward's father snorted. "That waste of time. No gentleman ought to sit still for so long when he could be at other pursuits. If it wasn't at Inglewood, I'd tell you to leave it be, Edward. But it's important to build good relations with our neighbors. Especially when they are earls, aye, Claude?" He chuckled and led their party through a gate, held open by the groom accompanying them to assist with such things. "How goes the progress? Is she about finished with it yet? What's it been—a week?"

"It's an oil painting, Father." Edward had to hide his impatience with his father's complete lack of understanding or interest. He hadn't perceived Caroline as a threat to his plans yet, despite Edward's daily absence. Edward needed to press the point harder.

"A painting of the magnitude she plans will likely take weeks to accomplish. Not a few days."

Edward's father jerked around, starling his horse into sidestepping with more gusto than necessary. "Weeks, you say? With Miss Clapham?"

"Yes. At Inglewood Castle." Edward feigned innocence in his tone and expression, pulling his horse to a stop as the other two gentlemen had halted their mounts completely. "I cannot see that it matters how long it will take. I could hardly deny both the countess and the daughter of a gentleman who have asked for my assistance."

"I suppose not," his father said, face scrunched up as though he'd tasted a lemon. "But, Edward—is it the done thing? Do you know, Claude? Women painting men to whom they are not related?"

Why would anyone appeal to Claude to ask if something was appropriate or not?

"I have never been asked to sit for a woman artist," Claude said, sounding rather petulant. "Though if a peer sanctions such a thing..." His words trailed away as he shrugged. "Never mind. It hardly matters to me. Are we here to exercise these animals or gossip about Edward's strange doings?"

"Weeks, Edward?" Mr. Everly repeated, his eyebrows raised. His mind was finally turning over the matter.

"As I said, Father. Thankfully, Miss Clapham is delightful in conversation and charming in manner. I will not mind the time in her company. Not in the least." Edward nodded to the field. "My cousin is right, though. We ought to get on with our purpose."

His father stared at him with open shock, and perhaps a touch of suspicion, but Edward let that be the last word on the matter as he put his heels to his horse and urged the animal to stretch its legs and run, galloping across the empty meadow, the wind rushing around them both.

Speculation about Edward and Caroline would begin in earnest at last. Starting with his own family, but likely spreading quickly through community.

And his name would at last stop being coupled with Mariah Kimball's, which would hopefully be all she needed to finally speak to her parents about whomever it was that already possessed her heart.

No one had paid attention to his comings and goings from Inglewood Castle. The earl's servants were far too loyal and tight-lipped. Edward's sisters had said nothing to his parents, likely thinking they protected him. If his father had needed a clear statement, perhaps everyone else did, too. He couldn't help grinning, as his horse flew over the meadow full of wildflowers, as he thought on the satisfaction of thwarting his parents' plans.

And the attractive idea of more time spent in Caroline's presence.

# CHAPTER 15

S unday arrived, and Caroline sat at the front of the church between the countess and Lady Fox. The ladies had their husbands at their sides, too. But no children, as all were deemed far too young to sit still for a sermon. Even if the man they referred to as "Uncle Jacob" was the one to give it.

Mr. Jacob Barnes was quite good at being a vicar, Caroline decided. Though her mind wandered more than it ought. Her thoughts lingered on the canvas she had started preparing the evening before—the canvas that would become her Atlas.

Every day for over a week, Caroline had sat with a sketchbook in her lap and studied Edward Everly's face and form. She'd sketched him from the shoulders up when he sat still on a chair. She'd drawn him kneeling, and he'd taken his boots off for her to better observe the turn of his leg, calf, and ankle. He'd often taken his coat off on every occasion, too.

And he'd made it easy for her to forget how uncomfortable she should be, as an unmarried gentlewoman, by talking to her of ridiculous things while she worked. He'd shared bits and pieces of his life, both at home in England and abroad during his time on the Italian peninsula. He never made her feel small for not having the same experience of the world that he had. And he didn't mind when she became curious. He answered all her questions to the best of his ability.

They'd talked of the cathedrals with their beautiful stone saints and glass windows. He'd described the Greek Sea to her, and the hills of Rome. Places she had only imagined or read of in books had come alive in his stories. Often, he'd described things to her by their color and texture—something her artist's heart truly appreciated.

Edward's visits had each lasted an hour. They'd worked in the library or a west-facing sitting room that had excellent afternoon sunlight, and Lady Inglewood remained in the room with them reading or pursuing her own artistic projects. The countess rarely spoke to them unless Caroline had a question.

Sometimes, Caroline completely forgot her mentor remained in the room with them.

Her hour with Edward was the best part of her day.

The women on either side of Caroline rose. Caroline leaped to her feet, too, confused by the sudden movement until she realized the sermon had ended and the choir had sung its last note. All while she daydreamed about her time spent with Edward Everly.

Certainly not the most unpleasant way to pass her time in church, though she doubted her mother or grandmother would approve.

Everyone shuffled down the aisle, exchanging greetings as they passed friends and neighbors, up until the moment they left the church entirely for the open air and summer sun. Ladies took out parasols, gentlemen squinted into the sun, and Caroline had an odd moment when she attempted to do both things at the same time and stumbled off the gravel path from road to church, a troublesome rock forcing her heel to slide forward.

A hand caught her arm in a firm grasp, steadying her, and Caroline nearly dropped her parasol in her surprise. A voice, sure and strong, murmured into her ear.

"I have you. Are you all right? Did you turn your ankle?"

Edward.

Caroline's heart raced, quite without her permission, and she pulled out of his grasp with a hasty movement. "Mr. Everly," she said, looking up at him and hugging her prayer book and parasol to her chest. "Goodness. I did not even see you behind me."

She had looked about during services and spotted him once, seated on the opposite side of the church and several rows back. Then she had tried to ignore him, only partially succeeding since she spent the entirety of the sermon thinking on their time together over the past week.

"You would have to have eyes in the back of your bonnet to achieve that feat." Edward grinned at her, not at all put out by her obliviousness. "I followed to ask after your work, Miss Everly. And a good thing I did, given the uneven ground's attempt at assassination."

"Let's not blame the entire ground. I think it was one stone that wished to end my life. Horrid little piece of rubble." She looked down at the offending stone, narrowing her eyes, not at all minding the ridiculous shift of their conversation. Anything to keep her blushes at bay, even while her heart continued its erratic beat. "Thank you for your assistance. I doubt the fiend will try such a thing a second time."

When Edward spoke again, it was a murmur so soft she barely heard what he said. "My mother and father are at the church door, watching me run after you like a fool. Can you manage to appear charmed by our conversation?"

Oh, they were playacting. She hadn't realized... How strangely disappointing.

She fixed a smile to her face meant to appear shy rather than friendly, and she tipped her chin down. "They are aware at last of our ruse?"

"Indeed. Though I thought they would have taken note of my comings and goings before now. I had to cease the subtlety. I told my father I find you quite charming." Her heart fluttered again. The silly thing. "Once they started asking questions, each one sounding more suspicious than the last, I switched tactics again. I have evaded most conversations on the point, which seems to pique their curiosity still more." The amusement in his tone was impossible to miss.

"I suppose that is natural, given that they are your parents, and they care for you." Caroline couldn't imagine her papa and mama ignoring her comings and goings had there been a young man involved. She twirled her parasol over her shoulder and tipped her head to the side, certain anyone looking from the church would see her smile.

"They are concerned about dictating my future. Not my present." Edward tucked his hands behind his back and nodded to the gate. "May I walk you to your carriage?"

Lord and Lady Inglewood had not yet exited the building. As had happened the weeks before, people sought after the earl and countess for conversation. "That would be lovely, yes, though there isn't any need to hurry."

"Then we will take our time." He offered his arm, and Caroline took it.

Edward's escort wouldn't go beyond twenty feet. Yet she wished it would go farther. Longer. Because she enjoyed his company. Ruse or no ruse.

"We are all to picnic at my sister's house this afternoon." Edward bent his head toward her in such a way that others might think their conversation more personal than it was. "They always invite Lord and Lady Inglewood to such things, as my brother-in-law and sister consider them family. If they come, do you think they would ask you as well?"

"I am certain they will invite me."

"Then please come." He smiled at her, his blue eyes sparkling with mischief. "And we will sow more seeds of romance between us."

Caroline raised her eyebrows at him, stamping out the tiny flutters of excitement that trembled within when he said the word *romance*. What was wrong with her?

"If I am invited, I will be present. Though I warn you, I am quite popular with the children, and I will be at their beck and call above all others."

He laughed. "We will manage, then. It often falls to me to entertain them, too."

Her heart returned to its hurried rhythm at the idea of him playing with the children and making them laugh. Men were always more attractive when they were fond of little ones. It was a truth even she understood.

Except, she *shouldn't* be attracted to him. Everything between them was make-believe. An exchange of favors. Nothing real. Had her daydreams run away with her ability to reason? He wasn't interested in courtship or marriage. He'd made that quite clear. And *she* wasn't interested, either. She wanted to pursue art. Not a man.

"Until this afternoon, then?"

She looked up at the carriage with the Inglewood family heraldry emblazoned on its side. The walk was over too quickly. "Until then," she murmured by way of agreement.

Edward took her hand and helped her step up into the carriage, then bowed and left. She watched his form retreat back into the church yard where his parents stood, arm in arm, staring at him.

Caroline's gaze swept across the rest of the open area between church and road, seeing the stares of others upon her. Including Mariah's cheerful smile, accompanied swiftly by a friendly wave. Caroline waved back with as much pleasantness as she could.

At least she was doing both Mariah and Edward a favor. Perhaps even a good deed. And there were only two more months of summer. Surely, two months would pass quickly. She would paint. Pretend. Impress the Royal Academy's president. And then return home to plan the next part of her life.

Two months was nothing. She could do anything for that long. Including pretend adoration of Edward Everly.

So long as her heart would stop its rapid beating beneath his stare, and her daydreams would stop veering into thoughts of her time with him, she would be perfectly fine.

When Lord and Lady Inglewood came at last into the carriage, the countess had a wide smile upon her face. "How would you like to attend an afternoon picnic, Caroline? Only a few of our closest friends and their families will be there, so it is an informal affair. We will bring the children, of course."

Caroline had her answer at the ready. "That sounds like a lovely way to spend an afternoon, your ladyship. I would very much like that."

Lord Inglewood took off his hat and dropped it to the seat beside him. "I certainly prefer the open air to my study on a day like today. It is far too stuffy indoors. No breeze to be had. Summer is the worst of seasons."

His lady laughed and nudged his arm. "You love the summer. Do not pretend otherwise. You would rather be on your boat in the waves than at home, and if you can have neither of those, then your friends are the next best thing."

He grumbled and folded his arms. Lord Inglewood had joined some sort of club which focused on the sailing of sleek, beautiful boats with tall sails. A *yacht*, he called it. The word, he had explained, was Dutch in its origin. The crafts were modeled after the ships that royalty had used for centuries to outpace attackers or journey in luxury from one side of the sea to another.

He seemed quite fond of the boat and enthusiastic to see the "sport" of yachting grow in England.

Caroline hadn't any thoughts on the matter, except that the sails of his boat made a pretty subject for a painting, with white triangles full of wind against a summer-blue sky. With that whimsical image held in her mind, Caroline entered the house and went to change into clothing more appropriate for being out-of-doors with small children likely to sit in her lap or take hold of her skirts to gain attention.

But there were hours yet to pass before they left for the picnic at the vicarage. While it might have been wisest to pick up a book to pass the time, or even take one of her mother's prescribed summer naps, Caroline instead went to the countess's painting room.

There had been improvements to her work, of course. There was more life in her depiction of the woods than she had managed in her depictions of orchards at home. But her canvas with the seascape still appeared rather dull.

What was different between the two? How could a lifeless boat sitting amidst trees have more to it than a sea with gulls floating above the waves?

She didn't understand it. When others looked at her work, did they see what she did? At all? Or did she imagine all the short-comings?

Lady Inglewood had reminded her, several times, that every artist of every medium was their own worst critic.

Caroline paced back and forth in front of two of her canvases, her hands clasped behind her back. She sighed deeply and muttered under her breath, "Why can't I make it work? Why can't I make them feel right?" She paused and turned to face her depictions of sea and wood, frowning at the images before her. "It's merely paint on canvas, no matter how hard I try to make it otherwise."

She picked up her paintbrush and twirled it between her fingers, debating if she had time to add a detail here or there before the others would be ready. Or if it was even a wise idea, given the dress she wore was for visiting, not for painting.

Best not, she supposed.

Then she stalked to the corner where a large canvas with blue-black paint covering its stretched expanse waited for her. Charcoal smudges, made lightly over the dried midnight paint, outlined the figure of a man kneeling on the ground.

The beginnings of her Atlas.

Even this frustrated her.

"Art is supposed to inspire a feeling," she whispered, imagining how she would fill in the shape with Edward's figure. Atlas seemed an apt enough subject, given the weight he bore. Edward knew about carrying the weight of his family's expectations. And Caroline? The weight of her hopes, dreams, and fears. It all weighed upon her. Crushing her spirits until she wondered, at times, if she ought to give it up.

She tugged a stool in front of Atlas's future place of torment, then she let out another deep sigh and sat down heavily in front of her canvas, her head in her hands. "How will this piece be better?"

Edward's grimace as Atlas filled her mind. The angry furrow of his brow, the light of defiance blazing in his eyes, the near-snarl he'd shown with a curl of his lip and jut of his chin... Truthfully, she hadn't thought he'd have it in him to convey a rebellious warrior. That he managed it told her things about Edward that made her heart twist.

He understood pain.

He knew determination.

He had empathy and imagination enough to put himself into the place of another.

Every hour she spent in his company added a new stroke to the picture of him in her mind, a portrait that became more vibrant and filled with depth with each passing day. Just as she reveled in the captivating hues and delicate brushstrokes that brought her art to life, so too did she find herself immersed in the intricate colors and shades of emotions evoked by her affection for him. Each thought of him was akin to an artist's brush, delicately shaping the contours of her heart, adding layers of warmth and richness she hadn't thought possible.

A long-case clock stood in one corner, the pendulum inside swinging softly. It chimed the hour, startling Caroline from her confused musings. Caroline picked up her sketchbook from the table, the one filled with Edward's profile, the way he held his arms, his figure while kneeling. She tucked it beneath her arm and left the room.

She had a picnic to prepare for, but while she physically removed herself from the painting, her thoughts lingered behind. Having her sketchbook with her was little consolation, but it was better than nothing at all.

# CHAPTER 16

W hen they arrived at the vicarage, children already littered the front garden. It took Caroline a moment to identify all of them. The vicar's eldest, Elizabeth, sat on a blanket in the shade of the tree in the front garden. The moment she saw Irene, Elizabeth leapt to her feet and waved ferociously.

Lady Fox was seated on a bench beneath the same tree, her youngest child, a boy, in her arms. Next to her on the bench was Mrs. Barnes, tying a bonnet beneath the chin of her younger daughter, Marjorie.

The older two children belonging to Lady Fox and Sir Isaac were Luther, a boy with red curls, and Faith, a child a little younger than Elizabeth and Lady Irene. Luther's eyes widened when he saw his cousin Isaac, named after Luther's father, was with them, and he came running to the older boy with a look of admiration on his little face.

"You came, Isaac. Mama said you would."

The earl's son puffed out his chest and grinned, the sight proving him every bit as much of a little boy as his friend, despite the fact he was properly referred to as Lord Marham. "Of course, I came. I couldn't let you be surrounded by all these *girls*." He gestured to the children in frocks and bonnets.

"We have Michael," Luther reminded him, pointing at the baby in his mother's arms.

"Yes, but until he's out of dresses, he can't have the fun that we do." Isaac turned to his father, his eyes glowing with youthful enthusiasm. "Papa, may we explore the back garden?"

"If Aunt Millie doesn't mind," Lord Inglewood said, sitting on a bench in the shade, where his wife had already settled.

"Not in the slightest," Lady Fox assured the boys. "Off with you both. And mind that you return without too much dirt on your trousers and elbows."

The boys bounded off like over-eager puppies. Caroline's heart gave a small twist, and she briefly thought of her brothers. They were only four years old, and rarely out of her mother's sight. Yet she could imagine them bounding away to find their entertainment in a garden full of insects and acorn tops.

Another chair waited for Caroline, and she took it after greeting the others.

There was no sign of the Everly family yet. What if they didn't come?

She glanced toward the road.

"Gardens are far more entertaining for children than for adults," Lady Fox said, her eyes dancing with mirth. "If Luther could permanently have an encampment of his friends in our gardens, I think he would never come indoors again."

"Have you ever allowed him to sleep outside?" Caroline asked, memories of her own childhood dancing in her mind. She tried to put aside thoughts of Edward Everly.

"Good heavens, no." Lady Fox laughed, though not unkindly. "I ought to suggest his father take part in that adventure, though."

Lady Inglewood grinned as well. "My brother would think it amusing. But if you allow Luther to sleep outside, then I will have to let my little Isaac do the same. And I cannot imagine Silas finding the prospect all that enjoyable."

Lord Inglewood had crossed his arms and leaned as far back as he could upon the bench, half-lounging upon it. "I am more than capable of sleeping outside of an evening. If it pleases the boys."

"That would certainly make an adventure of it." Lady Fox turned her attention to the ground behind where she sat, and when Caroline did the same, she saw the baronet napping on the grass with his arm behind his head. "What do you think of the idea, Sir Isaac?"

"I did my share of sleeping outdoors in the army," he said. "But I suppose, so long as no one else loses an appendage, I could see my way to enjoying it."

Lord Inglewood laughed quietly. "Must you bring up your missing arm at every opportunity?"

"Of course. It makes me a picture of masculine tragedy and a symbol of the British will to survive and adapt." Sir Isaac grinned back, unoffended, then pushed himself upright with his remaining arm. "But the camping idea. Perhaps we could make a tradition of it. Sleeping out-of-doors with our sons in the summer. It sounds rather glorious."

Caroline's gaze drifted away from the baronet and to the road again. Where was Edward? What if his family had decided not to come?

But it couldn't matter to her. Not really. Edward had presented this as an opportunity, but not a necessity. She could enjoy the afternoon without him. Indeed, she would enjoy it *more* because there would be no play-acting to be done.

"Caroline? Dear? Are you all right?" Lady Inglewood's voice broke through Caroline's internal muttering.

Turning swiftly away from the road, Caroline answered, "Pardon me, your ladyship. My attention slipped away. Did you ask me something?"

Lady Inglewood regarded her with a somewhat skeptical raise of her brow but repeated her question. "I was saying it was likely our daughters would want to mimic anything the little boys do. And I asked if you'd ever slept outside during your childhood."

Forcing a smile, Caroline gave a single nod. "I have, yes. In the barn and in my family's orchard a time or two. It was great fun."

"Sleeping outside when there are perfectly good pillows and beds to be had doesn't sound recreational, and not the least bit cozy." Lady Fox put her young son down to play in the grass and clover. He gleefully pulled up a handful of the soft, leafy plants and then stared at the dirt from one of the roots with puzzlement.

Another glance at the road proved it remained unsatisfactorily empty.

Mr. Barnes emerged from the cottage carrying a small table. "Is this how it is to be?" he demanded to know, putting the table down with a grunt. "The titled men lay about doing nothing, while the vicar waits upon them hand and foot? The two of you, come inside and help me carry out the trays at least."

Amid more good-natured protests and argument, sounding like men half their age, Lord Inglewood and Sir Isaac both followed their friend indoors while the women giggled at their antics.

"Caroline?" It was Lady Fox who spoke this time, drawing Caroline's attention away from studying a wisp of dust in the air above the road that might have indicated an approaching coach.

"Yes, Lady Fox?"

The red-headed noble woman studied Caroline with her brows arched, one corner of her mouth pulling upward before she spoke. "You seem distracted today, my dear. Are you quite well?"

Caroline's cheeks warmed and she forced a laugh that didn't sound nearly as natural as she'd hoped. "I thank you, Lady Fox. I am well. Merely thinking on a difficulty with my painting. I will do my best to set aside those thoughts for now." Caroline turned her attention to Mrs. Barnes to find the vicar's wife already studying her.

A glance at Lady Inglewood proved that lady stared at Caroline with curiosity, too.

Caroline took her fan from the reticule at her wrist and snapped it open. "It is quite warm today, is it not?"

The women surrounding her appeared to hold a silent conversation with their exchange of smiles, raised eyebrows, and then they looked as one toward the road as Mrs. Barnes said, "Where can my family be? My papa prefers punctuality above most virtues. Indeed, it is a wonder none of his daughters received *that* as a Christian name."

The other women giggled, and Caroline fanned herself with more vigor.

"Caroline," a child's voice sang out from the corner of the vicar's cottage. Caroline turned to see Luther Fox had returned. "Will you come help us with the castle?"

"There is a castle in your garden, Mrs. Barnes?" Caroline glanced to her hostess, who smiled and gave a merry shrug.

"There will be if the children have anything to say about it. You may go if you wish, Caroline, or remain here. Where you have an excellent view of the road."

The blush Caroline had attempted to stave off through willpower alone burst through to her cheeks, the heat in them rivaling coals from an oven. She stood hastily. "I think I will go see this castle for myself." She curtsied to the matrons and followed after Luther, her fan clutched in a firm grip.

That the women suspected she watched the road for a sign of Edward was evident. And really, since her eagerness for his arrival would assist in their charade, it ought not to have bothered her that they thought such a thing.

Why did she feel like squirming, then? Like fleeing from them before anyone could ask, directly, if it was Edward Everly she watched for with such focus she couldn't attend to the conversation?

"Because it is humiliating," she muttered to herself, entering the small garden. There were low-cut shrubs bearing yellow flowers, pots of marigolds, a table with chairs, and a low stone wall dividing the pleasure garden from the kitchen garden.

She had never been the girl with stars in her eyes, dreaming about a gentleman riding up to her cottage on a white horse with a bouquet of flowers and an offer of marriage. She made her own adventures, climbing trees and building sandcastles, reading books and sketching flowers.

Wasn't it rather silly, to hold one's breath in anticipation of receiving a glance or a smile from a man?

All she'd wanted was to paint. Though she had given some thought to her future, to a possible marriage and family, she hadn't wanted to depend on anyone else for her happiness. And what if she fell in love with a man who didn't support her art? Or couldn't afford for her to buy paints and brushes? What if he expected her to give all of it up to focus on a household and children?

She didn't object to the idea of children. She adored children. But was that to be her only contribution to the world?

Caroline kicked a small pebble off the path, her frustration twisting her insides. This was precisely why she avoided thoughts of matrimony. There were too many unknowns. At only nineteen, with a modest dowry, she had time. She could work on her painting. She could travel, perhaps, to fulfill commissions or work as an art instructor for families all over England. Perhaps even on the Continent. If only Sir Thomas found her work adequate.

And he would.

The children were toward the back of the cultivated land, beneath birch trees that had likely been planted at the same time as the woods on the Inglewood estate. The children, boys and girls both, were leaning boards against a low branch, creating a lean-to wall of loose lumber and branches. Luther had returned to picking up small stones and lining them up in a semi-circle around the front of their make-believe castle.

Pushing aside all thoughts of Edward, courtship, and marriage, Caroline joined their game, suggesting an addition of dried leaves to the floor of their castle. She also prevented the theft of a bean pole from the kitchen gardens, instead finding a long branch to hold the flag they improvised with Caroline's handkerchief.

Devoting herself to the children's entertainment, Caroline sat on the stone wall, weaving daisies into a crown. One for Irene, another each for Elizabeth and Marjorie, and a fourth for herself.

She was absorbed in the task, looping daisy stems over and through one another, when she noticed a strange silence.

Caroline glanced up, but the children all seemed well. They were covering their mouths, looking in her direction. As though they held back laughter. Had someone told a joke at her expense?

Raising her eyebrows, Caroline asked, "Is there something amiss, knights and ladies?" A few of them shook their heads, but their grins remained. She returned their wide smiles with one of her own. "Sir Luther?"

The red-headed little boy shook with giggles as he bowed. "All is well in our kingdom, Your Majesty."

"Excellent. I am glad to hear it." She took off her bonnet, despite the sun shining above, and lifted her now-complete daisy-crown to put it atop her head. "Queen Caroline declares a royal holiday. Celebrating—"

A hand covered her eyes, and her whole body jolted forward in surprise. This didn't alarm her assailant, whose arm looped around her waist, preventing her from toppling off the low wall and securing her back against a broad, warm chest.

A low chuckle near her left ear stirred wisps of her hair and made a trickle of warmth spread from that spot through her body and deep into her belly. She knew exactly who had hold of her before he even whispered, "Do you know me, Queen Caroline?"

Edward had finally arrived.

Her heart fluttered dangerously in her chest, as though it would burst free entirely and take flight. "You are a knave, for certain, and an enemy to the crown," she said, trying to sound firm and cringing when her words came out breathless.

Why hadn't she sensed him coming, as she always did with her little sister? The man crashed through brush with abandon but had somehow come through a kitchen garden without making a sound. Although, given the way the children were laughing, they had certainly seen his arrival.

Caroline put her hands on her hips, causing her shoulders to brush against him. "Are my knights going to stand for this assault on their queen?"

"We will protect you," little Isaac shouted, and a chorus of the other children's voices followed before she felt tiny hands take hers and pull her away from the wall.

Edward released her and immediately said, "*En guarde*, knights!"

Caroline, safely out of his grasp, let the boys tuck her behind them as she turned to meet Edward's gaze. He had both hands on the wall, leaning forward, grinning at her as though he'd stumbled upon the best game in history. The boys held up sticks meant to serve as swords and lances, brandishing them toward Edward and shouting threats of running him through, arresting him, and locking him in a tower.

Edward ducked behind the wall and came up again with his own stick, far shorter than any the children held, and then vaulted over the wall to answer their challenge.

The girls hurried forward and took Caroline's hands. "Quick, Queen Caroline. You must hide." Though she would much rather take up a stick for herself, Caroline followed the little ladies behind their make-believe castle and into the trees. She and Marjorie stood behind a narrow birch while Irene and Elizabeth hid behind a different tree, covering their mouths to muffle their giggles.

Isaac and Luther whacked at Edward's stick with their own, until one especially hearty strike broke Edward's weapon in half. He gasped dramatically and dropped to his knees on the paving stones.

"Alas, I am unarmed, and I must beg for mercy. Please, sir knights, spare me! I was only following orders."

Holding his stick outstretched toward Edward's exposed throat, Isaac snarled in his comically deepened voice, "What orders would those be, wicked knave?"

"Yes." Luther held his pretend sword up, too. "What orders?"

Even from her place behind the tree, Caroline could see Edward's eyes sparkling with amusement, and it made her heart do its distracting impression of a dragonfly again. Beating hard, fluttering, looking for a way to leave her behind and take to soaring above practical things like the ground and trees.

"I have been ordered by Lady Inglewood to fetch Queen Caroline for tea, and to inform her court that there are fruits and biscuits laid out for a feast."

The boys exchanged a look, then dropped their sticks and shouted, "Biscuits!" They started off at a run around the house.

Irene gasped. "They didn't even try to tell us! Hurry, 'lizabeth. Marjie! Or they'll eat all the sweets." Heedless of their dresses or gowns, and quite forgetting their queen, the three little girls burst from the trees and made haste through the garden. Elizabeth only slowed down for a moment to take hold of her little sister's hand to tug her along after them.

Caroline followed them, at a normal pace, calling out, "Careful not to trip!"

Edward came to his feet and bent over to dust off his knees. "My valet isn't going to be pleased with me." He glanced her way with a crooked smile.

Ignoring the twist of her stomach, Caroline folded her hands demurely before her. "That hardly matters when you made the boys as happy as you did with your dramatic surrender."

"Perhaps." He crossed his arms and swept his gaze from her hem to the crown atop her head. "It seems you have done your own share of entertaining the children. I'm not certain you are aware, but along with your fashionable crown, you have a twig and a leaf or two in your hair."

"Oh. I suppose that is to be expected when one hides in a forest." Her cheeks warmed and she raised her hands, but he stopped her by gently grasping one of her wrists. He wore gloves, yet she still felt the warmth of his fingers through the fabric in the brief moment he held her.

"No, here. Let me. You don't even know where they are." He smiled, his eyes briefly meeting hers. Then he concentrated on his task while he removed debris from her hair with a touch so light she barely felt it. Would not have felt a thing, in fact, had her hair not stirred with each removal.

Caroline swallowed, then said softly, "I thought you might not come today."

He raised his eyebrows, his deep blue eyes curious. "Did that distress you?" When she didn't immediately answer, he went back to his work upon her hair, and a dried leaf fluttered to the ground between them.

"Not really," she answered, tone cool. "The pretend courtship is more important to your plans than mine."

He smiled, drawing her gaze to his lips. Lips she had spent hours studying as they grimaced and frowned, snarled, and then smiled when he forgot he was Atlas. She thought she knew them quite well by now. Yet still, they fascinated her.

"How disappointing. I thought you were about to proclaim your heart broke at the mere thought of doing without me for an afternoon." As his mouth formed those teasing words, one corner went up a little higher than the other. Though it wasn't a smirk. More of a roguish grin. Much like the one her father wore when he wished to provoke her mother into one of their playful arguments.

She rather liked the expression on Edward. It suited him.

"I am only a pretend admirer," she said, meeting his blue-eyed gaze. "So it would be a pretended broken heart."

"I suppose I would have pretended to heal it, then."

They stood so close, yet she hardly heard him above the *not* pretended rapid beating of her heart. He stood so near. Closer than any man had before. That didn't stop her from swaying forward. No more than an inch, perhaps, before she caught herself.

His lips curled briefly upward in a smile, then he stepped away from her.

A sharp sting of regret pierced her chest.

"There. Her Royal Majesty is now free of nature's baubles, with the exception of her crown." He turned from her and went to the garden wall, where her bonnet still rested with its ribbons hanging down the stones. She pulled in a quiet breath, trying to compose herself while his back was yet turned.

He picked up her bonnet, still facing away from her as he said, "I apologize for the delay. We were ready to leave when my cousin decided he wished to join us. Good manners required that we wait while he readied himself for the outing."

Had she wanted him to kiss her?

Caroline swallowed and reasoned with herself quickly. Of course she hadn't wanted that. She was an artist. It was quite natural for her to admire the human form. Natural to study Edward so closely. It was habit by this point, really.

Calm. She had to be calm. What had he told her? Something about Claude making the Everlys late.

"That explains the delay, of course." She tucked her hands behind her, fingers twisting together. "I suppose we better not compound today's tardiness with our own. We ought to join the others."

Edward turned and held her bonnet out to her. "Yes. And I will be forced to introduce you to Claude."

She accepted the hat with one hand, then slipped the other through the crook of his arm. "Lead the way, knave. Your queen follows."

"Queen of the Sprites."

She wrinkled her nose at him but didn't rise to his teasing. If he meant to keep calling her that, the surest way to satisfy him would be to continue her protests. Before the two of them could take so much as a step, a man came through the garden door, without a hat on his bright copper hair, and wearing an expression of boredom. Caroline briefly tightened her hold on Edward's arm as his muscles went tight with tension.

She was about to meet Claude Everly.

189

IT WAS A VERY GOOD THING—DIVINE intervention, surely—that Edward hadn't kissed Caroline. Even though she'd looked as though she would not have minded. Even though his lips had been inches from hers. Because he would have still been kissing her when Claude arrived.

Somehow, Edward was quite sure of that. Because a single kiss with someone as passionate as his artistic sprite would kiss as beautifully as she painted. He had no doubt of that.

And no more time to spend thinking on it, as his cousin approached them.

When Claude had declared a sudden interest in joining them for the picnic, Edward had tried to leave ahead of his family on horseback. But his mother insisted they all wait for Claude to do whatever it was he needed to prepare for the outing.

Meaning, Edward hadn't had the chance to ride ahead to warn his sister of the addition to their party, and he certainly hadn't had the time to prepare Caroline for this first meeting. He'd told her about his relationship with Claude, of course, but hadn't anticipated an informal gathering would be the first time they had a conversation.

If anyone discovered their ruse, it would likely be his cousin, given the man's predilection for causing Edward trouble.

"Edward, Cousin Grace sent me to fetch you. Your sister fears you have forgotten your errand to fetch Miss Clapham. I assume this lovely creature is the artist I have heard so much about? Do introduce us."

It took some strength of will to maintain a polite tone of voice, but Edward somehow managed it. "Miss Clapham, this is my cousin Claude Everly. Claude, Miss Clapham is a guest of Lord and Lady Inglewood." That reminder might keep Claude in check.

"A pleasure, Miss Clapham." Claude bowed.

Caroline darted a glance at Edward as she curtsied in return. "It is good to meet you at last, Mr. Everly."

He bestowed a charming smile upon her, a keen interest in his expression. "As I said, I have heard much about you. I must confess that I envy Edward's good fortune in having such a charming friend. Although it surprised me to learn you have asked him to act as the model of a mythical Titan. You must be talented, indeed, to have the confidence to render him as anything other than what he appears."

Before Edward managed a retort, Caroline laid her other hand on his arm. Steadying him.

"I am the fortunate one. Most men are reluctant to volunteer for such projects. Your cousin is quite generous with his time."

"Truly?" Claude's eyes glittered as he turned them on Edward. "Is that all he is generous with, I wonder?"

Edward's hand balled into a fist, but Caroline spoke with a deliberately cheerful tone. "Mr. Edward's kindness and support have been invaluable to me. He has a marvelous respect for the arts." She nodded to the house. "We should return to the others before they send out yet another search party, should we not?"

Edward nodded at once, adjusted her hand upon his arm to give it a thankful press. "Absolutely. I must prove myself successful in my retrieval of you, Miss Clapham."

Caroline kept hold of Edward's arm, giving no opportunity for Claude to offer his own. Edward deliberately took the path that led around the house rather than through it. Claude followed behind them without a word, though Edward felt his cousin's eyes upon the back of his neck.

They arrived at the table after everyone else had seemingly filled plates with delicacies and foods provided by the vicar and his wife. The chairs that had been scattered about when Edward arrived were now arranged in more of a semi-circle beneath the shade of the large tree. The married couples, which included Edward's parents, and his unmarried sister already conversed and nibbled on the victuals.

Three chairs remained unoccupied, next to one another, on one end of the gathering. Edward swallowed his disappointment and sent a glance to Charity, who met his gaze and merely smiled at his meaning-filled frown.

She knew precisely how little he wanted to sit near Claude.

"Let me fill your plate for you, Miss Clapham," Claude said, suddenly at Edward's side with a plate in hand. "You have but to tell me what it is you desire."

Edward wanted to take the plate from his cousin and break it over his head. No matter how innocently meant, he never wanted to hear Claude use the word "desire" in any context regarding Caroline again.

"How kind of you to offer." Caroline released Edward's arm only to take one of the two remaining empty plates from the table. "But I cannot bear to be waited upon, Mr. Everly. Not during so informal an occasion. Please, see to your own repast." She made quick work of selecting items, and Edward followed along, while Claude put as little as possible on his own plate before trailing behind them.

Edward had every intention of sitting between his cousin and his sprite, but Caroline didn't hesitate to take the middle of the remaining chairs for herself. She settled upon it with a smile and gestured with her free hand to the tree above them. "What a glorious day for a picnic. Eating beneath the tree like this reminds me so much of home."

With some reluctance, Edward took the chair on the outside of the gathering. With luck, his brother-in-law, on Claude's other side, would keep his cousin occupied in conversation.

Grace, not many feet away, happily took up the topic Caroline had presented. "I cannot hope my single oak provides as lovely an experience as picnicking in an orchard of cherry trees. Do you find yourself homesick, Caroline?"

"At times," Caroline admitted, laying her gloves in her lap before plucking a tart from the plate. "But I am treated so well, any melancholy I feel when I think of my family and home does not last long."

Claude entered the conversation without pause. "Ah, the countess is known for her impeccable hospitality. I have never been fond of the country myself, but I have come to find the more charming aspects of this area, despite my infrequent visits.

Perhaps you would allow me to show you some of its hidden charms?"

Edward nearly choked on the sandwich he'd selected, and an embarrassingly long break in the conversation occurred as he tried to recover breath. Finally, he managed to get out, "I cannot think why anyone would wish for you as a guide." Edward didn't swallow back his words this time, and the way Claude smirked in response made Edward's hackles rise still more. "You have visited twice in the last three years."

"Perhaps my cousin is right, Miss Clapham. I may not be the best option of escort, but at least I could plan something suitable to your tastes, if you would permit. I would tailor an afternoon outing to your requirements, after careful thought and deliberation." He stretched his legs before him and crossed his ankles. "Though Edward isn't a much better option, given his propensity to dash into ventures without establishing any sort of plan for them."

"I may be impulsive, but I always find a way to make things work out in the end. And a tour of the countryside is hardly an expedition to China." Glowering at his cousin was hardly mature, but Edward didn't much care.

He also noted a distinct lack of chatter among the others present, though no one looked their way except for Grace. Her eyebrows had raised nearly to the point of disappearing beneath her bonnet's brim.

Poor Grace. She didn't enjoy conflict. And this was her picnic.

"Goodness." Caroline released a soft laugh, one that didn't seem in keeping with what Edward had learned of her in their time together. Yet her smile seemed genuine enough as she turned first to Claude and then Edward. "Thank you both for offering your assistance. I appreciate your concern for my enjoyment of the area. However, my time is best spent at work on my paintings. I wouldn't want to take unnecessary time away from that. But I do appreciate your kind offers."

"Oh, but Caroline, dear," said Lady Inglewood, on the opposite end of the bow-shaped line of chairs. "I have kept you far too much indoors of late. I think a drive around the country is a wonderful idea. Perhaps you ought to reconsider?"

Edward's jaw fell open. What in the name of all that was good was the countess *doing*? He stared at her heedless of hiding his shock at her proposal. Surely, she knew all about Claude. She must, given her friendship with Grace. Why would she place anyone under her care within Claude's grasp?

Lady Inglewood's smile turned in his direction, and that was when Edward saw her lift her eyebrows in a way that seemed to say, *Now what will you do, Mr. Everly?*

At his side, Caroline stared at her hostess with as much surprise as Edward felt, but as she began to speak, Edward's mind caught on a possibility. "Oh, but your ladyship, there is so much yet to do. I cannot take the time—"

"I would be honored to drive with you," he said in a rush, before Claude volunteered himself again. "And you could bring your sketchbook, if you wished, on the chance you are inspired while out."

Now it was Edward's mother who stared at the lot of them with wide eyes and a biscuit frozen midway to her mouth. She lowered it and looked at her husband, who had folded his hands across his rounded stomach and closed his eyes. Edward knew that position. His father had dozed off, lulled by conversation and the warm weather.

"That would be good for you, Caroline," Lady Inglewood said, somewhat dismissively, before she turned to Edward's mother with a wide smile. "Your son is a delightful conversationalist, Mrs. Everly. I have enjoyed having him in my home while he assists my protege with her art, and I have found his company quite enjoyable."

Caroline lowered her gaze to her lap, not yet accepting his invitation nor responding to her hostess with more than a shallow nod.

Had his attempt to save her from Claude making another offer displeased her? Edward shifted in his chair and nearly toppled his plate off his knees, losing a gooseberry off its edge before righting it.

"Thank you, Lady Inglewood," Mrs. Everly replied, her expression a little uncertain. "Though I confess, I did not learn about his offer of service until recently. He has always acted as seems best to him in the moment, I am afraid, and saves all explanation and reasoning for later. But I am glad he is able to be of use to you and Miss Clapham."

Claude chuckled, and a grin played at the corners of his mouth as he spoke. "Edward has always been impulsive, hasn't he? Sometimes it's difficult to keep up with him as he charges headlong into some trouble or another."

Why did the man derive such satisfaction from his subtle insults? Edward drew in a breath, ready to point out that Claude had the better instinct for finding trouble, when Caroline turned a little toward him, also speaking loudly enough for the company to hear.

"It is admirable that he follows his instincts, is it not? It takes courage to act on an impulse, to cast aside fear of whether society will deem your action appropriate, or if a risk will be rewarded. Perhaps in certain situations, it is wiser to act with swift decision instead of lingering in endless contemplation of the potential consequence."

Given her recent teasing about his headstrong behavior, Edward couldn't tell if she meant what she said or had only spoken in his defense. Whichever the cause, humor sparked to life amid the thorny frustration his cousin caused with his mere presence.

"Hear, hear," Jacob muttered, joining the conversation he'd hardly blinked at a moment before. Edward narrowed his eyes at his brother-in-law, who smiled back at him with a far too innocent expression. "Why do you look at me with such suspicion? I agree with every word Miss Clapham said."

"You are one of the many who have lectured me on the danger of rash behavior," Edward said, glancing at Caroline. "I am certain at least one of his sermons on 'careful contemplation' was directed at me in the past."

"I never sermonize to a single person. That is the swiftest way for a vicar to annoy congregants." Jacob turned his grin toward

Caroline. "And while it's true that Edward made trouble for himself in the past, I cannot think of any recent events that would warrant caution on his part that he has not taken."

"Really?" Caroline raised her eyebrows and leaned forward enough to look past Claude, giving Edward's brother-in-law her full attention. "Have you any examples of the more troublesome times?"

Edward didn't like where this conversation was going, but one glance at Claude's smug grin kept him from protesting. Best to pretend he didn't mind the stories rather than let Claude think he'd exposed a weakness. Even if Edward knew precisely which story Jacob would tell.

"When Edward was about thirteen years of age, several of the local boys developed something of a mania for climbing atop tall trees. It was a game, to see who dared venture the highest." He raised his eyebrows at Edward. "This lad thought that growing up climbing apple trees made him the expert. Never mind that apple trees are rarely more than fifteen feet in height. He joined the challenge when it was ash trees that were the favorite. Then someone dared him to climb the oldest oak in Alderton, standing behind the inn. That tree was measured by survey last year. It is sixty-seven feet tall. More than double the height of the ash trees. But that didn't stop Edward."

"Oh dear." Caroline bit her lip as she turned to look over her shoulder at Edward. "Did you make it to the top?"

"Not quite." Edward well remembered that day. "The limbs were large and the bark rough. It was difficult to get any purchase on the lower branches. So I snuck inside the inn, climbed out one of the windows onto the roof, then jumped into the nearest branch of the tree."

"I still say a prayer of gratitude that you didn't fall and break your neck that day," his mother said suddenly from the other side of the half-circle. "Honestly, Edward. It is a wonder you reached your majority."

"What happened?" Caroline asked.

Jacob continued the narrative. "He made it up high enough to get stuck."

"And nearly everyone ran off, afraid they would be held to blame if anything happened to me." Edward winced at the remembrance. He'd looked down through the branches to the ground and hadn't seen a single friendly face looking up at him. He'd never been more afraid in his life as he clung to a thin limb as tight as his thin arms had allowed. "Lucas Jones hadn't run away like the rest. He went to the innkeeper and then to the blacksmith, raising an alarm, and soon enough half of Alderton's residents were beneath the tree shouting up at me." He shook his head with the remembered misery. "I couldn't understand a word of it. My mind was wild with fear."

"First they found the tallest ladder they could and stood it against the tree," Jacob said. "Then they had Alfie Smith, the blacksmith's son, a strapping lad of eighteen, heft a rope over his shoulder and climb as high as he could."

"Then they passed Alfie a pole," his mother said. "By that time, someone had fetched his father." She glanced at her husband, who was lightly snoring, completely undisturbed by the recounted tale of Edward's reckless behavior. "Alfie tied one end of the rope to the pole and threw it like a javelin."

"It hit my shoulder." Edward shook his head. "On the first try. That made me focus, and I caught it on the second. I dropped the pole over my branch, and it slid back down to the ground, where the Blacksmith held it. Alfie kept hold of the other end. Then I climbed down the rope."

"As I said. You must have some sort of guardian angel, Edward." His mother placed a hand over her heart, as though the story still affected her. "We give the Smith family an enormous goose every Christmas to this day."

"And that isn't even the worst thing he's done," Jacob said with a broad grin.

Edward glowered at his brother-in-law. "I thought vicars were forgiving sorts who didn't dwell on the past mistakes of others."

The unrepentant vicar laughed at him. "It's the sins we don't dwell on, Edward. Childhood folly is fair game for a brother, even if the brother is a vicar." But he didn't torture Edward by sharing another tale. Instead, he turned with intent toward Claude. "You must tell me more about yourself, Mr. Claude Everly. We are kin through marriage, yet I cannot think we have spoken more than a few words to one another, and most of those when you were yet a child come for summer visits. I seem to recall some incident with a seagull when you were a lad."

Caroline leaned forward. "Another childhood mishap? Will this be an entertaining story with a rescue, too?"

Edward glanced toward Grace again to find her watching him with a raised eyebrow and tilted head. He smiled, putting as much apologetic feeling into the look as he could. She shook her head and turned her attention to her husband, who recounted a time when Claude had been under attack from seagulls for "no reason whatsoever."

Edward knew the reason. Claude had climbed up a low cliff where several seagulls had made nests, and he had tried to steal their eggs. He'd managed to get hold of one before the parent birds had swooped in, beating at him with their wings, knocking him about with the claws on the ends of their padded feet, screeching terribly.

Every time Claude had stepped on the beach the rest of that summer, the birds shrieked and swooped at him. Edward had found the experience highly amusing. He'd taken care to bring strips of dried fish and bits of pastry to feed the birds after Claude returned home.

Reliving that memory put him in a better humor, until the moment he saw his mother prodding his father awake and whispering in his ear. His father's disinterested expression swiftly turned serious, and his gaze swung up abruptly to meet Edward's.

He didn't appear pleased.

Rising with his plate, Edward gathered Caroline's as well. "Allow me, Miss Clapham." He returned the empty dishes to the table, where the children had come to stack their tin plates after enjoying their food. They were scattered about together in the grass yards away from the adults, giggling as they played some sort of guessing game.

One tin plate remained in the grass with them, and Edward hurried to fetch it. As he bent to pick it up, he spoke in an undertone. "Does anyone wish to walk to the beach with me? We can feed the gulls our scraps." Their response came in a chorus of excitement, their young voices blending together in their eagerness.

"Yes, can we?"

"Please, Uncle Eddie?"

"Yes!"

"Will Mama let us?"

"If you are looked after," he said, rising from his crouch. "I am happy to escort you. Perhaps we could ask Charity and Patience to come? And your Queen Caroline?"

Lady Irene was up in a trice, running to Caroline with her hands outstretched and shouting her invitation, "Will you take us to the beach, Caroline? Please?"

Little Isaac brushed off his trousers as he stood and narrowed his eyes up at Edward. "You want to take us to the beach?"

"Of course."

The child appeared more skeptical. "And you want Caroline to come?"

Perceptive child. "Don't *you* want her to come, too?"

Isaac shrugged one shoulder upward in a near-perfect imitation of his uncle and namesake, Sir Isaac. "I suppose. But no more kidnapping her if she's going to stay our queen." The boy squared his shoulders and lifted his chin upward. "You must promise not to steal her away. On your honor."

A weight the situation did not merit settled on Edward's heart. The boy's innocent demand, all part of a game, made him hesitate. He looked up, where Lady Irene and his little nieces had pulled Caroline to her feet, tugging at her hands and skirts as they spoke with excitement. Caroline smiled in his direction, laughter parting her lips and making her eyes dance.

Edward promised, "I will not kidnap your queen, nor make any attempt to steal her away. On my honor." The words didn't remove the pressure resting above his heart. Indeed, the feeling changed, sinking deeper within.

Caroline still wore her crown of daisies, and she left her bonnet behind on her chair as she came to meet them, her attention now riveted by the children skipping at her side.

"I suppose that's all right, then." The boy didn't sound as though he believed Edward.

Which was fine, really. Because in that moment, the possibility of stealing Caroline's heart had entered Edward's thoughts. A flutter of excitement stirred in his chest, and Edward's natural impulses, so trusted by him in all matters, didn't demand immediate action.

Instead, his heart and mind seemed to whisper one word in accord. *Wait.*

Despite listening to that instinctive demand, Edward's mind raced forward. What of his desire to travel? Her devotion to her art? He had nearly kissed her, and he had the feeling she would have returned that kiss. Even though no one had been there to witness their game of pretend. She had to have feelings for him.

What were his feelings for her? He couldn't be falling in love, surely. He had hated the idea of marriage. Of a chain around him, keeping him forever moored at the Refuge and the apple orchards.

But perhaps not all chains were the same?

*Wait.*

He could do that. He would do that. But while he waited, he'd go right on wooing Caroline. And for a little while longer pretend he wasn't falling in love with her.

# CHAPTER 17

When Caroline greeted Edward, nearly bouncing on her toes in her excitement, his less-than-cheerful smile gave her pause. Usually, he greeted her with enthusiasm. Today, it was with preoccupation.

"Am I late for our appointment?" he asked as he handed his hat and gloves to the footman by the large front doors. Caroline had intercepted him in the entryway of the castle rather than wait for a servant to bring Edward to her.

"No, of course not." Caroline approached Edward as the footman withdrew, somewhat hesitant. "Are you well, Edward?"

"Me? Of course." He tucked his hands behind his back, not quite meeting her gaze. "Where are we working today?"

"If you aren't in the frame of mind for this—"

Edward's hand slipped around hers, his bare fingers brushing across her knuckles before gently clasping her fingers. "Caroline." He said her name gently. "I am well. There is nowhere else I would rather be and nothing else I would rather be doing. My morning began with Claude needling me about the picnic again. The unpleasant effects of that conversation have lingered, is all. Now that I am here with you, things will be better." He punctuated his statement with an added squeeze of her hand, the pressure soft but reaffirming his words.

Caroline sensed the tension lingering in him, standing this close. When he took her hand, a jolt of warmth ran through her, and she couldn't quite explain the confusing mix of comfort and excitement that his touch brought her. She pushed the thoughts away and focused on the present. "Perhaps this will cheer you. Rather than spend the whole of your time sitting still, or moving about like a doll at my command, we are going on an exploratory campaign."

His eyebrows raised, but the dimness yet remained in his eyes. "Are we now? And what is it we are meant to be exploring?"

"Lady Inglewood suggested we start our day with a search of the castle attics. I'm hoping we'll find something suitable for your costume as Atlas." She paused, her gaze meeting his. Did he realize he still held her hand? There wasn't even anyone about to notice. The footman had left completely. "If the idea doesn't appeal to you, we could forgo the campaign entirely. I'm certain I can find what is needed another time."

The hint of a smile played at his lips, and finally a gleam of good humor returned to his eyes. "A treasure hunt in the castle attics with you? It sounds like an adventure I wouldn't miss for the world. Let's go and discover what hidden gems and ancient relics we can find up there."

Why did her cheeks grow warm beneath his smile? She had to get hold of herself. And begin by taking back possession of her hand. "I will be happy if we can find a toga or sandals." She stepped back, sliding her hand from his in the same motion, and turned to the stairs. "Come along, Edward. Our expedition begins with a climb."

"There are an alarming number of staircases in this castle."

"I am well aware." Caroline led the way up the first, relieved he sounded normal enough now. "I travel up and down several of them daily. Sometimes two and three times a day."

"The Refuge is but three floors. I find myself grateful for the more modest construction."

Caroline smiled to herself. "My home is a cottage. One flight of stairs. Two floors. No attics."

He spoke with feigned horror. "No attics? Wherever does your family store all their unwanted furnishings? All of the useless things their ancestors passed down to them?"

She laughed and took him down the corridor to another set of smaller stairs. "Is that what attics are for?"

"That is their exclusive use. Attics are where you put objects you feel obligated to keep even though you have no possible use or any affection for them."

Caroline glanced over her shoulder at him. "I suppose that is why orphans in novels are always made to live in them?"

"Precisely why." He grinned up at her, and relief made it easy for her to grin back. There, Edward was quite himself again. Which meant he wasn't likely to try to hold her hand. Except the moment she faced forward, he asked, "Have we no chaperone today?"

She missed the next step and tottered precariously, but Edward's hand was on her arm, catching her before she could humiliate herself with a fall.

"Careful," he warned, helping her stand upright again. "These stairs are more treacherous than I thought." He was only one step below, so turning toward him made her but an inch or two taller than him. She swallowed.

"Thank you."

His eyebrows raised. "You are most welcome."

Why did her laugh come out with a tremble? "Onward, then."

They had nearly climbed the last narrow flight of stairs when Caroline finally remembered to answer his question. "Lady Inglewood said she would try to join us soon, but she is visiting the nursery. Often, she forgets herself when she is with her children and hours pass before I see her again. Perhaps she trusts us both to behave ourselves while she is occupied."

"Very likely her reasoning." Edward's voice fell lower as he spoke, perhaps musing aloud to himself. "Our families have known each other for years."

Of course they had. And of course the countess trusted Edward and Caroline both. Why wouldn't she?

Inglewood Castle didn't match one's idea of a traditional castle, but Caroline had heard tales of far stranger homes in England. Inglewood looked rather like two smallish castles put together. One in gray and built with turrets meant to resemble the Tower of London, the other in brown brick but otherwise a mimic of the first, and the two were connected by something that resembled a grand house. The first castle had a Tudor-like quality to it, though it had been built over a hundred years after that dynasty came to an end.

"I have never been in this part of the old keep," Edward murmured from behind, pausing to look through a thin window meant to mimic an arrow slit. "Can you imagine purposefully putting these things here? I doubt this castle was ever under siege. These were a decorative decision."

Caroline kept climbing upward, having to hold her skirts up a little higher to avoid stepping upon them. "Can you imagine archers firing their arrows down on enemies from that angle?"

Caroline had toured the castle as a child and again after she arrived this summer. She knew all about the strange Inglewood earls and the even more eccentric barons who had added to their family estate whenever they fancied. The whole of it was a sprawling work of many generations, with towers from antiquity at one end and a modern glass-encased *studio* at the other.

"Caroline?"

She turned on the step to look down at him, noting Edward had stopped several steps below her, one foot on the next step. "Yes? Is something the matter?"

"I think it is time to tell people we are courting."

Her stomach dipped and she pressed her hand to the spot. "Do you?"

His eyes were dark in the shadowed stairwell, the light above them too far, the light behind casting most of his expression in shadow. She sensed more than saw the hesitancy in his expression. "We've known each other nearly a month. We've spent more than a fortnight meeting for your work." He ticked each circumstance off with an upheld finger. "And we have been flirting quite obviously after church and any time we meet in public."

"You are right, of course. It is time." She smiled at him and turned forward again. Her heart behaved strangely, and she found her chest had tightened. Likely due to climbing of so many staircases.

They said no more while on the steps.

Her fingers grazed the stone wall as they made their final ascent into one of the oldest parts of the house. It hadn't started as an attic, but as the third floor of the first castle. The ceiling arched above them, held in place by ancient timbers and expertly hewn stone.

The windows were large rectangles without glass. A servant had come ahead of them, sent by Lady Inglewood, to throw open wooden shutters and draw back thick, ancient curtains. The dust still danced in the air, lit by the late-morning sun.

Caroline's breath caught as she surveyed a long, narrow room filled on all sides with boxes, furnishings, wardrobes, and empty frames.

Edward stood behind her, near enough she felt his breath against the back of her neck as he said, "This could take a while. Unless we have a treasure map."

"The wardrobes," she said and wished for a cup of tea. Her throat had gone dry, somehow. She didn't shiver. Nor did she leap away from him. Caroline remained completely calm, outwardly. Inwardly, things were another matter altogether. Perhaps she ought to have waited for Lady Inglewood. "We might find old costumes there, Lord Inglewood said."

Edward stepped around her, and only then did Caroline realize she'd turned into a statue of sorts. He went deeper into the room, the boards creaking softly beneath his feet. "You hoped for a toga? White sheets or drapes would capture that effect, would they not?"

"And a belt," she added, finally stepping after him. "A dark cloak, too. Maybe some sandals. And sheets wouldn't work. The cloth will need to drape a certain way to look right. I can only do so much with my imagination without seeing true folds and sensing the weight of the robes."

He opened the first old wardrobe, a tall thing with a faded pattern painted along its doors. It smelled of lavender and dust. He reached inside and took out a bright green coat with gold embroidery on its cuffs and along the hem. "What in the name of all that is holy is this monstrosity?" he asked, holding it at arm's length.

Caroline gasped. "Oh my goodness. The earl's great-great grandfather wore that coat in one of his paintings. It's in the family gallery."

Edward shuddered and put it back inside, but his hand emerged again holding twin slippers he had taken from a shelf. They were a match to the coat, with thick heels of at least three inches height. He raised his eyebrows. "Was that earl's great-great grandfather especially short?"

She snatched the shoes from him. "No, you silly man. All the gentlemen wore heels in those days. The French started it." She placed them back on their shelf and then rifled through the rest of the fabric. "But we aren't dressing you like a man from eighty years ago."

"Thank goodness for that. Those shoes are a danger. I'd turn an ankle," he quipped, and she darted him another annoyed look only to find him grinning at her. He stretched to take a box from the top of the wardrobe and brought it down, pulling the lid off and then slamming it closed again. "I found his wig."

Unable to help it, Caroline burst into a fit of giggles. "No. Surely not."

"I did." He turned from her and opened the box, bent double, and then raised up again. He turned around, a massive white cloud of hair upon his head. The wig was impressive, or would have been were it not coming loose in several places.

"Oh, that's terrible." Caroline snickered and stepped back. "And it looks as though it's as heavy as a sack of flour."

"It's quite comfortable, actually." He grinned, and without warning started pulling his coat off. He had to raise his hand twice to steady the wig before he cast his coat aside, atop a chair missing one arm, and then went into the wardrobe to pull out the coat again. He put it on with ease, as it was quite voluminous. "There. What do you think? Forget painting Atlas. Turn me into a dapper gentleman from seventeen-hundred-and-fifty."

Caroline laughed aloud and then tried to smother the sound behind her hand. "Edward, you look ridiculous. Take all of that off!"

"You don't want me to try the shoes?" He feigned disappointment.

"No. Please leave the shoes where they are."

"But what of the pantaloons?" He reached inside and pulled out a pair of the most ridiculous looking trousers she had ever seen. There were *tassels* at the hem. "I shall look like a gold-gilded lime."

"A lime?" The image that conjured up in her mind nearly made Caroline fall over. But the color was right for it, and Edward laughed, too, before striking a heroic pose.

"There now. See. If I stare off into the distance, I am the very picture of a hero, am I not? Admiral Nelson, Herakles, that George Washington person the Americans are always going on about—"

"Edward, stop." Her lungs were beginning to ache with her effort to stifle the laughter that kept coming, especially when he held a hand over his eyes and pretended to be staring off into the distance. Heroically. "You are too horrid. We have work to do." She came forward and held her hands out to remove the wig herself, still giggling.

Edward bobbed his head away. "You will spoil all my fun, Cara. I must try the shoes!"

The use of a name she hadn't heard since leaving her family startled her. "What did you say?"

He grinned. "I will wear the shoes."

He hadn't realized what he called her. She glowered at him. Fine. She wouldn't bring his attention to it. But those shoes...

"Absolutely not."

"I shall."

"No."

"You cannot stop me."

She snatched the shoes from the wardrobe and danced out of his reach as he lunged for them, his wig nearly toppling off. He caught it at the last moment, then followed after her, casting the pantaloons aside.

Caroline wove her way through boxes and cloth-draped furniture, deeper into the attic and toward another wardrobe. "You may not have the shoes."

"You are very cruel." He grinned and sidestepped a stuffed dear's head that had alarmingly large glass eyes. "I thought we were friends."

"I am doing you and everyone who could possibly see you a favor." She pointed to the wardrobe, holding the shoes in one hand over her head. "Check in there for what we came for."

"Are you blackmailing me with footwear?" He held the wig, which looked more unkempt than before, in place with one hand and opened the wardrobe with the other. He shuffled things around inside, but blocked Caroline's view.

"Have you found anything useful?" she asked from behind a table, a bust of a scowling man, and a somewhat hideous statuette of a lion. At least, she thought it was a lion, but whoever had created the piece hadn't seen the same drawings of lions that she had.

"Perhaps." He glanced over his shoulder at her, then in a flourish he turned and twirled around a red cloak around his shoulders, the size of the cape made it terribly impractical for use. The thing had at least two feet of its length puddled on the floor behind him. "A Titan's cape?"

Oh. That might work. "That will do marvelously."

"Now may I have my shoes?"

Caroline wrinkled her nose at him. "Never."

Edward pounced. Despite the cape, wig, and distance between them. Caroline squeaked and tried to move out of reach as he cleared the edge of the table, his cape knocking everything off its top. But she didn't anticipate the speed of his attack.

Edward's arm came around her waist, and he tried to pull her back. He didn't know, however, that Lord Neil Duncan had trained his stepdaughter on how to evade someone of greater size and strength. He'd taught her for far more serious reasons, but his lessons came in use in that moment, too.

Caroline threw herself backward into Edward, startling him and knocking the wind from him, before dropping down out of his hold. He stumbled backward, catching hold of the table, and Caroline made to slip around him.

His dratted cape caught her slipper, though, and slowed her escape. Which gave Edward enough time to regain his balance and catch her wrist in his hand. The hand not holding the shoes, so she stretched the other as far away from herself as she could, keeping the dreaded footwear out of reach.

Edward pulled her closer, arm around her waist, pinning her to him, while his free hand stretched down her arm to grasp the heel of one of the ridiculous old shoes while the gold studded fabric glinted at them.

The look of determination he wore, coupled with the laughter dancing in his eyes, fully captured Caroline's attention. How could they not, with her pressed so near to him? His handsome face with its strong jaw, smiling lips, and high brow? She'd studied him for weeks, from every angle. And every angle was quite perfect. At least in her eyes.

He looked down at her, and his teasing grin faded slowly as he realized she wasn't engaging in the game anymore. Their laughter had faded away, and Caroline's heart was now the organ in most jeopardy. It thudded against her ribs, banging about like a hammer on an anvil, as loud as a military band's drums.

His arm stayed around her, and the hand reaching for the

ridiculous shoe touched her cheek instead. His fingers grazed the burning flesh, then traced over to just below her ear, then gently down to cup her chin.

"Sometimes," he whispered softly, "merely being near you feels like part of an adventure."

Caroline leaned into him without realizing it, and then she couldn't be certain if he bent or she raised on her toes first. But they both moved. And together, they met. His lips grazed hers, and she closed her eyes the instant before she kissed him back.

Warmth spread through her, as she lost herself in the moment. His kiss was soft and tender, yet full of promise, sending shivers down her spine. He held her close, cradling her chin as though she was made of glass, yet his arm was firm and protective.

It was everything she could hope for in a first kiss. Yet nothing she could have explained, written, or painted about with any accuracy.

They parted slowly, their eyes meeting once more as they both took a deep breath. Edward's gaze softened, and sudden panic wrapped around Caroline's heart. This wasn't supposed to happen. They were pretending. They had made a deal. The long summer stretched before her, with all her hopes pinned to a single painting and the man who would decide if she was good enough, if there was any hope for her dreams.

She had to put a stop to whatever it was that was happening. And when Edward's lips parted, as though to speak, she dropped the shoes to the floor with a clatter and stepped away from him.

"That didn't happen."

He blinked at her. "Caroline?"

"It never should have happened. I am terribly sorry, Edward. I haven't any idea what came over me. It seems I took the game too far." She spun away from him and picked her way through the relics of Inglewood's past. "Please don't mention it again. For my sake. It was terribly inappropriate."

"But Caroline, I—"

With several feet between them, she turned and glared at him.

"No, Edward." She spoke with a firmness she had never used before. Not on anyone. Vaguely, she realized this was what her mother had sounded like a time or two when Caroline had stepped too far out of bounds. "Nothing happened. We were playing a childish game and things went awry. It will not ruin our friendship, or our plans, or our arrangement. Promise me."

He slowly took the wig off his head and looked down at it, studying the white curls as though they would explain things to him. "I am making a lot of promises of late. They almost never work in my favor, I think."

She swallowed, though the tightness in her throat made it difficult. "Nevertheless," she whispered. "Nothing happened. Nothing has changed. Promise?" The word came out as a plea this time.

He released a humorless chuckle, then removed his cape with a sigh. "Very well, Cara. I promise."

He turned away without seeing her reaction to the shortened form of her name, the one she had only ever allowed her family to use for her. The familiarity of those two simple syllables, said in such a bleak tone, almost made her wish to take the promise back.

But she couldn't. Not now. Everything she dreamed of and had worked for would be ruined. Wouldn't it? He didn't want to marry. Marriage was a trap. Edward had said as much. And she didn't want the distraction of whatever else this thing between them could be. A harmless flirtation? No. It wouldn't be harmless. She couldn't kiss someone like that and not risk herself. Her heart. Her future.

Even if he did want to marry, *she* wasn't ready. She wanted to see the world. She wanted to paint, to create art and share the joy of that creation with others. Either through teaching or hanging her work in their homes and galleries. She started twisting her fingers together, chewing on her bottom lip. Her mind and heart raced, dipping and rising.

She couldn't do this. She had to bend her will, all her thoughts and feelings, toward her work. That was the only reason she had come to Inglewood.

Edward went to a large trunk and lifted the latch, rifling

through it before closing the wig inside. "Do you really think we will find Greek-inspired sandals up here?" He sounded almost normal again.

"I haven't given up hope yet," she answered, turning away.

She pretended she didn't hear him whisper, "Neither have I."

# CHAPTER 18

Days after the event in the attic, Caroline woke with her lips tingling from the memory of that kiss and the dream that had brought it back to her in exquisite detail. Trying to forget a thing as searing as Edward's kiss was more difficult than anything Caroline had ever done before. And the harder she tried, the more the memory of his lips pressed to hers filled her thoughts.

What had come over him?

With a groan, Caroline rolled over and pulled a pillow over her head in a failed attempt to smother her blush.

Throwing all the blame on Edward wasn't right. Every time she tried, her heart sped, and her traitorous mind teased her with the memory of rising up on her toes to kiss him. Perhaps she'd even been the one to start it?

She'd been playful, of course. He'd been ridiculous. No more so than two children playing at tag or make-believe Robin Hood games.

Everything had changed between them, too. Though she'd pretended it hadn't. They hadn't worked on the painting again, after finding the pieces they needed in the attic, shuffling about in the dust and boxes in an awkward silence. He'd had family obligations. She'd visited neighbors with the countess.

The time apart ought to have helped things, really.

But then there had been a dinner the night before that Mrs. Barnes had invited Caroline to attend. And she had. She liked Grace Barnes excessively. The woman was gentle, intelligent, and had a dry wit that surprised people around her quite often.

Edward had been there, too.

Grace Barnes was playing matchmaker. To a match that was already made. Or, at least as made as it would ever be. Those circular thoughts muddled Caroline all the more.

"You will not think of him," she muttered aloud, her voice muffled by the pillow still pressed to her face. "Not today, Caroline."

She removed the pillow from her head and stared at the growing light between the curtains. The maid would be in soon to wake her, dress her for the day ahead, and share the gossip from the servants' hall.

They'd become friends, of a sort. Perhaps one could never truly befriend a servant. Caroline wasn't certain. It was something she had asked her mother in the last letter she sent home, along with descriptions of all she was doing and the people she met.

She'd even written of Edward, in terms as plain and spare as possible.

Even while she'd strived to create a picture with no more than black ink on cream-colored paper, memory of the lightness in her chest and the fluttering sensation that had spread throughout her body brought a smile to her lips. All the things she didn't tell her family took up more words and lines than what she did tell them.

But she could hardly tell them about the man who made her heart race with both apprehension and excitement. What would her mother think of Caroline's kiss in the attic? Of Edward as a pretend suitor?

That horrid word, *pretend*, made her stomach tighten.

Would her mother, her papa, understand why she had come up

with the plan to help Mariah? To do what she had? They trusted her. They said that often enough. Perhaps if they knew about Edward, they would trust her less.

The whole of it made the kiss between them more problematic. Forgetting it would be easiest, even though it seemed impossible. And what had he said before the kiss? That being near her felt like part of an adventure.

Her stomach dipped in delight.

And here she was. Thinking of him again after telling herself, in clear terms, not to.

"It was a delightful moment," she whispered aloud as her room changed from blue-gray to warmer tones of gold. "But I cannot make it more than that."

She rose and readied herself for the morning. Today, Edward would come again. Unless she sent a note to delay him. To tell him she had no need of him until the next day. Would that worry him? Yet giving herself one more day's distance to fortify her feelings seemed wise.

She went to her desk and wrote the note.

The countess and earl had planned a bonfire for that evening. She could blame the delay on assisting them with that. The countess was unlikely available to chaperone them anyway.

That was the best course of action.

She signed the note with her initials. She did not seal it. It was not private. Anyone might read a simple deferment of plans.

Nodding to herself, Caroline opened one of her largest windows and took in a deep breath of the sweet summer air, salted and flavored by the sea. And she most certainly didn't think of that kiss, or the rather dashing gentleman who had shared it with her.

THE CURTAINS in Edward's bedchamber burst open, letting in bright morning light from the east. Edward winced and sat up, shielding his eyes. His valet had woken him this way before, but only after Edward had ruined a pair of trousers by catching them on a hook. He'd ruined his shoes, too, stumbling into a brook with a fishing pole he'd purchased on a whim.

But it wasn't his valet intent on punishing him with the early morning light.

"What are you playing at, Edward?"

It was his father.

Blearily, Edward rubbed at his eyes and then ran a hand across his face. "Playing at? Father, I'm still asleep. I can't possibly have done something to upset you today."

"Not yet, but the day is still young." Mr. Everly stomped from the window to the bed. "Where were you last evening?"

Edward scrubbed the top of his head with one hand, then smiled to himself as his memory caught up to him. "I had dinner with Grace and Jacob. I told Mother before I left."

"You were not the only guest. Is that correct?"

Gossip among the servants had moved faster than Edward thought possible. It took his mind a moment to catch up, and he effected a confused expression while he formed his response. Best to deliver it slowly, as though uncertain. "I suppose not. Mr. and Mrs. Bartlett were present. And Miss Clapham."

"Precisely!" His father paced away a few steps, only to turn again and hold out both hands toward Edward. "Miss Clapham. Is it not enough that you spend an hour every day at her side, but now you must go driving with her in the afternoons and be her dinner partner in the evenings?"

"We went driving once," Edward pointed out, sitting back against the headboard of his bed. "The day after the picnic, after the countess said it would be a good idea. And Mother insisted I take Charity with me. There was nothing inappropriate about that."

And no one knew about the kiss. The kiss that had left Edward permanently distracted, keeping him unfocused during the day, and

216

haunting his dreams at night. A kiss he'd promised to forget yet couldn't go even five minutes without thinking on it.

"But the dinner," his father said, shaking his head.

"One dinner." Edward held up a single finger. "At my sister's house. My sister, who you will recall, is married to the vicar. There is nothing untoward about that, either."

Mr. Everly folded his arms over his broad chest and glowered impressively at his son. Edward had grown too used to his father's severe looks to be affected by them. And truly, he'd done nothing wrong. Nothing his parents or anyone else would ever hear of.

"Grace invited me to dinner because she knew Miss Clapham and I are comfortable with one another—"

"Comfortable? Is that all?" his father interrupted, voice raised and tone incredulous. A twitch of his left eye gave further indication the man wasn't the least bit amused. "Edward, people are beginning to talk."

"People are always talking, Father." Edward sighed and threw his blankets off, wearing only his nightshirt as he shuffled to where he'd left a dressing robe on the back of a chair. He slid it over his shoulders, keeping his back to his father. "What are they talking about that has upset you?"

"Miss Clapham!" His father suddenly thrust a card out toward Edward. "This arrived for you today. Unsealed. By a servant at the kitchen door. 'Mr. E. Everly,' it says, 'please allow for a change in plans today. The house is busy with preparations for the bonfire this evening. May we resume our appointed meetings tomorrow? Lady Inglewood agrees.' And then she signed only with her initials. Her *initials.*"

Though his mind filled with disappointment—another day without seeing Caroline—Edward couldn't let his father know of that. Instead, he forced himself to chuckle as he cinched the belt of his robe and turned around. He hadn't let his father harangue him like this in some time. He'd avoided all conversations that had even the chance of gaining such a heated response for months. This one he couldn't avoid. Not if he wanted his plan to work.

And not if his father was going to turn up in his bedroom before Edward had even dressed for the day.

"Initials are a common way to sign a letter, Father. It doesn't allude to anything clandestine. And everyone knows I have been at Inglewood, posing for that painting of hers. It isn't a secret." He gave his father an amused smile. "Given that Miss Clapham is a gentleman's daughter, and the guest of a peer, I cannot imagine what people have to say about her or that note that would distress you this much. You have met her, Father. Several times. Grace adores her."

His father opened and closed his mouth, then huffed and went to the window, glaring out of it. "She doesn't distress me. Nor does this." He dropped the card onto Edward's bed before glowering at his son again. "It is that you are in her presence an exorbitant amount of time that distresses me. More than a month, Edward. You have called on her nearly every day for a month. Driven her about in a gig, directly through town. Everyone saw you. And this morning I learn you dined with her."

"At the house of the vicar, where we were both guests." Edward repeated the facts with a barely restrained grin. He folded his arms and leaned against the hearth. "Who told you of that, anyway? I didn't know she would be a guest until I arrived."

"You didn't?" His father whirled toward him, startled.

"I have never lied to you, Father." Though he had been keeping a great deal from his parents of late. Mariah's secret, his own desire to travel again, his agreement with Caroline.... "I was pleased to see her there."

The older man's chest puffed up again. "Now see here, Edward. You cannot lose your senses over some...some artist. Gentleman's daughter or not. She is likely a penniless woman destined for employment as a governess. I doubt a disinherited lord, who isn't even her father, has provided a dowry for her. She isn't the sort of woman you need as a wife."

"Wife?" Edward repeated the last word with incredulity, even though his heart skipped a beat to hear it spoken aloud. "Father. I haven't even begun courting her yet."

"Be that as it may—" Mr. Everly interrupted himself with a sharp turn of his head. "Yet? You haven't begun *yet*? Does that mean you intend to court her?"

Edward waited less than a second to reply. "Yes. I do."

"I thought you didn't wish to court anyone?"

Here came the tricky part of the conversation. Edward couldn't say more than he felt. More than he and Caroline had agreed upon. "I didn't wish to court Mariah Kimball. And she was the only option presented."

His father walked slowly through the room, past Edward, and to a chair before the still-cold hearth. He settled himself into the cushions slowly. Heavily. He fixed his gaze on Edward. "You still refuse to wed Miss Kimball? Even though she is the most sensible choice?"

Edward gave a single nod in response.

"What of her feelings on this matter?"

Again, Edward reminded himself to tread carefully. One misspoken word would reveal too much of a secret not his own. "I have known Mariah Kimball since her infancy. We have been friends for nearly as long. I have no reason to believe she expected a courtship or offer of marriage from me. Despite what you and my mother have hoped for."

For a long, sullen moment, his father merely stared at him. Saying nothing. Waiting, perhaps, for Edward to play more of his own hand or show some hint of what was in his thoughts. But Edward remained silent, his lips pressed together.

He was a terrible card player, after all.

At last, his father's shoulders fell. "You will ask Miss Clapham for a courtship?"

Edward's chin came up. "I already have." A pretend courtship. But in the days since the picnic, since herding children about on the shoreline and watching the way Caroline's smile lit the whole world around her, things had turned quite real for him. Even before the kiss, he'd begun considering what it would mean to do away with the pretense of their arrangement. To tell her he wanted to make things real between them.

Her initial return of their kiss had made him think he had a chance. Even if Caroline hadn't spoken of it again.

"What did she say?" Mr. Everly asked, the twitch in his eye punctuating his question.

"She agreed to it." Edward's chest tightened. "I intend to ask Lord and Lady Inglewood for their permission, and I will seek out Caroline's parents for theirs if things go well." The moment he knew if Caroline could return his feelings, if she had interest in pursuing something more, he would go directly to her parents. In person. Without delay.

The word *wait* still echoed in his mind.

He had to be careful. For all that everyone made light of his propensity to leap into action or trouble without a plan, sometimes he knew better. This was one of those times. Kissing her as he had... it had almost ruined everything.

"An artist, Edward," his father said, plaintively. "They are eccentric. Unreliable. What sort of wife would she be? What sort of mother?"

"Those aren't things you need to worry over, Father." Edward didn't hide his smile, though his insides twisted with anxiety. He'd been raised to please his parents. To bend to their will and honor their decisions for him. To go against that training made him itch with discomfort. "Lady Inglewood is an artist, and the earl seems quite content with his life."

Slowly, Mr. Everly rose from the chair. "You will exercise caution, Edward. Please. None of this jumping off a cliff without checking for rocks below."

At this, Edward managed to laugh. "Those reckless days are behind me." Even if he had worried over the same thing moments before. "I'm proceeding with utmost caution this time. I don't want to make any hasty decisions and risk spoiling what could be a promising future."

"I am not certain I believe it." His father shook his head and went to the door. The disappointment in his voice, in his expression, made Edward's gut clench most uncomfortably.

Edward had one question yet burning within. One that could not hurt to ask. "Will you send Claude home now?"

Mr. Everly hesitated, then looked over his shoulder. "Send Claude home?"

After a swallow, Edward said with confidence, "You invited him here in hopes it would persuade me to do as you wished. Did you not?"

Mr. Everly's eyebrows went upward, but he gave no other emotion away. "Is that what you think?"

It was exactly what Edward had thought. Up until that very moment. "I can see no other reason for him to be here. And I know you asked him to come. He didn't invite himself."

"Indeed. I invited him." Mr. Everly didn't appear at all guilty in his admittance. He stared at Edward a moment longer before he opened the door and took a step through it. Then he said, "I think Claude will remain for some time yet. I will see you at breakfast, Edward." He closed the door before Edward said another word.

Edward leaned against the wall, staring at the door. Perhaps he shouldn't have mentioned Claude. He tilted his head against the wall and looked up at the ceiling, a feeling of unease creeping into Edward's already bewildered heart. The dark hints Claude had dropped in casual conversation, his father's evasiveness, didn't sit right with him. There was an undercurrent of something between the two men that Edward sensed. He wished he understood it. Because he had the feeling that whatever it was, it was going to add yet another complication to his life.

# CHAPTER 19

What would a courtship with Edward look like?

Caroline turned that question over and over again in her mind ever since the day in the attic. She didn't typically mind questions she didn't have the answers to, because finding the answers meant learning and experiencing the world. But this question made her uncomfortable. And she'd yet to come up with an answer.

That afternoon, she had outlined Edward's form on her canvas, using the faintest lines of charcoal before daring to touch her brush to it. With each movement, each touch of the canvas, she remembered the feel of his hand cupping her face. His fingers twined with hers. The press of his lips. His scent. His taste.

When she'd finished for the day, she looked at the form emerging on her canvas with surprise. She hardly remembered what she'd done to put it there. Though her hands had moved, her mind had been far from her brush. Yet everything looked as she wished.

How very strange.

She'd left the canvas behind but kept thinking on Edward.

In the community where she had grown up, a man and woman may walk home together after church. That was when they were poor farmers, millers, innkeepers, or other tradesmen. Perhaps they would dance together at the assemblies, enough times for people to whisper about it behind their hands or fans.

Caroline sat in front of the mirror in her room, watching as Emily carefully braided her hair into a coronet around her head. She had decided to dress simply for the evening bonfire on the beach, hosted by the earl and countess for their friends. She wore a white cotton dress with minimal flounces and a lace-up, dark blue bodice. The maid helped her slip on a pair of half boots that the sand wouldn't harm, and Caroline stood up to survey herself in the mirror.

The curls peeking out about her face made her look elegant yet relaxed, and the dress was both comfortable and flattering. She twirled around a few times to make sure the skirt flowed just right, and Emily laughed at her playful display.

"You look beautiful, miss," the maid said with a smile.

Caroline grinned back, feeling less self-conscious than she had when Lady Inglewood had hosted that first dinner for her. Bonfires she understood. Evenings spent laughing and singing, telling stories, those were far less intimidating than a formal dinner. She had started making friends, too.

Edward would be there.

Caroline felt a flutter in her chest as she looked at the clock on the mantel. Minutes instead of hours separated them now. She couldn't deny that she enjoyed spending time with him, that his quick wit and bold spirit drew her to him. But what did all of that mean? Did he feel the same way about her? And even if he did, what would that mean for her future? Would she be content to be a wife, to set aside her artistic dreams for the sake of a husband and children?

Was that her future, exchanging one love for another?

Without romantic ambitions of her own, Caroline hadn't paid attention to who had a fondness for whom until bans were read in their village church. Even when Jill Martin's brother had started to visit more often, bringing her flowers or jam, talking to her of things he thought she liked, she hadn't felt he was *courting* her. He was being a nuisance. A sweet nuisance. But still. A nuisance.

Things with Edward were not like that at all.

Those questions plagued her and she sensed that she would have to make a decision about her future quite soon. But for now, she would enjoy Edward's company, and try not to think too much about what it might mean.

Focusing on Sir Thomas's impending visit would distract her from Edward, even though she had worried that Edward would distract her from the visit. Caroline no longer knew which man would hold her future in his hands.

She selected a light shawl to drape over her shoulders, knowing that the night air would cool quickly. As she left her room, she took a deep breath. Enjoying the evening was her only concern tonight and she would *not* overthink things. No matter what. All her worries would keep another day.

Caroline arrived at the beachfront while the sun remained hovering over the horizon. Walking through the gardens, she admired the colorful decorations that were strung up for the occasion. The bonfire had yet to be lit, but people were already gathering in small groups, chatting and laughing as they waited for the festivities to begin. The air was filled with the scent of roasted meats and spices, and Caroline's mouth watered at the sight of the delicious food protected by servants with fans. The earl and countess stood at the center of the main garden walk, in the place before the steps dipped downward to the sand.

As Caroline approached Lady Inglewood's side, the countess smiled and greeted her warmly. "Caroline, darling, you look lovely this evening."

"Indeed," Lord Inglewood smiled broadly at her. "Are you ready for one of our favorite celebrations?" They'd explained that they had hosted a bonfire night every July since their marriage, inviting friends and neighbors to tell stories and sing songs around the fire. Recently they had expanded their guest list to include merchants and their tenant farmers, people the community held in respect and were known to the earl.

"I think so." She brushed her ungloved hand down the front of her dress. "Is there anything I can do to help?"

"You are not to worry about anything," Lady Inglewood said. Then she glanced at her husband, who shared a smile with her. "Though there is something we'd like to address with you. You see, one of our guests arrived quite early to speak to us about you."

"Oh?" Caroline glanced between the two of them, then looked to where people milled about a table in the garden, selecting cups of lemonade and laughing with one another. She saw several familiar faces, but no one stood out to her. "Is something the matter?"

"Not at all." Lord Inglewood tucked his hands behind his back. "It was Edward Everly who came to our door, asking for an audience. He was shockingly formal about it."

Edward? But what did he need with—

"Oh," she breathed aloud. "He asked to court me."

Lady Inglewood exhaled and put her hand on her husband's arm. "I am relieved you knew about it. He said he'd spoken to you first, but you hadn't said a word to me."

The shame of lying to her mentor made it difficult for Caroline to speak for a moment. A harmless lie, she'd thought at first. Now others were being drawn into it, things were not as simple as she'd thought.

"What did you say?" she asked, gaze flicking from the earl to the countess and back again.

"Insofar as our guardianship extends," Lord Inglewood said with a crooked smile, "we approve."

"But we believe you need to write to your parents at once," Lady Inglewood added with raised eyebrows. "We can vouch for his respectability, and we will continue to provide chaperoned opportunities for you to get to know one another. But your parents must give their consent."

"Of course." Her stomach sank. Her parents would be surprised. They knew how much her work meant to her. Would they be disappointed she'd been distracted by a romance? Or, worse, would they be happy for her? And *then* disappointed when she inevitably told them it had led to nothing? "I will write them tomorrow."

Lady Inglewood sighed, and her expression turned amused. "Watching the two of you together these last several weeks made me suspect something more than friendship was blooming. Thus far, the two of you complement each other quite well."

"Thank you." Caroline wanted to sink into the ground and disappear entirely. They had only been friendly toward each other in Lady Inglewood's presence, hadn't they? They had laughed and teased. Did that count as flirting?

The married couple exchanged knowing smiles, then Lord Inglewood swept aside, clearing the path to the beach, with his wife on his arm. "Excellent. We will not keep you a moment longer."

"He's waiting for you on the beach," Lady Inglewood added, laying her head against her husband's shoulder. She spoke with a teasing lilt to her words. "Behave yourselves, my dear."

"Yes, your ladyship." Caroline curtseyed, then took the last steps down to the sand.

Torches dotted the sandy shore, ready to be lit the moment the sun fully disappeared beneath the waves. Benches and logs had been set up around a smaller fire, already tended by a servant, and the unlit bonfire.

Edward stood where the waves lapped gently against the shore, his shoes barely out of their reach, his back to the castle. He cut a fine figure, standing like that with the sun lining his form in yellow-gold.

Her heart forgot her guilt long enough to skip happily, and Caroline took a moment to gather herself. Yes, she found Edward attractive. Yes, she enjoyed his company. But she could not allow herself more. Their courtship wasn't real. He didn't want to marry. He wanted to travel, and never would because he feared his father's censure. He wouldn't do as he wished if it risked upsetting his parents, and they had thus far refused to understand what it was their son wanted.

Caroline had her own dreams to fulfill. Spending time worrying about his was pointless.

With a steadying breath, Caroline put a smile on her face and made her way to stand beside him. "Edward."

He smiled but did not turn to look at her. "Caroline."

"I understand we are officially courting."

He nodded, eyes still on the horizon, looking into a distance beyond what she could see. "I am certain the gossip will spread this very evening. Will you mind?"

"This was my idea, Edward. All will be well."

He raised his eyebrows and finally looked at her. The full force of his gaze made her stomach flip. She didn't see Edward alone when she looked at him now. She saw the strength in his shoulders, the determination in his gaze, the burdens of his thoughts as heavy on his soul as the globe had been resting on Atlas's shoulders.

"I have never courted anyone before, Cara."

There it was again, the familiar name that sounded so different when he spoke it. She needed to quell her ridiculous feelings before they ruined everything. "Perhaps this will serve as practice, then, for when you find the woman you wish to wed."

His lips twitched upward, and he lowered his gaze. "Practice. There's a thought." He held his hand up between them. "Will you accompany me to the refreshments, where I will look at you adoringly for all to see?" He punctuated the question with a smile that almost teased.

"You may." She took his hand, and he tucked it securely against his arm. Then guided her along to speak with others. No one mentioned a courtship to them, though Caroline intercepted several inquisitive glances as the evening went on. The fire was lit, logs and benches and stools were pulled up around it. A fiddle guided them in song.

Mariah Kimball arrived, a trifle late, which drew attention equally toward her and Caroline. She had settled on a long bench between Edward and Charity, who came with Claude and her parents since Edward had arrived early on his errand.

Caroline rose when she recognized Mariah, and her friend came at once to her side with a wide smile and bounce in her step. She looked far happier, freer even, than any other time Caroline had seen her.

"My parents heard the news that Edward declared his intentions," she whispered as she embraced Caroline, as though they were the oldest of friends. "My mama swooned, and Papa looked dreadful until I laughed. They thought I suffered a fit of hysterics." She scoffed and stepped away. "I told them it was about time Edward discovered who and what made him happy, and that I could not wait to congratulate you."

Caroline's cheeks burned, despite being distant from the fire by several feet. "Is the plan going to help you as you supposed?"

Edward slipped up beside her, wordlessly taking her hand in his and twining their fingers together between them. Was that for her benefit? His? Or for the people who might be watching? Caroline didn't know. She decided not to care.

"Yes. My mother tried to forbid me from coming this evening. She thought it would be better for me to shun you and Edward both. Yet here I am, after convincing both my parents that I am unhurt by his attentions turning to another. Mother thought you belonged to me, Edward."

"I am not sorry to disabuse her for that notion." Edward kept his voice low. "My parents weren't in raptures about this, either."

Caroline bumped his shoulder with hers. "Careful, Edward. You will wound my maidenly pride."

He chuckled, the sound rich and warm in the shadows cast by the fire. He ran his thumb across her knuckles, offering reassurance in that subtle touch. Caroline fought the sudden inclination to tip her head onto his shoulder as she had seen Lady Inglewood do to her husband at the beginning of the evening.

A scandalous thought. Resting her head on the shoulder of a man who wasn't her relative, and certainly not her husband. She nearly pulled away from him, but Edward's thumb stroked the skin on the back of her hand again, and Caroline didn't want to give that up. Not yet.

She doubled her effort to focus on Mariah, asking, "What does this do to your secret?"

"I think they are uncertain of what to do with me." Mariah tugged the shawl she wore closer around her shoulders. "Now that Edward is no longer seen as a viable option, I believe there is a chance to present my parents with the man who holds my heart. Slowly, of course. They must be eased into the idea." She brushed a stray curl from her eyes and grew solemn. "They had a map to guide me to happiness before, but the map is gone. This gives me the opportunity to try my own path. Mark my own way."

Edward's grin flashed in the dark. "You mean to ambush them."

"Edward," Caroline whispered, glaring at him. "That is a terribly unromantic thing to say to a woman in love."

Mariah Kimball laughed, "But it is an accurate description of my plan." A knowing smile that Caroline hadn't seen the other lady wear before appeared on her face. "It's as if a door that was once firmly closed has now cracked open, offering me an opportunity to show them the depth of my affection and the genuine qualities of the man I've chosen."

"Congratulations, then, Miss Kimball," Edward said with complete sincerity. "I am glad for you, and I wish you well in your search for happiness."

At this, Mariah folded her arms and fixed him with a skeptical stare. "Do you, Edward? I wish I could say the same for you. When will you seek your own happiness?" She turned to Caroline. "He hardly speaks of what it is he most wants."

"Indeed." Caroline looked up at Edward, studying him as she normally did when she painted him. "Even though he has asked me all about my dreams, he keeps his to himself."

# CHAPTER 20

Edward knew that look. It was the one Caroline wore while painting him. Peering inside him as though she wished to use raw emotion on the canvas rather than paint.

His stomach dropped and his lips suddenly turned dry. He couldn't blame the salt-laden air for either sensation. Only the foolish task he had set himself, and the foolish words he had said before when he'd believed love would cost more than it was worth.

"We all have our secrets, I suppose." It was an unimaginative answer and weakly spoken. The women exchanged a look heavy with significance, then let the matter drop.

Mariah lingered for a time, conversing with both Edward and Caroline. Everyone present would see she held no ill will toward the couple, laughing as she did with them. If Mariah Kimball didn't mind their courtship, there was less for gossips to say about Edward's constancy or lack thereof.

Surely, all they had to do now was maintain the ruse.

Across the fire, Thomas Oddsen sang a folk song played by the violinist, and other voices joined them. Mariah excused herself to speak to her friend, Miss Parr.

Edward kept his hold on Caroline's hand. "Our places on the bench were taken."

"Thank goodness." Her voice was soft as silk. "Shall we find some refreshment? It's so warm by the fire, I will not mind being away from it for a time."

People dotted the path between the bonfire and the castle. The gardens, lit with torches and lanterns, held knots of people conversing and laughing with one another. Here the innkeeper spoke with the earl, there a farmer's wife regaled Lady Fox with stories of her children, a gentleman listened raptly to advice from the milliner. The gathering was one of the most unique events Edward attended with his family. Lord Inglewood had reportedly started hosting the event, with an open invitation to half the county, as a way of strengthening relationships in the community.

Caroline seemed more at ease in this setting than she had at the formal dinner from weeks ago. As they approached the refreshment table, she smiled at a group of women standing nearby.

"Miss Clapham," one of them called. "Do you have a moment?"

She glanced up at Edward who released her arm. "I will fetch you a drink and something to eat," he assured her.

"Do not be long," she whispered, glancing toward the women. "I barely know those three. I'm not even certain I remember their names."

He chuckled and bent a little closer to her. "The tall one is Miss Thompson. To her right is Lady Daniels, baronetess. The last is Mrs. Ashby." Her grateful smile made his heart twist. He let her go and went on to the table he'd spied at the beginning of the evening. His mother was there, reaching for the ladle to serve herself punch.

Edward hurried his step and called to her. She turned, her eyebrows already high on her forehead. "There you are, Edward. I haven't seen you since I arrived. Have you been down by the bonfire all evening?"

"Before it was even lit," he told her, giving her a kiss on the cheek. "Let me pour your drink."

"Thank you, dear." She accepted the cup from him with her usual gentle smile. "And where is Miss Clapham this evening? After your announcement at dinner, I didn't know what to expect. I had some vague notion of finding you glued to her side." The way she said it didn't sound disapproving in the least. Edward relaxed somewhat.

"You think me that besotted, do you?" he asked, moving to the table with small plates, fruits, and cakes. "I am not certain whether to be offended or amused."

She accepted the plate he handed her and smiled when she saw he'd put strawberries, her favorite, at the center of the plate. "I think you are a passionate young man. You always have been. Headstrong, of course, which your father and I have worried over without ceasing. But you have a loving heart. I had so hoped you would make a match with Miss Kimball. Yet now I see how misguided I was." She gestured to one of the elegant benches near the same fountain where Edward had sat during the painting party. "Sit with me a moment?"

Edward went with her, holding her plate again until she had situated herself comfortably. She accepted it from him and picked up a strawberry.

"I am sorry to disappoint you, Mother." He spoke with sincerity. He'd always wanted his mother's approval and her happiness. Yet sometimes, when she aligned herself so closely with his father's desires, Edward couldn't help feeling he'd let her down in some way.

His mother blinked at him, then narrowed her eyes. "You haven't disappointed me. Not in the least. My dear boy." She laid her hand on his arm. "If I have given you that impression, I must correct it. As I said, I hoped for that other match. Because I adore Mrs. Kimball and her daughter, of course, but I also hoped Mariah would be the one to make you happy. She is so steady and certain, I thought that her character would be a complement and balance to your own. Now, of course, I see there was never any chance of that. Your affection for Mariah Kimball is that of a friend and nothing more." She gave his arm a gentle squeeze and picked up one of the strawberries. "You are quite a different man when in love. It is most obvious now."

Edward glanced away from his mother. "Am I? What makes it so obvious?"

"You must think me blind and inattentive to ask that." She laughed, whether at him or herself he couldn't say, but it wasn't unkind. "You cannot wait to leave our house, day after day, to spend more time with Miss Clapham. When you are with us, you are not truly present. Your mind is forever elsewhere. And when you *do* speak, you speak of her. Likely without even realizing. 'Miss Clapham says we are at the beginning of a new artistic movement.' Or something simpler, like when you said, 'I wonder if Miss Clapham has eaten as many cherries as we have apples.'"

He had said that when his mother ordered baked apples covered in cinnamon and butter for dessert one evening. What else had he said without realizing it? And here he'd thought he'd been too subtle.

"Chattering on about someone is a sign of love?" he asked, folding his arms and leaning against the backrest.

"The look in your eyes every time you say her name, and when I suspect you are thinking of her, is the clearest sign of all." His mother's tone grew wistful and when he looked again he found her studying him with gentle intensity. "The only time I have seen you as happy as you have been these past weeks is right before you left to visit Rome, and then in the months after every time you spoke of your adventure." She tipped her chin down the better to give him a motherly raise of her eyebrows. "Caroline Clapham is your new adventure, I think."

He lowered his gaze to his mother's plate, unable to say anything in response. Somehow, despite all the time away from home, despite growing from boy to man, his mother still had the ability to understand him as no one else could. Did all mother's possess such a talent?

"May I have a strawberry?" he asked, his throat tight.

She handed him the second-largest on her plate and he smiled. Then she said, "I think we should find Miss Clapham and find out if she would like a strawberry."

"An excellent idea." He helped his mother refill her punch, then put together a plate for Caroline. The two of them found her in the midst of a conversation with the same ladies who had called her from Edward's side. She smiled with some relief as he joined her, and then greeted his mother with enthusiasm.

Edward contented himself by listening to the ladies discuss portraits and gardens, watching the play of the lantern light on Caroline's face, noting how attentive she was to his mother. And how kind his mother was to her.

His mother had realized he was falling in love before Edward had known it. How long would it take for Caroline to see the evidence of his affection? He spent the evening following her about, practically as his mother predicted he would, satisfied to merely keep her company.

By the next morning, he suspected that all of Alderton would know that he, Edward Everly, was completely enamored with Caroline Clapham.

My Dearest Mama and Papa,

I hope this letter finds you in good health and spirits, and that our orchard continues to thrive. Even if I am not there to do all the cherry picking, as we all know that I am the most talented cherry harvester in the county. Yes, Papa, I know you will protest. But we both know it is the truth.

This letter isn't the usual sort. I am not certain how best to prepare you for news that I never expected I would have to write in a letter. There is something of great importance that I must share with you, and I trust that you will receive my words with an open heart and mind.

Recently, I have been presented with something rather unexpected. That sounds rather dreadful, doesn't it? Rest assured, all is well, and I am quite happy. Edward Everly, who I have mentioned in previous letters, has requested to court me. After careful contemplation, I have granted him permission. I hope you understand that this decision was not made lightly. You have raised me to be thoughtful in all things, especially in matters of the heart.

Mr. Everly is a kind and honorable gentleman, and Lord and Lady Inglewood have promised to act their part as my guardian by ensuring everything is appropriate in my conduct and in Mr. Everly's.

I am grateful for his friendship and the help

he has given me in regards to my painting. However, I must confess that deep in my heart, I am unsure if this courtship will lead to anything substantial. While I value his company, I believe that our paths may diverge in due course if I am to continue my artistic pursuits. Mr. Everly is his father's heir, and his family has placed both responsibilities and expectations upon his future. I tell you this because I wish to keep your expectations in check and shield you from any unnecessary disappointment.

Please trust in my judgment and know that I would never embark upon such an endeavor without considering all that you have taught me. I hold your love and guidance in the highest regard, and it is with this trust that I confide these matters now.

Rest assured, my dear parents, that I am mindful of your hopes and dreams for me. I tread this path with caution, and I promise to keep you informed of any significant developments. Your happiness and well-being remain my utmost priority.

With all my love and devotion,

Caroline

My Darling Caroline,

Your letter has reached us, and I must say, it has sparked a range of emotions within my heart. Your papa and I are of an accord on this matter. While we respect your independence and trust your judgment, our concern cannot help but arise in such matters. Lady Inglewood's letter reassured us all was well. We are grateful that she and Lord Inglewood have promised to look after you.

Your casual mentions of Mr. Everly in your last several letters piqued my curiosity. You will think I exaggerate. How can someone infer such things from a letter? Yet I sensed a flicker of something more profound beneath the surface. A mother's intuition, perhaps? I confess that I suspected there might be more to your interactions than you wrote, and your revelation has not come entirely as a surprise.

While I urge you to exercise caution, my dear, I want you to know that your papa and I have complete faith in your ability to navigate this courtship with grace and wisdom. We trust that you have considered the consequences to your heart and have embarked upon this path with a clear understanding of where it may lead.

Do keep in mind, my love, that relationships between men and women can be intricate and unpredictable. Though you expressed some uncertainty, I hope you will approach this situation as you do all things you love. With your whole soul. Will there be risk? Of course. But the reward will be great if Mr. Everly is the one your heart desires. As you proceed, remember to be open to the possibilities that lie before you. Life has a way of surprising us, and sometimes, the most unexpected journeys lead to the most extraordinary adventures.

I hope you will write more about Mr. Everly. I am understandably curious about him. And your papa wishes to know how the gentleman managed to secure your good opinion. Please keep us informed of any significant developments from henceforth. Your happiness is our ultimate wish, and we will be here for you, regardless of the outcome. Lean on our love, our guidance, and our unwavering trust as you explore this uncharted territory.

With all the love and encouragement a mother can offer,

Your Loving Mother & Papa

# CHAPTER 21

J uly drew to its end, and Caroline had nearly finished her portrait of Edward. Day after day he came, even when she didn't need him for her work, to sit in the library or in the studio with her. Of course, she refused to let him see the canvas until she completed it. But when she had to wait between coats of paint, she entertained him by handing him a sketch and telling him to copy it. The results were always amusing, as he inevitably added details for the sole purpose of making her laugh.

He'd given a mouse the ears of an elephant, and a large mustache to a rabbit. He put a dragon on a teacup, rather than the flowers she had painstakingly recreated from the original. And he added a swing to a tree before asking her to drive with him to his family's home, where a real swing had hung for years.

She went, of course. The day was fine and enjoying it with Edward made it all the better.

He walked with her after church, carrying her parasol. He told her jokes and loaned her books from his library that he thought she might enjoy. And Caroline lost the ability to discern moments of friendship and their pretend romance. Sometimes, she forgot they pretended at all. Even though he didn't kiss her again. Neither of them spoke of that moment, though Caroline caught herself remembering it often. Especially in the quieter moments, when Edward wasn't looking directly at her, and she had a moment to study him without him knowing.

Something was shifting and changing within her, and between the two of them. And it both terrified and elated her. If only she could tell someone what was going on, and ask for advice. But the nature of Caroline and Edward's arrangement kept her from knowing what to ask without giving away too much of their secret.

The first week of August surprised them with a heavy rain. Caroline sat with Lady Inglewood in a room with windows facing the sea, though they couldn't catch a glimpse of the waves for all the gray clouds and sheets of water. Lady Inglewood's children played quietly on the rug in front of the hearth, wooden blocks and animals marching along the patterns of the rug.

Caroline couldn't help thinking of her family. Her brothers with their animals on the floor, or her father making up strange sounds for each wooden member of the menagerie to make. Was it raining in Dunwich too?

She held an open book in her hands without reading a single word.

The door to the sitting room opened, and Caroline's back was toward it. She looked over her shoulder, to see if the earl had decided to join them, then gasped and dropped her book to the floor.

"Papa!"

Neil Duncan's light hair was damp on the ends, making it curlier than usual, and his green eyes danced with merriment. He wore traveling clothes and tall boots, but had already shed hat and gloves. Caroline forgot herself completely. She wasn't a guest in a countess's sitting room, she was a little girl who climbed trees and ran about barefoot in the summer. She ran to her stepfather, arms open and tears springing to her eyes as she jumped into his embrace, wrapping her arms around his neck and burying her face in his rain-damp coat.

The strong, familiar arms of her papa wrapped tightly around her, squeezing just enough to secure her there with her feet dangling above the ground. He kissed the top of her head, as he had since he'd married her mother.

"Had I known I'd receive such a welcome, I would have come weeks ago," he said, his voice thick with emotion. He lowered her to her feet and stepped back, grinning at her. "Shame you haven't grown an inch. You're as short as ever."

"Papa," she protested, wiping at her eyes.

"Tears?" He whipped a handkerchief out from his coat. "You're meant to be pleased to see me, you know."

She accepted the large square of linen, one she had embroidered for him with green little frogs in one corner. The sight only made her eyes water more, and suddenly, Caroline burst into a sob. Neil's teasing ceased entirely and he pulled her close again, running his hand up and down her back.

"It's all right, *ma fille*. Whatever it is, it is all right." Yet she couldn't seem to stop. How had he known she needed him? That she missed everyone at home? That she felt lost and confused, and that her heart and mind were so full of anxiety she could barely think? She heard him speak above her head, "Lady Inglewood. Good to see you."

"And you, Lord Neil." The countess's voice was soft. "I am glad the rain didn't delay you. The room across the corridor has a fire burning. You two will have privacy there."

"Thank you." Her papa stepped back, tucking Caroline's arm through his, and led her away without another word. They entered another sitting room, this one facing westward and overlooking the drive where a carriage was being driven toward the stables. Neil sat down, tugging Caroline with him, onto a couch angled toward the fireplace. "What are all these tears for, Cara?"

"I hardly know," she confessed, trying to laugh and failing. "It has been a long two months. And I have been so happy. I swear to you I have. But I was thinking of the twins, and Amelia, and you, and mama, and all the sudden you were here." Her throat closed up again and she shook her head, unable to say another word until the emotion passed.

Neil held her hand, requiring nothing of her, and began to speak. "Your mother misses you terribly, and I think she has read every letter you sent at least a dozen times. She carried the most recent one with her in a pocket or apron. She tells everyone how proud she is of you and of your hard work. Sometimes, she walks to the sea cliffs all on her own to read your letters when they first arrive. We are both so proud of you."

She sniffled and grinned at him. "Thank you."

"Alfie and Victor have grown at least two inches, but their French is still terrible." That made her laugh, and he smiled as he kept talking. "They have convinced your mother to let them adopt a duck they found with a wounded wing. They have even had the creature sleep in a box in their room at nights. They named it Gingersnap. Amelia is convinced that if you are an artist, she must be a musician. She has doubled her efforts on the pianoforte and asked if she may learn the flute next. Your grandmother is well. And I am here because there is some scoundrel named Everly trying to court you, and I need to have a good look at him, even if your mother and I trust your judgement on such things. It will reassure me, if nothing else, that he knows you are a woman of worth."

Worry dried up the last of her tears. She lowered the handkerchief and twisted it with both hands. "Papa. I wrote to you all about Edward. So did the earl and countess."

"And I happen to remember the fellow from years ago, when he was a gangly youth getting stuck in trees."

A watery giggle escaped her. "I have heard that story."

"It wasn't long after that his sisters caused me a broken arm," he added with a wry twist to his smile. "Yes. I am well acquainted with the Everly family. But that doesn't mean I am ready for one of them to court my little girl. Especially given all the cautionary words you wrote." His eyes narrowed. "Your letters about him sound as though you both want us to approve and dread the moment he will break your heart."

"I wanted to spare you from potential disappointment. In case things between Edward and I do not end as you may hope." As she spoke, she laced the handkerchief through her fingers, tugging it and twining it until she inadvertently put a knot through it.

Papa leaned back against the arm of the couch and fixed her with a look she had seen before, the one he reserved for fatherly lectures or difficult truths. One of his eyebrows lifted, rather imperiously. "All we hope for is your happiness. The way you seem to anticipate this courtship leading nowhere has concerned me that you aren't happy at all. Or you anticipate having your heart broken."

"My heart is safe enough," she murmured, looking down at the knot and wondering if she ought to tug it loose again.

"Is it, Cara?" He covered her hands with one of his, bringing her gaze up again. He stared into her eyes, a weight in his gaze that pressed on her already overburdened mind and heart. "We have always told you that you needn't marry unless you wished, and that you ought to marry where there is love and respect. Courtship is a path to marriage. I thought you didn't wish to find a husband yet?"

"I didn't think I did," she said. "I'm so young, Papa. And there is still so much I want to see and do."

"Would Edward Everly support your dreams or would he prevent you from achieving them?" he asked, all teasing gone. This was the question that mattered most to him, it would seem. And he had come to it rather pointedly.

She took in a shuddering breath. "I do not know," she said at last. "Because he is a man who puts everyone else's expectations before his own. The things that he wants most, he will not do. He doesn't want to risk upsetting his parents by going against their wishes and hopes for him."

"I have heard that can be difficult. Though I never cared a fig for what my parents wanted me to do." He sat back again and crossed his arms, turning his stare to the hearth. "But not everyone can run off and marry a beautiful heiress with a cherry orchard."

That brought a smile to Caroline's face. She ran her fingertip over the little green frog in one corner, its long legs stretched as it hopped upward. "Why do you still have this? It must have been five years since I gave you this one."

"I've never used it, so it is as good as new."

"What?" She looked up at him with wide eyes. "Papa, handkerchiefs are *meant* to be used."

"I carry it about from time to time," he said with a shrug. "But the linen is too fine to mop my brow while I am in the fields or orchards. Besides. I like the reminder of you." He took it gently from her. "But see here, that doesn't mean you can go about tying it up in knots." His large fingers pried the cloth loose before he folded it carefully and returned it to his pocket. "No more tears, Cara. Show me what you have busied yourself with this summer. I am under strict orders from your mama to tell her *everything*. I may need to take notes."

She rose and held her hand out to him. "We have plenty of paper, if you need it."

He took her hand and followed her through the house while she told him of her summer. The parties, picnics, painting, and days spent on the beach. He listened, occasionally interjecting when he recognized the name of a family.

Before they entered the conservatory, Caroline asked, "Did Lady Inglewood know you were coming?"

"Indeed. I asked her to keep it a secret." He grinned at her. "She was happy to oblige."

They stepped inside, and Caroline took him to the canvases that were hers. Fields of flowers, a boat incongruently in the middle of a clearing of trees, and the earl's yacht with it's white sails against the blue backdrop of sky and sea.

"But this is the most important piece," she said, moving to the last canvas. The largest. Covered with a sheet to protect it from dust and prying eyes both. She hesitated a moment, hand gripped to pull the protective covering away. Caroline looked at Neil. "You cannot be upset. I am given to believe some fathers would rather their daughters never paint a man they are not related to."

"Since when have I ever been *some fathers?*" he asked with that raised brow. "You warned us in a letter that your Atlas is 'barely clothed.' Your mother laughed for days about whatever she imagined she saw on my face. I assure you, though not an artist myself, I completely understand the need for recreating the human form." He spoke with the accent of a well-educated lord, sounding snobbish enough that she could imagine the sort of person he had been when he'd been more *lord* than farmer.

"Very well." Caroline gathered the cloth up in both hands, then gently pulled it from the easel and the canvas, revealing a portrait three feet tall and twenty-two inches wide. A background of black with faint pinpricks of light, distant stars, made the foreground image stand out in brightness and complexity.

Caroline held her breath as her papa studied the portrait, watching him rather than looking at the image she knew well enough to sketch it with her eyes closed.

At last Neil spoke, his voice soft and tone almost reverent. "Caroline. This is magnificent." He turned to look at her, and she saw tears and wonderment in his eyes. "You did this?"

He had only ever seen her portraits of the people she loved and had known since childhood. Her landscapes of sheep and sea. Studies of flowers and baskets of puppies and kittens. Nothing like this. Caroline had never attempted anything like this.

"It has exhausted me," she admitted to him. "I have never worked this hard on anything, Papa." And she didn't know if it was good enough. Wouldn't know, until someone with authority told her so. Nor did she think she could ever make something so full of human emotion again.

"You are a marvel, Caroline Clapham." He put his arm around her shoulder and turned her, so they both looked at the painting. "I have never seen anything so captivating." They stood in silence a long while, with Caroline looking for every fault and weakness in the work she could find. With her papa's arms around her, she didn't find them as easily as she usually did.

"It isn't finished," she whispered at last. "There are details still to add to the globe. To his cape."

Neil kissed her forehead. "I only wish I had a place worthy to hang it, where everyone could see what you are capable of, and what you have already done."

The words soothed her heart, and Caroline looked up at her father. "I'm so afraid that Sir Thomas will not like it, Papa."

"And if he doesn't?" The imperious eyebrow rose again. "He is one man. An important one in his field, but still just a man. And this piece would impress most, I think."

"Especially since it's done by a woman."

"Bah. There will come a day when women artists are as well known as men. When it won't matter who did the work, only that the work speaks for itself." He squeezed her shoulder. "It will be people like you who make it so."

"What if I marry and my husband doesn't want me to paint? Or if children come and take all the time and energy I have? What if—"

"Lady Inglewood manages. She has a painting hanging at Kensington Palace."

"A countess has more resources than I do," Caroline pointed out.

Neil huffed and looked around the room at the evidence of that statement. "So she does." He narrowed his eyes at her. "As to the husband trouble, we will hope you choose wisely. There will be someone who loves you and wants you to succeed, my dear. And if that is not Mr. Everly—" How had they got around to talking about Edward again? "—I hope you will put an end to that courtship. Love is important. So are dreams." Neil picked up the cloth from the chair where she'd draped it and put it over the canvas again. "Do you love him?"

Did she love Edward? And if she did, when had she stopped pretending? Caroline didn't give an answer, and her father didn't press her for one. "He is coming this afternoon. Would you like him to stay for dinner?" she asked.

Her papa's smile turned into something dangerous, and a gleam came into his eye that Caroline wasn't certain she liked. "Yes. If our hosts do not mind. I would like nothing better."

Hopefully, Edward would feel the same.

# CHAPTER 22

The knowing gleam in Neil Duncan's eyes as he received Edward's introduction from Caroline did nothing, absolutely nothing, to calm Edward's nerves. He'd meant it when he told his father he would speak to Mr. and Mrs. Duncan. But he'd thought he'd have time to tell Caroline the truth, and to find out if she held him in any kind of affection, before that moment came.

Being in the midst of a pretend courtship while meeting a woman's father made an already complicated introduction that much worse.

Though Edward had known Caroline adored her stepfather, seeing the way she looked at him, with such trust and love, caused his heart to ache. He didn't have that sort of feeling toward his own father, a man who had always been in his life, related to him by blood.

They weren't working on any paintings today. Caroline didn't hand Edward a sketchbook to amuse himself or a volume of myths to read aloud to her as she worked. There would be no spontaneous carriage rides or walks along the shore. Instead, the three of them walked through the rain-dampened gardens. Caroline on her father's arm and Edward at her other side, with both hands tucked behind his back.

"I am only here for a day," Mr. Duncan said. He'd insisted on that form of address rather than Lord Neil. Edward couldn't work out if that was a good sign or a bad one. "Then I will go back to our home, gather up the rest of the family, and return here in time to meet Sir Thomas."

"You needn't go to all that trouble, Papa," Caroline assured him, though her gaze fell to the path. Edward knew it would mean the world to her, to have her family there at the culmination of her summer's work. "I will come home after Sir Thomas's visit and can tell you everything then."

"We wouldn't miss this, Cara. Your mother and I want to share the triumph with you." He raised his gaze to Edward. "You will be in attendance for the presentation, will you not, Mr. Everly?"

"Yes, sir. Of course." Nothing would keep him away. "Your daughter has my complete support." That sounded not the least romantic. But did a father wish to hear a suitor wax poetic about his daughter? "I look forward to meeting Mrs. Duncan and the children, too. Miss Clapham has spoken of your family often and in the warmest terms."

Caroline gave him an odd look.

"I am glad to hear it. I rarely say a word about my family." Mr. Duncan smirked. "And I have no intention of seeing them during either of these visits. They have never been what you would call supportive, I suppose. They are rather miserable to be around, in all truthfulness. I have done all in my power, as has my wife, to ensure our children never have reason to feel that way about us. What of your family, Mr. Everly?"

The abrupt question caught Edward slightly off guard. "My family, sir? I think you know most of them."

"Your elder sisters were in the same circles at times, but no. I do not truly know any of them. Though as I reminded Caroline, I can thank Hope and Grace Everly for a broken arm that, even mended, has given me the ability to anticipate a coming storm."

Edward wasn't sure if he should smile or not at that. "I have heard that story, sir. It is something of a family legend these days."

"Indeed?" Mr. Duncan's tone was amused even if Edward couldn't read the man's expression. At least Caroline seemed at ease. "Aside from your now married sisters, how does your family get on? Do you enjoy their company? Do they enjoy Caroline's?"

"I am quite fond of all of them," Caroline said with a bright smile. "Mrs. Everly and her daughters, married or not, have made a sincere effort to come to know me."

Mr. Duncan nodded to his daughter but kept his questioning gaze on Edward. Waiting for his answer to the question. Was this some sort of interview? Or a test?

"We make an effort to enjoy one another's company," he said at last, wincing at the uncertainty in his tone. He wanted to give the answer that would make Mr. Duncan stop watching him with that strange, penetrating stare. "We are not so close as some, but no one doubts they are cared for in all the ways that matter."

They had come to the fountain with its thick walls of hedges and elegantly curved benches. Caroline sat and her father gestured for Edward to join her. "Do sit, Mr. Everly. I have been in a carriage for hours and would prefer to walk about while we converse."

From there, Caroline took over the conversation. She spoke with animation and a brightness that often made Edward want to keep her talking just to watch her expression. She gestured with her hands as she spoke, the movements graceful.

"If Sir Thomas will write a recommendation for me," she said, "I could easily make a name for myself as a tutor, or use it to gain instruction or meetings with other artists. Any introduction into the world, even as a novice, would present numerous possibilities."

"Ah, and that will be when the difficulties begin," Mr. Duncan said with a crooked smile. His daughter narrowed her eyes at him.

"That seems a silly thing to say."

He exchanged a glance with Edward heavy with significance. "My daughter is often brought to a standstill when she is presented with two or more options that are equally good. Give her a good and bad, no difficulty. Two terrible things to choose from? She takes one and meets the challenge head on. But two very good things? She cannot ever decide between them."

Caroline protested. "That isn't always true."

"Nine times out of ten," her father countered. "The best thing to help her along in decisions of that sort, Mr. Everly, is to make one option ever-so-slightly sweeter to her. Something I suppose you will need to learn before long." Then the gentleman gave Edward another probing look. "Which do you think best for Cara? To become a teacher or to search out masters to increase her own knowledge?"

Everything was a test.

"Caroline will know the best course when the time comes," Edward hedged, uncertain if that was correct. "I am certain she will make up her mind without any help from me."

A frown met that response. "And what will become of your courtship?" Mr. Duncan asked.

"Papa," Caroline protested. "We haven't spoken of such things. There isn't any need yet."

The man's gaze softened when directed at her. "No matter what Sir Thomas has to say about your talent, Caroline, you will have important decisions to make. Whether you will travel, find work, or return home must be decided. And if the two of you are serious about your courtship, these are things you must at least discuss. Should you decide to spend your lives together—which I am not saying you must declare any time soon—that will change everything."

Edward's hand found Caroline's between them on the bench. He covered it with his own and she looked at him with some surprise. He stared into her eyes and smiled, and when she returned the expression the tilt of her lips wobbled uncertainly.

He needed to speak with her. Soon. And tell her everything. Because Mr. Duncan was right. If Edward wanted to be a permanent part of Caroline's life, there were a lot of decisions to make.

"I LIKE HIM," Papa said in a whisper to Caroline as they sat in the library after dinner. Edward had sent home for appropriate clothing to attend the meal when he was invited, and they'd spent the late afternoon hours playing cards and talking of orchards. Sir Isaac and Lady Fox had come, too, and the baronetess had spent part of the evening sharing stories of the first time she had met Lord Neil as a guest in his family home.

Edward stood examining a shelf across the room from where Caroline and her father sat. He frowned at the book spines, and Caroline wondered if he fought the urge to rearrange them as they had the night of her welcome party.

"I do, too," she whispered back. "Very much."

"Have you told him so?"

Caroline felt her cheeks warm as she shook her head. "Only that he is a dear friend. That I enjoy his company."

For the first time in ages, her father's eyes darkened with disappointment. "You need to tell him how you feel, Cara. Holding back those words, those feelings, can cause harm."

"I am not certain of his feelings yet," she protested.

"And if he refrains from telling you for the same reason?" he asked, arching one eyebrow at her.

Caroline lowered her gaze. She didn't have an answer for that. "I didn't come here to fall in love."

Her papa bent to catch her eye. "Love involves vulnerability and taking chances, even if there is a possibility of uncertainty or rejection. You must be as courageous in your feelings as you are in your art. Growth comes from uncomfortable moments and truths. If I hadn't dared to tell your mother how I felt, even though I had nothing to give her but my heart, we wouldn't be sitting together this evening."

Sir Isaac and Lord Inglewood had been talking in low tones, and the baronet finally raised his voice. "Duncan, I have been challenged to a duel. Will you be my second?"

"Duel?" A lazy smile stretched over her papa's face, and Caroline caught another glimpse of the past as he swung his stare toward them. "What sort of duel?"

"A duel of billiards. Inglewood thinks he can best me at the table. Care to come see to it the rules are followed?"

"I am not known for caring overmuch about rules. But why not?" Papa rose and winked at Caroline. Then said, "What about you, Everly? Do you enjoy billiards?"

"I do," Edward said, his expression pleasant but somehow not as open as Caroline was used to seeing. "But the hour is late, and I must rise early in the morning at my father's request. We are taking my cousin shooting. Again."

"A shame. But familial duty must be done." Papa went to him and held his hand out. After a moment's hesitation, Edward clasped it in his own. "It was a pleasure to meet you, Mr. Everly. I look forward to introducing you to my wife and my other children in a week's time."

"Thank you, Mr. Duncan."

"Caroline? Why don't you escort Mr. Everly to the door. The two of you can finally speak to one another without your father listening to every word."

Lady Fox and Lady Inglewood both gasped, the baronetess protested on Caroline's behalf. "You must stop teasing the young people, Neil."

"Not at all sporting of you," Lady Inglewood agreed with a grin. "Run along and play billiards with your friends and leave the poor children alone."

He held up both hands as though to ward off their words, then left via the doorway the other gentlemen had already disappeared through.

Edward's ears had turned red, and Caroline knew her own cheeks were a shade to match. But she gamely joined him at the bookcase and took his arm. "We may as well make our escape now, before he comes back." She needed to talk to him, of course, but hadn't wished to make such a scene of it. His smile didn't reach his eyes as he allowed her to lead them from the room. Once in the corridor with its softly burning wall sconces, Caroline slowed her steps. He matched her pace, but kept his gaze trained ahead of them both.

"You have been so quiet," she said at last. "All afternoon. Is something troubling you?"

He heaved a sigh and lifted his shoulders in a shrug. "I didn't expect to meet your father so soon. He asked a great many questions, too."

"He likes you."

"Does he?" Edward's smile lasted less than a second. "I wonder how swiftly that would change if he knew the truth. I cannot imagine he would be happy to know I have used his daughter's kindness for my own benefit."

The words were brittle and strangely sharp when they touched Caroline's heart. She stopped their progress altogether and released her hold on Edward's arm. "That isn't what you have done. Not at all, Edward. You cannot see it that way still, after all these weeks we have spent together. We have helped each other, as friends do."

He winced, though she could not guess why. "This hasn't been easy for you, though. Lying to them in your letters, and now face to face. And your mother comes next week."

Caroline shook her head. "I don't understand you, Edward. Do you wish me to tell them the truth? To end our relationship?" She wanted to take him by the shoulders and make him look at her, but refrained. "What will that do to Mariah?"

"I find I do not care as much as I did before," he said, and Caroline gaped at him. What had happened to Edward? Why had he grown so solemn, so horribly glum? Right as she was feeling more content with the world, comforted by her father's visit and reassurances.

"Edward, how can you say that? Mariah is your friend."

"Mariah should have told her parents the truth from the beginning and spared me making a ridiculous promise to her." If he had spoken with heat or anger, Caroline might have understood. But he seemed so lost and his voice was too quiet.

She needed to bring him out of whatever fog had overcome his mind. "You are not one to speak of such things, given your refusal to tell your father the truth."

That brought his gaze to hers at last, and she caught a flicker of something in his eye. "What do you mean?"

"Your dreams are withering here, Edward," she said, taking one of his hands in both of hers. "As I have come to know you, the closer we have become, the more I have seen the desperation in your heart and mind. You aren't happy. You refuse to speak of what you want, to stand up for yourself, and it is eating away at you. Why won't you tell him you want to travel? That you have places you wish to see and things you want to do with your life before you take on management of the estate?"

The spark flared brighter, and too late Caroline realized it was anger. He drew his hand back. "You don't understand. I cannot tell him anything about it. I barely managed my trip to Rome, and he still brings that up time and time again, calling it a waste and me a fool for thinking such a journey was necessary. It didn't matter that those were the best weeks of my life. Asking to leave again, to go anywhere, would drive a wedge between us as it did between my father and his, between my uncle and my father. I would be admitting that he failed to make me a man of reason and responsibility."

Caroline let his words flow over her, listening and struggling to understand. "You aren't like them at all. Your father must see that. You are honorable and kind, certainly responsible. If you would talk to him, tell him—"

"I cannot, Caroline. I will not." He shook his head slowly and took one of her hands, then started walking again toward the stairs. "And we needn't discuss it."

"We do," she insisted, pulling her hand from his grasp. Fear caught her around the heart. Papa had been right. She needed to tell Edward how she felt. She had to take the risk. If she didn't, he might not think her worth taking a risk of his own. Edward deserved so much more than what his father wanted for him. "Edward." She put her hand to his cheek and his eyes widened, one hand came up to cover hers. "I cannot watch someone I care about so deeply lose what they most desire."

"Caroline, I—".

She stood on her toes and pressed a kiss to his lips. It was gentle. Over in an instant. Not at all like what they shared in the attic, and yet it marked a moment she would never forget. "If you will not fight for yourself, how will you fight for me?" She stepped back, her heart racing. "I love you, Edward. Please. Don't ask me to give up my dreams *and* yours."

Turning away and racing down the corridor to disappear into another room, out of his sight and before he could say a word, would be cowardly. Though perhaps wiser than standing there in a dimly lit corridor waiting for him to respond. She had laid her heart at his feet. Her future, too.

"I am tired of pretending," she whispered when he said nothing, staring at her as though he didn't believe his eyes or his ears. "Aren't you?"

Edward gathered her in his arms, still staring at her with that somewhat dazed expression. "I haven't been pretending for a long time now. Since before the attic."

Relief encircled her heart and flowed through her, and for one glorious moment everything took on a softer aspect, a glow that she wished she knew how to add to canvas, the better to save that instant of happiness for the rest of her life. She tipped her chin up, smiling, ready for another kiss and hoping for many to follow.

But Edward wasn't smiling. Even though he was there, holding her, he didn't seem happy. Why? What had she done wrong?

"Cara." He rested his forehead against hers and closed his eyes. "You deserve so much more than I can give you. You need to see Paris and Rome, Florence, Amsterdam, Vienna. I want to be the one to take you. To promise you everything. And I can't." His voice broke on the last word.

She stepped out of his arms, her heart threatening to crack. Caroline took in a deep breath. She needn't make demands of him. That wasn't love. Her papa and her mama showed her, every day since their union, what love was.

"Think it through, Edward," she said at last, holding herself together and forcing her lips to turn upward in a smile.

"I thought I could make this real," he said, voice soft. "But the way your father spoke of your hopes today as things already bright in your future, things you have spent your whole life preparing for, changes everything. Your dreams are part of you, Cara. I cannot give you those things."

"Of course not," she answered, wrapping her arms around herself. How could she make him understand? "My dreams hang upon my talent and my willingness to work for them. I only want one thing from you, Edward."

He stared at her, his deep blue eyes full of sorrow. "If it is in my power, it is yours, Caroline."

"You, Edward. Just yourself. And we will make everything else work as best we can." She stepped away. They could get nowhere else tonight. Her emotions were too taut, her heart disappointed. She had been brave and declared herself. And he hadn't been able to do the same. Not really.

Some risks were not immediately rewarded.

Summer wasn't over yet.

They were at the top of the staircase.

"Good night, Edward." She took a step back. "I will see you tomorrow. At our usual time." He didn't move, so she gave him one last smile before stepping around him to retrace her steps to the sitting room. She looked back only once, before she opened the door, and he was already gone.

# CHAPTER 23

S leep evaded Edward.
*"Aren't you tired of pretending?"*
Caroline's voice echoed through his mind and haunted every heartbeat. Yes. He was exhausted. Not of her, not of pretending at their relationship. Tired of pretending the life his father had chosen for him was what he wanted. Yes, as the only son of an entailed estate, he would have to run it someday. He would have to live at the Refuge, tend to its business, see to the tenants, the farms, the orchards.

The time would come when his father would need Edward's help. And on that day, Edward would face his responsibilities with the knowledge and training he'd received since childhood.

Until then, he'd planned to remain with his family. Develop a routine. Petition his father to make changes. Perhaps convince the stubborn man to give some of the daily responsibilities to Edward.

A dull, gray existence stretched before him. He loved Caroline. He'd thought that would be enough. That he could court her and convince her to love him, too. Then he would wed her and fill his home with paints, brushes, canvases, and all the things she needed to be content. He would do as the earl had for the countess. He would take her to London, to galleries and museums. And that would be enough.

*"Don't ask me to give up my dreams and yours."*

She'd known what he would ask. Perhaps she'd even be willing to sacrifice some of her own expectations and hopes, but she wouldn't give up on both of them. It made him love her all the more.

She didn't belong in the gray with him. Caroline needed light, life, and all the most vibrant hues in the rainbow. She needed dazzling purple sunsets in Spain, crystal blue waters of the Mediterranean, the silver frosts of Switzerland.

She deserved a golden horizon. He wanted to be the man standing beside her as she stepped into her dreams, traveling and painting, learning, exhibiting her art, meeting and conversing with others who saw the world through the prism of color and light as she did. He wanted to sit beside her on beaches while she sketched children playing in the sand, or stand with her in the *Musée Royal du Louvre* as she gazed on works of art the likes of which he'd only read of in history books. He wanted to give her the world. And all she had asked him to give her was...him. Edward.

*"If you will not fight for yourself, how will you fight for me?"*

He gritted his teeth and rose from his bed, going to the window and throwing it open to breathe deeply of the cool night air.

A potent combination of frustration, resentment, and a burning desire for authenticity churned within him. The years of repressing his own dreams and desires had taken their toll, and a profound weariness had kept him quiet and compliant. Yet, within the depths of his soul, a flicker of defiance had kept his hopes alive, an ember of self-determination that refused to be extinguished.

Loving Caroline had breathed life into his dormant aspirations, reigniting the dormant flame of his true self. In her presence, he found solace and inspiration, and felt more himself than he had been in years. Watching her work, her dedication to achieving her heart's desire, made him wish he possessed the courage to confront his own inner battles.

She saw him for who he truly was, beyond the expectations and judgments of his father and society. With her by his side, did he have the ability to break free from the shackles of conformity and pursue his own dreams, unapologetically and authentically?

With each passing moment, the realization grew stronger within Edward that he could no longer deny his own desires and sacrifice his happiness to uphold an ideal that wasn't his own. Caroline deserved more.

He looked up at the stars and whispered, "I deserve to be happy on my own terms, even if it means risking my family's disappointment and disapproval. I can't keep sacrificing my own happiness for my father's demands."

He would have to confront his father.

What was the worst that could happen? His father wouldn't disinherit him, though he could refuse to give Edward access to the family coffers. Did that matter? How much did Edward need to travel with Caroline? They could make do, so long as she had the ability to purchase art supplies.

The stars glimmered, fading away into the gray of dawn. Had he been awake all night? His turmoil had lasted an eternity, yet time moved far too quickly. He had a plan to make. Did he have the time he needed to accomplish it?

Giving his heart and Caroline's permission to wander the world wouldn't mean they were forever rootless. He knew that. A day would come when they would want to settle, to call a place home again. When that day came, the Refuge would be waiting.

When they went to Spain, he would stay with his sister and the ambassador. He had friends in other places who would open their homes to him, he felt certain. Knowing that one day he could repay such favors. If he went through his belongings, the things that were his and his alone, selling everything, he could keep them well enough for a year.

If Caroline sold paintings, as he knew she would when others saw her inspired work, that would help with their travels, too. If she would have him still. If she thought they could live such a life together. He wouldn't demand such a thing of her. He would put his plan together, estimate expenses and the worth of his belongings, and present her with all the facts.

Then, if she realized she needed more than Edward could give, he would let her go. Even if it shattered what was left of his weary heart. Then he would take those steps into the world without her, proud to have had her in his life for one glorious summer.

The sun crept into view, a soft yellow and gold, bringing light and life back to the countryside. The birds were singing and had been for an hour. The trees in the distant orchard stirred with the morning breeze coming in from the sea. A world that looked like the old but felt entirely new stretched before him.

Caroline had said she loved him. And Edward, with his plans laid out before him, would be able to tell her the same.

There wasn't time to waste.

As Edward sat down at the desk in his room to meticulously map out his future, a wry smile tugged at the corners of his lips. The image of his former impulsive self, the one who had always embraced spontaneity and leapt into the unknown without a second thought, now planning every detail of his life, brought a touch of irony to his heart. He couldn't help but chuckle at what those who knew him best would think.

He used a pencil, the better to write quickly without the need to worry over ink smudges. He used a sketchbook Caroline had sent home with him, filling the margins around his weak attempt recreating the sketch of a mouse she had handed him. He'd added the elephant ears with the hope it would make her laugh.

He adored her laughter.

The realization that he was embracing a more measured and calculated approach to his future, all for the sake of building a life with Caroline, filled him with both awe and amusement.

He barely registered when his valet came into the room and paused, likely shocked to see Edward not only out of bed but bent over a book and writing as though possessed by a frenzied muse.

After a time, Peters cleared his throat. "I have your clothing ready, sir."

"Excellent. Thank you." Edward dropped the pencil in the book and closed it, tying it shut with a ribbon. "I will need my hat and gloves, too. And my horse brought around. I need to go into Alderton straight away."

"Yes, Mr. Edward."

He would consult with the town's only lawyer on the best method of selling his belongings. Perhaps the man would even give him an estimate of the prices Edward could expect to fetch for the sale of his horse, his stickpins, and the odds and ends he wouldn't need to take with him on his journey. He would be thorough.

Caroline deserved the best he could provide her. She had declared that all she desired was Edward. Very well. He meant to offer her the best version of himself, even if that meant working at becoming that man every day for the rest of his life. Because she deserved nothing less than the very best in all aspects of life.

All his dreams included her now. And he dared hope she felt the same about him.

# CHAPTER 24

E dward left the lawyer's office with his head swimming in numbers and his sketchbook filled with calculations. There was more work to do than he had thought possible, but if he bent his mind to the task he would have everything ready in the time it took to read the banns.

If Caroline would have him.

He hated thinking there could be an if. Hated that he had left her when he'd given in to a moment of weakness and doubt. Caroline deserved so much more.

"Edward Everly? Is that you?" a familiar voice called.

He turned just short of where he'd left his horse to see Mariah Kimball standing in front of the apothecary, arm-in-arm with a man Edward had grown up with. The apothecary's son, who had gone away for two years to learn the work of a physician. Lucas Jones.

"Mr. Jones," he said, bowing slightly. "I hadn't heard you were home. Have you completed your studies? Is it Doctor Jones yet?"

The other man shook his head, his smile tempered with weariness. "Not yet. I have another two years, at least, before they will declare me fit to practice. I am home for a few weeks only, at Miss Kimball's request, in fact." He looked down at Mariah with a somewhat accusatory raise of his eyebrows. "And, I am told, had I not come speedily, she would have allowed herself to be married off to you, Everly."

Edward stiffened and readied himself to protest, when everything about what he saw before him suddenly made sense. He nearly swore aloud in his shock, but Mariah's far-too-innocent expression kept him somewhat reasonable. "Mariah. You're in love with Lucas Jones?"

"Don't sound too shocked, Everly," Jones protested. "She could do worse. She could have thrown her lot in with you."

Mariah's smile was brighter than Edward had seen it in a long time. "Stop, both of you. I cannot bear to be teased. We still have to tell my parents. Lucas only arrived last night, and I am whisking him away this instant."

"Why would your parents object to a physician as a husband?" Edward asked, shaking his head as he looked from her to Jones. "I had started to think she'd given her heart to a fishmonger."

Jones's brow furrowed. "Thankfully not. Did she really make it sound that terrible?"

"No. Edward is exaggerating." Mariah glared first at Edward then up at the man she had apparently fallen in love with. "And you held yourself in such low opinion, you may as well have been a fishmonger."

"I still don't understand." Edward tucked his book away. "But then, I haven't had much sleep. Perhaps you are both making perfect sense."

"I doubt it," Lucas Jones muttered, then sighed. "Mariah's had my heart since we were children. I didn't think I had a chance with her, though. Not unless I made something of myself. An apothecary may be a respectable tradesman, but her parents wouldn't allow her to marry beneath her. And I didn't think she'd pay me any attention, either."

"He told me before he left for Scotland the first time," Mariah added, her expression growing somber. "I had six months to think about it, to be angry with him, before I saw him again."

"You called me a presumptuous lout," he reminded her, looking down at her with an adoration Edward immediately understood. He felt almost certain he'd looked at Caroline like that before. "You forbid me to become a doctor if I was only doing it for you."

"He was home for two months," Mariah said, tearing her gaze away from Jones to smile at Edward. "Do you remember? Likely not. But I made every excuse I could think of to visit the apothecary. I was so frustrated at first. I kept asking if he'd made up his mind about things yet. Do you know what he said?"

Edward slowly shook his head, hardly believing the story unraveling in front of him. "I cannot even make a guess."

"He said he'd only made his mind up about loving me, and everything else would work out one way or another." Mariah's whole aspect brightened. "I was quite in love before he left again. And now he's returned, and he's stopped saying nonsense about not being good enough for me. My parents are in a terrible state at the moment, thinking I will never marry."

"Mariah thinks they will be desperate enough to accept me as a son-in-law, even though I haven't finished my studies."

The love in Mariah's expression was unmistakable. "But you will." She beamed at Edward. "He's very good at his work. And Alderton needs a physician."

"It does, indeed." Edward studied the two of them. Lucas Jones was tall and trim, with dark hair and freckles. They'd played together as children, and he'd been one of the boys who had tried to convince Edward *not* to climb the tree behind the inn. And the one who'd run off to find help. "Congratulations to you both. I hope everything goes well when you speak to the Kimballs."

"As do I," Jones muttered with a grimace.

"Hush. Everything will be perfect." Mariah gave Edward a final smile. "Isn't this wonderful? Now you and Caroline can stop pretending. If you wish to, that is." She batted her eyelashes at him, and the gleam returned to her eyes. "Of course, after what I have seen these last weeks, perhaps you will continue the ruse a little longer."

As the only other person aware of their act, Mariah would be the only person who saw through it. Edward wouldn't give her the satisfaction of admitting to the truth of things. Not yet. He had too much to accomplish. Including telling Caroline this news.

"It was good to see you, Jones. Miss Kimball." Edward bowed to them once more. "I will not detain you from your purpose, and I have an errand of my own to see to. Good day to you both."

They said their goodbyes, and Edward mounted his horse with one destination in mind. He needed to see Caroline. And he didn't want to wait the hours between that moment and their usual meeting time. He wanted to see his sprite at once and reassure her of his feelings. Some things simply couldn't wait.

BIRCH TREES WERE NOT MEANT for climbing. They were tall and stately trees, with slim branches that might make for decent handholds. But they were not comfortable to climb for long, and not a single branch was thick or sturdy enough for one to sit upon.

It was a shame, really. After the night and morning Caroline had been through, she wanted very much to climb into a tree and hide from all the world. As she had when she was a little girl. Instead, after bidding her father farewell after breakfast, she contented herself with being among the trees rather than in them.

She sat in a boat, on a narrow bench seat, in the middle of a clearing in the earl's birch wood. She'd cast off her bonnet and gloves, leaving them piled atop her parasol and sketchbook. She simply sat there, with her face turned upward to catch the warmth of the afternoon sun.

All was quiet, except for the sounds of birds and squirrels, and the leaves rustling with the wind. She settled in the clearing looking for escape and solitude, yet the longer she sat, the lonelier she grew.

Until a crashing in the woods drew her out of her thoughts.

Her heart sped faster, and she looked in the direction of snapping twigs and crackling leaves. A smile of anticipation escaped her, and she bit her lip to keep from calling out. And then, Edward appeared.

"There you are," he said, a grin splitting across his face. Immediate relief flooded her. She hadn't been certain what to expect when she saw him again. More morose frowns and melancholy, perhaps. Or he wouldn't come to Inglewood at all, she had supposed. "I thought we were to meet at the usual time and place," he said, "which would be two hours from now at the castle. How did you know I would be here?"

"I might ask you the same." Perhaps she could call it coincidence, or a gift from Providence. "Have you still not learned how to walk quietly through the woods?"

"Haven't the patience for it," he said, coming across the grass to the boat. "Permission to board?"

"Permission granted." She didn't move, and he took the wooden plank seat across from her, their knees nearly touching.

Edward held a book in his hand. A sketchbook she had given him weeks before, telling him to occupy himself with drawing while she worked on her paintings or her own sketches. He opened it and took out a pencil. "Though I know sprites prefer the woods to stone castles, I didn't know you would be here."

"I didn't, either. I meant to walk to the beach. But the trees seemed more welcoming today." She noted words on his page surrounding his dragon-teacup. "What are you doing?"

He tilted his book up slightly, concealing it from her. "Never you mind, Mistress Sprite. I am hard at work, and that is all you need know. Oh. And that I love you, too. But I think you suspected as much." He said the words softly, a note of teasing in his voice, but the earnest warmth in his eyes bore witness to the truth of them.

Caroline stared at him, lips parted in surprise. This was not at all what she expected after their emotional parting the previous evening. What had happened to transform him from a burdened, defeated man into this? And in a single night!

"Edward." She couldn't get out another word. Only his name. And in a most accusatory tone, too.

His expression softened. "I will tell you everything soon. I promise. But I thought it best that we be clear on that account before a minute more passes. I love you. With everything I am or will ever be." He came off his seat enough to place a kiss on her forehead, sealing a promise and his words, then he sat down and went back to his book. "I spoke with Mariah this morning."

Caroline's curiosity shifted immediately, as his tone seemed somewhat strange. "Already? You have been busy this morning. Did she have anything of interest to say?"

"Yes." He glanced up at her, his blue eyes bright with laughter. "She is taking her suitor to see her parents. They might be standing in her father's study at this very moment, proclaiming their love."

Caroline's gasp startled a squirrel above them, and it darted away with several angry chirping sounds. "Who is he?" she asked at last.

"His name is Lucas Jones. He's the apothecary's son."

"The one in Scotland?" When Edward raised his eyebrows at her, Caroline explained, "I visit the apothecary quite regularly. He carried some of the ingredients we need to enrich our pigments. He told me all about his son at Edinburgh, learning how to be a physician. That is extraordinary." Then she shook her head at him. "Why would Mariah think her parents would disapprove of him?"

Edward explained what the two of them had shared with him, along with his own suppositions. Some class distinctions were difficult to cross, and though the Kimballs weren't excessively proud, they had married several daughters off to men of fortune and property. Mariah Kimball had done as she thought best, and perhaps their ruse had helped her after all. And it was a very good thing they had already admitted to each other that they had already stopped pretending.

Caroline was still turning over the love story in her mind when Edward spoke softly from his side of the boat.

"What will you work on today, sprite?" He'd opened his book

and was writing in it, not quite looking at her. She studied his bent head and then the book tilted carefully on his knees, its pages hidden from her sight.

Impatience and curiosity pinched at her, but she dismissed them with a contended sigh. "I finished Atlas last night. When I could not sleep."

He raised his gaze to hers. "If I was the cause of any anxiety, Cara, I apologize. I did not leave in the best frame of mind."

She smiled back at him. "You seem much better now." She picked up her sketchbook from where it rested on the ground. "You will tell me why later, will you not?"

"Indeed." He winked at her. "Just as I will be certain to kiss you as you deserve to be kissed. Later."

Her heart skipped and warmth simultaneously pooled in her belly and burst into her cheeks. "I can hardly wait," she said, breathless. He chuckled and went back to his work. It seemed the kissing would come *much* later. What had happened to her spontaneous Edward? The mystery would wait, she supposed. Along with the kissing.

Patience quite suddenly seemed like a most overrated and unnecessary virtue.

# CHAPTER 25

Caroline fussed with her hair in front of the mirror one last time, and her mother stood beside her with an amused smile crinkling the corner of her eyes. Papa, Mama, Amelia, Alfred, and Victor had come in a coach that morning. Tomorrow, Sir Thomas would arrive in the afternoon. And tonight, they dined with the Everly family.

"You look charming, my dear." Mama put her hand on Caroline's shoulder and turned her gently away from the mirror. "Edward certainly already thinks the world of you. It was good of him to be here when we arrived, and he was so thoughtful with the children."

He had gifted the boys with tin soldiers from his childhood collection, for their exclusive use while they visited Inglewood. Then he'd treated Amelia as though she were a lady of sixteen instead of six, winning her over by inviting her to take tea with his mother and sisters in two days' time. But the moment he had taken with Mama, bowing as though she were a lady of high rank rather than a gentlewoman farmer, had been lovely. His every word had been sincere.

Caroline remembered them well, and always would. *"It is an honor to meet you, Mrs. Duncan. Your daughter has told me of how much she admires and loves you. I hope we come to know each other well, someday. I would consider it a privilege to have you as a friend."*

Then he had taken a walk with her parents while Caroline settled the children into the nursery. When they returned, Papa had seemed impressed. Perhaps Edward had won him by finally acting as his normal self. Whatever had passed between them, her parents hadn't said a thing to Caroline about it.

Would it be terribly foolish for her to sigh in contentment every time she thought of him? The girl who had never dreamed of being swept off her feet had turned into a woman who enjoyed the situation greatly.

Teresa Clapham adjusted the pearl necklace around Caroline's neck, then kissed her daughter's cheek. "I am happy for you. One can tell at a glance how deeply in love you are."

"Surely not," Caroline protested, wrinkling her nose. "I look as I ever did." Yet she saw it, too, when she glanced in the mirror.

"You glow with it, my dear. As though you have been lit from the inside, like a lantern." Mama led the way from the room, and they met Papa in the corridor. Mrs. Everly had sent the invitation for a family dinner, including Caroline, her parents, the Barnes family, and all the Everlys at home. Someday, Caroline would meet the only one of Edward's sisters not present. She couldn't guess when.

Edward had remained secretive about his book and his plans. And just as spare with his kisses. The week had flown by with preparations for house guests, with Edward taking her for rides through the country, meeting his sisters for tea, and even sitting beside her in church. Mrs. Kimball had stopped glaring at them both, too, and Mariah's smile had turned brighter.

Despite the anxiety of Sir Thomas's visit, Caroline had never been so happy.

They arrived at the Everly home at the same time as the vicar and his wife, their gig ahead of the borrowed Inglewood carriage.

Papa and Mr. Barnes exchanged bows and polite greetings, while Mrs. Barnes actually embraced Caroline's mother.

"You must be so proud of Caroline," the vicar's wife said as she took her husband's arm. "I have seen some of her work. She has talent and dedication, and she is such a lovely person to know."

"We are very proud of her," Mama said, her chin tilted up. "Thank you for welcoming her into your home."

"Ladies, we can exchange pleasantries much more comfortably in the house," Papa said with an arched eyebrow. "Barnes. Any words of warning from the vicar before we enter the lion's den?"

Caroline shook her head while Mr. Barnes chuckled and took his wife's arm. "It will not be too terrible. I have managed as an in-law for several years now. Do not fear, Miss Clapham."

"I hadn't thought I had reason to," she replied, following behind the married couples and into the house. They gathered in a sitting room Caroline had visited earlier that week to read with Edward's sisters. The room was pleasant and large, with tall windows framed in ivory curtains and furniture in green and gold.

The Everly family had already gathered, with the exception of their visiting cousin, and all had risen when the guests entered. Once everyone had been introduced to Caroline's mother, the only remaining stranger to the Everly family, they found their places again.

Edward came immediately to Caroline's side and threaded his fingers through hers. Despite their gloves, her fingers immediately tingled from the contact. She lifted her gaze to his and then raised her eyebrows in some surprise. "Are you well, Edward? You look... nervous about something."

"Nervous? Me?" He squeezed her hand. "Likely because I am. Quite nervous, in fact."

He reached into his dinner jacket and withdrew the little sketchbook. He pressed it to his heart, then held it out to her. "This is for you. Inside, I have written all my hopes and dreams, all my plans, and how to make them a reality. Every moment I have not been with you, I have worked at ordering my life. And now, I have an announcement to make. I have just one question for you first."

It didn't matter that there were others in the room. In that instant, nothing existed outside of the two of them and the place they occupied. The universe had contracted around Caroline and Edward, making them the sole occupants of a work of art, perhaps even a masterpiece, as he held her hand and searched her gaze for an answer to the question he was about to ask.

"Yes," she whispered.

His smile quirked upward. "Now who is leaping before they look?"

"One of us obviously must take that role, and it certainly hasn't been you of late. Planning, organizing, and scheming, Edward?" She tipped her head to the side and sighed. "Very well. If you must. Ask."

"Ask what?" a voice said beside them. An annoying sort of voice, too. Claude Everly had arrived and stood less than two feet from them, a smirk on his face. "If he has trod on your foot, perhaps? Does Miss Clapham enjoy it when you loom over her like that, Cousin?"

Before Caroline could worry herself over Edward, he laughed. Actually laughed about Claude's terrible timing. Then he tugged her with him to the center of the room, and the talk around them ceased entirely. Edward didn't pay anyone else attention, though. His focus remained on Caroline, while she blushed and smiled at her parents before returning her gaze to his.

"Will you marry me, Caroline Clapham, and let me come on all of your adventures? May I come with you, as your husband and friend, as you travel and share your talent with the world? May I grow with you, in talent and experience, as we open our hearts and minds to all the beauty that lies beyond our door?"

It was more than she expected. Edward wanted to marry her, and he wanted to give Caroline her dreams. Her eyes filled with tears. She didn't know how he'd managed it. The answers to all those sorts of questions would be in the book pressed against her chest. All that mattered was that he'd found a way for both of them. Whatever came of Sir Thomas's visit, Edward would stand with her, loving and supporting her.

Marrying her.

"Yes, Edward. The answer was always yes."

Papa spoke first, and loudly. "Well done, son."

Edward's grin appeared, and his eyes promised a more apprecia- tive response would come. But not in front of their parents or his sisters. Or his cousin. Who surprised her by adding his congratu- lations.

The only one who remained less than enthused was Mr. Everly. He said the right words, but without any warmth. He appeared confused at first. They went into dinner, and Caroline didn't protest when Edward insisted on changing the order at the table to keep her by his side. He likely would have held her hand throughout had she not needed it to enjoy her dinner.

Nothing had ever tasted so delicious. Would everything be like this, now that Edward had declared himself? All her senses were more awake and alive. And she suddenly realized what he had spoken to her parents about that afternoon.

She turned to look at her father and then her mother, before saying out loud, "You both knew he would ask this evening, didn't you?"

Mama and Papa, on opposite sides of the table, exchanged their knowing smiles. "Of course we did," Mama said with an elegant shrug. "He had to ask for our blessing first, didn't he?"

"Good of him to follow that tradition," Mr. Everly said at the head of the table, tone somewhat of a grumble. Caroline smiled at him, determined not to let him intimidate her. He noticed and tried to smile. "You will be a charming addition to our family, Miss Clapham."

"Indeed." Edward's voice and expression were full of an infec- tious joy Caroline couldn't help but feel, too, the moment she glanced his way. "After our wedding trip. Which will be a lengthy one, since we intend to see all the best works of art in Europe."

Mr. Everly's knife clattered to his plate and the room went quiet. "What did you say?" he asked, more shocked than angry.

Caroline's eyebrows rose with some surprise. Whatever plans Edward had made, he hadn't included his father in them. Considering how long he'd lived trying to win the man's approval, it was extremely brave of him. "Thank you, Edward," she said, her voice ringing through the stillness. "I cannot tell you what such a gift means to me."

Conversation resumed, with Edward's sisters telling them they must visit Spain to meet the rest of the family. Caroline's parents teased her that all the language lessons she had detested as a child were about to be put to good use. And Caroline basked in Edward's love and attention, bestowing her own on him. Before the evening drew to its close, when they sat together after dinner, she asked if Mr. Barnes would marry them after the banns were read. His wife burst into tears as he said yes.

As Edward handed her into the carriage that night, his heart in his eyes, she looked over his shoulder to where his father stood in the doorway. Waiting.

"Never mind him, sprite," Edward whispered, giving her hand a squeeze. "I promise, all is well. Get your rest, as best you can. Sir Thomas will be here tomorrow, and you will want all your wits about you."

Sleep didn't seem possible. Yet all the excitement, the wonder and joy, had done enough to balance the worry and anxiety. Caroline managed to slip into a most contented rest, with dreams of Edward beside her wherever she wandered.

EDWARD FOLLOWED his father into the office, noting Claude's presence with some annoyance. He brushed that aside. Nothing

Claude did or said could possibly upset Edward. Not now. "What is it you have to say to me, Father?" he asked.

"That display before your mother and sisters," Mr. Everly said, glaring at his son. "Before our *guests*. It was disrespectful to all of us to announce your intentions that way. You put me in a difficult position."

He stiffened. "I fail to see that perspective, sir. I announced my intentions to marry and travel with the woman I love. I wouldn't call either of those things disrespectful."

"I am your father, and I knew nothing about it." His father went to his desk and stood behind it. "How did that make me look? My position as head of this family is not to be ignored."

"And what of my position?" Edward asked. "I am your son and heir. I have passed my majority. I have done everything you have ever asked of me, Father. All I ever wanted in return was to see more of the world than you would have me see. We cannot all be content to live and die in the same spot, without ever seeing what else the world has to offer."

"You speak as though you've been locked in a dungeon," his father said with a scoff. "You went to Rome, did you not? We cannot afford to indulge your whims—"

"That isn't what you said to Lord Neil," Claude said from his place in the shadowed corner. "Or what you have given me to believe."

Mr. Everly's gaze snapped to his nephew. "Our finances are adequate," he snapped. "Because they have not been used up frivolously. I saved this family from ruin. I kept our name upheld in honor and respect."

"Have you?" Claude asked, and Edward had to remind himself to ignore the man. What business did he have to witness this argument between father and son? An argument long in the making, with Edward always putting his family's needs and his father's desires above his own.

"I have done better at the feat than your father, Nephew," Mr. Everly said between clenched teeth. "Else you wouldn't be here."

Claude came forward, into the dim light of evening and fire. "My father was a decorated officer of the British Royal Navy. What harm did he ever do to your precious family honor?"

The feel of the room shifted. Edward became aware of a tension between the other two men that he hadn't sensed before. Something went on here that he knew nothing about.

"What harm will I do to it by seeing something of the world?" Edward added, eyeing Claude with suspicion.

"You are both too young to understand anything of the world and how it works," Mr. Everly snapped. "You cannot go, Edward. I forbid you wasting time and funds. There is nothing for you out there that you cannot find at home. You may take a wife of your choosing, and you will settle down. Whether that is Miss Clapham or someone else, I care not."

"I asked Caroline for her hand in marriage," Edward said coolly. "You were there. She said yes. There is no one else." Caroline was right. He had to stand up for himself. For his dreams. And for hers, too. "I will not trap her here when she holds the same desires to experience new cultures and ideas as I do. We are young, as you say, and we will not postpone our dreams until we are too tired to enjoy them, on your say-so. You are content to be where you are, but I want to see what else is out there. And I will not need your help to do it."

Claude chuckled and raised his hands to applaud Edward, a twist to his lips that wasn't at all complimentary. "Well said, cousin. Such an impassioned speech." He looked at his uncle. "I wonder, though, if your father will appreciate it? He has fought so long to prove he and his offspring are nothing like our grandfather. Nothing like my father. When my father made a similar speech in favor of adventures found far from English shores, what did you do to him, Uncle?"

A chilling silence fell, and Edward's father stared at Claude as though he wished him to drop into the depths of the sea at that moment. "You will not speak of that in front of my son."

"You mean your heir doesn't know where the fortune that will be his came from?" Claude's smile curled slowly upward. "I thought you were proud of both paying the family debts and filling your coffers."

Edward looked between both men. "My mother's dowry paid our grandfather's debts," he said, looking at Claude with confusion, then to his father. Bits and pieces of conversation he'd overheard, of words spoken that didn't make sense, came forward in his mind. Trying to connect to one another. "And there was the investment."

"Yes. The investment." Claude looked down at the floor. "The investment made the same morning my father told his overbearing older brother that he wouldn't bow to his wishes anymore. That he had a way out from beneath Samuel Everly's thumb at last." Claude smirked at Edward, a chilly note in his tone as he spoke. "Your side of the family has always been so perfect. So honorable. You've been dedicated to maintaining that facade as long as I've known you. Bowing to all of your father's demands to ensure everything remained just so. What if it is all a lie, Edward? Would you want to know? Ask him what he did to my father, if you do."

Mr. Everly said nothing.

"What is he talking about, Father?" Edward demanded, looking from his cousin's cold fury to his father's shameful frown. The contrast in the two men made Edward's blood run cold. "What did you do to your brother?"

"Nothing," his father muttered, not meeting Edward's gaze. "I did nothing to him."

"You stole from him," Claude accused, the heat and snarl back in his voice. "You tricked information out of him then used it for your own benefit, and you left him with nothing."

"He owed me money," Edward's father protested, though his voice was weak.

"Ten pounds." Claude glowered at him. "And the information he gave you was worth five-hundred times that."

Edward sucked in a sharp breath. "Five-thousand pounds," he said quietly. He'd heard the story. A story that occurred when his father was young, about to marry a woman whose dowry would pay

SALLY BRITTON

off the debt left by *his* father. Edward's grandfather. "A return on a wise investment is what you called it."

Edward's father sank into his chair behind the desk. "My brother had many vices," he said. "And I knew them all, because they were the same as our father's. They were both reckless. Heedless of everything except their own entertainment and pleasure."

"And you were so righteous, were you, Uncle?" Claude demanded, leaning against the window frame. "What did it matter that you took advantage of him?"

"He would've gambled it all away." Edward's father mustered up enough indignation to glare at his nephew. "That money would've slipped through his fingers the way it always did. Until he joined the navy, your father was a worthless drunk."

"Hurrah for the navy," Claude said with a mock salute. "They did what his own brother wouldn't do. Showed him how to be a better man. Gave him a sense of worth. And he *thrived*. Despite your greed."

"What happened?" Edward asked, though he suspected he had enough information to guess. He needed to hear it. From his father.

Claude didn't wait long for his uncle to break the silence. "My father was acting as secretary to a well-informed member of parliament," Claude said, each word spoken with ruthless sincerity. "A member of Lords with lots of money and enough connection and investments to manipulate trade on a national level. And he meant to use his information to quietly purchase several shares of stock in a shipping company. The risk was high. But my father knew it would be a matter of days before the reward came in."

"How did my father get the information?" Edward asked, no longer looking at his parent but at his cousin. A man he'd hated he suddenly trusted more than he did his own father.

"He bought him a drink," Claude said with deliberate slowness. "Then another. And another. All while lying to him. Flattering him. Telling my father all the ways the two of them could use an enormous amount of money to explore the world together. They would put their differences aside and build new bonds of brother-

284

hood. A thing which had always been my father's dream, since he suspected his older brother hated him."

Edward's heart dropped. He ran a shaking hand through his hair and looked at his father again to find the old man had dropped his face into his hands with his elbows upon his desk.

"Once my father was drunk enough, my uncle bought him a room for the night. He left a note. My father kept it with him his whole life. Did you know that, Uncle? I nearly buried him with it." Claude reached into his coat and pulled out a small case, the size of a snuff box. He opened it and drew out a yellowed piece of paper. He stormed to the desk and threw it on the surface. "Do you remember what it says, Uncle? I have it memorized."

It was like watching a play unfold in front of him. A tragic, horrible play that was all too real.

Edward's father reached a shaky hand toward the small square of paper, its edges dark and ragged. He laid his hand atop it but said nothing.

"'Consider your debt paid, Matthew. Be comforted in knowing you saved our family's home and reputation.' That was all. The comfort of saving your inheritance was supposed to make up for what you cheated him out of. While my father slept off the alcohol you had given him, you went to a bank and borrowed against your wife's dowry. Using the marriage contract in your possession to secure a loan of five-hundred pounds. And you bought every single stock you could. There wasn't anything left for my father when he arrived at the Subscription Room after it had closed. The next morning, the news was out. The price rose. My father didn't have enough money in his pocket for even one share."

"Father." Edward couldn't move. His body had turned to stone. "You didn't keep it all. Surely not." He sounded like a child begging for comfort after a nightmare. Comfort that wouldn't come.

Claude slammed his fist into the desk, making Edward's father startle. "Tell Edward the truth, Uncle."

"I didn't give Matthew anything," he admitted at last, voice raw. "And he disappeared. For months, I didn't know where he'd gone.

And one day, someone came on his behalf. An old friend. Another younger son. He asked if I would give him the money to buy a commission for Matthew."

Claude's eyes narrowed. "The friend's name?"

"Walter Lansbury." He swallowed twice. "Your father wasn't to know. I didn't think he'd take it if he knew. I regretted my actions by that time. But I was married. The estate needed attention. The twins were barely a month old—"

Edward was shaking his head with each excuse. "You could have gone to him. Brought him here."

"He was a gambler and a drunk, like our father," he argued. "I regretted my actions. But I wouldn't invite him back into my life."

"So you sent him to sea," Claude said, tone thoughtful and laced with bitterness. "To live or die by the sword, in fact. But here my worthless, drunkard father proved himself at last. He rose in the ranks. Became a first officer. By the time Napoleon started making trouble, my father received recognition for his service by the admiralty." Claude's voice steadied as he spoke until it held more pride than pain. "And he gained a small fortune through prize money."

"A fortune you have squandered," Edward's father said without any real heat.

"Have I, Uncle? Or have I only let you think that?" Claude walked around the desk and Edward tensed, ready to physically defend his father if Claude acted in any way violent toward him. "I have my fun," he said as he opened one of the drawers in the desk. "I gamble. I flirt. I drink. I travel. And now, I am to marry and leave all of that behind. And all of *you* behind. All you self-righteous Everlys with your sanctimonious honor."

Claude was engaged? Edward's mind took on that surprise without the shock the news would have caused him a mere hour ago.

His cousin removed a case from the drawer. "It is all here?" he asked, splaying his hand on the lid. "One-thousand pounds? And my grandmother's wedding ring?"

Edward's jaw dropped open. A family heirloom he'd seen on his own mother's finger and a small fortune was in that box.

"All of it," his father confirmed. "Take it and go to the devil, along with your father and mine both."

"Where we will eagerly await you, Uncle." Claude tucked the box beneath his arm. "You can keep the note. I don't need it anymore." Claude made his way back around the desk and stood before Edward. "I never had reason to like you," he said, meeting Edward's shocked gaze with his own clear-eyed stare. "And you made it clear you despised me. I doubt we would have rubbed along well even if we were strangers rather than cousins. I haven't the patience for someone like you. You worry too much about pleasing others. Let this be a lesson to you, cousin." He tapped the box with his free hand. "Take what you can get and don't wait for anyone's approval. Now. I'm off to my wedding. None of you are invited."

Claude left them. The carpet in the hall made it impossible to hear his receding steps, but he whistled as he went, and the whistle slowly faded away. The distant sound of the front door closing reverberated through the house, a solemn resonance that filled the air and commanded attention. The sound, though not forceful, carried an undeniable weight. Its echo permeated every corner of the house, reaching Edward's ears with a distinct sense of finality.

They would never see Claude Everly again. And Edward almost smiled. Because Claude had left on his own terms, with chaos in his wake. Some small part of Edward admired that.

"I never want you to repeat what you heard in this room," Edward's father said, his voice stronger than it had been beneath Claude's glare. "Not to anyone. Your mother must never know. Your sisters cannot have reason to doubt their heritage."

"I am going to travel," Edward said quietly, as though his father hadn't spoken. "I have wanted to travel all my life. To see the wonders of the modern world and the remnants of the ancient. And I'm going to do it, with or without your blessing."

"Why are you so insistent about this?" His father stared at him in bewilderment. "You already traveled."

"Three weeks in Roman cities hasn't filled my soul. So few people have the means or the desire to do what I want to do. I have both. And I'm not waiting anymore." Edward looked at the square paper, still on his father's desk. He leaned forward and picked it up. Unfolded it. Read the faded ink in his father's familiar hand. Decades had passed and his father had always put an odd loop at the top of his C's.

"How long?" his father asked in a tone of defeat.

"I don't know. A year. Perhaps longer. I will write when Caroline and I decide." He tucked the note into his waistcoat pocket. Claude might not need the reminder of Samuel Everly's selfishness anymore. But Edward might.

"We need you here. The estate needs you."

Edward smiled, though he couldn't be certain why. It didn't seem the time to smile. "Not yet. You're still here. And we both know you haven't wanted me to interfere with the way you do things."

His father's expression turned sad, almost bleak. "When will you go?"

Edward knew precisely when. "After my wedding."

"And what of Miss Clapham?" his father asked, shoulders sinking along with his gaze. "Do you wed her to spite me, too?"

"I love her." He wouldn't let his father cheapen that. "And I know her heart as well as I know my own." There was more to life than what Edward's father valued. It wasn't better. But it wasn't less, either. "Even had she said no tonight, Father, I wouldn't stay. Claude was right. I have cared too much about making you happy. I am going to look after myself for a while." He stared at his father, who wouldn't meet his eyes. "I know you thought you were protecting me. But you were wrong, Father. I have learned from every mistake I made, and I never made the same mistake twice. I am not like your father, your brother, or you. I am my own person."

His father heaved a sigh and turned away. "It's late, Edward. I am going to bed."

The dismissal didn't hurt. His father had faced his own hubris and weakness, he'd had his shame thrown in his face, in front of his only son. He was an old man. Tired and unbending. Nearly broken by a decades' old lie. Perhaps one day, Edward would forgive him. "I will turn in as well. Good night, Father."

"Good night."

Edward left the office, heavier with knowledge yet lighter in step. Whatever came next, he would be ready. And, hopefully, Caroline would be, too.

# CHAPTER 26

Standing in the entry hall of Inglewood Castle, Caroline twisted her fingers together behind her back, over and over again, twining and untwining them, lacing them one way and then another. Were they ribbons, they'd have been knotted into a hopeless mess never to be undone.

Edward's hand covered both of hers, warm and reassuring. He disentangled her left hand, joining it with his, and looked down at her from the corner of his eye. "Steady on, sprite. The work is done. The wait is almost over."

The carriage in which Sir Thomas Lawrence rode had been seen not long ago from an upper window, and everyone staying at the castle had assembled to greet the president of the Royal Academy. Edward had arrived early, while breakfast had yet been on the table. Somehow, he'd sensed that she needed his steadying presence.

Mama and Papa stood with them, and the earl and countess were at the forefront.

"He will not even see the painting today," Caroline whispered aloud as the sound of wheels clattering on stone reached her ears. "He will want to rest after his journey. Then have dinner. Then the light won't be right, and he will wait until tomorrow."

Edward raised his eyebrows at her but made no comment.

The doors opened, and a gentleman of middling height entered the castle. At three and fifty years of age, he still had an exuberance about him that surprised Caroline as he walked with a straight back and light step directly to Lady Inglewood. He swept off his hat, revealing a distinct lack of hair atop his head. His dark eyes sparkled with mischief as he approached.

He bowed low and Lady Inglewood extended her hand, which he kissed with an air of fondness. "My dear countess, it is an honor to be in your home once more. And my lord." He bowed to the earl, who returned the gesture with a shallow bow of his own. "Perhaps this time I will persuade you to part with your wife's painting of Herakles?"

Caroline blinked. There was only one painting of the Greek demigod in the castle, in the library. It depicted the ancient hero wrapped in a lion's skin and looking into the distance at the far away Mt. Olympus. Lady Inglewood had painted that? But then, her model had to have been someone to whom she was close.

"That painting will remain with the castle," Lord Inglewood said, and Caroline noted a slight redness at the back of his neck. "Though I appreciate your compliment to her ladyship's skills."

"I do not give praise freely. You can be certain of that," he said, then rocked backward on his heels and turned his smile to the rest of the gathering.

Lady Inglewood made the introductions in order of precedence. Mr. and Mrs. Duncan, Mr. Everly, and at last: "Finally, this is Miss Caroline Clapham. My friend and protege. It is for her sake that I asked you here this month."

Sir Thomas bowed to Caroline as she curtsied deeply to him. "It is a pleasure to meet you, Miss Clapham. There are too few female artists, you know, who put themselves forward. Their parents seem to believe it undignified for a woman to have any skill outside of the music room." He shook his head as though deeply offended by that idea. "Well now. Let's see what you've done, shall we?"

Caroline's heart seized and her chest went tight. "Oh, but, Sir. You must be tired from your journey. I wouldn't want to rush you."

"Nonsense. I remember well what it was like to have my work on display. I will not be the cause of a lady suffering anxiety one moment longer than she ought. Though the countess has told me enough that you likely have no reason to be concerned." He smiled, and Caroline had the impression he had used that smile to his advantage for many, many years.

"We have arrayed her work in the long gallery, where the light is best," Lord Inglewood said, extending his arm to his countess. "If you are ready, Miss Clapham?"

"Y-yes," she said, and felt a gentle touch at her elbow from Edward. It was enough to cure the warble in her voice. "I am ready."

Sir Thomas offered her his arm. "Then lead the way, my dear."

When the earl and countess waited, along with everyone else, watching her, Caroline nodded to the staircase. "This way, Sir Thomas." How had she ever come to this? Walking ahead of an earl, in his own castle! Yet no one seemed to mind. She was midway up the staircase when a sudden fear gripped her that she would forget the way to the long gallery, where the earl's family portraits stretched along the wall.

The man at her side kept talking, pleasantly, of the artwork they passed. He knew most of the artists of note and their subjects. "I painted my first work of significance in 1787, of course, and showed them at the Royal Academy's exhibition. But it was the portrait of Queen Charlotte in her blue gown that won the interest of the Crown Prince." He gave her a kind smile. "I was twenty years of age. I am given to understand that is close to your own at present?"

"Yes, Sir Thomas." Somehow, she had led them to the gallery, and footmen ahead of them were opening curtains to flood the room with light.

"Age has very little to do with talent," he told her, pausing a few steps inside the room. "There are many other factors at work. Education, determination, passion, and a single-mindedness that will drive you toward betterment." He patted her hand on his arm, and the warmth in his eyes reassured her. "But experience is important, my dear. Experience of the world, of people, of broken hearts, and all the struggles and triumphs of humanity. I say this to you so you will know, when I look at your work today I am not making a life-long pronouncement."

Caroline nodded once. "There will always be room for improvement."

His smile returned. "Indeed. And, between the two of us, had I Queen Charlotte's portrait to do again, it wouldn't look at all the same. In thirty-odd years of painting, I have learned much about my own weaknesses and strengths. Whatever your work tells me today will be about today only."

Her heart calmed somewhat, and she nodded. "Would you like me to show you each piece?"

"Walk with me, Miss Clapham. If I have a question, I will ask."

They went to the first picture upon its easel.

All of Caroline's displayed pieces, fourteen items, were in frames borrowed from Inglewood's attic. Each chosen by her, dusted carefully, polished, and holding her work. Sir Thomas asked few questions. He studied her pastels, her watercolors, and her sketches with interest. His nose hovered sometimes so close to the canvas as he studied a detail that it nearly touched the dried paint. Then he would take several steps back and look again. He went down the line with an expression Caroline couldn't decipher. She didn't try. When her heart threatened to leave her chest and go racing away, she looked for Edward.

He waited with her family at the end of the row, facing the single painting still covered by a white cloth. Each time their eyes met, he would smile, and her heart calmed. No matter what happened, she had Edward. His strength, his love, his encouragement. And soon, his hand in marriage.

They came to that last easel, and Caroline paused before it. "This is my most recent piece," she said, her fingertips brushing the cover. "Lady Inglewood informed me that you have a personal preference for pieces that are challenging and depict stories or themes that are awe-inspiring, legendary, and provoking. I cannot say that this will be a work that you will find favorable. But it has challenged me, mind and body, in ways I have never been challenged before."

He had listened with patience, nodded as she spoke, then turned expectantly to see the unveiling of her summer's work.

"I call it the *Defiance of Atlas*."

Sir Thomas did not move for a long moment. He simply took in the painting, his eyes on those of the angry Titan staring back at him. Edward's handsome face had transformed into an angry warrior's, his battles lost, his daughters taken by the enemy, his dreams dashed to pieces. His blue eyes dared the viewer to look away from him without knowing his pain and frustration.

And Caroline felt small, uncertain, and untalented.

"I painted something like this, once," Sir Thomas said, his voice so quiet Caroline barely heard him. "I was young. I displayed it at the exhibition the year I finished the work. And another painter, a man I respected, said he would pay the Academy one-hundred pounds to have it removed." Sir Thomas turned to look at her, and she saw a strange glimmer in his eyes. "I never did anything like it again. Though I am still proud of it—of what I attempted with it. Perhaps I will try to display it again, someday."

Then he stepped closer and began his examination, as he had on all the other pieces. Caroline waited, looking at Edward, who watched her with an expression of open adoration.

"Very well. I am ready to share my initial thoughts. Though I will likely view these several times over the next few days." Sir Thomas Lawrence turned to address the people gathered. "You are all important to Miss Clapham, and you obviously believe in her and support her. That is more than most artists of her age and sex can hope for. I hope you will continue to offer your encouragement. As to her talent. Well."

He looked down the row of work. "Miss Clapham has a remarkable talent at such a young age. This is truly promising and speaks volumes about her potential as an artist. Her ability to convey depth, emotion, and masterful use of light and shadow is truly commendable. Though I would classify several of these pieces as safe, or even common, there are others that show an emotional understanding of the subject that intrigues me. The old man seated on a bench with his pipe is one such painting. I should like to see it in our exhibit next year."

Caroline had never swooned in her life, but her knees went weak and threatened to give her that first experience. Edward, beside her now, had his arm around her waist in an instant. That old man in the painting was one of their neighbors. A man who had told Caroline ridiculous stories every time she saw him at the public house or on the village green.

"Your landscapes and depictions of nature are graceful, Miss Clapham. They are gentle and pleasant. Pastoral scenes are calming and welcome in homes across the kingdom. If you wished to sell any of them, you would find willing buyers at several levels in society."

No one breathed a word as he turned again and looked at Atlas. "As to your *Defiance* piece, I can see that it has stretched you to the very limit of your talents and capabilities. It is passionate and truly commendable. The mastery you display in capturing the interplay of light and shadow is striking. Your ability to convey rage and sorrow both—truly remarkable for one of your age and inexperience."

Edward's arm tightened briefly around her, and she saw his lips curl upward in a smile.

"While the painting as a whole is a testament to your talent, there are places wherein the details appear slightly less defined, which could be further developed to enhance the overall depth and atmosphere of the scene. With continued dedication and refinement, you have the potential to achieve even greater heights." He turned to look at her, and his gaze flicked momentarily up to Edward's. He smiled. "Atlas, I presume?"

"Yes, Sir Thomas." Edward's cheeks reddened but his shoulders straightened. "It was my honor to pose for the work."

"Her love for you comes through the paint, Mr. Everly. There is as much heart as there is oil on that canvas." He then addressed Caroline again, his expression turning almost stern. "Lady Inglewood has told me something of your studies up to this point. Considering that you have made do with traveling artists and a yearly visit with the countess, you have achieved much." Here he tucked his hands behind his back. "I cannot help but envision the incredible growth and refinement you could achieve through travel and exposure to the world's artistic wonders. Experiencing different cultures, landscapes, and the works of great artists from various eras can have a profound impact on an artist's development and perspective. You could improve on your own, but it will be difficult. You need more experience and guidance, Miss Clapham."

It wasn't a declaration of genius. But Caroline hadn't truly expected such a thing. And she wasn't disappointed. If anything, her heart rose to the challenge. "I intend to spend at least the next year traveling, Sir Thomas. On the Continent."

"With this fellow, I presume?" He glanced again at Edward and then at her.

"Yes. Mr. Everly and I are to be married."

The man nodded once. "When you have returned, come to the Royal Academy. I would like to see how your work has changed. And I would like you to study there, as often as you wish. I will draw up a list for you of places you ought to visit, and I will prepare letters of introduction, if you wish, to some of my acquaintances in the arts."

"Thank you, Sir Thomas. That is kind of you." Her heart was doing flips and twists, and she felt as though she could leap for joy. But she forced herself to stay still, with Edward's hand on the small of her back, anchoring her to the moment.

"I do not give compliments to just anyone, Miss Clapham," he reminded her with the slightest of smiles, his eyes crinkling at the corners. "You have a gift, and you have done well. But there is so much more for you to learn. My hope for you is that you will know your worth, and you will not let anyone prohibit you from achieving your potential." Then he spun on his heel and held both hands out toward the countess. "You promised me an excellent new talent, my lady, and a delightful seaside holiday. You have delivered well on the first point. How shall we ensure the second as well?"

Lady Inglewood sent Caroline a triumphant grin, then took Sir Thomas in hand and led him from the gallery. Lord Inglewood followed after them with an amused smile and a quick nod to her parents. Caroline wanted to sink to the ground and lay down, flat on her back, and not get up again until her body stopped trembling.

Her papa swept her up in his arms, as he had since she was a little girl, and gave her a tight embrace that lifted her toes off the ground. "Remarkable," he said in her ear. "Graceful. Of course he would see those things, Cara." He set her down and released her to her mother's embrace.

"My darling, I am so proud of you." She kissed Caroline on both cheeks, then held her daughter's face in her hands. Caroline had surpassed her mother's height by several inches, yet she never failed to feel like a little girl beneath her mother's loving gaze. "Letters of introduction, my dear. What adventures you will have!" Then she looked over Caroline's shoulder. "The *both* of you will have."

Edward's hand found Caroline's again. She looked up to find him staring at her with unconcealed pride. "I am fortunate she agreed to have me along with her."

Mama touched Caroline's forehead again and furrowed her brow. "You are flush with excitement. Edward, be a good man and take your betrothed out on the balcony. She needs fresh air. Goodness. With all this excitement, I think I need to rest."

"Summers are for picnics and naps beneath the trees," Caroline reminded her with a smile.

"Truer words were never spoken." Papa took her mother's arm. "Come along, Teresa. Let us find you a proper place for a nap."

Edward didn't even wait for them to leave the gallery before taking her to the set of glass doors that opened onto the balcony. It faced inland, westward, but the air still tasted of the nearby sea. He took her to the rail, then put his hands upon her waist as she faced him.

"This is only the beginning," he told her, his grin familiar and welcome. "You have so much ahead of you, Cara. My sprite. My love."

"*We* have so much ahead of us." Her hands went to his shoulders, then slid around to lace her fingers together behind his neck. They settled there quite nicely. "My dreams have changed this summer, Edward. I still want to paint and travel. I still hope to gather commissions, and I want to teach others to pass on all that I have been given. But now, all my dreams have one thing in common."

He bent his head toward her, his voice softened as he asked, "Will you make me guess?"

"I think you know." She tilted her chin upward, and her eyes fluttered closed. "It's you, Edward. I want always to be with you."

Their kiss sealed her words and made her senses reel. Even with her eyes closed, as his lips caressed hers, and as she drank him in, Caroline's mind burst with color and texture, from the white of winter's first snow to the deepest blues and blacks of night, they filled her mind with dreams as Edward filled her heart with his love.

Perhaps art and love were part of the same thing. They both required that a person look outside of themselves to find beauty, meaning, and truth.

# EPILOGUE
## NOVEMBER 1823

*Paris, France*
*Musée Royal du Louvre*

"You, Monsieur Everly, must write this down. I have said it more than once, but no one ever writes it down," Monsieur Eugène Delacroix spoke with an air of superiority that seemed quite common among the Frenchmen Edward and Caroline had met thus far, but Edward dutifully opened the notebook he carried when he accompanied Caroline on her visits to the *Louvre*, a French palace turned museum.

"I am ready, Monsieur Delacroix."

"The artist who aims at perfection in everything achieves it in nothing." He nodded smartly. "One day, you will see, I will be quoted often for saying such things." The enthusiastic young artist looked about. "Where did Madame Everly disappear to?" He looked down the long gallery and Edward turned to sweep the area with his gaze, too. Patrons sat on benches, some had brought their own chairs and sketchbooks, admiring art from masters dating backward hundreds of years.

Edward didn't see his wife. "Perhaps we lost her in the statuary in the last room?"

"Ah. We will divide and conquer. I will search backward, you will go forward." Delacroix slapped Edward on the back and went off. Edward tucked the notebook away and hurried through a small door, where he had glimpsed the edge of a dark blue gown he suspected belonged to his wife.

The former palace was a maze of corridors and hallways, chambers and antechambers, and they had barely seen what little was open to the public. Most days they had rooms to themselves, but others there were artists from other parts of the world. Even American artists and students of history.

The *Louvre* was an architectural marvel. The sheer number of items housed in its growing collection seemed impossible to comprehend. Art and historical artifacts were on every wall, in every corner.

Edward found his wife in one quiet little corridor, standing before a modest sized portrait of a woman. He came closer to her, and after he ensured they were quite alone, wrapped his arms about her from behind. The French were far less stuffy about displays of affection than the English, but he'd found few chances to show his wife his affection that day.

"What are you doing in here, sprite?" he asked softly. "Hiding?"

She briefly tipped her head back to look at him, smiling. "Enjoying a moment of quiet. And look what I found." She pointed to the woman who sat quietly, looking out of her portrait at them, a small smile barely touching the corners of her lips. As though she knew a secret. "The plaque says they have proven she is one of Da Vinci's. Can you imagine? Three hundred or more years ago, she was alive. And someone great painted her, so she could never be forgotten."

Edward kissed his wife's forehead. "She seems a little serious, though."

"I rather like her. She looks like she would be quite good at keeping a secret."

"Like ours? You still haven't told anyone we began the whole thing as a game of pretend."

Caroline laughed and turned in his arms. "Neither have you. I think that is the sort of thing we admit on our anniversary."

"Really? Which one? I intend to have several of those with you." He admired the curls framing her lovely face, and the dark eyes reflecting his love for her back to him.

"I haven't decided. Someday, we will tell everyone how it began. I am only grateful with how it ended."

"Ended?" Edward shook his head. "We are only in the next chapter, Cara. And we have entire volumes left to fill. Or, given I am speaking to an accomplished artist, I should say we have entire canvases still to paint."

His wife wrinkled her nose at him. "I have seen your paint, my love. You had better leave that part of our story to me. I have no intention of letting you put an elephant's ears on my portrait, thank you very much. No matter how much I love you."

"What about rabbit ears? I am getting quite good at those."

Caroline's glare dissolved into a giggle, and the twinkle in her eyes wasn't a thing Edward could resist. Since the only one watching was the woman in the painting, he swept his wife into a kiss.

Caroline Everly tasted like the adventure of a lifetime.

# THE INGLEWOOD BOOKS

### The Inglewood Series:

*Rescuing Lord Inglewood | Discovering Grace*

*Saving Miss Everly | Engaging Sir Isaac*

*Reforming Lord Neil*

If you enjoyed this story and haven't read the first series set at Inglewood, all five are available as ebooks, paperbacks, and audiobooks! Learn how the Earl and Countess were forced into marriage and faced trials and hardship together. Find out about the time Grace and Hope Everly switched places, leaving Grace to fall in love with her best friend and Hope stranded on a desert isle with a handsome castaway. And, of course, find out how Lord Neil became Caroline's beloved Papa when he fell in love with a woman who lived on a farm.

### Return to Inglewood:

*Romancing the Artist*

More Inglewood Titles Coming Soon... Sign up for Sally Britton's newsletter on her website so you won't miss a single announcement!

# FROM THE AUTHOR

Once upon a time, I wrote a series about five childhood friends who had to grow up. Every word I wrote about Silas, Jacob, Grace, Hope, and Isaac made me love them more. I even found a place in my heart for their one-time antagonist, Neil. When I finished the last book, I already knew I would want to visit them again. Years later, when they were all grown with children facing the same dilemmas their parents encountered on their paths to happily ever after.

My readers have waited three years for this book, the first that follows the next generation of Inglewood romances. I hope it was worth the wait. Those who followed my progress closely know how many times this book was planned, promised, scheduled, and rescheduled. I'm writing this author's note only hours before the story is due. As such, there will likely be little mistakes that I'll have to edit out over time. I hope everyone will be patient with me on that account.

The truth in the fiction: The Mona Lisa was in the Louvre in 1823, returned quite recently from time spent in one of Napoleon's residences. Though several in the art world admired it, the portrait hadn't gained the fame or notoriety is has today. It was one of many paintings on the wall, unknown by many, cherished by few.

Sir Thomas Lawrence was a real person with an interesting life story. The painting he mentioned that was considered a failure would be considered daring even to this day. He was a genius of his time, and the Prince Regent was one of his most important patrons.

Why was Caroline an artist? I hadn't really written an artist before. As someone who isn't visually creative at all, I wanted to challenge myself. Alas, that is the downfall of many an author. I enjoyed learning about this time period in the world of painters. It was the beginning of what we now call the Romantic Movement, and someone of Caroline's age and enthusiasm would've been right at home with the new emphasis on portraying greater emotion on the canvas.

**Will there be more Inglewood stories?** Absolutely. I have several planned, and you will see all those lovely little children I mentioned in this book grow up and find their place in the wide world and each other's hearts. You won't want to miss it.

My favorite part of finishing a book is this part. Writing my notes and adding my thanks to the people who made this possible.

I was coming out of a difficult season of life while I wrote this book. Creatives and non-creatives alike have heard the term "burnout," and everyone should dread it. Mine had come without me realizing it. I started this book while in the middle of it. I finished the book after coming out on the other side. I hope the story benefitted from this time in my life. Because of the muddle I was in, I relied on friends and family for so much.

Marilee Merrell, to who this book is dedicated, was a phenomenal cheerleader, help, and friend. She kept me on task and made sure I didn't neglect my wonderful readers. I cannot express how much I needed her, and I'm grateful she rose to the challenge. By the time she reads this finished version of the story, it will be the fourth time she's read through it. Maybe the fifth. But who's counting?

Shaela Kay, my dear friend and cover designer, had to listen to me talk about this book for YEARS. She created the cover ages ago and kept begging me to get these stories written. Finally, Shaela, here is the first.

Jenny Proctor, my friend and developmental editor, talked me down from throwing in the towel. Many times. She gave up precious hours talking me through story points and reading my book to make sure it wasn't garbage. She is the best.

My oldest child, Lucy, who is unlikely to see this for some time. She is an inspiration to me in so many ways, and I look forward to the day the rest of the world can behold her creativity and brilliance.

My other three children, who were so patient with me and cheered me on, will always be the inspiration for the youngest characters in my books.

And, as always, I am most grateful to my husband. He is my happily ever after, my best friend, and my greatest adventure.

Thank you for coming on this journey with me, dear reader. It takes both of us to tell a story. I hope you enjoyed your part of the tale.

# ALSO BY SALLY BRITTON

**Castle Clairvoir Romances:**

*A Duchess for the Duke* | *Mr. Gardiner and the Governess*

*A Companion for the Count* | *Sir Andrew and the Authoress*

*Lord Farleigh and Miss Frost*

**The Branches of Love Series:**

*Martha's Patience* | *The Social Tutor*

*The Gentleman Physician* | *His Bluestocking Bride*

*The Earl and His Lady* | *Miss Devon's Choice*

*Courting the Vicar's Daughter* | *Penny's Yuletide Wish*

**Stand Alone Regency Romances:**

*The Captain and Miss Winter* | *His Unexpected Heiress*

*A Haunting at Havenwood* | *Her Unsuitable Match*

*An Unsuitable Suitor* | *A Mistletoe Mismatch*

**Hearts of Arizona Series:**

*Silver Dollar Duke* | *Copper for the Countess* | *A Lady's Heart of Gold*

# ABOUT THE AUTHOR

Sally Britton, along with her husband, their four incredible children, their tabby Willow, and their dog named Izzie, live in Oklahoma. So far, they really like it there, even if the family will always consider Texas home.

Sally started writing her first story on her mother's electric type-writer when she was fourteen years old. Reading her way through Jane Austen, Louisa May Alcott, and Lucy Maud Montgomery, Sally decided to write about the complex world of centuries past.

Sally graduated from Brigham Young University in 2007 with a bachelor's in English. She met and married her husband not long after and started working on their happily ever after.

Vincent Van Gogh is attributed with the quote, "What is done in love is done well." Sally has taken that as her motto, writing stories where love is a choice.

All of Sally's published works are available on Amazon.com and you can connect with Sally and sign up for her newsletter on her website, AuthorSallyBritton.com.